MASTER BERNARD

MASTER BERNARD

(*Maître Bernard*)

ÉLIE BERTHET

TRANSLATED BY

GERALD BRIGGS

WILDSIDE PRESS

For Élie Berthet, a 19th century author,
whose exceptional writing deserves to be
better known in the 21st century.

ACKNOWLEDGEMENTS

My sincere thanks to my patient editing team headed up by my old friend and pod mate, Cynthia Ploski and my faithful cousin, Patty B. Copp (both with publishing experience), as well as Heather Briggs, an eagle-eyed niece. These three burned up the e-mail trail on the internet to help me get this work into readable shape. I also owe them many thanks for their encouragement and support.

A special note of appreciation to Jean Marc Ferrer, Managing Editor of LES ARDENTS EDITEURS in Limoges, France, for his advice and support during the translation process, and also to Denis Ségalat, ARDENTS' graphic artist, for graciously providing the basic design for the cover of this book.

Finally, my thanks to John Betancourt of Wildside Press, LLC, for accepting this manuscript and making its publication possible.

I am grateful to you all…

—Gerald Briggs

INTRODUCTION

Master Bernard (in French; *Maître Bernard*) is a historical novel which reflects what actually happened during the terrible religious wars between the Roman Catholics and the Huguenots (Reformed/Calvinist Protestants) in France during the second half of the 16th century. The principal character is a real person: **Bernard Palissy**, master potter, craftsman, writer, researcher and lecturer who lived from 1510 to 1589. Many of his glazed pottery masterpieces can be found today in the Louvre and other major museums around the world. This is a story which vividly describes the customs of that time and how Palissy and his family were drawn into one of the bloodiest chapters of French history. It is estimated that three million persons perished from the violence, famine or disease during that period.

The conflict between the two religions took place during the long reign of Queen Catherine de Médicis, widow of Henri II, and involved a power struggle between the fervently Catholic House of Guise (claiming descent from Charlemagne) and the less powerful House of Condé (a branch of the House of Bourbon) who were sympathetic to the Calvinists. The Catholic Queen sided with the Guises and this struggle came to a head in 1572 during what is known as the *Saint Bartholomew's Day Massacre*, in which mobs killed between 5,000 and 10,000 Protestants in the Paris area alone over a period of several weeks. Sadly, this horrendous conflict lasted until 1598.

Palissy, a fervent and outspoken Huguenot, after gaining fame as a creator of a revolutionary technique which resulted in a stunning new style of pottery, was taken under the protection of Queen Catherine de Médicis for his artistic talents. With an official title in her Court, he and his family were temporarily sheltered from the persecution for heresy which cost the lives of many of his closest Protestant friends. His historically documented proximity to the Queen placed him truly in the front line of this historic and tragic conflict.

The author closely followed events as described in Palissy's own autobiography which gives the reader an almost first-hand experience.

* * * *

Élie Berthet (1815-1891), the author of this work, although not well known today, was one of France's leading writers in the 19th century, having produced over 100 novels about Paris, French history and other subjects. His books have been translated into a dozen languages and one of his works was re-published in France as recently as 2007. *Master Bernard* was first published in 1875. It is said that in his day, he was better known than Alexander Dumas. I am pleased to mention that Élie Berthet was my maternal great-great-grandfather, which played a key role in my wishing to translate this particularly exciting and colorful work.

* * * *

Translation Issues: There was an exceptional challenge in dealing with the French vocabulary of an author writing in the 19th century about 16th century events. There were many words used which took considerable research to decipher. Berthet only included a half-dozen footnotes, but due to the subject matter and historical aspects which might not be familiar to English speaking readers, I have taken the liberty of inserting additional explanatory footnotes where I felt they would be useful. I also tried to maintain the author's style, punctuation and syntax to immerse the reader, as much as possible, in the mood of that era.

I believe that readers will enjoy this book as much as I enjoyed translating it. It has action, intrigue, humor and heartbreak. In addition, it is also a historically accurate and educational document relating to an important period in French history.

—Gerald Briggs
May 29, 2018

PART ONE

THE POTTER

I.

THE HOUSE OUTSIDE THE GATES

At the outset of those terrible religious struggles that ravished parts of France, notably the Saintonge region, two horsemen, approached the town of Saintes on a dark October night, the darkness was profound and due to the torrential rain and driving winds, the two were wrapped in heavy cloaks. However, under those folds, one could hear metallic sounds signaling that these travelers were armed and could be men of war.

They were approaching the town by a heavily muddied road and were beginning to discern the dark shapes of the first homes in the town's outskirts when one of the voyagers' mounts suddenly lost its footing. It slipped on the edge of a water-filled ditch and fell. The rider, expert in the art of horsemanship, kept control and in spite of his bulky clothing and large spurred boots, managed to rapidly regain his footing. He pulled the horse up by its bridle, shouting encouragement, and succeeded in raising the animal. However, as he prepared to remount, he realized that the poor horse was limping badly and had either broken or severely damaged one leg.

"Devil take me!" he shouted in anger. "Courtaut is injured. He is incapable of carrying either his harness or myself. We have a serious problem!"

The other rider had now also dismounted.

"Indeed, father," the other replied in a vigorous and clear voice that announced his youth. "This is a regrettable accident. Fortunately, we are not far from the town. Take my horse and I will lead yours by its bridle until we reach the nearest inn."

"An inn! Where in heaven's name do you think, Gaston, that we will find an inn at this time of night? I do not know this area and everyone is sleeping. It is past midnight… and if we do reach Saintes, I seriously doubt that the guards will open the gates for us without specific permission from the Governor, even with the orders that the Constable has provided us. We will be obliged to wait at least two hours in this terrible wind and pouring rain at the foot of the drawbridge…. This damned Huguenot country is disastrous for good Catholics!"

"All the more reason, father, to demonstrate our Christian resilience.

Why not go knock on the door of some of these houses?"

"Hmm, they are lovely these houses," grumbled the father, observing in the darkness the state of the miserable hovels. "As needy as we are, we would hope to… But, Ventrebleu![1] what is that light over there?"

He pointed to a red flame that shone on the side of the road some distance away. This flame was of good size and all the more striking in that in this dark night, it was the only point of light visible.

"With all due respect, father," said Gaston excitedly, "we are perhaps not as unfortunate as you thought. That red flame looks like the fire of a forge. And as you know blacksmiths are often able to heal the wounds of horses. Not only that, but a nice hot coal fire would be most welcome to warm us up and dry our clothing."

"Well said, Gaston, my son. Let us proceed in God's name! This wind is glacial, and the water entering my collar will soon fill my boots."

Father and son, leading their horses by their bridles, headed towards the flame, which, as indicated earlier, did not seem to be that far away.

Their progress was slow and difficult. Blinded by the swirling rain, they had trouble keeping to the path that was gullied, slippery and full of potholes. In addition, the wounded horse could only move forward with extreme difficulty and its master did not wish to pressure it more than necessary. In spite of all this, the two travelers soon found themselves nearing the fire that had served as a beacon.

Its brilliance shone from the middle of a large field that bordered the public path. At some point a palisade and a hedgerow had provided protection from passing travelers, but the foliage had now disappeared; either having been torn up or suffered the ravages of the weather. As for the hedge, all that remained were bouquets of thorny vegetation with gaps sufficiently large to permit the passage of passersby into the rough enclosure. Our travelers, seeing no habitation, simply entered through one of these gaps.

The ground was now crevassed and littered with all kinds of objects, and it could become dangerous to move forward in this unknown space. After several steps, the father and son halted to try to understand exactly where they were.

The fire came from a stonework furnace built in the middle of the clearing with flames escaping from the chimney, providing the glow of light that they had seen from afar. One could recognize one of those kilns in which potters fired their products and which remained lit several days and nights consecutively. The master of this oven must have been very poor,

---

1 **Ventrebleu,** one of dozens of almost untranslatable exclamations (usually of surprise) of that time, many ending in 'bleu', i.e. morbleu, sacrebleu, corbleu, parbleu etc. etc. In this case the literal translation would be 'blue stomach.' The suffix 'bleu' was actually a transformation from the less acceptable use of the word 'dieu' (God).

as contrary to normal practice, there was no roof to protect its owner from the vagaries of weather while surveying the progress of the baking process. Moreover, he was probably lacking wood as he had gathered some stakes from neighboring vines to feed the fire.

The owner himself merited close attention. He was a man of about forty-five years of age, well built, tall, but astonishingly pale and thin. His face was narrow with sunken cheeks partially hidden by an unruly and greyish beard. However, his facial expression reflected dignity and intelligence; his deep-set eyes glowed with a spark of fever or genius, or a combination of both.

His clothing was miserable. He wore on his balding head a small cloth cap. His doublet was so outrageously patched it hid its original color. The breeches were held together with stitches that certainly did not come from a tailor. Finally, the linen stockings that covered his thin legs had even more repairs, and on his feet were cracked clogs. In an attempt to add protection to his tattered clothing, he had thrown over his shoulders an old wool blanket that was so damp that steam rose from it when he approached the furnace.

The poor devil seemed unaware of his sad state. He surveyed his oven with meticulous care, and from time to time, fed the fire with the pieces of stakes that he was using to nourish it. When he had a moment, he would reach under his woolen covering and pull out a small book that he read attentively by the light of the flame while carefully protecting it from the rain.

The travelers took all this in at a glance, and as the circumstances did not lend themselves to prolonged observation, the elder of the two rapidly approached.

"Greetings friend, by the horns of Beelzebub[2], who are you and what are you doing here?"

Upon hearing these rude words suddenly coming out of the darkness, the worker exhibited more surprise than fear. He hurriedly hid his book in the folds of his clothing, and before answering opened a small door of his furnace which immediately released a bright light illuminating the area. In turn, he now examined the travelers. Recognizing by their appearance that they were of an upper class, he doffed his cap and said with a mixture of politeness and soft melancholy:

"I am a potter of clay, at your service, kind Sires, and as you can see, I am exercising my profession."

"Good God, Master, your profession is not at all enjoyable on a night like this! But you must have a home not far from here. Could you possibly provide us shelter for a few hours; ourselves and our horses?"

The question seemed to cruelly embarrass the potter. As he was slow to reply, the traveler added:

2 **Beelzebub,** another name for the Devil, similar to Satan. He is known in demonology as one of the seven princes of hell.

"You have nothing to fear from us. I am the Baron de Massac, Lord of Puy-Néré and other places, and this is my son, Gaston, who has finished his apprenticeship. We are both attached to Sire de Montmorency, Constable[3] of France, and we bring orders for Captain de Pons, Governor of Saintes. My horse has suffered an accident that prevents us from proceeding further. If you can take us into your lodgings until the gates of the city are open, I will find some silver coin in payment.… But decide quickly. There is no point in standing here babbling in a wind that could blow the horns off a bull!"

This explanation did nothing to diminish the potter's hesitations; however, he replied in his usual polite and soft manner:

"You are well known in this area Baron de Massac; and I am aware that you are a true gentleman and… a zealous Catholic. My house is over here" (and he pointed towards a building that one could just see not too far away.) "I have never refused to provide hospitality under my roof; but I am poor, and all is lacking in my humble home. And as it says in the Holy Scripture; 'my door is shut and my children are sleeping. 'You would be wise to search for an inn.…

"Corneboeuf! friend," interrupted de Massac, furrowing his brows. "You cite Holy Scripture.… Are you a member of the so-called Reformist religion, by any chance? If I believed so… but once again, enough talk.… Is there an inn nearby?"

"There is one near the walls of the city but perhaps you may have trouble finding it in the darkness of this night. Unfortunately, I cannot leave my work to lead you there because this batch, which is my entire fortune, will be lost."

"Then my poor Courtaut, with his crowned[4] or broken leg, I'm not sure which, will never make it that far. Look my man, we won't be difficult; we only need a few of hours until daybreak. You must have a corner of your stable to protect the horses from the rain. And all we need is a stool near the fireplace in your house."

"Fireplace!" repeated the potter with a groan. "Alas, my good sirs, this is where I lack the most. My stock of wood is almost gone, and my pottery is far from baked.… If I completely run out of wood… oh well, I warned you of my poverty. Now the rest of what I have is yours. Come with me to my home, Sires. However, I cannot, like the widow of Sarepta,[5] offer you a piece of bread with a bit of flour. However, my home will protect you from the rain and the wind. And my stable, which has long been empty, will shel-

---

3 **Constable, (Connétable):** Chief military officer of France and a functionary of the Royal household.

4 **crowned**, from Couronné, a veterinary term for a wound on a horse's knee from a fall.

5 **Serepta,** reference to the widow of *Zarephath*, the woman mentioned twice in the Bible for having shared her last morsel (1 kings 17;8-24 and Luke 4:25-26).

ter your horses."

These words were pronounced with great humility and Baron de Massac appeared quite touched.

"Come now, Master," said Gaston. "Do not worry. Neither your family nor you will regret having provided us your hospitality, and you will be free to complete your pottery."

II.

THE INVENTOR'S FAMILY

First the potter led the horses into a kind of dilapidated shed that would serve as a temporary stable. The roof and the walls were sound. There was no box for fodder, but some straw was scattered on the ground. Certainly, if the Baron de Massac had seen in what a sad enclosure his favorite steed had been placed, he might have sought another refuge. But the obscurity and distance from the oven's light prevented him from noticing those details. The potter, having led the poor animals into the shed and attached them, he loosened their saddles and straps, lifted the stirrups, and announced that he would return shortly with a lamp and some materials to treat them. He also announced, to the great joy of de Massac, that he had knowledge in the veterinary art, and that he would apply a poultice to the wounded horse's leg that could do marvels.

They left the horses to themselves and approached the house.

The master of the dwelling had only to lift the door's latch to introduce his guests into what seemed to be a rather large room. He lit a lamp and cried out in a manner as to be heard in a nearby room:

"Woman, get up along with your daughter Esther, and both of you come help me receive noble travelers who do us the honor of stopping with us."

Several voices, including those of several children, responded in the other room; then the sound of furniture being moved and the shuffle of feet indicated that preparations were in progress to respond to this request.

Under the glow of the lamp, the travelers cast curious glances around their surroundings.

The room contained a large variety of objects, some of which could be quite surprising. In one corner stood a potter's wheel along with one of those kilns used by artisans who paint on glass and create ceramics. The owner of this space appeared to be both a laborer and a scholar. While the brick flooring was cluttered with piles of modeling clay, there were also various molds and fragments of glazed pottery, some of which were brilliantly colored. Furniture and shelves lining the wall were covered with carefully labeled mineral samples, all types of seashells; and in glass jars, serpents, lizards and frogs that undoubtedly served as models for an artist. Vases half-filled with water contained plants freshly picked from the fields. In addition, drawings executed with the care and precision of a surveyor or a painter of decorations were posted on a bare wall; and on a wood plank that served as a desk, one could see not only writing materials, but several books, bulky manuscripts and innumerable sketches which bore witness to an all-consuming activity.

However, the furniture that was almost entirely covered with this confused mass of objects seemed pretty basic; a worm-eaten wardrobe, some benches and several dilapidated chairs were the principal pieces. Under the mantel of the vast fireplace were several utensils made of pottery principally used for household cleaning purposes. However, no hams or sides of bacon hung from the ceiling; the large sideboard contained nothing that could satisfy an appetite, and the dented salting pot contained only shards of stained glass.

The travelers contemplated this unexpected scene with stupefaction while their host struggled to rekindle the flame on the grate. Since they were tired, and soaked to the bone, they soon turned their attention to their own state. Removing their cloaks, they moved to the fireplace.

The Baron de Massac was one of those rugged soldiers that civil and foreign wars had created from the ranks of nobility. He wore a breastplate made from buffalo hide and neck armor made of steel and his huge spurs jingled on his boots. This military demeanor suited his facial appearance; tanned, lined, and adorned with a thick grey mustache. However, his clear blue eyes did not reflect the toughness implied by the harshness of his words.

As for his son, Gaston, he was a handsome adolescent or, as they used to say, a young aristocrat; capable, elegant, refined and open. He smiled often and his smile was full of grace. He also wore a buffalo-hide breastplate but a starched ruff replaced the neck armor, and this innocent vanity perfectly reflected his youth. Like the Baron, he wore a felt cap topped by a feather that was slightly damaged by the wind and the rain. Like him, he was armed with a sword and a shell-hilted dagger. Father and son each wore around their necks a rosary that identified them as fervent Catholics, not to be confused with Huguenots.

The potter, having succeeded in rekindling the flames, moved two old wooden chairs closer and said to his guests:

"Please be seated Sires, I would like to provide you the hospitality that you deserve, but I warned you that I am but a simple artisan, and earn, by the sweat of my brow, just enough bread to feed my family and myself. Even so, the bread is sometimes wanting! For now, permit me to look after your animals."

"Yes, yes, take care of Courtaud," responded the Baron de Massac who like all true horsemen, had a soft spot for his favorite mount.

The potter went to a corner of the room. One could hear the rustle of containers as he withdrew the medicines he would need. Next, having selected a candle, he was preparing to go out when an inner door opened and two women entered.

The mistress of the house did not appear to be older than thirty-six, but worry, privations and the fatigue of childbirth had wilted her complexion, hollowed her cheeks and removed the spark from her dark eyes. An austere, almost gloomy expression characterized her features. There was something impatient and irritable in her manner. She had hastily put on a homespun shift that was rather threadbare in appearance.... Several locks of hair appeared under her coarse linen head covering. Her footwear consisted of wooden clogs that resonated on the brick floor.

Following her came a young girl, almost a child. She was blond, with the dark eyes of her mother and the noble and intelligent stature of her father. Her high forehead with arched eyebrows glowed with innocence. Her ruby lips seemed destined to open only to pronounce soft words. Her attire consisted of a shirt cruelly patched but exquisitely clean and tied at the collar by a ribbon, and her skirt was a bit short. Her arms and legs were thus partially bare, and while these retained the charms of a child, they were white and well formed. Her hair was luxurious and held in place by a ribbon that allowed natural curls to fall on her shoulders.

The charming child seemed completely oblivious to the deficiencies of her clothing and expressed no shame. After having made a brief curtsy, she turned her attention, with wide eyes, to the visitors whose military arms and feathers excited her curiosity.

The mother once again attracted attention. She approached, with furrowed brows and an impatient step. However, when she realized that the visitors were of an upper class, she in turn curtsied, and said in a reserved tone:

"May God protect you Sires, and all welcome to you here; but you have not been told… Bernard, Bernard, are you not ashamed to have these respectable Lords witness our misery?"

As the potter was left speechless by the vehemence of this declaration, the Baron replied with a hearty laugh:

"By the devil's horns, woman, do not mistreat your husband, as it is not exactly of his free will that he brought us into your home."

"And," added Gaston de Massac, "he warned us that his lodgings were cruelly bare. His family must not be concerned by our presence. A warm spot near your fireplace until the gates of your city are open is all that we seek."

The young damsel gave a fleeting smile to Gaston to thank him for his reassurance.

"It is Bernard's fault if we cannot properly receive travelers," angrily replied his wife, "Thanks to his follies, we are in a state of suffering and desperation…and we have six children, most of whom are small."

These reproaches painfully touched the head of the household. However, he forced himself to reply in a firm manner:

"Patience! woman, patience! Better times are ahead. God, until now, has chosen to test us. Soon, perhaps in a few hours, I will find the rewards of sixteen years of toil, research and suffering. If my latest batch is successful, as I hope it will be, you and these poor children will have everything you need. We will become rich, and the entire kingdom… but I must return to my oven. The least inattention could ruin the batch, which is our last resource. You and Esther, stay with our guests to keep them company. Give them everything that our home can provide… but do not abuse me as I already have a broken heart and I need all the courage that I can muster!"

A tear glistened in his sunken eye. Esther saw the tear, and as the potter was about to leave, ran to him and standing on the tips of her tiny bare feet, threw her arms around his neck and said to him through her own tears:

"Have confidence, father; God who grants victories to soldiers will grant success to the laborious artisan, I am sure…. Poor father," she added. "How tired you are, and your clothes are so wet!"

A smile appeared on the potter's face.

"Do not worry about that, Esther," he replied, giving his daughter a kiss. "You are good. You give me the strength to achieve my task. May heaven's blessings be upon you…."

And he dashed out the door where the rain and wind continued to rage in full force.

The two gentlemen had seated themselves, as we previously mentioned, near the fire whose and bright and sparkling flames comforted them. The mistress of the house settled herself on the side; but remained silent, no doubt frustrated at having nothing to offer their guests. Esther, however, skipped around the room searching for ways to be useful. She had laid their coats on a bench to facilitate their drying. She sponged off their felt caps and brushed the damp feathers. She wiped the large swords and the scabbards that the travelers had placed on a table. At the slightest movement of either father or son she would attempt to foresee their needs and react accordingly.

Gaston discreetly observed the movements of this gentle creature. The elder Massac, who was beginning to feel drowsy under the effects of the fire, yawned and said:

"My good woman, what is your husband's name?"

"Master Bernard Palissy," responded the mother.

This name, which would later become famous, was unknown to the two

Massacs.

"He is a potter of clay, I believe?" continued the Baron, more to combat his sleepiness rather than expressing interest in his hosts.

"He has been working for a number of years to become one," replied the Mistress Bernard with some animation. "Bernard was formerly a glass-painter; he was also employed for a time by the King's tax commissioners as a surveyor to map the salt marshes of Saintonge. He was quite skillful. When we were first married he earned a good living and we lacked nothing. But since that time, the sight of a beautiful glazed vase from Faenza turned his life upside down. He convinced himself that if we could produce such beautiful pottery in France as was produced in Italy, not only would we become rich, but he would be famous. And so, he has been working night and day. He abandoned a career to follow this dream. He is ruined and deeply in debt and has imposed upon us as well as himself the hardest of privations, spending cold nights outside, often on an empty stomach. Several times he believed that he had succeeded, but there always was an accident, or unexpected circumstances that would occur to ruin his hopes. Today, after all these failed attempts, so many disappointments, he still hopes to succeed. But like the alchemists and the searchers of the philosopher's stone,[6] perhaps he is doomed to ruin and shame!"

Esther rushed to her, sat on her lap and putting her arms around her neck as she had done with Master Bernard, she cried:

"He will succeed, mother, he will succeed. Do not doubt…. It would be like raising doubts about goodness, justice and Providence!"

Then turning towards the two Gentlemen while still maintaining her touching perch, she said with conviction:

"Perhaps, Sires, you will be witnesses to the success of my father…. Ah! You cannot imagine with what persistence and energy he will have earned it. He is so knowledgeable…. He has travelled widely, studied extensively. He is familiar with minerals, herbs, and animals from many lands…. He could write volumes on divine creation. He has seen, done and understood so many things and he speaks with such eloquence, goodness and tenderness! The prophets of the Old Testament must have spoken in this way to teach the people and lead them in the way of righteousness!"

The lovely child had lost herself in this vivid admiration of her father, and her face glowed with pride, when Mistress Bernard suddenly interrupted:

"Keep quiet, little idiot!" she said. "Would you believe dear Sires, that it is she who encourages Bernard in this erroneous path that he has taken. He taught her how to read and write, and now she helps him with his books and writings, and while they each continue to live on their cloud, we are in

6 **philosopher's stone**, is a legendary alchemical substance capable of turning base metals such as mercury into gold or silver.

distress and suffer a lack of food and clothing. This evening, the family went to bed without supper because our last piece of bread was reserved for the smallest of the children… who have still not had enough… and are crying their hunger. Do you not hear them?"

She pointed towards the room next door where one could indeed hear the complaints and cries of children. She was about to go there to calm them when the exterior door opened and Bernard entered the workshop, accompanied by a blast of wind and rain.

The potter was pale and trembling, less from cold than fright. His emaciated face reflected total desperation.

"Esther," he cried, "are there any pieces of wood left in here? I am out of wood and my oven will cool…. If this happens, it will be our ruin and our death!"

"What! Father, are there no more of those stakes and sticks that you thought would be sufficient to finish the batch?"

"None, my child: the bad weather obliged me to use more fuel than I expected. My God, the fire is already slowing down and if in five minutes I don't add another armful of firewood…. But," he added, his eyes fixed on some bits of wood that remained in a corner, "do you have a little left?"

And he reached out towards the miserable pile with hungry hands; Esther stopped him:

"What benefit, father, can you get from these scraps? And are you thinking of these Lords to whom you have offered our hospitality and who must remain until morning?"

"This is true," said Bernard, turning away to resist temptation. "Our guests come first, but what shall I do? If I had the time I would tear down the stable to burn its material."

"Yes, what to do?" repeated Esther, distraught.

"Oh! What's the difference," said the mother bitterly; "Die a few days earlier, or die a few days later, isn't our death near and certain?"

Gaston de Massac rose up:

"Do not despair in this manner, good people," he said with pity in his voice. "With the permission of my father, my wallet is at your service."

He plunged his hand in the pouch hung at his belt and withdrew several coins. Mistress Bernard hesitated and made a movement to take what was offered. However, Esther's face became red as a beet and the potter said with animation:

"A thousand thanks, young sire. Ah, if it were daylight and if I could, with silver, obtain what I needed, I would bless your generosity…. But in the middle of the night, with all the neighbors asleep… Holy Spirit! Inspire me!"

He closed his eyes as if in contemplation or prayer. Suddenly, he opened them and rapidly looked around him. He rushed to the oak bench that was the principal piece of furniture in the workshop and loaded it on his shoulder. With his other hand, he grabbed an axe and charged out into the night.

"Good God, that's all that was missing, that he burns our furniture! What will we become?" cried the mother.

Overcome by grief and anger, she fled to the other room where her children continued their lamentable wailing. The young girl, in tears, closed the outside door, and she could hear the sounds of the axe as Bernard broke up the bench to throw the pieces into the furnace.

Esther returned and sat in a corner. Now the moans of the mother had joined those of the children in the other room, and this noise, mixed with the howling winds of the storm outside, began to irritate the elder Massac, who was increasingly feeling the lack of sleep.

"By the head of Saint Martial!" he said, squirming in his chair. "Satan himself led us into this house of misery.... One cannot eat, drink, or even rest in peace.... May the Devil take this house and its inhabitants!"

However, Mistress Bernard had managed to calm her brood, and the Baron, succumbing to fatigue, finally dozed off.

III.

THE VIGIL

There was a moment of silence. Esther, who as we said, had settled in a dark corner of the room, remained very still, her face hidden in her hands. Finally, however, she sat up, pushed aside the curls that fell over reddened eyes, and turned towards the travelers. The Baron was decidedly asleep, and the glow of the fire, playing on his lined and mustached features, made him seem even more formidable. As for the younger man, who was leaning forward in a graceful pose, he was observing the lovely Esther attentively, and perhaps without realizing it, tears of sympathy moistened his eyes.

The girl once again noticed these tears: she moved towards him and asked with an adorable innocence:

"It is because of us that you are crying, is it not? It is for my father who is so patient, courageous and grand, for my mother whose misfortune has embittered her and for me who is suffering due to their suffering…. Oh! You have a good heart, Master Gaston!"

"Gaston!" repeated the young de Massac with delight. "You know my name, Miss Esther?"

"You also know mine! I heard your father call you thus…. Your father frightens me; but not you, Sire Gaston; I understood immediately that you have a tender heart, with pity for those who are suffering."

"You may add that I admire what is beautiful, noble and worthy of respect, and seeing you so young, so charming and already so unhappy…."

"You say this," replied Esther with some confusion, "because you arrived here just at a moment of crisis where all the dark spirits seem aligned against us…. But an inner voice tells me that this will change. The science of my father, thanks to divine protection, will overcome the evil influences. The name of Bernard Palissy will become known all over the world. Then my mother will no longer cry, will cease to be irritated, and will become as nice as she was before…. And each day I will thank the heavens for the happiness and glory he will have brought to those I love the most!"

Esther spoke with a sort of religious fervor and with a confidence that left no room for doubt. Gaston de Massac could not hide his astonishment.

"Upon my word, Miss, what a pleasure it is to hear you…. Angels must sound like this when they descend to earth. You have such a melodious voice and generous thoughts. You have been given an education that considering your youth and present circumstances is totally unexpected."

"I have never had any other teacher than my father," replied Esther not without a touch of naïve pride, "and he will teach me many more things. I would be so happy if I could reflect the wisdom and divine sentiments that inspire him! I gather his words and engrave them in my memory. Often, when he is there working on the designs for his pottery, I read aloud to him from his favorite books. We enjoy discussing passages of the Bible, which contains all the basic precepts of wisdom; then, to rest ourselves and raise our hearts towards God we sing those lovely psalms of David, put into verse by the poet Marot.…"

Gaston de Massac, who until that moment had succumbed to the charm of listening to Esther, suddenly leaned back. His face clouded and he abruptly said:

"You read the Bible in French, Miss? And you sing psalms put into rhyme by a heretic? Myself, I have never read the Bible except in Latin, and the Church forbids…"

"Oh! Sire Gaston, how would I know the Sacred Scriptures if I did not read them in French? I don't understand Latin, and my father himself, to his great regret, does not understand it either. Should we, because of this ignorance, be deprived of the sovereign precepts, the holy lessons, the infinite comforts contained in this sacred book? Its verses are so beautiful, so melodious! When we are broken-hearted they restore our courage, our strength, our hope!"

Esther had raised her voice. Gaston de Massac made a sign of dismay, pointing towards the sleeping Baron:

"Hush! Miss, Hush! For God's sake! My father must not suspect…. If you only knew the mission he is on at this moment.…"

Esther, surprised and concerned, was about to question the young de Massac when the front door opened once again and Bernard entered.

"More, more!" he cried in a feverish voice, "this worm-eaten wood burns at an inconceivable rate. Fortunately, the rain and the wind are diminishing, and I have just made sure that the glaze is beginning to melt. The heat-resistant bricks and the 'cazettes,'[7] which I invented, worked very well; a final effort and I will succeed."

"Well, father, there are still some items here that you can burn."

---

7 **cazettes**, (or casettes) are fireclay boxes in which items are placed as a protection from the direct action of the flames and kiln during firing. Invented by Palissy, his system is still used today in a process called 'encastage.'

While saying this, Esther was clearing the table, which Bernard hoisted on his shoulders, and in addition she brought him the stool on which she had been sitting moments before. The potter, bent by his double load, was about to leave, when Mistress Bernard, undoubtedly alerted by the noise, re-appeared on the doorsill of the second room. She was nursing a baby.

"Bernard," she said in a vibrant voice, "if you need more wood, you should not forget to take the cradles of your youngest children.... Then the little ones will sleep in my arms!"

Palissy responded with a low groan and left rapidly, while his wife returned to the other room slamming the door behind her. The Baron, awakened with a jolt, gestured with impatience and mumbled:

"Triple shades of Lucifer! Is it not possible to get a moment of rest? May lightning strike... and the plague destroy..."

The rest degenerated into a series of indistinct words, and the gentleman fell back asleep.

Gaston, his eyes fixed on the flame in the stove, remained as in a trance. Esther, having lost her seat, sat down on an old reversed earthen pot. At this distance from the fire and because of this tempestuous night, she was regretting the flimsiness of her clothing. Her frail body shivered and her teeth chattered.

Gaston finally noticed her discomfort. He rose and approached her.

"Esther, poor little one," he said kindly, "you are so cold.... Please come sit by my side."

And, taking her by the hand, he led her to a stone seat set in the side of the chimney. He held the little hand that trembled for a moment. Esther timidly said:

"I thought, Sir Gaston, that you despised us because we were of the Reformist religion."

"I could not despise you, Esther, but I pity you.... Yes, I pity you with all my heart. Not that I understand the differences between the religion of the Pope and that of Calvin, but, you and your family will be exposed to the cruelest persecution.... Listen to me.

"For the past several years, the Protestant ministers who came from Germany have made many converts in your Saintonge. Until now, we have left them in peace, as well as the other Huguenots in the nearby provinces. We have tolerated their clandestine meetings and we limited ourselves to going after the more audacious or more turbulent followers. However, as of today, this leniency comes to an end. My father is gentleman-in-waiting to Sire Anne de Montmorency, Constable of France; and I, since my education has been completed, am attached as personal Secretary to Sire de Montmorency who became fond of me, and not knowing how to either read or write, uses me often for his secret correspondence. So, at this very moment, the

Baron is bringing letters from King Henri and the Constable for the Governors of the cities in Poitou and Saintonge. These letters ordain that as soon as received, these Governors must seek out with utmost vigor all Protestants regardless of sex, age or condition who are found in their area of responsibility. They are then to be tried, and if convicted of heresy, confiscation of their effects, imprisonment and the most terrible torments will await them, unless they agree to recant.... These are, poor child, the orders that are about to be handed in a few hours to Master de Pons, Governor of Saintes. You understand now why I am concerned that my father not learn of your religion and that of your family. He is not lacking in indulgence about most things, but he is an ardent Catholic and his zeal sometimes leads to excesses. It is to protect him from the consequences of this zeal that I obtained permission to accompany him.... And I have already proven to him that if I feared danger for him, I do not for myself."

Esther Palissy listened, with gaping mouth. The shivering from the cold had suddenly ceased and now perspiration appeared on her brow.

"Good heavens!" she murmured grasping her hands together. "Will persecutions begin? Will they no longer permit us to worship God as we wish and according to our conscience? My father told me many times that since the arrival of the Protestant ministers in this country, men have improved, workers have become more industrious, and morals are purer."

"This is a falsehood, Esther," said the young de Massac who seemed to have a good dose of the paternal zeal himself; "but I beg of you, do not forget the fearsome clauses of the edict.... Neither sex nor age, that is to say neither frailty, nor innocence will be a safeguard against torture."

"So be it Gaston," responded Esther. "If primitive religions have had their martyrs, why would the Reformist religion not have theirs? If death comes because of my beliefs, I am ready!"

This was said with a simplicity that signaled an unshakeable resolution.

"Poor child," continued Gaston, "are you sure of being able to maintain this certainty in the face of torture? And do you think that even if you remained strong in the face of your own suffering, you might not remain so in the face of that of your father, mother or your brothers and sisters? Look, in the Provinces that we have just visited, these terrible edicts have caused great agitation among your fellow religionists. The majority have already armed themselves, and perhaps a bloody civil war may ensue. Aren't you afraid that Master Bernard, for whom faith is so vital..."

"Oh! As for that no, Master de Massac, I have known for a long time what my father's sentiments are on this point, and he would never participate in a civil war. He has shown in many instances great courage; but he would never take arms to kill his fellow man in the name of peace, religion or love. He would accept martyrdom; though robust and brave, he would, like a lamb, bare his throat to a cutlass but he would never strike with a sword, even to defend his religion and his God!"

Gaston de Massac felt a real admiration for this gracious child who expressed herself with such nobility, and for the father who had inspired in her such worthy thoughts. He was about to try once again to bring Esther back down to reason when Bernard made his third entrance.

The poor potter looked exhausted. His cheeks were paler, his eyes more sunken. His hair was plastered against his head by rain or perspiration, and water dripped from his miserable clothes. However, at this moment there was a smile on his face.

"My batch is done," he cried. "I only have to slow down the fire and wait for the oven to cool.... However, I need a little more wood to make sure the cooling process is not too rapid."

This time he took away the drawers and the door of the old cupboard. By now the only pieces of furniture left in the workshop were the two seats on which the de Massacs, father and son, were seated. Palissy announced that from all appearances, he would not need to return, and he left with his burden.

For several moments, one could hear the heavy breathing of the Baron. The old gentleman, used to a rude life, slept in a chair the way he might have done in a bed. Esther had become motionless and quiet, and suddenly a small moan escaped her lips, she paled and moved her head from side to side. She leaned against the wall and one might have thought that she was about to fall on the ground.

Gaston took her in his arms.

"Esther, what is the matter?" he asked. "Good God! emotions, fatigue, lack of sleep...hunger perhaps?"

The girl feebly murmured:

"Nothing! It is nothing.... The moment has passed... useless to alert anyone, I feel better now."

Gaston carefully settled her into the chair where he had been sitting until now and where the arms and the elevated backrest provided support. Then he began searching around the object-filled room for a cordial, some wine, or perhaps a bit of food that might help revive this young person. He found nothing that met his need except for a cracked pitcher that contained some water. He filled a pewter goblet and brought it to Esther. She took two or three swallows and a few indistinct words escaped her violet lips.

Gaston sat on the stone bench at the corner of the chimney. On his shoulder leaned the blonde head, with its floating curls, of the young girl, while he waited for her to regain consciousness. Esther made a soft sweet sound, and tried to move her hand, but once again became comatose.

Gaston did not dare move for fear of disturbing this innocent creature who was now so totally under his protection. However, he began to worry about her prolonged loss of consciousness when he noticed that her breathing had become easier and more regular. Her eyes were closed under the shadow of her long eyelashes; she was sleeping.

Gaston de Massac, who himself had all the naivety of early manhood, had a sense of bliss. For this frail child, sleep provided an escape from pain, past and present, and the recovery of lost strength. He therefore was careful not to disturb this precious rest, and he found an immense charm in the sensation of the lovely head leaning on his shoulder.

A certain time passed. All was quiet in the potter's house. Crying and whimpers could no longer be heard coming from the room containing Mistress Bernard and her children. Gaston felt the breath of the young girl on his cheek, breath that was slightly warm and perfumed like a Spring breeze. In her sleep, Esther had thrown her arm around the neck of the young man, as she would have her father or mother, and when Gaston moved, she once again made that soft plaintive sound.

Gaston continued to be careful not to move, despite the fatigue brought on by this posture. One might have thought that he could have tried to sleep, but his eyes remained wide open, and holding his breath, he appeared to be counting the beats of the young heart that throbbed next to him.

The lamp, for want of oil, had burned out, and the unattended fireplace gave off only a vacillating glow. However, a white tint coming from the exterior signaled the start of day, when Bernard entered the workshop.

At the sound of his steps, Esther woke with a start. The obscurity prevented her from realizing what had been supporting her during her comatose state; moreover, in the first few moments her ideas were vague and confused.

Palissy walked with difficulty and without seeming to know what he was doing or where he was. However, he cried out with an exaltation that resembled madness:

"Hosanna! My daughter, Esther... My work is accomplished! I am letting the fire to go out and the oven cool. Soon I will know my fate.... In the meantime, let us praise God!"

Esther, rapidly brought back to the realities of the current situation, responded with sadness:

"Beloved father, I am always ready to praise God with you, but we would need to know if we are to ask for forgiveness or pray for the courage and patience to face new challenges!"

"This time, my daughter," Bernard exulted, "everything is arranged; I have no more doubts, and my heart is full of joy.... Esther Palissy, your father whom you have seen contrite and so miserable that he has been ridiculed by his neighbors, cursed by his family, rejected by all, your father has just invented the *rustic figulines.*[8] A new art form has come to France. The temples of Christ and the palaces of kings will be embellished with the results of my work. The Lord lowers the great to raise the humble…. Esther my darling daughter, this is a hymn of thanksgiving that we must offer to God above. Sing with me Psalm 104 that celebrates the magnificence of creation and the goodness of the Creator."

Esther was electrified by his enthusiasm, which her energetic and ardent nature lent itself to sharing; but then she remembered the presence of the two gentlemen and how such a demonstration of piousness could have terrible consequences for Bernard and the entire family.

"Father," she said timidly, "I pray of you to calm yourself…. We must respect the slumber of our guests. Later we can thank Divine Providence."

However, Bernard was in such a feverish state that nothing could prevent the explosion of his feelings and words. He had totally forgotten about the two Massacs.

"Glory be to God! Glory be to God!" he cried. He began singing the psalm put into verse by Marot[9] and Théodore de Bèze[10] that ends as follows:

> *As long as I have life in me*
> *There will always be songs for thee;*
> *To my true God, in all Thy glory,*
> *Psalms will be witness to Thy story.*
>
> • • • • •
>
> *Up, up, my heart, with God, where good abounds*
> *To praise Thee… All praise with joyful sounds!*

This poetry is perhaps a bit dated now, but Bernard put in so much ardor and devotion that one could not listen to it without feeling emotion. Esther soon joined in and mixed her melodious and melancholy voice to his deep tones. Then, from the depths of the adjoining room, silvery voices, those of the children, brusquely awakened but recognizing the sounds familiar to their ears, joined in like a distant echo, singing the song of David. This humble concert, in the surrounding calm, in the dark of night, had a pious and sad effect capable of stirring the imagination.

Most certainly Gaston de Massac had a feeling of compassion; but he immediately attended to his father who was beginning to stir uncomfortably in his chair. The old gentleman was doing his best to come back to his senses and understand what was going on around him. No doubt memories

---

8 *rustic figulines,* Bernard Palissy's name for his creation. He later received the title of "Inventor of the King's Figulines" in official documents.

9 **Clément Marot**, (1496-1544) Famous 16th century poet put into verse biblical Psalms that were sung all over France.

10 **Théodore de Bèze**, ((1519-1605) French Protestant theologian, translator of the bible, professor, ambassador and poet.

returned slowly as the chanting had been going on for some time, when suddenly his boot with its heavy spurs hit the floor and he cried out with a voice hoarsened from sleep:

"By the Devil's tail! What is going on! What is this strange music that is insulting my eardrums. Great thunders, are we at a Sorcerer's Sabbath, or a Huguenot ritual?"

And since in the fervor of their zeal the singers did not cease, the Baron jumped up repeated in indignation:

"It is a ritual; it is a Huguenot ritual, Sacrebleu!… Where are my sword and my dagger! Long live the true Mass. Hell to Luther and Calvin! One does not dare sing psalms in the presence of the Baron de Massac."

His powerful pronouncements finally imposed silence upon Bernard and his family; poor Esther held herself close to her father and searched out Gaston's eyes to implore his support; but she only succeeded in catching a vague glimpse of him on the far side of the room.

While the old gentleman struggled to find his arms, Bernard responded coolly:

"What is the problem between us, Sire? You and your son, you are my guests; you have had the last chairs that I have, the last glow from my lamp, the last fire from my stove. Why are you troubling our last actions for grace? Why prevent us from thanking God in our own manner for the favors he grants us?"

"I will not tolerate Huguenot rites in my presence. You don't know me yet. I will have you burned, and may hell forgive me! I will teach you that one does not pray to God in French…."

"And yet it is in French that you blaspheme Him," replied Bernard with irony.

"Cursed Protestant, you want to argue with me? I will not lower myself to chastising you, but in a few hours, you will realize…."

Gaston rushed to intervene.

"Father," he said, "with all due respect, allow me to remind you that Master Bernard Palissy is in his own home, and it is not for us who have taken refuge here…. Any violence or insult on our part would be unworthy of us as Gentlemen!"

The father, in spite of his fanaticism, had a great respect for Gaston who had superior intelligence and knowledge, and whom he adored. He therefore calmed down immediately.

"So be it," he said, "but if anyone dared propose having me attend a Protestant ritual…. Come, my son," he continued, "there is nothing to retain us here. This house is situated such that we should have little trouble leaving it, and we were fortunate to have dined yesterday evening passing through Nérac…. Day is breaking, and the gates of Saintes will soon be open. Let's get on with it. And you, Master Bernard, bring us our horses…. Doubtless the poor animals have not been treated any better than us in your house of famine!"

"However, Sire, for you as for them, I gave all that I could give…. There remained in my stable a few bundles of straw left in the hayracks. I was able to draw from the well several buckets of water…. As regards the horse that had been hurt and on which I applied a poultice of my creation on his leg, it might be dangerous to make him walk for the moment, even if only to go to the town…. But I affirm that if you can leave him in the stable for another twenty-four hours, not only will you be able to ride him, you will be able to continue your journey as though he had never had an accident."

The elder de Massac opened wide his eyes.

"By Saint Martial! Is this possible?" he blurted, "The poor animal was *crowned* for God's sake!"

"Yes, it was *crowned*, but I repeat, Sire, that by tomorrow it will be well."

"My father has knowledge, said Esther with pride, "about the healing powers of stone, metals and plants, and he possesses many surprising secrets."

Gaston exchanged a few quiet words with the Baron. Finally, he spoke to the potter:

"It is agreed Master Bernard; my father will take my horse while I will follow on foot. Since we must remain in Saintes one or two days, Courtaut will stay with you until our departure. On the day after tomorrow, we will return to get him, and if he is well, as you predict, then you will have performed a truly miraculous cure…. In the meantime, since your four-footed guest will create some expenses, you will not refuse to take this."

He then reached into his belt and withdrew several coins that he tended towards the master of the house.

At that time no one, even those not of the servile classes, was ashamed to receive money from a person of the upper classes. This was the perfect example of how certain high scruples now common, were then nonexistent. However, Palissy and his daughter looked away with pride.

"My house is not an inn," said Bernard, "do not be offended by my refusal, Sires; I do not accept payment for my hospitality."

Gaston de Massac could not believe that in the family's state of destitution this gesture could be sincere, so he was about to insist. However, Mistress Bernard, who had slipped unnoticed into the room, threw herself upon the outstretched hand, taking what it contained, saying fiercely:

"Give, give…. *They* are honorable, but we do not only need hay for the horses, we need bread for the children who will soon awaken whimpering from hunger…. He," continued Mistress Bernard, pointing to her husband, "has not had a bite to eat in the past twenty-four hours. Would you believe that in spite of his his pride, he would not ask for food? Thank you, my good Lords. Esther and he may be offended, but I bless you!"

Neither Palissy nor his daughter dared say a word. Moreover, after this declaration, Mistress Palissy hurried to re-enter her room as though she feared that someone might take back what she had obtained for her family.

The two Massacs had gathered up their swords and put on their cloaks. Day was breaking and they went out to the open courtyard where the potter's furnace was located. Palissy and Esther accompanied them to the stable.

The horses were found to be in better condition, and this vision delighted the elder de Massac.

"On my word as a Gentleman," he said, "Courtaut looks much better… nurse him well, my man, and if by tomorrow you have put him back on his legs, as you have promised, you will have no need for repentance."

"You may count upon my word, Sir Baron, and tomorrow morning I will return him to you in good health…. At that same hour," continued Bernard, glancing over to his furnace where a few last pieces of coal were being consumed, "I will remove my pottery and discover finally if God has blessed my work…. May the heavens grant that my confidence in myself is not a vain presumption."

"What? Father," said Esther terrified, "you mean you are not certain of the result?"

"Doubts return as the moment of truth approaches," replied Bernard with a sigh.

During this conversation, the healthy horse had been taken out of the stable and harnessed. The Baron de Massac mounted him and they exited the enclosure by the gap by which the voyagers had entered the previous night. One could see in the distance, the city of Saintes built on a rise with its ramparts, towers and turrets becoming visible in the morning mist.

At the moment that Bernard and his daughter, who had accompanied the travelers to the road, were about to leave them, Esther, shivering in the chilly early morning breezes, said in a low voice to Gaston:

"In spite of your religion, Master de Massac, you are a good person. I have the proof. Please protect my father from the persecution that threatens us."

"I will try," Gaston hastily replied, "I will try because of you, but on your side, I beg of you, do not, Master Bernard and yourself, play the martyr… because no human effort will be able to save you."

And he set out towards the town with his father, while Bernard and Esther, having bowed humbly, returned toward the house.

As they were about to enter, they heard the slam of the door that gave on the public path and saw Mistress Bernard running towards the first houses on the approach to the town. Palissy halted, astonished.

"Does my wife have the same idea as I, and is she thinking of warning…. but of course not, she is only thinking of her children and their hunger and is going to buy some bread with the money from these gentlemen…. Well, I admit that I too feel exhausted, feeble unto death, and would accept a piece of bread, even if it came from charity!"

"I would also accept, father," replied poor Esther, "and I feel ashamed that I have so little courage."

"Come now, my child, you will soon be satisfied thanks to the foresight of your mother…. But pending her return, do you think that you might have the strength to perform a task that would be pleasing to God… and to me?"

"What does this involve?" asked the youngster, feigning strength and a tranquility that she did not really feel.

"You are aware of the terrible edicts that these gentlemen have been charged to give to the Governor of the town. Perhaps even today persecution will be unleashed upon our brethren in religion, and the most immediately menaced will be our honorable Pastor, Master Hamelin, who lives nearby. If you, who can come and go without attracting attention, could hasten to the home of Master Hamelin and tell him what is going on… you could save our young and respected pastor, as well as the other members of our poor congregation from great misfortune."

"You are right, father; I am going," said Esther. She threw on a woolen shawl that was her warmest covering and headed for the pastor's home.

As soon as she left, Bernard collapsed on the floor of his house, broken by fatigue, suffering and hunger. When his wife returned, she found him there in a state of semi-consciousness.

IV.

DISCUSSIONS AT THE CHATEAU AND ENVIRONS

For the entire day, there was great agitation and noise in the city of Saintes. One could hear the beating of drums and the sound of trumpets. At the same time, squads of soldiers, musketeers, on foot and on horseback, roamed the city leading people in chains. Several of these squads entered the surrounding villages and did not leave without obtaining a number of prisoners, as one could judge from the cries of anguish which came from all sides. This was the result of the orders brought that morning by the Baron de Massac. These orders, as we know, specified that the Governor of Saintes arrest all persons known to be of the Protestant religion and deliver them to the Bordeaux Parliament, which at that time, proved itself to be intractable towards heretics.

That night there were a number of meetings at the home of Master de Pons, the Governor, who lived in the ancient Gothic chateau that had replaced the "Capitole", built by the Romans. They had just finished their supper, served in a large room with a vaulted ceiling held up by pillars and walls, adorned with trophies of armor. Sitting around a massive oak table, still covered with a substantial amount of food, jugs and bottles, were, in addition to the two Massacs, the Governor, a youngish man with a fresh face; several local personages and church dignitaries from Saintes. This group was discussing the events of the day when a soldier wearing armor and a steel helmet entered the room. This was the Captain of the King's troops, who had presided over the arrests and was coming in to report on the results of the searches.

"By the Cross, Raby," asked Master de Pons good humoredly, "did you accomplish your task successfully with your troops against those cursed Huguenots, as was ordered by the King and the Constable?"

"I did not tread lightly, Sire Governor," answered the Captain while saluting. "However, I'll be damned, but I am sure these rascals were warned because the majority had left their homes before my arrival. However, I did bring in about a hundred of these heretics to the Chateau's prison. For once, I could do no better!"

"We must not allow peace or respite to these pariahs!" cried with violence a somber-looking monk who was the Father Superior of the town's Dominicans. "We must crush this nest of vipers. Captain Raby, I thought you a better Catholic and I had hoped that you would show more zeal in combatting ungodliness!"

"I am very saddened, Reverend Father," replied the soldier in confusion, "at not having met your expectations, but by the guts of... pardon, I meant to say that tomorrow, I will do better."

"Don't forget your promise; I have been told that you are guilty of many sins, Captain Raby. During the wars in Italy you burned down a number of Churches and Convents, and tortured monks and nuns.... It is only by your zeal in the pursuit of heretics that you have a chance of obtaining indulgence and forgiveness."

"I am not lacking in zeal, Reverend Father, and by the horns of... Sorry! Once again, but it is not my fault if I failed to put my hands on that prophet of the Devil, the young minister Hamelin."

"What? That servant of Satan was not captured with the others?"

"I had specifically informed you, Captain," said the Governor, "that this man was to the Reformists as a clarion call is to rebellion."

"So you did, sir, and I lost no time in hurrying to his home with a half-dozen good men. Unfortunately, we searched his house from the cellar to the attic in vain.... That infidel had either left the country, or perhaps been taken away by his friend, Satan."

"He has not left," said the Dominican. "He is too obstinate to desert his dammed cause so rapidly, and if you are vigilant, you will be able to snatch him in one of his hiding places.... But at least you have placed that fanatic, Bernard Palissy, in safe custody, have you not?"

As soon as his name was pronounced, a silence fell upon the room. Raby snickered nastily:

"Oh! By the Saints," he remarked, "that one is not difficult to find.... We can have him when we want him, as easily as catching a chicken in its feathers; but this morning Master de Pons expressly forbid me to..."

"This is true," replied the Governor, slightly embarrassed; "in deference to the de Massacs, who lodged with Master Bernard this past night, I recommended to Captain Raby that he not menace this inoffensive artisan... an unfortunate soul who has a mania of singing psalms in French!"

"And that of abandoning honest work," said another, "to experiment with shards of pottery at the expense of his ability to feed his family."

Gaston de Massac straightened and said quietly, but with conviction:

"With your permission Sires, Master Bernard Palissy does not merit being held in such mediocre esteem.... Aside from his religion, which I detest, he impresses me as being industrious, experienced, learned and he believes that he has just discovered the secret of the beautiful and renowned de Faenza pottery. Tomorrow morning, when he opens his oven, if he has succeeded as he expects, much will be said about his discovery. Sire Constable, our master, is already familiar with this artisan, I am told, since he has already employed him as a surveyor to map the salt marshes of Saintonge, and as he greatly appreciates beautiful objects... he will certainly take Master Bernard under his personal protection."

"Gaston is right," added the Baron de Massac, always in deference to the opinions of his son. "Sire Constable, who is acquiring treasure upon treasure for the chateau he is having built in Ecouen, would certainly... moreover, Sacrebleu! that man promised me that he would cure my horse, Courtaut, who had crowned his leg when he fell, within twenty-four hours; and I will be damned if I let anyone mistreat Master Bernard before that Protestant has had the time to keep his promise!"

The Dominican, whose name was Father Desmazures, rose suddenly, his bulging eyes full of menace.

"There you have it!" he exclaimed, "This is how the defenders of the Sacred Church interpret their duties! One is only worried about his horse, the other only concerned about trinkets of porcelain or glass, like the idols of the heathens! Here are the miserable interests we place before those of the Guardian of the heavens! Men of little faith, I repeat, put an end to your impiety and do not make a pact with the Devil.... Baron de Massac, your horse will not be cured, but if he is thanks to sorcery, he will only lead you to the loss of your soul.... As for you, young man," continued the monk, fixing Gaston with a baleful look, "how dare you defend this heretic, known only for his wild imagination and failed experiments for which he has sacrificed the well-being of his family? He has already announced his success to all a number of times, but God, who is his enemy, has confounded his arrogance, destroyed his expectations and humbled his miserable being. Tomorrow it will be the same as it is only those who serve the Church that can attain success on earth and reach the glories of heaven."

He spoke with such vehemence that no one dared even make the slightest objection. Realizing his advantage, Father Desmazures pressed on:

"What is the use of waiting? Tomorrow perhaps the blasphemers will have escaped. The Governor, who to my regret demonstrates insufficient zeal for the defense of the State, has only to authorize that the city gates be opened, and Captain Raby can this very night seize these monsters of impiety; Palissy and the supposed Pastor Hamelin."

Master de Pons, hearing himself accused of having taken a lukewarm approach to the persecution of heretics, furrowed his brow as this kind of reproach could have repercussions. Actually, he was not of a cruel disposition, but he was concerned that pressuring the Huguenots, who were in large numbers in Saintonge, might lead them to revolt, as they actually did later. Not wishing to encourage this approach, he responded:

"Now, now, Father Desmazures, there is no rush, and little reason to infringe upon the regulations of a fortified city. Tomorrow will be soon enough to get our hands on these persons… if such is deemed necessary…. The pastor is no doubt in flight, and Master Palissy is certainly not thinking of leaving his home. You reproached me, Reverend Father, for not having enough zeal; I reproach you for having too much…. But, Corbleu!" he added in another tone of voice, "I feel like going over there for the opening of that famous oven from which will emerge such beautiful objects…. If the announced discovery turns out to be true, we will determine what indulgence can be granted to a worker with talent and who is a useful inventor. However, if Master Bernard Palissy turns out to be a useless dreamer as well as a heretic, I will stop defending him and you can do with him as you wish."

"As for me," said the Baron de Massac, "what is most important is knowing if the potter has cured my horse, Courtaut, as he promised, for if he has failed, I will consider Palissy an imposter, a rascal, and I shall ask that he be severely punished."

"I shall also be there," said Captain Raby, stroking his red moustache with one hand and toying with his heavy sword with the other. "If Master de Pons orders it, I will not let pass the occasion to make up for my sins."

Decisions having been taken, the participants agreed to meet in the morning to accompany the Governor and the de Massacs to the home of Bernard Palissy. Father Desmazures, although unhappy with the manner in which Master de Pons had treated his request, promised to be there, but with the secret intention of making any act of kindness impossible. Then they separated.

Gaston, who could see the storm forming around Bernard, but incapable of doing anything to prevent it, murmured to himself; "My God! If that poor man cannot keep his promises, what will happen to that innocent child who has expressed so much confidence and faith in me?"

* * * *

The next morning there were a large number of neighbors and curious passersby milling around the home of Palissy. The rumor had spread through Saintes that after sixteen years of unsuccessful efforts, the potter had finally succeeded in his efforts. So, in spite the grave concerns shared by a number of persons, quite a few of them wished to be present for the opening of the oven.

Palissy and his children moved back and forth between the enclosure, the house and the stable as though occupied by a number of tasks. All were dressed in their finest for the solemn event in preparation. The father with his unruly beard and his feverish eyes wore an old quilted doublet and patched up shoes that underscored his emaciated state. He said of himself at that time: "my arms and legs had lost all form, and I was so thin that after attaching my pantaloons, if I moved, they would fall to my heels." His two sons, Mathurin and Nicolas, ten and eight years old respectively, had begun to assist Bernard with his work in spite of their young age. They were dressed in clothing that was badly worn and had become too small for them. As for Esther, she had put on stockings and shoes; shoes that were too large for her tiny feet. One could see on her shoulders the short cloak that hid the lightness of her clothing. However, the hood, which was thrown back, made it possible to admire her abundant hair and adorable child's face with its soft eyes and an expression that was both chaste and serene.

In spite of the preparations for a celebration, Bernard and his family, as noted earlier, appeared anxious, and as the morning progressed, Bernard's state of agitation increased. Several times he approached his oven, checked the heat, and then went away nodding his head.

After a while he was obliged to remain in the enclosure as his neighbors and acquaintances were arriving in numbers. The news that the Governor and other notables were going to be there for the opening of the oven had generated a considerable amount of curiosity and there was nothing to prevent the access to the enclosure of unwelcome visitors. In fact, Bernard had good reason to carefully handle inconvenient visitors; the majority had done him favors, and a few were his creditors.

Therefore, he suffered their presence with resignation, and seated on a rock opposite the oven with all its grates open, holding his head, he listened distractedly to the various conversations being held around him.

Some of the remarks were anything but flattering, and his daughter, standing beside him, seemed to suffer as much as he.

"By the Cross! Brother Palissy," said derisively a neighboring potter who had never produced anything but kitchenware, "the great day has arrived! This is the day you dethrone those ceramic makers from Faenza! Marvelous, only you will be dragged before the Guild for our profession and you will be fined for having manufactured pottery without being a Master Potter."

"But I am a Master Glazer!" replied Palissy.

"It doesn't matter, the Syndicate regulations are specific, and they will not tolerate…."

"Now, now," interrupted a man who had a short jacket on one shoulder and leaned on a cane with a silver knob. "The regulations of the Syndicate would not apply to Bernard since he has never produced an item of value…. It will be so this morning as it has been for a number of years. Yet I would not be displeased if he succeeded, as he would pay me back the twenty ecus[11] I was foolish enough to lend him four years ago at Chandeleur."

"And I," said a large man whose clothes were covered with flour and who owned a mill on the Charente. "He owes me eight bushels of wheat."

"And I," cried the tailor, "a doublet for him and a petticoat for his wife, not to mention several items of clothing for his little ones...."

"Brideau, you were probably able to include the cost of the children's clothes in the price you got for the doublet and petticoat, so you owe him a discount, neighbor," chortled another in a strong Gascon accent.

The person who had just spoken was Master Toupinac, barber-surgeon for the surrounding area. Small, thin, always in movement, he had a sly and malicious expression but sometimes tried to look serious. It was difficult to judge his age, but one could imagine him young although he had been in the area some number of years. He was born in Lectoure, in the center of Gascony, and was called familiarly "the little Gascon."

Brideau, the tailor, did not particularly appreciate the barber-surgeon's attempt at humor.

"Parbleu! Master Toupinac," he said, "you didn't even advance Bernard a beard trim or a haircut because one could swear that neither scissors nor razor have approached his head in months."

Everyone laughed at the expense of poor Palissy who remained impassive.

"Neighbor Brideau," Toupinac said "if I neglected the outside of his head, it was to take care of the inside.... Bernard is a dogged Huguenot and I am working to convert him. I am killing myself to convince him that his misfortunes, miscalculations and other miseries come from his wretched religion.... The more he toils, the more he sweats and labors, the more he sinks in a quagmire. I want to bring him back to the true path; him, his wife and all his household., including the little Esther who from day to day becomes nicer. I do not stop repeating to him that when he rejects these unholy and heretic doctrines, all will change for the better."

The barber-surgeon, as one can see, was one of those "converters" who proliferated during these periods of religious conflict. Unfortunately, his strange appearance, manner and language contrasted with the role he wished to attribute to himself. As soon as he used the phrase "I want to convert him," laughter broke out again.

Bernard Palissy finally stirred from his impassiveness and frowned.

"You care too much, Master Toupinac," he said coldly; "I did not request your good services.... Moreover, it is not with phrases but true Christian actions that one could achieve my conversion."

"Do you question my qualifications?" said Toupinac, vexed. "I am a

11 **ecus**, gold coins introduced by Louis IX in 1266, and various versions remained as official currency until the beginning of the French revolution (1789).

Master Barber-Surgeon, colleague, and I have been tested by the doctors of the Faculty of Bordeaux, as proven by my diploma. I am therefore as apt as a cleric or a monk to inform you of the dangers of erroneous and perverse beliefs which are contrary to the faith…"

"Hey Colleague!" interrupted the miller with false naivety, "would you have used that same knowledge to have treated the boil I had on my leg during the last mowing?"

Toupinac, thus reminded of the requirements of his profession, was about to answer impatiently, when someone cried out:

"Here is the Governor and other noble gentlemen arriving from the city."

"And Captain Raby and his troops are marching behind them," added the miller.

All eyes turned towards the public way. Indeed, a number of persons, the majority of whom wore velvet coats, starched ruffed collars and plumed hats were rapidly advancing. This first group appeared peaceful enough, but the second one, which was composed of about forty disorderly mercenaries armed with muskets and pikes with axe-heads, appeared much less friendly. At a sign from their Captain, three or four dropped out at intervals to check on houses in the village that were known to be inhabited by Huguenots.

V.

THE RUSE

Bernard stood up and looked with the others. At the appearance of Raby and his cutthroats, he could not hide a shudder of fear.

"They have released the tigers and the leopards," he murmured. "God, protect our children."

He leaned over to his daughter and spoke a few words in a lowered voice. Esther replied briefly and then ran towards the house and closed the door behind her.

Master Bernard seemed to wait impatiently for her to come back, but before she could return, the Governor and his retinue entered the enclosure by the gap in the hedge, while Raby and a dozen of the ruffians who remained, headed towards the house as though they were going to conduct a search.

The two Massacs and several other participants from the previous evening accompanied the Governor, as well as Father Demazures who was looking around him suspiciously. Master le Pons, his wide-brimmed felt hat placed aside, one hand leaning on his cane, the other on the hilt of his sword, waddled forward. He said to Palissy, who bowed in respect:

"Good day, my friend. It is said that you have invented a fabulous pottery. These gentlemen and I, we wish to see it. Therefore, please show it to us, and rapidly, as we do not have much time to lose on such trifling matters."

"With your permissions, my dear de Pons," said Baron de Massac, "Would it not be better to first attend to my horse? This fellow swore that he would return Courtaut to me fresh and healthy, and if he fails to do so, upon my word, I will break his bones."

"These threats are unnecessary, Sire de Massac," replied Bernard. "Your horse will be returned and you will find him to be healed as promised.... As concerns the request of the Governor," he added sadly, "I cannot yet give him satisfaction; my oven is still too hot for me to remove the pottery before another hour or two."

The Governor slammed the ground with his cane.

"What is this, you peasant?" he cried. "Are you mocking me? Ah! Corbleu, you and your assistants can burn your hands to do your duty. It is not my concern!"

"If it only concerned the burning of my hands," responded Palissy. "Exposing the pottery too soon to cold air risks causing it to break, and my work will be lost."

"I will not accept such excuses," said de Pons in a fury; "It no doubt is repugnant to your Huguenot pride to satisfy the wishes of a good Catholic and the Royal Governor of the city of Saintes.... Do not push me too far or I will call in Raby who already does not wish you well...."

"Once more, my dear Governor," repeated the Baron de Massac, who pursued his idea, "let us first take care of the horse. This will give time for the oven to cool."

"Sire Governor is too fair-minded to hold Master Bernard responsible for something he cannot control," said Gaston with humility. "I have indeed heard that objects heated excessively can shatter when cooled too rapidly."

"And I agree with Master de Pons," said Father Desmazures: "Master Bernard has always rebelled against earthly authority as well as divine authority, and he perhaps has a secret reason..."

"I have no other motive than unchangeable necessity," answered the poor Bernard, who was losing patience. "Oh well, if it must be so, I will ask you for a little time...and in the interim, I will get Baron de Massac's horse."

"Yes, yes, that's fine!" happily responded the Baron. "Let us rapidly see Courtaut.... By my sword," he continued, speaking to the others, "a horse with a *crowned* leg cured in a few hours will be most surprising!"

Palissy continued to look worried and disconcerted, glancing towards the house where Captain Raby and his gang were prowling expectantly. Nevertheless, he walked slowly towards the stable while the Governor and his friends chatted and laughed among themselves.

Soon he reappeared leading the Baron's horse by its bridle. The animal, fully saddled, held its head high and walked with a firm step, although the damaged leg had some form of bandage.

Massac, his son, the Governor and the other gentlemen present, who all greatly appreciated the veterinarian art, carefully examined the horse which had been so seriously hurt two days earlier. The noble animal, having recognized its master, perked its ears, made several joyful movements and whinnies.

"He is cured.... He is cured, Corbleu!" cried the Baron beside himself. "My poor Courtaut brought back to health... Man, you must provide me with the formula; I would give you fifty pieces of gold! Or if you prefer, I will defend you against all the monks and all the mercenaries of the kingdom, even if you are a ten-fold Huguenot and have participated a hundred times in their rituals, or Devils' assemblies or a Sabbath of sorcerers!"

Upon hearing these blasphemies, Father Desmazures wanted to protest, but all those gentlemen present shared de Massac's enthusiasm.

"It is an astonishing secret," the Governor was saying. "All the horses that I have lost due to crowning and sprains. You must also give me the formula, Master Bernard, and upon my faith as a Christian, you will be rewarded."

"Give me the same, Bernard!" they all chimed in.

Palissy did not reply. While listening to the congratulations of his noble visitors, he continued to look out of the corner of his eye in the direction of his house to see what was going on. An individual wearing a large hat, a short jacket on his shoulders as was the current fashion, had just appeared at a ground floor window, and jumped out into the enclosure. Two of Raby's men were outside and obviously assigned to watch the potter's house, but the mystery person had not made any noise and the guards had their backs turned. He was obviously attempting to join the milling crowd without attracting attention.

Such was the secret preoccupation of Bernard when Father Desmazures, irritated by the enthusiasm of the Governor and his friends for the Huguenot potter, said somberly:

"Beware, good Catholics, of the illusions of the evil spirits. Perhaps this animal has been given the appearance of being healthy by magical means which will only last a few moments.... The foolhardy person who mounts this horse will have his neck broken, or the horse itself will become lame and kill itself with its first steps."

Such declarations were easily accepted during this period of excessive gullibility. Therefore, a number of persons backed away with fear from the poor Courtaut. The Baron de Massac made the sign of the cross.

"Do you really believe this, Reverend Father?" he asked. "However, I am not worried about trying. I would really like to know if Courtaut is capable of trotting and galloping as promised."

In the meantime, Palissy had realized that the stranger had succeeded in losing himself in the crowd; but suddenly some frenzied cries came from the house. The door opened and the Captain emerged gesticulating, his sword in his hand. He was followed by three or four of his men, then by Esther and Mistress Bernard. Raby was furious with his men and seemed to be berating them for their negligence.

The potter did not need an explanation to realize what was happening. He therefore said in an unusual tone:

"Yes, yes, sires, you can mount the horse and assure yourselves that he is completely healed! You! Prove it!" He was speaking to the stranger, still hidden under his hat brim, who had sidled by his side. He added a few words in a low voice.

Palissy had taken Courtaut by his bridle, and either by chance or by plan, had placed the horse between the attending nobles and the mysterious visitor.

What occurred next happened in the blink of an eye. The stranger jumped onto the saddle, seized the reins without taking the time to put his feet in the stirrups, and kicked the horse with his heels. At that same moment, Palissy cried:

"Attention Sires, now we will see if the horse is able to gallop!"

Instinctively, everyone backed up as Courtaut plunged through the hedge and onto the public way.

At that same moment, the Captain ran over.

"Alert!" he cried, "Stop that man.... It is the Huguenot pastor who was hiding at the home of Palissy, and who slipped through my fingers with the help of that cursed family."

"It is Hamelin!" said Father Desmazures; "What a disaster! That pariah will escape."

In fact, the rider, who had until this moment kept his well–known features hidden, was galloping up the road.

No one had a horse with which to pursue. Moreover, Courtaut scampered away with a vigor and lightness that would have made catching them most difficult. The Governor was furious:

"Sacrebleu! he said. "That damned Huguenot is mocking us; making his escape right under our noses!"

"Hmm, a pretty good trick," murmured one of the others, giving a wink....

"Captain Raby," continued de Pons, "what were your musketeers thinking? Shoot! Shoot! That servant of Satan... are you on his side?"

The Captain, furious at having been tricked, had indeed ordered his people to fire on the fugitive, but it was no little task to shoot with the heavy and awkward muskets in use at the time. One had to blow on the lit fuse to get rid of the ash, then trim it to give it the right length before the flame reaches the barrel. After these preliminary actions, which took time and care, one then took aim and pulled the trigger for the perfect shot... if it went off.

The musketeers had reached the road and three or four loud detonations were soon heard, but the rider and his mount were already far away and no doubt did not have much to fear from these shots. The Baron de Massac ran over.

"Halt your shooting," he cried. "Don't you see that you might hit Courtaut? By the Mass... he is galloping beautifully and you would think he had never been hurt.... But when will I get back my horse?"

"Have no fear, Sire," said someone next to him. "Reverend Hamelin is not a thief. Soon your steed will be returned to you."

The person who had spoken was Mathurin, Palissy's oldest son. Massac wanted to question him, but Mathurin had dashed out of the enclosure and appeared to be in pursuit of the rider who had by now disappeared around a bend in the road.

In the meantime, there was quite a tumult around Bernard Palissy who had been rejoined by his wife, Esther and the smaller children.

"Rascal!" the Governor was saying, "You will pay dearly for this audacity.... Facilitate, in my presence, the escape of an enemy of the King and the Sainted Church! I don't know what keeps me from having you shot on the spot and send to jail all your wretched family."

"I am at your orders, Sire Governor," said Captain Raby, "and I will particularly recommend to the jailer that little Huguenot." (He was pointing to Esther, who pale and trembling, was hiding behind her father.) "Persons in the village had warned me that the so-called pastor had taken refuge in the home of Palissy, and I had the house surrounded.... But while the little devil was amusing me with sweet talk and mush, she gave the other the time to slip out by a window.... Sacrebleu! If she is to be taught a lesson, I will be pleased to do so."

And the horrible mercenary reached out as if to grasp Esther. Gaston de Massac moved resolutely between him and Palissy's daughter.

"One moment, Captain!" he said with authority, you will wait for orders from the Governor."

De Pons again addressed Bernard:"Good God! Will you explain, wicked Protestant? What have you to say in your defense? How did this so-called minister come to be in your house? How could you dare make me a witness, and therefore an accomplice to his escape?"

"Nothing was premeditated, Sire Governor," replied Bernard with serenity and straightening himself to his full height. "Hamelin, who is my friend, sought refuge in my house. Could I reject him? He was discovered and pursued. Could I hand him over? God provided him with a means of escape when he was in danger. Could I oppose myself to the will of Heaven? Now Hamelin is certainly in a safe place. If anyone is to be punished it is me alone."

"Marvelous! In this case Raby will teach you to..."

There was an explosion of cries and weeping. His wife and children encircled him with their arms as if to protect him. Palissy pushed them away gently and resumed speaking with his majestic serenity:

"Sire Governor is the master of my life, but first, I pray that he remembers that he came here with his noble friends to see my *rustic figulines*... and I am ready to open my oven."

Master de Pons, who was perhaps not as terrible as he seemed, replied in a gruff tone:

"All right, so be it; let us see your *rustic figulines*, as you call your inventions. But take care, if you betray our curiosity as it is said you have done a number of times, you will be cruelly punished."

"I am staying!" said Raby.

"We can see your potteries," continued Massac, "while my horse is being returned… if he is being returned."

"Sires, I will obey you," said Bernard.

He removed his doublet, and assisted by his family, prepared to remove from the oven the objects that had generated so much curiosity.

VI.

THE RUSTIC FIGULINES

Esther, and especially Mistress Bernard, appeared as nervous as ever. After so many dashed hopes and sad disappointments, they were terrified at the thought of the ramifications of another failure. Nevertheless, they hastened to the task of assisting the potter with the delicate removal of the contents of the oven. The smaller children had been placed in the care of a neighbor, as little by little, the enclosure filled up with the local inhabitants; then Esther and her mother began to carefully place on flagstones that served as tables, the objects that Palissy and his son successively withdrew from the oven.

At first glance, the results confused them. Each piece had been enclosed in container of baked clay that Palissy had invented to protect the glazed pottery from cinders, and which is still used in the manufacture of fine porcelain under the name *cazettes* or *gazettes*. Bernard, though certainly impatient to know his fate, did not rush to open the *cazettes* for fear that the cold air might damage the contents. Therefore, the observers saw only oddly shaped grey forms which some of them mistakenly took to be the final result of so much study and effort.

It was only after the oven had been half emptied that Bernard decided to begin opening the *cazettes*, starting with the first ones to have been removed.

He selected first a piece of dinnerware called a *salière* which had numerous compartments designed to hold the various spices popular at that time. The bottom and the sides were painted in vivid colors, and in relief were flowering plants, delicately veined ferns, fish with brilliantly colored scales, scarabs with blue wings and rose or pearl-colored crustaceans. Next, he brought out an elegant ewer, with two half-naked nymphs forming the handles and mythological figures painted on the vase itself, surrounded by tasteful decorations that were raised from the surface. Finally came a series of beautifully ornate dishes and magnificent platters on which appeared, always in relief, crayfish, lizards and reptiles surrounded by greenery that had the form, freshness and grace of nature.

Admittedly, Palissy's first efforts did not have the abundance of detail and richness of color that later characterized the works of the master. However, there already existed as much of a difference between these and the pottery previously known in France, as there is of a Raphaël painting compared to a cabaret poster. Moreover, a ray of sunshine had fallen on the delicate figurines, those gilded fish, the luxurious vegetation and the lightly colored, dazzling and varied enameled pieces, making them sparkle like objects in a gem cutter's shop.

As these marvels appeared, a stunned silence had fallen upon the assembly. Noble and plebian, bourgeois and artisan, men and women, contemplated in wonderment the superb collection that was before them. As Palissy opened each new *cazette*, revealing a new masterpiece, a murmur of admiration and respect emanated from the crowd. Soon cries of excitement and joyous exclamations exploded on all sides.

The Governor had picked up the elegant ewer and was handling it with great precaution, as though he could not believe his eyes.

"Good God!" De Pons said, "I could not imagine one could create such objects from clay and glass.... I would like to have this pottery that will be beautiful in my chateau. How much are you asking, Master Bernard?"

"Whatever pleases you, Sire Governor," said the potter, delighted with his success.

"Well, twenty... no, thirty ecus.... Is this enough? Here they are."

And he took from a purse that hung on his belt several pieces of gold, which he handed to Palissy.

The other gentlemen were expressing a similar desire to own some of the art objects laid out before them.

"I," said Lord de Burie, "would really like to have those two lovely platters covered with beautiful green, red and yellow creatures with all that greenery and flowers of Saint Jean.... Master Bernard, would you cede these to me for twelve ecus?"

"Twelve ecus for two such perfect gems?" cried the Count de Maulévrier, one of the richest residents of Saintes, and an ardent supporter of Bernard. "You are joking, Burie.... I wish to make them a gift to my mother, and I offer twenty-four ecus."

"And I thirty," immediately responded Lord de Burie; "By the fox's belly, I would rather sell my gold necklace than let these pass into another's hands!"

"If I were not travelling," said in his turn the Baron de Massac, "I would also purchase some of these lovely potteries.... But I cannot consider it."

While these other gentlemen were discussing the bids for the works of Bernard, Gaston approached Bernard and said with some emotion:

"I salute you, Master.... This noble invention will bring you honor and riches, as well as honor and riches to the entire kingdom."

These simple words gave more pleasure to Bernard than the coins that he threw into his wife's apron as soon as he received them. He thanked him with an eloquent look, while Esther, who had heard the compliment, said in a low voice while shedding tears of joy:

"Ah, Sire Gaston, you are the most generous of all these Lords. You have understood. Money does not suffice to reward the poor artisan, who thanks to his will power, knowledge and talent succeeds in creating such masterpieces!"

Soon all the pieces of pottery that had been removed from the oven were sold, and Bernard, with the aid of his family, continued the process of taking out the rest. With the appearance of each new object, cries of admiration could be heard, and it seemed that each was more beautiful than the last. And the bidding would begin again in a sort of frenzy. The desire to own at least one example of the *rustic figulines* was now shared not only by the Governor's friends, but also by the bourgeois who were crowded behind the more privileged spectators. The Dominican monk himself, despite the horror that the Huguenot worker inspired in him, could not resist acquiring for the convent of his church, a superb enameled basin; and Captain Raby, the coarse and ferocious partisan, had paid three ecus for a lovely plate which represented lovers, which he took for angels, that he planned to give to his 'sweetheart' in a local township.

Finally, the oven, which was not very big, was now empty, and its contents had become the property of the participants in the event. Only a few minor pieces were left which Palissy was happy to keep as samples of his first successful batch. All the coins that came from the purses of the Governor's friends, as well as those of the Governor himself, had found their way into the apron of Mistress Bernard. In addition, several of the gentlemen had indebted themselves to Palissy for fairly important sums. The enthusiasm continued to increase as the potter's surprising creations were carefully examined and a number of the acquirers, wishing to decorate their chateaux and manors with his marvelous works, placed important orders with Bernard for his next batch.

In the middle of all this general excitement, one person remained cool and distracted; this was the Baron de Massac, whose interest in art could not distract him from his obsession.

"With all this going on, my horse has not reappeared," he was saying. "That damned Huguenot minister is capable of having taken it with him to hell.... Sacrebleu! I am going to need Courtaut since tomorrow morning I must leave with my son to continue our task as ordered by the Constable."

No one responded and no one seemed to have heard him. Courtaut, the minister Hamelin, the Huguenots and the Constable's orders; all had been forgotten. They were discussing the finesse of a figurine, the coloration of an insect or a lizard. Palissy extended his arm towards the nearby road and, smiling, said to the Baron; "Look over there, Sire Baron de Massac, Courtaut is not in hell, that is certain."

Indeed, less than fifty meters from the enclosure, a horse was approaching at a rapid trot, ridden by Mathurin, Palissy's son. A moment later, the boy dismounted and was making his way towards them through the crowd of spectators. The Baron, very happy, retook possession of his beloved Courtaut, who was healthy, alert and as proud looking as before.

"Little boy," cried de Massac, "You have maneuvered nicely…. But how did you manage to catch up with my brave animal that the heretic scoundrel was riding away with at such a rapid pace?"

"As I told you," Mathurin replied boldly, "Master Hamelin is not a thief, and I was certain that once he was out of range of those… musketeers, he would hastily abandon the horse. Indeed, less than a half league from here, following the main road, I found this animal tied to a tree next to a forest of pines…. I mounted and brought him back to you, but not too rapidly so as not to tire him."

As he spoke, Mathurin was looking at his father who gave him an almost imperceptible sign of assent.

The return of Courtaut had created a diversion and reawakened the hatred that had abated. Father Desmazures approached Mathurin.

"Boy," he said in a severe tone, "reply to me without lying. Did you see the despicable man who tried to steal the mount of Sire de Massac?"

"As I said, the horse was attached to a tree and I saw no one."

"No doubt this has been agreed upon in advance, and you have been assigned your role…. Curses on those who teach children hypocrisy and lying! Sire Governor," continued the Dominican with menacing irony, "these pretty objects, whose splendor, I admit, seduced me as it did others, will they make us forget the specific orders of the king against these sacrileges?"

"Cornebleu!" said Captain Raby, "the *rustic figulines* do not prevent Bernard from misinterpreting the faith!"

There was a moment of anxiety among those assembled. Master de Pons, having been given notice in this way, could not avoid executing the edict. He therefore seemed irresolute and uncomfortable, as though his duty was in contradiction with his secret wishes.

Bernard's wife and children had once again protectively surrounded the head of their family when help arrived from an unexpected source. Baron de Massac, his arm hooked through the reins of his horse, forcefully exclaimed:

"Sires, I have always presented myself as a loyal servant to the king and a zealous Catholic… but if my worthy friend, Master de Pons is willing to follow my advice, he will think twice before treating as a simple mumbler of psalms, a man so learned and who possesses such marvelous secrets. As for me I cannot forget that Bernard Palissy was my host for one night, and if any gentleman other than the Governor attempts to molest him, by the holy mass and blood, I will take him to task on the spot!"

"And I," said Gaston, raising his voice, "I dare say, with my father's permission, that Sire Constable, Duke of Montmorency, for whom I have the honor of being Secretary, will hasten to send a guard to protect Master Bernard as soon as he learns of the merits of this excellent artisan. Everyone is aware that the Constable is interested in paintings, stained glass and statues; not only will he place Palissy under his protection, he will give him large orders for the Chateau d'Ecouen which he is in the process of building."

"This is true," resumed the Baron; "Sire Constable greatly appreciates persons with talent. He has already enlisted Jean Bullant[12] and Jean Goujon,[13] and he will certainly like to have Bernard Palissy.... Beware of crossing swords with Sire Constable!"

This was all that was necessary to convince the Governor. Actually, he was inclined towards indulgence, but like many functionaries, he was not unhappy to have it seem that his hand had been forced to cover his responsibility. Satisfied on this issue, he did not fear expressing his true sentiments.

"My friends de Massac are right!" he cried. "I will not allow, for either a religious or any other cause, the mistreatment of an artisan who has just enriched the kingdom with a marvelous discovery. I am therefore placing Master Bernard and his entire family under my protection; this means that he will be able to work in the city of Saintes, or in all the territory under my governance, on the condition that he does not involve himself in any act of revolt or scandal."

A murmur of satisfaction could be heard from the gathering.

"Thus," said the Dominican with indignation, "the Governor of Saintes sacrifices God's interests in favor of mundane considerations? Impiety will lift its head with impunity!"

"Triple Devil's head," scolded Raby. "How can I redeem my sins if one does not give me heretics to mistreat for my salvation and theirs?"

"Peace! Raby.... Pull in your claws, old wolf!" said Master de Pons. "As for you Reverend Father, you are once again forgetting that your robes, which make you respectable and holy, do not authorize you to give orders...."

"So be it," replied Desmazures: "A day will perhaps come when all Christians demand that the Cardinal of Mayenne establish the Inquisition in

---

12 **Jean Bullant**, (1515-1578) French architect and sculptor who built the tombs of Anne de Montmorency and Catherine de Médici. He also worked on the Chateau d'Ecouen.

13 **Jean Goujon,** (1510-1565) French Renaissance sculptor and architect.

France, and then we shall know… but I have nothing more to do here in the company of heretics, and I say *raca*[14] on their persons as on their works!"

At the same time, he threw to the ground the dish that he had bought; then without even turning his head, headed up the road alone towards the town.

This temper tirade had made quite an impression. The Prior of the Dominicans benefited from considerable credibility and no one knew how much secret influence he might have that he could put into play to revenge the affront that he had just received. Master de Pons himself was a bit concerned, however his dignity would not let him show it. He spoke with an exaggerated lightness:

"Bah! The good Father will calm down eventually. As for you, Captain Raby, you will take your revenge on the Huguenots who proliferate in the town and its environs…. Arrest and imprison them without pity or mercy; I give you carte blanche…. It is well known that I do not like the Huguenots!"

"At last!" cried Raby. "Corneboeuf! I will immediately get to work, and if that cursed minister is anywhere nearby…. Let's go, my musketeers. Let us fill both the prisons and the gallows!"

He gathered together his band of cutthroats and departed with them to continue the arrests.

Bernard Palissy listened with ill-disguised horror to the Governor's orders. As soon as Raby was no longer present, he spoke to the Governor with boldness:

"I thank you for your kindness towards me, Sire, but I would not want it to be the cause of a redoubling of severity towards my co-religionists. I would a hundred times prefer offering myself for slaughter."

"That is enough, Master Bernard," the Governor interrupted drily; "Say as little as possible about your religion, believe me, and do not give me a reason to regret having granted you this indulgence. Think about your *rustic figulines*, my friend; work, produce masterpieces like these, and do your best to make us forget that shameful sect to which you belong. Take this as friendly advice."

"However, Sire Governor…"

Gaston de Massac and the Count of Maulévrier began to lead the potter away.

"For God's sake Master Bernard," said Gaston in a low voice, "are you forgetting how precious your life and your liberty are to your children?"

Palissy finally understood that his insistence could not possibly lead to a favorable result, and he resigned himself to silence.

Master de Pons and his retinue soon departed, loaded down with their magnificent acquisitions. Before rejoining them, Baron de Massac who had

---

14 *Raca*, Biblical term of Aramaic origin meaning worthless, empty.

remounted his precious Courtaut, said to Palissy:

"We will meet again, Master; tonight, you will give me the formula as you promised...."

"With your consent, father," said Gaston, "it is I who will come to get it."

The Baron gave a sign of agreement, and then father and son also took to the road leading to the city.

After the ovation from the nobility for the inventor of the *rustic figulines*, came the ovation from the populace. The bourgeois and the artisans, whose respect for the Governor's presence had prevented them from expressing their admiration, now crowded around Bernard showering him with praise. They even fought over pieces of broken pottery; each fragment becoming for its new owner a veritable treasure. The creditors and the neighbors who had crushed Palissy with their sarcasm were not the least to cover him with compliments and caresses. The vision of the silver and gold coins which filled the apron of Mistress Bernard no doubt contributed considerably to the exalted and universal enthusiasm of the moment.

"Dear colleague," the potter was saying to Palissy, "You need not worry about my remarks concerning a Mastership. All this can be arranged with the Guild and you can count on me to arrange this. On the other hand, you, dear colleague, you should share with me the secrets of the creation of those beautiful colored enameled pieces...."

"Never," interrupted Bernard with energy. "Those secrets I acquired after sixteen years of hard work and suffering. I learned to create this science 'with my teeth.'[15] I would only share this information with my sons."

The assembly laughed at the potter's crestfallen expression.

"Master Bernard is right," said the man with the short jacket. "By keeping for himself the secret of his discoveries he will earn great sums.... If he needs more money to exploit his new invention, I will provide as much as he needs and become his associate... so no more mention of his back debt which was a trifling matter."

Bernard did not listen any more to the second interested proposition than to that of the potter.

"I do not need an associate and I will repay all my debts."

"I hope that you do not say that for me, Master Bernard," resumed the miller in a fawning tone, "I never tormented you about the eight bushels of wheat... and if you ever need eight more, or twenty, or one hundred, they are at your disposal, neighbor Palissy."

"And if you need a new doublet, or clothes for the children," said the tailor, "you don't need to worry about it, Master Bernard."

---

15 **Author Berthet's original Note**: '*with my teeth*.' Expression from Palissy himself.

"You would also do well, Master Bernard," said Toupinac, the barber-surgeon, "to take care of your appearance now that you will have to deal with so many handsome nobles and grand ladies.... You have forgotten the path to my shop, neighbor; yet you know that my razor and lancet are always at your service."

Palissy did not deign respond to these courtesans of success. "Ah, neighbor Bernard," continued the little Gascon, taking an inspired pose and lifting his eyes to the sky, "You persist in avoiding me because I wish to convert you... My heart is bleeding to see you following the path of error; you, your wife and your little ones.... And now you should be thanking God who helped you achieve such an extraordinary success."

Palissy did not listen any further. He felt broken with fatigue and wished to collect his thoughts after so many shocks. Leaving his neighbors to exchange their observations, he entered his home with his family.

There, occurred an intimate scene that brought him sweet delight. We know that Mistress Bernard, though an honest woman and excellent mother, had not ceased in recent years to shower him with bitter reproaches.

As long as she was in the presence of strangers, she succeeded in restraining herself, but once home, she gave free reign to her tears, knelt down before her husband and clasping her hands, said:

"Bernard, my sweet Bernard, can you ever pardon my blindness, my hardness, my injustice against you? While you, under divine inspiration, put up with the cold, the heat, the hunger, the vigils and the fatigue, I heaped insults upon you and drove you to desperation with my mockery and anger!... Forgive me Palissy, whatever you do; I will never again doubt you! My children, beg your father, who loves you, to forgive your mother, who has treated him so cruelly."

After this touching declaration, all the family began to cry. Palissy himself had tears in his eyes, but replied smilingly:

"Get up, dear woman; it was maternal sentiment which made you act in this way; and in reality, by pursuing my long and expensive experiments, I, as a father of a large family was not without blame.... Now our suffering is over. You will no longer suffer privation or misery. Embrace me and let us mutually forgive each other the past."

They embraced each other with emotion, while Esther proudly said:

"Ah! father, I never doubted you!"

VII.

NEW DANGERS

That evening, approximately one hour before the closing of the gates of the city, Gaston de Massac, alone and on foot, crossed the Charente by the old bridge decorated with a Roman arch, and headed towards the village inhabited by Palissy.

The rapidity of events has not permitted us to properly acquaint the reader with Gaston, who despite his youth, was far superior to the gentlemen of his epoch. He was brought up in the Chateau de Massac by an erudite teacher of great intelligence. The Baron, with whom we are already familiar, was basically a man of war, subject to the prejudices of his time, and his role in the education of his son was limited to teaching him the equestrian arts and swordsmanship. However, Gaston had a mother full of goodness and wisdom who helped him develop the most noble and delicate instincts. Having been called to the service of the Constable of Montmorency, to whom the Baron was already attached, Gaston was able to complete his education through these new contacts. The Constable, who was known for his astuteness, soon learned to appreciate the qualities of his secretary. We have already mentioned that the Duke Anne de Montmorency did not know how to read or write. Therefore, he appreciated all the more the services of a young man who was educated, enlightened, and devoted until death. We can assume that the son was closer to the secrets and good graces of the Duke than the father himself.

Gaston de Massac, with so many brilliant qualities and the protection of one of the most powerful Lords of the kingdom, could aspire to a high destiny; and his handsome face and elegant appearance would certainly work in his favor in the stylish Court of Henri II and Catherine de Médicis.

However, what attracted Gaston to the Palissy home at this hour was not only to obtain the famous formula promised to his father. Any lackey of the Governor could have been sent to claim it. He had given in to the desire of seeing the charming Esther, still present in his mind, before his departure planned for the following morning. Was he already in love with the daughter of Master Bernard? We cannot be certain, but as we said earlier, he had the simplicity, freshness and vivacity of early youth, and he could not forget that night spent under the potter's roof.

Daylight was beginning to fade as he approached the house, and he was already searching for Esther's gracious form. The lovely child did not appear, but Gaston suddenly found himself face to face with a villainous personage that he did not expect to meet.

It was Captain Raby, who, standing under a tree on one side of the path, seemed to be on the lookout for someone or something. Around him prowled a number of rough-looking men dressed in metal helmets and knee-length buffalo-hide coats who were part of his gang.

His mysterious appearance and presence a stone's throw from Bernard's house, inspired certain suspicions in Massac's mind. He did not hesitate to address Raby.

"What's this, Captain," he said in a light tone, "are you still chasing after Huguenots? You are forgetting that it is getting late and the gates of the city will soon be closing."

"Oh? Cornebleu! you seem to be forgetting it as well my young gentleman," replied Raby, looking at him defiantly. "Well, it could be that my good men and I do not return to Saintes this night…. One notices things here that merit further attention."

"Bah! What is it, then, Captain Raby?"

"I am not exactly certain, but I have sent out my finest hounds and I will be informed soon. You can be told," said the Captain, lowering his voice, "I suspect that a meeting of Huguenots is in preparation nearby; a preaching or *conventicle,* as they call it. We have seen a number of persons pass by, though not known as Protestants, who are clearly suspect. All were headed this way (and he gestured towards the countryside), leading me to conclude that they will gather not far from here. By my innards! They will surely not begin their Sabbath before nightfall, and it will be possible for me and my men to fall upon them at the moment they expect the least."

Gaston was aware of the strictness of the royal orders against the Protestant assemblies, and Raby's zeal did not seem untimely.

"Courage then, Captain," he resumed, "and do your duty. However, remember that you were specifically ordered to spare Bernard Palissy."

"Yes, yes, I will not cross the threshold of his house, this is understood… but by God, if I meet up with him in a fight, he, or a member of his family…"

"You will spare him under all circumstances, Captain," Gaston interrupted drily, "Palissy and his family are under the protection of Sire Constable, Master de Pons, the Governor… and I will add, if necessary, under mine, which I know how to assure."

Then, not deigning to discuss further with the chief of the band of cutthroats, he touched his cap and continued on his way.

Raby watched him depart.

"Hum! I do not care much for that bird," he grumbled; "and regardless of what he says, if I find an excuse to take my revenge against that potter... however, here is one of my searchers coming in to report on his mission. We will have work to do, no doubt!"

And he moved towards a musketeer who was running towards him appearing distraught.

On his side, Gaston had reached the house, which bordered the main path. This side of the house, as well as the other, looked rather miserable and its annual rental must not have cost Palissy very much. As there was no bell or knocker on the door, and one could hear voices inside, Gaston simply lifted the latch and entered.

This room of the dwelling, though not as cluttered by a thousand strange objects as was the case in the workshop situated in the next room, looked just as poor. Several beds and two cradles, the contents of which included more straw than horsehair or feathers, constituted a sort of dormitory for the family. A worm-eaten chest and some stepladders completed the furnishings which two days earlier could have been fed into Palissy's oven without much financial loss provided they could replace them. A ray of feeble and insufficient light entered by two windows on each side of the door.

At that moment, an extraordinary abundance reigned. One could see on the table an enormous loaf of white bread, bacon and fruit, as well as a container full of wine and some pewter goblets. Around this sumptuous feast, some sitting, some standing, were Mistress Bernard, her two sons Nicolas and Mathurin, and others who were younger. The mother had a child breastfeeding on her lap. Palissy and Esther were absent, but no one seemed concerned by their absence and were eating with an avidity that proved that fasting had been frequent in the potter's home.

The sudden appearance of a visitor produced a sudden commotion. Mistress Bernard gave a start and sat up with concern. Two days earlier she would probably not have been afraid as she could handle a robber; but now that she possessed a considerable sum, she feared the beggars and vagabonds who infested this remote area. However, her children, after a first reaction of surprise, resumed with enthusiasm their chewing exercises as though nothing was seriously capable of distracting them from this delightful occupation.

The mother, on her side, quickly recognized her guest of two nights ago. She arose and gave him a deep bow of reverence; then offering the seat that she had occupied, humbly said:

"May God be with you, kind gentleman... please sit and accept our welcome.... You wished to see Palissy; he has gone out but he did not forget his promise to Sire Baron, your father, and here is what he tasked me to give to you."

At the same time, she presented Gaston with a paper; it was the famous formula for treating the "crowning" of horses. Gaston simply glanced distractedly at it.

"Many thanks, Mistress Palissy," he replied, "but I did not come here only for this. I expected to see Master Bernard, congratulate him on the brilliant success that he obtained today. And then…"

He stopped with an embarrassed expression.

"Ah! Yes, my gracious Lord. Bernard is very happy. Who would have thought that the bourgeoisie, nobles and the Governor himself would fight over the fruit of his work? I am the first to accuse myself of having made life difficult for this poor man; but I asked his forgiveness and I hope that God does not punish me for this injustice. What can one do? Esther was the only one who had faith in her father. She alone understood and admired him, while the others…"

"Esther is indeed an exceptional creature," interrupted Gaston with warmth, "but why do I not see her?"

"She accompanied her father," replied Mistress Bernard distractedly, seeming to survey her famished children. "I must tell you, Sire, that the two are seldom separated. Esther is Palissy's right hand and executes all his wishes…. For example, it is she who wrote out the formula for the sick horses, and if one leaves it to her, she will become a scholar herself."

Gaston now examined with greater attention the paper that he had been given. The writing was delicate, very readable and without errors in spelling. Not many high and mighty ladies in this period of ignorance could have written as well.

Massac soon resumed:

"All this is wonderful. I have some information I wish to obtain, either from your husband, or from Esther…. Let's see, why don't I just wait for them. They should be returning soon."

Mistress Bernard appeared to be quite ill at ease.

"I would not dare assure you of this," she replied. "They may be back very late…. And you must return to the city before the closing of the gates."

"There is no worry on that point…. I foresaw that possibility and the Governor has provided me with an order to open a special guard entrance whenever I present myself."

"What power you have! Nevertheless, I urge you not to wait as Bernard and the little one will be gone a good part of the night."

Gaston, sensing her fears, decided to insist without mercy.

"Where are they at such an hour?" he asked. "See here, Mistress Palissy," he added, lowering his voice. "Be frank, are they not providing assistance to the Protestant minister who was hiding in your home this morning and who escaped in such an odd manner?"

"What! Sire, are you suggesting…"

"Do not challenge me…. I have given you sufficient proof of my good will."

This time, it was Mistress Bernard who took on a mysterious air.

"Good God! Master de Massac," she asked, "are you secretly one of ours? This happens often in the times of crisis such as ours; there are times when fathers and sons do not feel the same way about religion…"

"I think exactly as does my father," replied Gaston in a forceful tone, "although I feel a bit more indulgent towards those who have lost their way…. So, Mistress, I was not mistaken, and your husband, as well as your daughter, have gone to some remote location to meet with this… minister of your sect?"

"Well, when that occurs, Sire, would you blame them for coming to the aid of an outlawed Christian who is persecuted and does not have a roof over his head?"

"He is an enemy of the King and of the Church," replied Gaston drily, "but so be it…. The true religion orders us to be charitable, even towards heretics and infidels…. However, is it not possible that Palissy and Esther are meeting with other persons than Pastor Hamelin in the place that he is hidden?"

"Why this question Master de Massac?"

"I have reason to believe that not far from here, a meeting of Huguenots is in preparation where there will be singing of psalms, and where there may be planning to resist Royal authority…. Tell me, woman, is it not to an assembly of this sort that Palissy and Esther have gone?"

"Hush! Hush! Sire, how could you suppose… how could you know…. But when it is known, would you betray poor people who hide to pray and to weep?"

"I am neither a spy, nor a betrayer. But nearby are persons who are much less indulgent…. What would you say, for example, about Captain Raby and his rogues?"

"Raby and his infernal gang! May the almighty God preserve us! At this hour, they have certainly gone back to the city and are unlikely to come out as they are about to close the gates."

"I have just encountered the Captain very near to this house, and he informed me that he is not about to return to Saintes. Finally, I must admit it, Raby suspects what is happening and has sent out several of his rascals to find out, and perhaps he already knows the location of the meeting."

"My God! Spare your humble servants," murmured Mistress Bernard lifting her eyes and hands towards the sky; "That Captain is like the lion that prowls around your home…. Happily, my husband and daughter have found powerful protectors."

"I would not like to frighten you, but you should not count too much on the safety that has been granted them. It would be effective for them here, in your home. But if they were to take part in a public scandal, if they were found participating in one of those ungodly assemblies it is said are often held in the forest, God knows to what they may be exposed…. Captain Raby and his regulars are famous for resorting to horrendous excesses."

"Oh, Mercy! What to do?" said the poor woman, wringing her hands in desperation. "The saints of Israel will be scattered, loaded down with chains…. Blood may flow! My poor Bernard, with whom I have been so unjust and who has become our pride… Esther, my beloved daughter…. Good heavens! What is going to happen?"

Gaston de Massac rose to his feet resolutely.

"Your suffering touches me, Mistress Bernard," he resumed. "I too would be devastated if misfortune struck this honest young girl and her impudent father…. I can still save them by warning them of the danger and preventing this disastrous assembly that may perhaps end in carnage…. Give me the location of the meeting and I will go there and warn Bernard."

"You, Master de Massac?" cried mistress Palissy with a mixture of surprise and defiance; "You, a Catholic who brought to Saintes those ruthless edicts…."

"But I have never committed myself to implementing them, Mistress Bernard," replied Gaston haughtily. "I swear to you on my honor as a gentleman, that I have only good intentions for your husband, for Esther and even for those poor fanatics…. But you must hasten to furnish me with the necessary information; the night is falling and each passing minute increases the danger."Nightfall was indeed becoming noticeable in the room. Mistress Bernard approached Gaston and looked at him intently.

"A handsome face and loyal!" she murmured. "Clear, limpid eyes incapable of lying…. All right, Master de Massac," she continued, "even if you were a pack of devouring wolves threatening the flock and the pastor, I put my trust in you…. The meeting is to take place in the moor of Brassac, the other side of Bois-Aigu, which we also call the forest of pines. As the preaching… I mean the meeting, will only begin two hours after sundown. You should undoubtedly arrive soon enough to warn the Protestants of the dangers which await them."

"Good, I will leave immediately…. Explain to me the route as I am not familiar with the countryside."

"You will follow the road to Cognac for about a half-mile; then you will follow the path to Jard until you reach the Seugne, and then… may heaven have pity on us! It will be completely dark when you arrive there, and you risk getting lost…. How to avoid losing time when the consequences could be so serious?"

Suddenly, she was struck by an idea.

"My son, Mathurin, will accompany you," she resumed. "He knows very well that area and will be a perfect guide for you…. Moreover, he does not lack courage or finesse as he proved today. If you agree, Mathurin will lead you."

"So be it. Let us hasten."

Mathurin did not seem very happy about leaving a copious meal to go running around the countryside at this late hour, and he made a nasty grimace. But the mother had no patience for issues of obedience. She spoke to her son in a severe tone and seemed to give him instructions. She finally reconciled him to his task by cutting a large piece from the loaf of bread that he could nibble on during the trip.

Now equipped against the challenges and fatigue of the trip, the youth silently joined the stranger and they set off.

Mistress Bernard, standing on the doorsill, followed them with her eyes as long as she could.

"What have I done?" she murmured; "This Master de Massac is an ardent Catholic, and if he were to betray us…. One should not put one's trust in facial expressions!… I will myself pray, and have the little innocents pray as well!"

VIII.

THE PREACHING

It would be supremely unjust to render Catholicism responsible by itself for the appalling excesses that were committed in its name during the terrible religious discords of the sixteenth century. The Catholic concept, which had provided the unity, the strength and the greatness of France from the origins of the monarchy, was superior to its actors and dominated them from its heights.

But at that time, customs were still barbarous, morals crude and savage, passions frenzied. As a consequence, methods of execution were often odious. The Protestants, when they took arms, did not last long against the opposition and were defiled by violence, excesses and cruelties that brought France to the edge of its own destruction. It took all the energy of Richelieu to destroy this '*State within a State* which menaced the kingdom with near dissolution.

The events which we have described and those that we will describe concerning Bernard Palissy will not serve to prove either for or against the religious principles then in conflict. The two parties were sincere in their beliefs; and if the methods of attack and defense shock us now, one must understand the character of a generation that did not admit consideration or respect of the conscience of others.

This said once and for all, let us return to Gaston de Massac.

* * * *

At the moment that Gaston and his young guide left Palissy's home, the night mists were beginning to envelop the picturesque countryside which remained luminous from the direction of the setting sun. It became difficult to distinguish the trees, the shrubs and the vines that lined the path. A profound silence reigned everywhere; however, one could hear, at intervals, the steps of persons hastening towards the gates of the city before they closed,

Gaston had placed the velvet jacket that he normally wore on his left shoulder, as was the custom of the day, so as to cover his face, and forced his large felt hat down over his eyes. Thus disguised, he was unrecognizable, and the sword, which protruded from his coat, implied that it might be imprudent to disturb his incognito.

As it turned out, these precautions soon proved unnecessary. The gentleman and Mathurin found themselves under trees that formed a line on both sides of the route making it almost impossible to distinguish anything. At each moment, they passed mysterious individuals who were all travelling in the same direction. Were these persons friends or enemies for Gaston? He did not know and it did not seem that he wanted to find out, and they, in turn, sought to hide in the shadows.

A quarter hour went by in this manner. As Massac and the boy were walking quite rapidly they had covered at least a half-mile. Mathurin had not said a word and seemed to have forgotten his companion. He contented himself with biting into his piece of bread from time to time and mixing the sound of his chewing with a sort of monotone humming that resembled the singing of a psalm.

They had attained the spot where they were to leave the main road to take a shortcut that dropped deeply into the undergrowth. The young guide was about to plunge in without hesitation, but Gaston, more prudently, preferred taking stock of the situation around him, and placed his hand on Mathurin's shoulder to signal him to come to a halt.

The countryside continued to be silent and the sunken path appeared deserted. However, about a hundred paces away, along the continuation of the road that they were about to leave, a bright light shown on the ground floor of a house, and at the same time could be heard the faint murmur of voices in the calm of the night.

As Gaston was observing this light, the only one in sight, a shadow passed before it and one could glimpse a metal helmet, similar to those worn by Captain Raby and his men. Leaning towards Mathurin, Massac said in a low voice:

"What is that house, my boy?"

"The Saint-Antoine cabaret… a house of sin, where on Sundays, the townspeople come to drink new wine."

Gaston judged that the cabaret was very well placed to serve as a meeting place for the mercenaries of Raby's regulars. He ordered Mathurin to follow him towards the suspect house.

"It is not there that we must go, Sire," murmured the young guide, surprised and alarmed; "my mother did not tell me."

"Well, Sacrébleu! I am telling you; come…. We will only stop for a moment."

The boy did not appear at all satisfied with this breach of the instructions he had received and accompanied Massac reluctantly.

The closer Gaston approached the more he felt the necessity of getting more information about this solitary house. Now he heard a loud voice that spoke in a menacing tone, and in that voice, he believed he recognized that of Raby.

He stopped when he was within a few steps of the cabaret; thanks to an open window, he was able to see and hear what was going on in the lower room.

Indeed, Captain Raby was there with a dozen of his men.

"By all the devils!" he was saying, "Are you mocking me, my men? While I thought that you were out following the trail of the Huguenots, you are here carousing and getting drunk! Death and blood! At this hour, the heretics must be meeting, and it is time for us to bid them welcome.... I swear to God that the one of you that does not put himself energetically to the task will receive fifty lashes of the belt on his back!"

But his mercenaries knew their chief too well to be overly concerned by this threat.

"Patience, Captain!" replied one of his lieutenants, a toady old rascal who enjoyed good relations with Raby; "You do not need to resort to lashes to get us moving.... However, you cannot refuse having a drink or two of this excellent Saintonge wine... a truly smooth drink!"

And he offered Raby a cup filled to the brim.

"Drinking is appropriate, by Satan!" replied the Captain. "Are the muskets loaded? Are the fuses lit? We will encircle the infidels and we will shoot them in a full volley.... And really," he added taking the cup with hesitation, "is this wine as good as they say?"

"Even better, Captain," said the rascal, drawing up a chair upon which Raby let himself settle distractedly. "Our duties should not let us forget to take care of our bodies. Now, now! We have not lost any time and will come upon the Huguenots presently."

Without ending his ruminations, Raby began drinking with his men.

Gaston de Massac knew enough.

"We will arrive before them," he murmured, thinking that he was speaking to Mathurin; "Take me quickly to the moor of Brassac."

There was no response. Palissy's son had disappeared. Either he had been frightened by the proximity to the cutthroats or he suspected the gentleman of bad intentions.

Gaston was very annoyed. How could he locate the meeting place on this dark night and in unfamiliar countryside without a guide? While returning along the path towards the shortcut, he called out Mathurin's name cautiously, but his calls remained unanswered. Decidedly, Mathurin had fled.

However, realizing that he had no time to lose if he were to get there before Raby and his gang, Massac plunged into the deep path where reigned, as we said, almost total obscurity. He hoped that with the vague directions given by Mistress Bernard that he would reach the pine forest that borders the moor, and perhaps on the way he might encounter someone who could inform him.

He was almost groping his way, listening for the slightest sounds. He soon caught up with someone whose class or age he could not discern, but who stopped upon hearing his steps. Gaston asked softly:

"Mathurin Palissy, is it you?"

"No," responded a male voice. "You, my brother, you must be a member of the persecuted church?"

"I am going to the moor of Brassac," replied Gaston evasively.

"And I as well; we can travel there together if you permit it."

Gaston could not ask for better, as one could expect, and the two moved forward side by side.

Each appeared anxious to know with whom he was dealing; but the narrow path, bordered by heavy shrubbery, was still very dark, and one could not perceive the slightest facial detail or the person's clothing. However, they soon reached an open spot where there was a faint glow from the sky, and they examined each other avidly.

One can imagine Gaston's surprise! His travelling companion was equipped exactly as he was; large felt hat, short velvet jacket, long sword which identified him as a gentleman, and like himself, had brought his jacket up to his face.

Finally, the stranger asked:

"You seem to be waiting for someone, Sire, and it would seem this countryside is new to you?"

"Indeed; but as a precaution I had taken a young guide, but we were separated in the dark."

"And this guide whom you named a moment ago, is the son of Bernard Palissy, the potter?"

"Exactly; do you know Bernard, Sire?"

"Who does not? However, if Bernard lent you his son to guide you, it is that you are one of us, and that you can be entirely trusted."

At the same time, the stranger let drop the fold of his cloak, and although the obscurity was still too great to be able to see his face, Gaston did not wish to abuse the trust of his companion.

"I am not what you think, Sire" he replied. "And I have other motives than to listen to sermons and psalms in going to the moor of Brassac."

The stranger rapidly leaned towards Gaston and stopped.

"You are the son of that ardent Catholic, the Baron de Massac, who arrived in Saintes two days ago!" he cried. "Upon my faith, Sire, does a gentleman come in the night to spy on miserable religionists, to later turn them over to prison and torture?"

Gaston blushed at this suspicion.

"Sire" he replied vehemently, "I detest heretics and heresies; but to accuse me of such an infamous role…. If you are a gentleman, you should trust me."

"If you do not have such odious plans, then what sort of affair brings you to the moor of Brassac?"

"I do not wish to reply."

"In that case," resumed the stranger, leaning back against a pine tree on the edge of the forest, "I will go no further and I will not allow you to pass."

"This is what we shall see, Sire," said Gaston, drawing his sword which gave off a spark of light in the night.

The stranger, on the contrary, did not move.

"If your intentions were good," he asked ironically, "would you use such methods to express them?"

"Whatever my intentions, I intend going where it pleases me…. On guard then, Sire, or by all the devils, it will be with the flat of my sword that I will strike you!"

The Protestant in turn drew his sword.

"So be it!" he said, "I will not allow an enemy to sneak into this peaceful assembly where there are only the weak and the innocent."

He threw aside his cloak and the point of his rapier touched that of Gaston producing a sinister clicking sound.

The two adversaries could barely see each other and the success of such a duel could only be the result of chance. However, Gaston assured himself that the stranger was a man of a certain age, of good appearance, and Gaston thought that he had seen him somewhere recently, although he could not remember where.

They clashed swords for a few minutes without result. Finally, Gaston, anxious to end this haphazard duel, made a rapid move and lunged, striking his adversary who dropped his sword, his arm pierced.

Gaston lowered his and stepped back.

"I imagine, Cavalier," he said, "that you have had enough…. Now you will no longer refuse to guide me…."

"I am at your mercy, Master de Massac," replied the Protestant, whose arm bled profusely. "But even wounded and disarmed, I defy you to make me advance one step."

And he sat down at the foot of a tree.

"I shall at least know who you are," replied Massac, examining the wounded man. "The Count of Maulévrier," he added immediately, "friend and dining companion of the Governor of Saintes! I remember now, Sire Count, that on various occasions you warmly protected the interests of Bernard Palissy… and some Protestants."

"My secret is in your hands, master de Massac," replied the Count of Maulévrier dejectedly; "I do belong to this forbidden religious sect, although certain duties and expediencies prevent me from making known my membership.... I am not the only one among the nobility who cannot confess his beliefs and I dare to hope that a generous enemy will remain silent on this matter."

"You have my word, Sire.... I regret the progress of this detestable heresy; but I can now say that I had absolutely no evil plans against your co-religionists; On the contrary, I wanted to give them information of the greatest importance."

He then related the visit to the home of Bernard, his dual encounter with Captain Raby, and explained how because of his interest in Palissy and his family, he wanted to warn the Protestants of their imminent danger.

"If you had said this earlier, Master de Massac, you would have avoided for yourself, a needless act of violence, and for me a cruel wound!"

"Could I give in to a stranger who spoke to me in a menacing tone?"

"It would have been wiser.... But is it certain that this villain Raby and his gang of assassins are preparing to attack the Protestants?"

"Here comes the proof," said Gaston, pointing towards the narrow path.

From that side came a confused sound like that produced by troops advancing, a clanging of arms knocking against each other, raised voices and badly muffled laughs. Raby's regulars had never been well disciplined; and at this moment, in spite of the need for silence, the wine that had been consumed at the Saint-Antoine cabaret had overexcited this rabble of ferocious soldiers. There could be no doubt as to these persons' intentions, and Maulévrier gave a movement of alarm.

"Let us leave immediately," he said; "For the love of God, Sire, help me to get up."

Gaston hurried to lift him, but once on his feet, the Count felt that it would be impossible to walk.

"My legs are buckling; my head is spinning. Leave without me."

And he rapidly gave Gaston the necessary instructions.

"Sire," said Gaston, "I cannot abandon you here alone and wounded."

"Leave, do not worry about me; I will obtain some help nearby.... However, do not forget that you have promised me to keep secret our encounter."

The murmur of voices and the clanking of arms were rapidly approaching; one could even glimpse the sparks from the lit musket fuses.

He could no longer hesitate. Gaston gave a sign of regret and launched himself forward, while the Count of Maulévrier crawled from tree to tree so as to not be in the path of the Captain and his troops.

But Gaston, mindful of the danger to Palissy and his daughter, did not worry any further about his unfortunate adversary; he pursued his way, and soon he stopped hearing Raby's gang, which proved that he was gaining ground.

Despite the Count's instructions, he once again encountered new difficulties. He was now in a dense forest dominated by pine trees. He was obliged to follow several side alleys before arriving at the meeting place, and he wondered how he would recognize it in the darkness. After several minutes of walking, he decided to halt once more to orient himself.

Unfortunately, he was lacking in points of reference. He had entered a path that seemed quite long to him. There was a luminous area over his head, but it did not permit him to see directly around him.

Afraid that he was once again lost, he remained still, when suddenly he heard a singing, distant and muffled, but soft and harmonious, which appeared to come from a large number of voices. It seemed to be church music, and Gaston made out one of the psalms that Protestants sing together during their sermons and their secret assemblies.

These sounds mixed with the light breezes of the night permitted him to recognize which direction to follow, and he continued his way.

The singing was interrupted in intervals, but then soon resumed, always at a timid and plaintive rhythm, and it guided Massac through the forest. Soon it became stronger and more distinct and finally a great light that reflected on the tips of the trees indicated that the traveler was approaching his objective. In fact, when Gaston reached the end of a last alley, an image, as strange as it was picturesque, appeared before him.

This alley opened upon a clearing where the sterile and rocky land formed a sort of moor.

The forest completely surrounded this open space, except at one point, where a river flowed between willow trees and an embankment. A great number of torches shone here and there. Most were made from branches from the pine trees and released, with a red glow, aromatic odors.

About a hundred persons of both sexes, all ages, and all classes were gathered on the moor. In the center was a bare rock that could have been deposited there by nature, but could also have been a *standing stone,* or one of those *dolmens,* the erection of which was attributed to the druids and which in any case were used for worship by Gallic priests. On this one that roughly had the shape of a table, and rose a few feet above the ground, stood the minister presiding over the assembly.

This minister, whom Gaston would have recognized as Master Hamelin if he had had time to examine him the previous morning, was a man of about twenty-five years of age, slim, pale and who exhibited great religious exaltation. He was dressed simply in black; his hair long and swept back, moving with the breeze. Bible in hand, he was singing with great enthusiasm. His expression was both serious and sad which added to the character of this striking nocturnal scene.

The participants were either standing or sitting on the heath. Certain families were crowding around their leader who held the book of psalms, while other persons illuminated the congregation with torches or even lit candles. The overall picture was a true representation of a nascent and persecuted religion, obliged to hide itself, at night and in the wilderness.

However, Gaston de Massac was little moved by the poetry of this banishment. Stopped on the edge of the woods, he sought out, in this crowded gathering, the only two participants in whom he had an interest; Esther and Palissy. Not seeing them, he wondered if they were there, and he hesitated to give the alarm to save sectarians who were odious to him. Moreover, whatever he did, two steps away from the crowd, sword in hand, no one paid any attention to him and continued singing.

A sentiment of generosity finally triumphed over Massac's hesitations. He threw himself into the midst of the assembly, waving his hat, and yelled in a thunderous voice:

"Disperse, save yourselves, good people! Captain Raby and his regulars are arriving."

Such was the fervor of the Protestants that only a few grew quiet and looked at this stranger who suddenly appeared among them. The others continued their singing, and their minister himself, eyes flashing; one arm lifted to the skies, added to the echoes the accents of his inspired voice. On the other hand, a young girl who was sitting near the rock, arose and cried in a tone of surprise and terror:

"Good God, it is Master Gaston de Massac!"

"Master de Massac!" repeated with force a man seated next to her and who jumped to his feet.

Gaston recognized Palissy and his daughter. He ran towards them, while the pastor, who had decided to interrupt his singing, spoke to him in indignation:

"Godless desecrator, why do you come here to trouble our sacred ceremonies?… You have your churches and palaces; why do you not leave us the forests to adore Christ according to our faith and our wishes?"

Gaston, who had now rejoined Esther and Bernard, replied animatedly:

"By the Saints! I do not care about this Huguenot circus and its pastor…. But you, Master Bernard, and you, Esther, leave this place immediately! Raby and his rascals are very near. Esther, take my arm, and I know well how to protect you."

"My God! What is happening," said the young girl trembling.

"Master de Massac," asked Palissy in turn, "how is it possible…"

But it was not the right moment for explanations. Total confusion reigned in the assembly. The singing had completely ceased. All the participants were on their feet; some had hurriedly put out their torches, others were beating a hasty retreat. The young minister, who did not realize the cause of this alarm, was trying to restrain them.

"One moment! My brothers," he was crying, "let us not panic before we know the source of this questionable warning...."

He did not have the time to say more; a dark and mobile mass had appeared at the place from which Gaston had just come. At the same time, one heard Raby who was yelling:

"Here are the Reformists.... Fire, fire! my lads. Scatter them! Kill them! No mercy for these heretics!"

The loud detonations of a dozen muskets immediately resounded. The flash of the powder illuminated the old pines and the heath of the moor, and the terrified crowd that was fleeing. Then darkness fell once more, but the piercing screams that could be heard, the panic and the terror of the Protestants were witness that the shots had attained some victims.

However, this horrendous success did not appear to satisfy Captain Raby. He let out a laugh and added:

"Now my braves let us get those who remain! Prepare the spikes and your swords.... Death to the Huguenots!"

And, followed by his men, he fell upon the miserable Protestants, who had fallen, or were incapable of resistance, while the rest, thrown into panic by terror, sought refuge in the forest.

IX.

THE SEPARATION

Bernard and Esther, giving in to the urging of Gaston de Massac, were going towards the forest, when they were knocked over by a group of fugitives. They had difficulty in disengaging themselves due to the tumult and the darkness. As soon as they succeeded, Palissy once more dragged his daughter into the undergrowth where he met the Pastor Hamelin, who said to him in a trembling voice:

"My brother Bernard, save this chaste and pure child.... Get her away from these sons of the Devil.... She is too young to suffer and die!"

"And you as well, Pastor Hamelin," said Palissy taking him by the arm; "Come with us, you will help to protect her."

"Let us flee, let us flee!" cried the girl frantically.

At that moment, the Captain and his men burst onto the moor. They were shouting savagely and were attempting to reach those fleeing with their swords and halberds. Raby, who was leading them, noticed poor Esther.

"A woman!" he cried. "By thunder, if she is pretty I am marking her as mine.... You realize, my comrades that I will gladly take care of converting attractive Huguenots? It is my duty."

"Ha! Sacrebleu! Come and get her!" said someone in a defiant tone.

At the same time a man with a cloak over his shoulder and a rapier in his hand, stood before him.

Raby did not recognize Gaston, and to tell the truth, he could not have imagined that the personal secretary of the Constable of Montmorency would dare challenge the implementation of an edict that he had himself brought. He simply replied with a sneer:

"Eh! Incredible! A Huguenot who swears and who fights? This is new! By the belly of a fox! We must give him his just reward."

The two blades crossed and a new blind dual began. Undoubtedly, Gaston had profited from his experience during the preceding struggle, as after several passes, he was able to insert his blade between the leather doublet and the neck armor of the soldier, cutting him near the neck. The wound may not have been serious, but Raby began to reel, saying in a faint voice:

"Devil take this rogue! It is a traitor's blow! Tear the soul of his body with your four-pointed spikes.... Show no mercy!"

As he was staggering, several of his men rushed to support him, while others were advancing towards Gaston shaking their halberds. Gaston avoided them with a leap to one side; then nimbly moving to face them, he dealt a strong blow to the arm of one which caused him to drop his halberd, then gave another a swipe of the flat of his sword against his metal helmet which gave off sparks and laid him out. After having struck this double blow, he ran as fast as he could towards the edge of the forest.

It was not the number of adversaries that motivated his retreat; but in addition to wishing to rejoin Palissy and his daughter, he was afraid of being recognized during this bloody fray which could place himself as well as his father in a very embarrassing situation.

Raby, despite his wound, had observed, with the tenacity of hate, the progress of that struggle.

"Catch him!" he ordered, "We must apprehend that damn Huguenot, or at least learn who he is.... Ten pieces of gold to the man who catches him, dead or alive!"

Thus motivated, the cutthroats launched themselves like a furious pack of hounds on the trail of Gaston. The young Massac, as agile as he was vigorous and skillful in fencing, jumped over obstacles with an unbelievable lightness. The soldiers, heavily equipped and further hampered by the wine that they had consumed at the cabaret Saint-Antoine, soon fell back, and Gaston finally reached the thickets and threw himself headlong into them.

He stopped for a few seconds to catch his breath. He was now under some large trees that provided a deep shade. In addition, a number of Protestants had sought to escape into this area and one could hear them running through the undergrowth. Gaston could also hear the soldiers who were continuing their hunt, and he wondered in which direction he should flee, when suddenly someone seized him by his coat and said:

"Is that you Master de Massac?"

Gaston recognized Bernard.

"It is I," he replied, "but let us speak in a low voice. It is important that no one know who I am."

"Come, then," murmured Palissy, pulling him away.

They followed a footpath that in spite of its twisting and turning seemed familiar to Bernard. The tumultuous sounds became progressively less distinct and eventually were but a distant murmur. Now reassured that he would not be recognized, Gaston asked with interest:

"And your daughter, Master Bernard, where is she? Surely you did not abandon her?"

"God forbid, Sire; we will rejoin her shortly. While I returned to find you, she remained under the protection of the worthy Master Hamelin; they should be waiting for us at Chêne-Brùlé."

Gaston could not hold back a gesture of anger.

"Upon my faith! Master Bernard," he resumed, "You are an over-confident father! Your minister Hamelin seems to me quite young, and to entrust him with your daughter, at night, and in the middle of the forest...."

"Your ideas, Master de Massac, are those of a worldly man, used to the bad actions of these evil times. But Pastor Hamelin is like a spiritual father to this child, and furthermore...."

He suddenly interrupted himself.

"What do you mean," asked Gaston.

Bernard smiled.

"Nothing," he replied, "but here are the ones you were speaking about without knowing them well... the ewe and the shepherd."

In fact, they were arriving at a turn in the forest. Under a large tree that had lost most of its leaves, one could just see two persons standing without moving. As they did not speak, probably from fear of being in error, Palissy addressed them.

"Thanks be to God," he said. "Like us, the protector of our persecuted church was able to escape our mortal enemies!"

"Thanks be to God! Thanks be to God!" repeated Esther, wringing her hands.

Hamelin turned towards Gaston trying in vain to examine him in the obscurity.

"I have been told, Sire," he said, "that you are not a member of our religion. The service that you have rendered to this unfortunate flock and me is all the worthier of praise. Charity should be a part of all Christian communities, and our gratitude..."

"Do not thank me, Sire," replied Gaston de Massac. "It was not for you or your followers that I turned myself into a defender of the Huguenots, and that I spilt the blood of my brethren in religion.... I came here only to protect Master Bernard, who has been my host, and his innocent daughter, Esther.... Now that they are saved, I am little concerned about the others."

"Oh, do not speak this way, Master de Massac," said Esther in an imploring tone. "You are just and generous; you have given further proof of this."

"Esther is right," continued Palissy, "and I regret that a young gentleman that the heavens have blessed with so many gifts, is still plunged in the ignorance of the ancient doctrines. But how could Master de Massac have known... "

Gaston told them briefly about the events of the previous evening.

"Now, Master Bernard," he continued, "it is important that you return to your home as rapidly as possible. As for me, I must get back to the city as my father must not know of my presence here, and as you know, tomorrow we are leaving Saintes."

"Yes, yes," replied Bernard, "let us start walking again; we may not be out of danger."

They moved with precaution onto a path. One could hear leaves rustling, hurried steps and the murmur of voices. Several times, they glimpsed shadows that crossed their path, and they anxiously stopped; however, the strangers seemed to be alarmed themselves and hastened to move further into the depth of the undergrowth, so they continued to advance.

Gaston de Massac had taken Esther's arm and was supporting her while occasionally giving her words of encouragement. Palissy and the minister, who seemed very familiar with the countryside, were walking with attentive eyes and ears.

Finally, after several alerts, they found themselves on the main road to Saintes. They halted once more and waited until the public way was deserted and Gaston brusquely said to Palissy:

"Now! Master Bernard, I hope that you will not invite into your home any dangerous guests! You have already strongly compromised yourself on the subject of the minister; if they discover him again in your lodging, no protection exists that can save you."

This warning dismayed Palissy and his daughter.

"This gentleman says the truth, Master Bernard," continued Hamelin; "I must not expose you to further dangers by accepting your hospitality. Thanks to your charity and that of Esther, my daily bread has been delivered to me today, to which you have added alms that allow me to meet my needs for several days. It is therefore time for us to separate.... Perhaps I will find a hiding place in the vicinity, with one of our brothers. And if necessary, I will spend the night in the open air.... I am prepared for all hardships and suffering."

As Palissy did not immediately reply, his daughter did so in tears:

"Oh, I beg of you, my father, do not abandon our poor pastor. Right now, he has no refuge, and you know it. Raby's soldiers have pillaged his home and none of our brothers dare receive him. It is true that while waiting for better times he could search for a sanctuary in certain neighboring regions that are less exposed to this one from persecution, but if he is found on these paths by these ruthless men who are relentlessly tracking him, he is sure to be arrested."

Her sobs interrupted her words.

"Thank you, Esther," replied Hamelin. "However, I will not sacrifice the life of an honest family for my safety."

"However, my brother Hamelin," said Palissy, "Esther is right; I could not, without cowardice and a bad conscience, leave you alone and without shelter. Once more this night you will rest under my roof, and God will protect us all!"

"I will not follow you my brother Palissy. I am overwhelmed with appreciation for your devotion, and that of Esther, but I would consider it unworthy of me to... "

During this debate on generosity, Gaston de Massac was alerted once again by the sound of voices and steps that were rapidly approaching.

"Shush! Listen," he said.

They all jumped behind some blackthorn and elderberry bushes that were on the side of the road. The heaviness of the steps and the clicking metallic sounds indicated that these were Raby's troops.

And so it was; six robust soldiers carried in their arms the wounded Captain who moaned from time to time. As they were passing slowly past the hedge, one of the group, probably a sub-officer, was saying to his companions:

"It would be best to take him to Toupinac, the barber-surgeon, who lives near here.... This Toupinac is almost as skillful as a Master Surgeon, and he is a good Catholic. He will cure our poor Captain."

"Yes, yes, he will cure him," said another, "and in a week, our valiant chief will swear and drink as in the past.... In the meantime, my friends, we must take revenge. Tomorrow, when the gates open, we must carefully examine each Huguenot who tries to re-enter the city; but tonight, it would be important to visit, one by one, all the suspect houses in the vicinity...."

"We must deal with these heretics," resumed the first one. "In my opinion, we should start our search with the house of that crazy potter, Bernard Palissy."

"Ah yes! We might discover some strange birds in that place."

The remainder of the conversation was lost in the distance.

"Well Sires," resumed Gaston with some irony after a moment of silence. "Do you still doubt the reality of danger?"

"My decision was already made," said the young pastor in a calm voice. "So, I will say my farewells to my generous friends, and if I do not see them again in this world, then we will meet again, I hope, in a far better one."

"What will become of you?" cried Esther with desperation.

"Providence will protect me."

Esther turned to Gaston.

"Master de Massac," she said with vehemence while clasping her hands. "Have pity on him, I beg of you, in the name of all the Christian sects, come to the aid of a good man! I am sure that you can help him if you have the desire to do so. It is this desire I am begging for. Protect him, save him... and I... I will love you!"

This last phrase was pronounced with such simplicity that no one would imagine the least sentiment of guilt. Gaston, in spite of himself, felt moved hearing this lovely and innocent child say to him: "I will love you." He could not see her expression in the darkness, but he imagined an angelic one, and sensed the aura of her soft gaze.

He hesitated before answering.

"I am already quite guilty," he finally said in a brusque tone. "I cooperated tonight with the odious Reformist cause. I spilt the blood of the defenders of my faith, and I will have to do penance later. However, I cannot resist the touching prayers of Esther Palissy.... At the risk of being taken for a renegade and a traitor, I will try to answer her prayers."

"I knew it!" cried the young girl. "You are good as well as powerful!"

"Sire," continued Gaston speaking to the Protestant minister, "did I not hear said a while ago that you hoped to find a safe haven outside of this region?"

"This is true; either at La Rochelle, or in Niort, where we have many co-religionists.... "

"I am not asking you where you wish to take refuge; I do not want to know.... However, I can provide you with a way to travel in all security once you have left the Saintes area."

"Is this possible?"

"Listen: I am about to do something reprehensible that could bring me severe rebukes; however, out of respect for the Palissy family I will impose silence on my own scruples.... I have with me several pre-signed documents of authorization from my illustrious master, the Constable of Montmorency; they were entrusted to me for purposes that I need not explain to anyone. I will write your name on one of these documents which will become one of safe-passage for you, and wherever you go in this kingdom, your life and liberty will be protected."

"Yet the Constable is our mortal enemy!" murmured Hamelin sadly.

"I am all the more reprehensible for placing you under the protection of this respected name.... However, I repeat, this safe-passage will not be effective here where you are known. You must therefore leave immediately since tomorrow morning you will be sought and pursued on every route, so you must leave the Sainte region as rapidly as possible. If you lack money for your travel costs, I can furnish you...."

"Thank you; my brother Palissy has already provided some.... As for my travel preparations, all I need is to cut myself a walking stick from the nearby undergrowth.... From you, Sire, I will only accept the safe-passage of which you speak, and your generosity towards a person that you probably hate merits all my gratitude."

"Master de Massac," said Bernard, "has as much greatness of soul as he does of righteousness, and if he belonged to our religion...."

"Ah, my father," said Esther warmly, "why not hope that one day his eyes will open to the true light. Then as Naomi[16] once said, "we will have one people and one God...."

This reference to the Bible caused Gaston to frown; however, he expressed the desire to prepare without further delay the safe-passage document so that Hamelin could be far from Saintes by daybreak.

Esther had a small resin candle to help her read her book of psalms during the services, so she hastened to light it. As for Gaston, he retrieved from a secret pocket, under his cloak, a leather wallet that held vellum parchments containing various stamps and seals. In his role as Secretary he also had with him a long slim writing case similar to the ones that clerks carry on their belts and which contain ink and quill pens. They placed the candle behind some bushes; then Massac hurried to fill in the blanks of the safe-passage. He only had a few words to write, and although he was hunched over in an uncomfortable position, it only took a few minutes to complete the task.

Shortly, he presented the Protestant minister with a perfectly legal document that should be effective wherever royal authority was recognized.

Hamelin thanked him warmly, while Palissy and his daughter, on their side, gave thanks in prayer. They then hastened to put out the candle lest the flame attract unwanted attention; and Massac having made his wallet disappear, said with severity:

"Now, Sire, nothing retains you.... Leave now before I have time to reflect upon my weaknesses.... My conscience is already in revolt. Take care that it does not cry too loudly!"

"This is just, Sire," replied Hamelin humbly; "I will begin my voyage... but first, I would like to give my brother Bernard certain instructions concerning my unfortunate and dispersed flock that I must leave behind... perhaps forever."

And he began speaking with Palissy in a low voice as they walked towards the potter's house. Gaston de Massac was following a few steps back with Esther.

"Dear little one," he said presently, "It is especially because of you that I have done so many things tonight which are contrary to my beliefs and my duty. Do you remember that as a reward for having made these sacrifices, you promised to love me?"

These words in the mouth of the young gentleman were as chaste as those that came from Esther. She accepted them in this manner in answering with naivety:

"Oh! Yes, yes, Master de Massac; I have certainly not forgotten the

16 **Naomi** is Ruth's mother-in-law in the Old Testament Book of Ruth.

services that you have rendered us…. My God! How, in such a short time, did we manage to inspire in you such a serious interest and such complete devotion?"

"I saw you suffer with such resignation and courage, Esther; I admired your affection for your father, this noble artisan, and the serene confidence that you had in him when he was so overwhelmed…. And," he continued, lowering his voice, "I still think about the night when, broken with fatigue and sadness, you slept with your head on my shoulder, as if placing your innocence and weakness under my protection!"

"What are you saying, Master Gaston? I do not understand…. I had a fever that night, and I do not remember… "

"Do not deny this moment of abandon, even if involuntary; as for me, I will never forget it, and you will never invoke the memory in vain."

Esther did not reply, she was crying. After a pause, Gaston continued:

"I believe, Esther, that peaceful times for Master Bernard and his family will follow this crisis. His brilliant success, the protection of the Governor and the admiration of the highest nobility of Saintes, will open for him a period of prosperity. On my side, as I have told you, when I rejoin my master, the Constable, I will recommend to him the sublime artisan that has just been revealed. However, I do not doubt that dangers can return. This disastrous sect to which you belong will involve you in dangerous hostilities in the future."

"What can we do, Master de Massac? Neither my father, nor I, nor any of my family will be willing to renounce our faith."

"And this, my poor child, is what terrorizes me. Everywhere around us fierce hatreds are accumulating. Merciless fanatical passions abound and I foresee a terrible shock that may result in this part of the kingdom being covered with ruins and blood…. Perhaps when this catastrophe occurs, I may be too far away from you and unable to come to your aid; nevertheless, take this… (and he slid into her hand a small object.) It is a signet ring, without monetary value, but which comes from my mother, and therefore is precious to me…. Keep it, in memory of the brief moments I spent in your home; if, one day, you find yourself in great danger, you or your father, send me this ring and I will come to your assistance…. It will always be easy to learn where the Constable, the person to whom I am attached, is residing. No matter where I am, I will come to you, and you will then know if time and distance have erased you from my memory."

Esther had hastened to hide the ring in her clothing, and said, while still sobbing:

"May God grant your wishes and guide you, Master de Massac!"

They had now arrived within sight of Palissy's house, and Bernard and Pastor Hamelin had just stopped to bid each other farewell. The two young persons stopped as well and were silent. Somehow the hand of the little Huguenot remained imprisoned in that of the young gentleman without either making an effort to move.

Hamelin bid to Bernard and his daughter very touching goodbyes. In spite of the safe-passage from Gaston, his situation remained precarious, and his friends really had reason to fear they might never see him again. Moreover, a secret sentiment seemed to make this separation particularly heartrending for the young minister, and when he left Esther, there was in his expression an unspoken suffering.

Bernard seemed very moved, and Esther who succeeded in freeing her hand, did not hide her tears. Gaston himself turned his head away in embarrassment.

Suddenly, Bernard spoke in a firm tone to Hamelin:

"Courage! Friend.... The storm will pass, and you will know better days.... When you return among us, and I hope that this time will come soon, we will resume the project that you and I have discussed, brother Hamelin. Esther, by then, will no longer be a child and will be able to become the companion to a good man, a minister of the Gospel, where earthly emotions find their place after divine emotions."

"My father, my father, what are you saying?" murmured Esther in confusion.

"Bernard," said Hamelin, troubled, "Do not speak to me of eventualities which will make me weak and lukewarm towards my duty. Esther has all the perfection of a woman and a Christian; perhaps her image has appeared too often in my thoughts, in my mediations.... And how would I dare ask her to share my fate, me, a minister to a banished religion...."

"That religion is mine, Sire," said Esther, "and perhaps it shall triumph later.... Meanwhile, I pray of you to be prudent, and believe that your life is precious to your friends, and to your faithful Protestants."

"Esther, Esther," asked Hamelin with ardor, "do you wish me to understand that you do not disapprove of Master Bernard's project?"

During this conversation, Gaston de Massac became violently agitated.

Until that moment he had looked upon Hamelin simply as the priest of an oppressed sect, and as odious as the sect was to him, he could not prevent himself from having a form of pity for this martyr to a religious conviction. However, upon learning about the idea of marriage between the young pastor and Bernard's daughter, all his esteem for Hamelin abruptly evaporated. He was no longer for him a miserable outcast, but a vulgar lover. The thought that this love was the charming Esther Palissy, who perhaps he himself loved, could only add to his repugnance and contempt. He therefore felt like jumping on Hamelin, wresting from him the document that he had just given to him, arresting him with his own hands and turning him over to the soldiers. He needed a major effort of will to resist this temptation. He succeeded; even more so, seeing an armed group cautiously approaching the home of Palissy, he said harshly:

"You have stayed too long, Sire; here come the soldiers who are resuming their search."

A glance by the others convinced them of the validity of the warning, and the necessity of separating as rapidly as possible. Hamelin hoped to say a few more words to Bernard and his daughter; but they did not give him time. He merely said in a stifled voice:

"Farewell! Farewell! May heaven protect you all!"

And he lost himself in the darkness.

As Bernard and Esther were not moving, Gaston resumed with an impatience that came from anger:

"What? Are you not going in? If the soldiers do not find you in your home, they will have no difficulty in guessing where you were a short time ago."

"You are right," said Palissy. "Let us go in, my daughter."

Gaston followed them to the house, where one could see a feeble light.

"I will in turn take my leave of you," he resumed in a halting voice, "as you no longer need my services.... Bernard, think about the fact that a father is as much responsible for the souls of his family as is a minister of an Orthodox or Reformed church.... As for you, Esther," he continued in a lower voice, "do not forget what has been said between us."

He added while Bernard was leaning over to open the door:

"Above all, do not forget that if you ever marry that little Protestant priest, I will kill him...and you as well!"

Esther gave a little frightened cry; Bernard attributed the terror to the approach of the soldiers... and hastened to push her in the house after having given the young gentleman a final sign of farewell.

Gaston waited until they had closed the door. Then he walked resolutely towards the soldiers, who were preparing to invade the home of the potter, and spoke to them with authority:

"You know me; I am Gaston de Massac, Secretary to the Constable.... I have spent the evening with this talented artisan, Bernard Palissy, who possesses so many marvelous secrets, and I expect that you will not disturb his rest. Therefore, leave here. I take responsibility for him and his family."

The contingent recognized Gaston, having seen him with the Governor.

"That suffices, Sire," said the Lance Corporal who was leading them. "We thought... and our poor Raby believed.... But when a Lord of your stature puts himself forward for Palissy, we cannot argue. Let us go, comrades," he continued, "We are not lacking in other Huguenot homes to visit... and let us hope that we come across one where there is something to drink!"

Muffled laughs responded and the entire troop turned on their heels to depart.

Gaston waited a moment just in case they changed their minds. Reassured on this point, he set out walking towards the city.

As he advanced, tumultuous feelings that he had held in check until now overwhelmed him. "Is this not due to the influence of evil spirits that in such a short time, I betrayed my master, my king and my religion? Tonight, I attended a preaching, I protected these odious Huguenots, I spilt the blood of defenders of the faith, I misused a document that been entrusted to me by the Constable…. I am guilty, and I too deserve the fires of hell…. Ah! Do I love this little bare-footed Huguenot dressed in rags? Should I go fight for her with this ridiculous singer of psalms? It would be a disgrace, and my father, who has such a deep tenderness for me, would strangle me with his bare hands if he knew the truth."

He remained pensive for a long time. Finally, as he was approaching the archway, he resumed with resolution:

"One thing is certain, I have been under the influence of the Devil, I have been bewitched; but my guardian angel has now taken control…. I want to forget this girl from a detested clan. When the sun rises, I will have left this area, and undoubtedly, I will never return…. May all the events of this cursed night be erased from my memory!"

PART TWO

THE BOURGEOIS FROM SAINTES

I.

THE PROMENADE

Several years had elapsed.

The religious quarrels seemed to have quieted down, and Saintonge experienced intermittent periods of calm that precede the great religious wars.

Protestantism continued to spread, but a sort of tolerance currently reigned in the province. However, it was true that here and there some Huguenots had been imprisoned or hanged. Palissy himself, in his writings, reported that the purity of the Protestants' lifestyle, their peaceful appearance and their patience, seemed to touch the population and the local authorities. Their ceremonies were often held in the middle of the night, and one could hear them returning to their homes in the city; however, no one asked them to explain these nocturnal sessions although there spread the most scandalous and ridiculous rumors. Therefore, despite certain signs that could lend themselves to fears of a renewed conflict, an apparent truce was maintained between the two parties.

Palissy and his family took advantage of this period of appeasement to attain a high level of prosperity. Master Bernard was no longer that poor starving devil, reputedly crazy, who lived in a miserable hovel in the outskirts. Now he took the title of *honorable gentleman* Bernard Palissy; some even said Bernard *de* Palissy; as if by reason of his status as Master Glazier, he had the right to the status of nobility. In the heart of the city of Saintes, at a location still named *Tuilerie de Palissy*, he had a large facility where he employed many specialists and workers. From there flowed a steady stream of charming works of art, that after having been admired by privileged local gentry, shipped out all over France spreading the reputation of the inventor of the *rustic figulines*.

This sumptuous establishment was especially due to the donations of the Constable, the Duke of Montmorency, who had become Bernard's most generous and loyal protector. Anne de Montmorency, as has been mentioned, was having the Chateau d'Ecouen built that was to equal the magnificence of the grandest of the royal palaces. Palissy was not only responsible for the ceramic art for Ecouen; the chapel's stained-glass windows, which a seventeenth century historian described as having an incomparable splendor, as well as the floor tiles and sixteen ceramic pictures representing the *Passion of Christ as* done by Albert Durer, were the work of the illustrious potter. He produced all these marvels in the Saintes workshop from whence they were transported to the Ecouen Chateau.

Furthermore, it was not only the Constable who appreciated Bernard's talents. In Saintes itself, and the entire Saintonge region, people fought over his works. Even the humblest of squires wished to have some *rustic figulines* in his manor. All the nobility of the province converged towards Palissy's workshop. He was pampered, flattered and showered with excessive expressions of admiration. They went so far as to close their eyes on his heresy, which was not a small concession in those times of religious fanaticism.

Master Bernard did not let pride go to his head; and if we follow him on a day when he was going for a stroll with his family in the outskirts of Saintes, we will have the proof that success did nothing to change his noble simplicity.

It was a Sunday, and at that time, it was the custom for both Reformists as well as Catholics, to take a stroll in the countryside after having fulfilled their religious obligations. Therefore, almost all of the city's population could be found outside the gates on the day we are describing.

Palissy was almost fifty years old. His height, bald head and long greying beard gave him a patriarchal air. The youngest of their children were running around their mother, while Esther, their eldest daughter, who was his favorite, walked besides her father. Mathurin and Nicolas, who had become robust and handsome young men, wandered to the right and left of the path to pick up wild flowers, various insects and pieces of rock which they brought back to Bernard. The sons and their father were dressed uniformly in a dark fabric without trimmings but without ornamental plumes on their hats, as was the local custom. Minimally, each wore a thin brilliantly white starched collar. The girls and their mother wore dark dresses that were slim and without the wire hoops known as farthingales. Their headdress was a bonnet of flat linen that only let pass a few strands of hair. The family, thus dressed, might have had a rather austere look, but their faces all had an expression of peace and contentment.

Palissy and his little group, having crossed the Saintes Bridge, were following the picturesque path that borders the Charente. It was the loveliest season. The sun shone in all its brilliance on a charming countryside, irrigated by two rivers, the Seugne and the Charente and dotted with meadows, orchards and vineyards. On the horizon, one could see the city, placed on the side of a hill, with its ramparts, bell towers and remains of Roman monuments.

Soon the Palissy family came to a halt on the banks of the river under a clump of poplar trees and weeping willows facing an island that resembled a basket of lush vegetation. It was quite warm and they had settled down on the grass. The younger children, who were tired, had grouped around Mistress Bernard who had become as calm and respectful of her husband as she had been ill tempered in earlier times. The smallest child had fallen asleep in her arms. Mathurin and Nicolas, whose activity did not fit with this rest period, continued to wander around the area. A short distance away from the rest of the family, Bernard and Esther were chatting with affection.

Esther was no longer the pale and frail child of earlier times. She was now almost twenty years old and she glowed in the blossoming of her virginal beauty. Her high-necked strictly cut dress, in spite of itself, revealed a slim and supple form. Her linen bonnet, which could barely contain her luxuriant stresses, framed a perfectly oval face, fresh and pink, but with a slightly melancholic expression. It goes without saying that she now wore shoes as one could judge from the tiny feet that peeked out from under the rough folds of her skirt.

The young lady was now leaning towards her father, examining with him some freshly collected plants and Bernard was trying to combine the colors in order to obtain the harmonious combination that distinguished his glazed pottery.

"You see, my child," he was saying, "I will place this pretty fern, with its brown veins next to the willow branch with its silvered back; I would combine them with some tufts of aquatic moss which have soft colors, and I would sprinkle them with some green and brown insects that your brothers have brought me.... The effect will be charming, and I am sure that this work will satisfy Sire Constable."

Esther became pensive upon hearing the name.

"Father," she asked, "has it been a long time since you have received a letter or a message from Sire Constable?"

"No, my daughter; rarely a month goes by that the Duke does not send me an order to fill new needs.... But all his letters are written in the hand of his personal Secretary, Master de Massac, and have only the seal of Master de Montmorency. Besides, we do not need doubt that the benefits that we have been receiving from this powerful Lord are thanks to the recommendations of young Master de Massac."

"Do you think so?" asked Esther with a vivacity that she immediately suppressed. "Master de Massac did not indicate in any of his letters that he retained any memories of his time with us."

"This is true; but in the custom of these grand people of the Court It would not be proper for a Secretary to add a personal note to a letter dictated by his master.... Moreover, on several occasions, Sire Constable has asked for news about our family and I felt obliged to provide some details about each of you. You will remember that last year when I painted the stained-glass windows of the Ecouen chapel I used you as my model for the Virgin, and if I say so myself, your likeness was excellent. I was so pleased with it that I reproduced it on a lovely dish that was destined to decorate the sideboard in the Constable's dining room. Our illustrious master, in seeing it, was so delighted, that in his next letter, he asked where I had found such a lovely model.... I had no difficulty in admitting that the model was my daughter, Esther, who is as modest as she is beautiful."

Esther blushed up to her ears.

"Oh! Father, Father," she stammered, "do you want me to become conceited? However, it is no less true that these Sires de Massac, father and son, especially the son, who rendered us such marvelous services while they were here in Saintes, seem to have completely forgotten us, in spite of their promises."

"The father, who I am told, has become old and broken, lives on his lands in Massac, at about a dozen miles from here, and he is limited to running his hounds and flying his falcons.... As for his son, he rarely leaves his master, to whom he is indispensable; and judging from the frequency of our correspondence, one can see that his function as Secretary is not a simple one."

"And then, Father," continued Esther, dropping her eyes, "although Sire Gaston most certainly saved our lives, ourselves and Pastor Hamelin, it is said that he is a powerful enemy of the reformist religion, and doubtless his memory of us inspires horror.... The Constable himself, if one believes reports from Paris, furiously persecutes our miserable brethren...."

"I have heard speak of this," replied Bernard, his expression darkening; "He is considered to be a wise and honest man of high morals, and the protection that he has accorded me proves that his heart is not closed to pity and justice."

"Above all, it proves, dear father, that this Lord really appreciates your masterpieces.... Up to now your superior talents have been our protection for us all, but can this remain so for long?"

"It shall always be so," said Palissy, with the naivety of genius; "in fact my daughter," he continued, lowering his voice, "I am so confident of the present and the future that I have written to Pastor Hamelin to bring him back to Saintes."

"Do you really think so, Father? On two different occasions Pastor Hamelin has attempted a return to his city of birth; each time the ardor of his zeal caused great resentment, and he had to leave hurriedly.... This time do you have sufficient authority to protect him?"

Master Bernard was a bit disconcerted by the vehemence of his daughter. However, he replied smiling:

"Ah, little one, you seem to take a great interest in the safety of our young minister.... Come now, there is nothing to be ashamed about.... There are honest sentiments that are blessed by God.... You are approaching twenty, and you already have the grace of Rebecca,[17] and the beauty of Rachel.[18] Hamelin, like Jacob, has been waiting for a long time for his betrothed; he is becoming impatient, and if one must say it, it is he who is pressing me to allow his return to Saintes."

Esther appeared agitated; she alternately paled and blushed, while turning her head. Finally, with an effort, she said:

"Father, all that you do is just and good."

At this moment, Mathurin and Nicolas returned with a new collection of herbs, butterflies, beetles, shells and shiny pebbles that they had collected in the surrounding area. They settled down with the family, and Bernard, so knowledgeable in natural history, explained the species and properties of the various objects; animal, vegetal and mineral, that they had just brought. At the same time, as an artist, he gave them an idea of the ways he would use these in the creation of his works. Palissy was very eloquent and had an admirable literary style[19] and everyone, even the prosaic Mistress Bernard, listened to him with respect. He was careful, however, not to abuse the patience of his listeners, and soon he interrupted himself:

"Now, my children," he said, "let us sing a psalm and return to the city."

"Which one, Father?" asked Esther.

"A canticle of joy; you should know why.... Look for psalm 81."

A little book came out of Esther's pocket, and the young woman having leafed through it for a moment, the entire Huguenot family began singing the psalm in French.

The song had lasted several moments when one heard from behind a nearby hedge a sudden derisive laugh, full of provocation.

The Protestants, at that time, were accustomed to taunts and normally put up with them with an inalterable patience. Therefore, the singing continued, but the laughter became so loud, insolent and mocking that Mathurin and Nicolas became impatient:

"With your permission, father!" they said.

And they launched themselves towards the hedge where the scoffer was hiding.

One could hear behind the bushes a burst of voices, then the sound of a

---

17 **Rebecca,** appears in the Hebrew Bible as the wife of Isaac and the mother of Jacob and Esau.

18 **Rachel,** was the favorite of the Biblical patriarch Jacob's two wives as well as the mother of Joseph and Benjamin, two of the twelve progenitors of the tribes of Israel.

19 **Alphonse Lamartine,** (1790-1869) French writer, poet and politician frequently praised Palissy's style, and considered Bernard as one of the leading French writers.

brief struggle; finally, Mathurin and Nicolas returned, each holding the arm of a small man with a scrawny neck, dressed like a bourgeois in his Sunday finest. He was vainly struggling to resist the two robust adolescents who were bringing him to their father. This bourgeois was Toupinac, the barber-surgeon that we had previously seen in the first part of this story.

Recognizing him, Bernard could not resist a gesture of disdain.

"What! Is that you, Master Toupinac?" he said; "Is it you who insults us because we are singing the praises of God?"

"Well! Master Bernard," replied the barber, "if I do not appreciate that you sing, then you do not appreciate that I scoff, and we are even… but why do these youngsters dare put their hands on me?"

"Release him, my sons," said Palissy.

The two young men, accustomed to absolute obedience, released their prisoner.

"About time," continued Toupinac, recovering his confidence. "So we can tell you now, Master Bernard, you may be singing today, but your song will shortly cease."

"Really! We will be returning to the city, and if you wish, Toupinac, on the way, you can give me news which you seem to have in abundance."

"Yes, yes, very fresh news," said the barber, rubbing his hands, "news which will make as much noise as all the canons of Saintes booming together."

Palissy was not unduly worried as the *Little Gascon*, as Toupinac was called, was often the source of the silliest of rumors. However, he indicated to his family that they should get up and they set off towards the city while Palissy, Esther and Toupinac followed a short distance behind.

They first travelled in silence. The barber was now feigning a somber demeanor.

"Well, friend," soon asked Master Bernard, "what do you have to tell me?"

"Ah, Palissy, neighbor Palissy, the moment has come to renounce your errors; if not, I shudder to think of the calamities which will come upon you, upon lovely Esther, upon your entire family… including these two young ruffians with such firm grips!"

This last observation caused Mathurin, who was walking slightly ahead with his brother, to turn his head and emit a low growl. However, Bernard remained impassive.

"Come now, Master Toupinac, do not keep me in suspense and tell me right away the reason for these lamentations."

Thus pressured, the barber agreed to tell all he knew.

The previous year, the King had issued an edict that condemned *all* Protestants to death and which forbid judges from lightening the sentence.

However, since this edict had not been applied in all of France, one could expect that it would remain unheeded like many previous edicts. However, the Bordeaux Parliament, upon which Saintes and Saintonge depend, had just ordered the implementation of this terrible edict. Toupinac had heard the news that very morning from a clerk at the provincial tribunal who had come into his shop for a shave, and the news had already created a great agitation in the city. Only Palissy, who had remained shuttered in his house until the time of their walk, had not heard speak of this serious event.

Indeed, it was serious, and if Palissy had heard it from a source other than Toupinac, he would have been extremely alarmed. However, believing that this was an exaggeration, or even some nasty trick by the barber, he did not show much concern.

"I thank you for your advice, neighbor," he continued. "However, I have difficulty imagining that that they could mistreat poor people like ourselves who have embraced the Reformist cause. It is certain that the gentlemen of the Council Chamber of Bordeaux do not like us very much, but it is something else to declare an edict enforceable, or to implement it. In Saintes, there are only softhearted and benevolent civil servants. Master de Pons, our worthy Governor, shows great kindness towards me. Master de Burie, and especially the Count of Maulévrier, who hold the highest rank here, only wish to use the most peaceful of methods with us. There is no one, including Father Desmazures, formerly our most relentless persecutor, who has not realized that severity and torture cannot affect souls. He has definitely recognized his error and is now kindness and charity towards us; he will protect us if necessary.... Moreover, Captain Raby and his militia, who had caused us so much trouble, were sent away from the city two years ago."

"All this could be true, my friend Bernard. The Governor and the authorities are lukewarm, I agree. But they cannot refuse the orders of the King. It has been announced that a Commissioner from the Bordeaux Parliament will arrive here shortly with extraordinary powers.... As for Captain Raby, whose militia has increased fourfold, he is currently at the Chateau de Taillebourg, a few miles from here, with a German cavalry. Raby, since having been wounded by a Huguenot at the moors of Brassac, a wound that was perfectly treated by someone I know, and more furious than ever against you; and if called... in fact, public rumor has it that he has been called and will soon arrive from Tailebourg with his soldiers and the Germans, even angrier than they are."

Bernard was horrified as these facts had the ring of truth. Poor Esther was listening and trembling. As Palissy was quiet apparently lost in thought, Toupinac continued:

"As for you, Master, you think yourself strong because of your protectors. I agree that many of these high personages are full of admiration of your marvelous glass and ceramic products, but do not count on this, and rather consider renouncing your heresies.... You never want to listen to me; if you only had a few moments of patience, I would prove to you by irresistible arguments...."

"Thank you, my friend," replied Palissy with a mocking smile. "It is true that I have been able to resist the arguments of Father Desmazures who comes to see me often and is a man of great science; but I am familiar with your superior eloquence, and a poor man such as myself would not dare argue against it."

"Well, you have your pride; and then you are too old, too stubborn to listen to the voice of reason. But," continued the barber, eyeing Esther, "if this lovely young lady ever expressed the desire to return to the right path, I would spare neither my counsel nor examples. I would even finish by finding for her a husband who is a well-established bourgeois of high morals."

"I do not wish to marry, Master Toupinac," interrupted Esther with impatience, "and if I did, I would only accept counsel from my father."

"Esther is right," said Palissy in a dry tone; "You are showing a little too much zeal, my friend.... And we are now where we must separate."

They had arrived in the neighborhood where the barber lived, and as Palissy was returning to the city, they had to take separate directions.

"Goodnight, Master Bernard," continued Toupinac in a sugary tone. "Your blindness saddens me. Goodnight to you too, Esther. Do not forget my good feelings towards you when the moment arrives..."

"What moment, friend?" demanded Palissy.

"That moment when you will die from the *heat,* Satanic Huguenot!" replied Toupinac, giving free reign to his fury.

And he fled from the scene.

It was known that in the language of the time, "dying of the heat" meant "being burned alive".

Bernard had simply shrugged his shoulders, but Mathurin and Nicolas approached their father saying:

"What is going on?"

"Nothing, nothing, my sons. Do you not know that the barber is a buffoon whose words are not worthy of consideration?"

As they were approaching the city Bernard thought that the faces on the passers-by expressed fear. As they were about to cross the draw-bridge which led to the main gate of Saintes, he saw a gentleman who was approaching at a rapid pace and seemed to be heading in their direction. It was the Count of Maulévrier, who, you will remember, was a secret member of the Reformist religion and had been wounded by Gaston de Massac. Palissy, aware for some time of the excessive prudence of his fellow religionist, pretended not to see him. However, Maulévrier, having made sure that no one was near enough to eavesdrop, spoke rapidly to him as he passed:

"Things are going badly…. Be careful!"

And he continued on his way, without turning his head.

This new warning, in spite of its brevity, re-doubled Bernard's fears; the potter, however, was not at the end of his concerns. Having passed under the darkened arch of the gate, while the snickering guards watched, they had plunged into the narrow and dark streets of the city when a man wearing the clothes of a skilled worker, ran up to them. Palissy recognized one of his employees in whom he had total confidence and was one of his most loyal retainers.

"You here, comrade Daniel?" he asked in surprise; "why have you left the house that I left in your charge during my absence? "

"It is you that I was searching for, master," replied the worker lowering his voice. "There are new events in your home;"

And he whispered several words in Bernard's ear, which caused him to shudder.

"Well, that is all that was missing!" he said.

Then, he turned to speak to his family:

"You do not need to rush," he continued, "I will go in advance with comrade Daniel, and will enter by the door to the workshops. We shall meet later."

"Father, dear father," asked Esther anxiously, "what have you learned now?"

However, Palissy simply gave her a quick nod, as if to recommend prudence, and left with Daniel.

II.

JOSÈPHE DE SENNEVILLE

Bernard Palissy's production facility, as we have said, was of consider-able size. In addition to a residential home, in a sort of park surrounded by walls, it also included several vast hangars, each containing a variety of ovens and workshops. One could enter by one of several doors, some low and discreet, others rather high and large enough to allow passage of loaded wagons.

It was in front of one of those discreet doorways in a squalid alley, of which there were many in Saintes according to Agrippa d'Aubigné,[20] that Bernard and Daniel stopped. Bernard withdrew a key from his pocket and opened it; then the two men crossed an immense hall where the receding daylight was settling into dusk.

Because it was Sunday, there was total silence where during weekdays reigned a feverish activity and the master set the example. All the ovens were shut down; not a worker or apprentice circulated among all this mate-rial which included tools, molds, stained glass frames under construction and tablets of earthenware scattered on the floor.

In truth, Bernard Palissy was very protective of his production pro-cesses. Having, as he said himself, acquired the knowledge 'with his teeth,' everything made him suspicious, and with the exception of his sons and certain devoted workers like Daniel, he did not communicate with anyone about his discoveries. In his absence, the workshops were closed and no one was allowed access. He was suspicious of even simple curiosity seekers and did not reflect upon the fact that even if they stole the secrets of the materials he used and the methods he employed, they could never steal his art, talent and exquisite taste which made his works unique masterpieces.

As he walked, he shot inquisitive glances left and right to assure himself that all was in order. Satisfied, no doubt, by this scrutiny, he asked his com-panion in a lowered voice:

"Where did you take them, Daniel?"

"To the modeling workshop for which you gave me a key, master. Quite

20 **Théodore-Agrippa d'Aubigné,** (1552-1630) Renowned French Protestant poet, propagandist, and chronicler.

a few persons came to your home today as the bad news is beginning to spread, and I felt it would be imprudent to let visitors see the new arrivals."

"You did well, Daniel. I am not worried about letting anyone into the modeling workshop; these persons are not likely to care about my sketches and models."

They finally reached a doorway at the far end of the main hangar. Palissy dismissed Daniel after having given him some instructions and hurriedly entered.

He now found himself in a fairly large room, illuminated from above like our modern artists' workshops. Bernard Palissy was a sculptor as well as a painter, and one could see some roughly shaped blocks, bas-reliefs, animals, busts and even individual statues or groups destined for Ecouen and other stately residences which he was charged with decorating. Some of these works, still in their early stage, were in clay or plaster, while others, completely finished, had their resplendent adornment of ceramics. The furniture consisted of two or three long tables and several wooden chairs of humble appearance.

In this studio, a precious work sanctuary, two persons seemed to be waiting for him. One was a man of modest appearance, dressed in black, without a sword or plumed cap, with a soft face and sad expression that was completely shaved in spite of the current vogue. The other was a woman, enveloped in a mantle and wearing a velvet cowl that covered a portion of her features, without hiding that she was young and quite beautiful. Tall and slender, she had well-arched black eyebrows, a ruby mouth and a curled lip. Despite the modesty of her clothing, one could note by her attitude an element of pride that promised a young woman of quality.

Upon the appearance of Master Bernard, both arose, but while the unknown lady, after making a slight bow, remained standing in front of her chair, the man rushed forward with open arms, exclaiming:

"Ah! Palissy, my dear Palissy, I am truly happy to see you again! May Almighty God grant you his favors, you and yours!"

It was Pastor Hamelin. Bernard affectionately returned his embrace.

"May you also receive his blessings, my son Hamelin!" he said in return. "You will need them in these troubled times in which we are living.... I perhaps rushed too much in urging you to return, Hamelin, considering that our persecution threatens to reawaken!"

"Yes, yes, I learned about this upon my arrival in the city... but I have girded my loins and strengthened my heart; may God's will be done!... But this is not about me, Master Bernard," he continued in a different tone, "It concerns this noble lady, who has most recently become our sister in religion, and for whom I implore your support... Miss Josèphe de Senneville."

Bernard acknowledged her politely.

"Senneville," he repeated, appearing to search his memory; "did not a family of that name live in a chateau located several miles from Saint-Jean-d'Angély?"

"Precisely, Master Bernard," replied the young woman in a tone that did not lack firmness. "The chateau of which you speak is the one where I was born and which I left two days ago.... Do you know it?"

"I visited Senneville many years ago," continued Palissy, "and I have never forgotten what happened to me there. I was then a simple journeyman and I was ending my tour of France. I had travelled successively the entire kingdom, Flanders, the Netherlands and a portion of Germany, travelling on foot and stopping occasionally to instruct myself and to earn my keep."

"I was therefore returning from these long travels and on my way to Saintes where I planned to settle definitively. One night, several miles from Saint Jean-Angély, I was overcome by a great fatigue and was extremely hungry. I looked around me and saw, a short distance from the road, a village, or rather a hamlet that was dominated by a feudal manor with two large towers...."

"That was indeed the Chateau de Senneville," interrupted the young woman.

"At the time, I was unaware of its name," continued Palissy; "but I did not have the strength to continue further and I decided to stop in the village. Unfortunately, I did not have any money, and when I presented myself at the only inn, I was rudely rejected. I attempted to obtain shelter with the peasants, but they were either too poor or too inhospitable to receive me. Rejected everywhere, I had sadly settled on a rock by the side of the road. Without shelter and without food, I was wondering how I was going to survive the night which was threatening to be quite cold and rainy."

"Suddenly I heard the noise of a group approaching. A gentleman and a lady, both on horseback, followed by several servants, were going towards the manor. They appeared to be returning from a bird hunt as each held a falcon and one of the servants held several hounds on a leash. I assumed they were the masters of the manor. When they approached, I arose and saluted them in silence. The lady spoke several words to her husband and they stopped. The gentleman asked me who I was, and what I was doing in this place. I did not hide my distress from him. He looked at his wife whose features were warm and friendly."

"Sacrebleu! Milady," he said to her, "we cannot allow this poor devil to suffer from hunger and cold on our doorstep.... Would it please you that we give him assistance?"

"The lady immediately gave her consent and I accompanied the group to the chateau. I had an excellent supper and a warm bed that restored my strength. The next morning, after a meal, they gave me provisions and an ecu. Thus, I was able to arrive in Saintes.

"My benefactors were the Lord and Lady of Senneville...."

"These were my father and mother!" cried the traveler, breaking down in tears. "Everyone in the countryside loved and blessed them.... Ah, if they were still alive, I would not be in this sorry state!"

Bernard sat next to her.

"If you are the daughter of this worthy Lord and generous Lady," he said, "I will be happy to repay the debt of gratitude which I contracted with them so long ago.... Therefore, speak, how can I be of service to you?"

Miss Josèphe de Senneville appeared embarrassed as if she feared touching upon some delicate aspects of her past life; she therefore asked Pastor Hamelin to lay out the facts that that were necessary to explain to Bernard. Here, in a few words, is what Hamelin recounted:

The Lord and Lady of Senneville, who had shown themselves so charitable towards Palissy, had two children, a son, older than Josèphe by five or six years, and Josèphe herself. The father and the mother having passed away some years ago, Josèphe had continued to live in the chateau under the guardianship of her brother, who had become Lord of the domain.

Moreover, she was independently possessed of a fortune, as the parents' will stipulated that if she were to marry, the brother was to pay her a dowry, the size of which was considerable for that time.

There was nothing that allowed one to suppose that a serious disagreement could arise between brother and sister. Senneville led the quiet life of a gentleman farmer and left Josèphe to manage the household. However, with the young gentleman having decided it was appropriate to choose a wife, the situation took on a new face.

The new Lady of Senneville could only look with jealousy upon the influence exercised at the chateau by her sister-in-law as rival to her own. She was stubborn, despotic and the tenderness of her husband encouraged her to claim her rights. On her side, Josèphe, formerly spoiled by her parents, used to her independence, and somewhat haughty in character, perhaps did not know how to deal with her sister-in-law's susceptibilities. The result was the development of a great deal of bitterness between the two, and the husband sided with his wife.

Another issue increased their mutual animosity. We have mentioned that Josèphe had the right to claim from her brother a sizeable dowry. This obligation seemed hard to the couple, who already had one child and whose family could increase further. In order to avoid the eventuality of a marriage, everything had been done to convince Miss de Senneville to take the veil in a convent and abandon her dowry. However, this plan was not at all to Josèphe's taste; she had energetically resisted the proposals of her brother and her sister-in-law and the situation in their home soon became extremely difficult.

While this was going on, Pastor Hamelin, who continued to lead a wandering life, had settled near the chateau. Josèphe had met him several times at the home of an elderly lady that she frequented and who had secretly adopted the Protestant faith. The minister's eloquence had had a profound effect on Miss de Senneville, who little by little, developed a passion for the Reformist doctrines. Finally, one day that they were pressuring her more than usual to take the veil, she became carried away and haughtily declared that not only did she not feel the slightest vocation for the cloisters, but that she viewed Catholicism with horror and had become Huguenot.

One can imagine the effect that this declaration had on the brother and sister-in-law. Aside from the question of religion, there was a question of their interests that could not help but awaken their anger. The ensuing result was a frightful scene. Senneville threatened to kill her or throw her into the dungeon; Madame de Senneville screamed that she never in her life wanted to see again this horrible heretic; and while the implementation did not immediately follow the threat, Josèphe understood that for her safety and her peace of mind, it was important that she leave the Manor as rapidly as possible.

She took advantage of the most favorable moment to go to the home of her elderly confidant, where she met up with Pastor Hamelin. She informed them about what had happened and they agreed with her that she could no longer remain at the chateau. But where could she go? The relatives, upon whom she would have counted under normal circumstances, were on the brother's side, and she did not know where to find sanctuary.

It was just at this moment that Bernard Palissy had written to Hamelin to recall him to Saintes, assuring that by his merit, by his immunity attached to his home, he could offer him a safe haven. Hamelin shared this confidence and proposed to Joséphe to take her to Palissy's abode. She accepted and set about to act as soon as possible. It was agreed that the elderly lady, under the guise of going on a trip, obtain a curtained litter[21] supported by two mules. Miss de Senneville was to hide herself in this, with a local peasant guiding the coach while Hamelin would follow on foot. All these arrangements were so well made that the next evening, while those in the chateau believed that Josèphe was shut up in her room, she slipped out of the house, climbed into the coach, bringing with her the few precious objects which she owned, and left with her small escort. Having traveled all through the night, it was thus that they arrived unannounced at the home of the famous potter.

Master Bernard listened to this story with attentiveness.

"From the point of view of human prudence, Hamelin, my son," he said,

---

21 **litter,** an enclosed chair for one person, carried on two poles by two men or two animals, one in front, one in back. Also called a 'Sedan Chair,' in French: 'litière' ,

"in spiriting this young lady away from her family, you have committed an act which can have consequences disastrous for her, for you, for our sacred cause itself…."

"I did not concern myself with human prudence, my father Bernard," replied the minister fiercely. "I wanted to save a pious soul from persecution and protect her innocence and frailty; I do not regret my action."

While Hamelin was speaking, Josèphe was contemplating him with a naïve admiration and had lifted her hands towards the sky, as if to give thanks for having such a protector. Palissy soon continued:

"I cannot reproach you, Hamelin, as I myself was wrong to inspire your confidence which today has been proven wrong by recent events. The hostility of a powerful family can only increase our difficulties."

Josèphe, who, as we have already had occasion to notice, had an impetuous character, suddenly stood up. "If my presence at the home of Master Bernard is troublesome," she said, "I could leave. I have a little money and some jewels; I can easily find in this town an honest house where I can stay until circumstances become more favorable."

Bernard contented himself with a sad smile.

"You have not understood me, Miss," he replied. "I have no intention of reneging on my debt of gratitude that I had contracted a long time ago with your father and mother, and their benevolent memory; and it would be a shame for me to deny my support for a sister in religion…. However, in the interest of your security, we will be obliged to take certain precautions that perhaps may prove cumbersome for you. During the week, my house is invaded by a great number of workers, and as confident as I am in these brave people, the presence of an unknown lady could attract a dangerous curiosity. You will have to adopt some sort of disguise and leave the room that I will have prepared for you as seldom as possible."

"Is that all, Master Bernard? I am ready for anything… Alas, in recent times I was almost a prisoner at Senneville!"

"As for Master Hamelin," continued Palissy, "as recently as yesterday I believed I could openly bring him into my home where everyone knows him; but due to the events that occurred today, we are obliged to act with great prudence. Therefore, I will urge our dear pastor to remain hidden in the home of mutual friends for several days until he can show himself in Saintes without danger."

"I will exactly follow your advice, my father Palissy," said Hamelin; "I will take up residence at the home of one of our brothers that you designate and will keep quiet until further notice, providing that I see you and yours often… especially your charming Esther."

Miss de Senneville gave a start.

"Esther!" she repeated.

"She is my eldest daughter, Miss," continued Bernard with a touch of pride, "she will henceforth be your companion and when you get to know her, you will certainly grant her your affection.... Master Hamelin must have sometimes spoken to you about Esther?"

"This is true, but I did not imagine..."

"I understand his reserve, but there was nothing to prevent him from admitting that that certain arrangements existed between us.... Everyone is aware that if things calm down, he shall receive, according to our rites, the title of son that I already give him with such pleasure."

Josèphe fell back in her chair giving a sigh that resembled a moan.

"Now," continued Bernard, "I will inform my family and make the necessary arrangements.... Be patient, I will come back to get you in a while."

And he went out.

As soon as he had gone, Josèphe animatedly asked Hamelin:

"How is it, Sire, that you never spoke to me earlier of your engagement to the daughter of Master Palissy?"

"Ah, Miss," replied Hamelin with candor, "what do my personal sentiments have to do with my obligations towards you? I told you that Palissy had a young, educated and pious daughter.... What was the need to say more?"

"True," Josèphe replied with a wry smile; "in any event, you love her no doubt?"

"Yes, I love her!" exclaimed the pastor, whose eyes were flaming; "You shall see her, Miss; never has a more beautiful, noble and saintly creature appeared on earth.... There is something celestial about her.... But no, no," he immediately added in confusion, "I am allowing myself to admire a creature as if she were the Creator.... I ask pardon for this fault to He who punishes reckless and mundane thoughts!"

He fell silent and seemed to be praying mentally. Miss de Senneville continued:

"And she, Sire, this... Esther, does she share the sentiments that she inspires in you?"

Hamelin hesitated.

"I do not know," he said finally; "I have seen her so seldom in recent years! But she is submissive to the will of her father, and she is full of zeal for our cause, and perhaps..."

He did not have time to finish his phrase. The door had just opened, and Bernard entered with Esther. Palissy's daughter, learning that a young lady, who was noble, Protestant and persecuted by her family, had taken refuge in her home, hastened to greet her. She approached the visitor, a smile on her lips, and kissed her on both cheeks before Josèphe could react.

"Miss," she said, "welcome to our home.... My father and my mother will love you like their daughter; allow me to love you like my sister!"

Josèphe replied with a haughty coolness at these gestures.

"I thank you," she said; "I do not intend abusing for long your hospitality, and as soon as I find another refuge…"

"Good!" interrupted Master Bernard; "you will stay with us the time necessary…. Well! Esther," he continued, speaking to his daughter, a little disconcerted by this reception, "you have nothing to say to our dear pastor?"

Esther turned towards Hamelin:

"I am pleased to see him!" she murmured, blushing.

Hamelin rushed towards her and took her hand, which he held tenderly in both of his.

"Oh! Esther," he exclaimed, "how you have become grown and beautiful…. But," he added hurriedly, "it is not yet there that I should be thinking…. My God, take pity on my human weakness."

The two young persons remained silent, embarrassed, while Josèphe observed them oddly. Bernard continued cheerfully:

"Let us go to the house, where the evening meal awaits us…. Everything has been arranged with my wife and Esther. Miss de Senneville will pretend to be one of our cousins from Bordeaux, where we have relatives, and we will only call her Josèphe. We are preparing a room next to Esther's and will try to render her captivity as bearable as possible…. As for you, Hamelin, directly after dinner, I will take you to the home of Savinien, the plumber, who is completely devoted to us…. Another important item: where is the coach in which Miss de Senneville traveled, and what became of the man who accompanied you?"

"We did not judge it prudent," replied Hamelin, "to enter Saintes with the coach, as it would have attracted attention…. We stopped at an inn in the outskirts, and after having generously paying our guide, we dismissed him suggesting that he return home as rapidly as possible, which he promised to do."

"Yes, but did he keep his word? If the gates were not closed at this hour, I would go to make sure. We cannot take too many precautions to ensure that they do not find your trace, as they will certainly follow you. In any case, let us hope that all goes well."

They left the workshop. Esther hastened to take the small bundle which comprised all the luggage of the visitor; then without being offended by Josèphe's continued coolness, which she attributed to timidity, she took Miss de Senneville's arm, while her father and Hamelin preceded them speaking in low voices.

As they were reaching the area of the buildings occupied by the Palissy family, the sound of horses could be heard in a neighboring street. One would have judged that a large cavalry was passing by, and the clamor and disorganized movements of the troops indicated that they were not the most disciplined.

Concerned, Bernard halted; but from where he was placed, he could not see anything, and the exterior noises soon faded as they moved away. The worker, Daniel, ran up quite frightened.

"What is happening, comrade?" asked Palissy.

"The calamities have been unleashed again, Master," replied Daniel. "The German cavalry from Taillebourg has just entered the city, and they say that Raby's musketeers are supposed to arrive tomorrow. Woe upon us! It is not for nothing that these men of blood have left their den!"

"The least insect cannot die without the express wish of Providence," replied Palissy austerely. "Now go in peace, comrade Daniel; and remember that we must resume our work tomorrow before daybreak."

In spite of the confidence that he exhibited, Bernard was concerned during the dinner; his family and his guests were in an equally restless spirit.

III.

THE REVELATIONS

The next day, the agitation increased in Saintes. Raby's musketeers had just arrived as announced, and these roughnecks, mixed with the horsemen from Taillebourg, who had arrived the previous evening, filled the town with their turbulence. At the same time, the most sinister rumors were circulating. It was said that the leaders of this military rabble and certain important personages were meeting at this moment at the home of Master le Pons, the Governor, to discuss the measures to be taken to assure the implementation of the dreaded edict. Serious situations, related to the increasing audacity of the Huguenots and their disdain for civil and ecclesiastical authority, had been reported to the Council, which certainly did not dispose them towards indulgence. In addition, emigration was increasing in Saintes; an important number of Protestant families were furtively leaving the city, taking their most precious possessions. The storm had not yet arrived, but no doubt would soon be upon them.

In the middle of this general terror, Bernard's house retained its customary appearance and activity. All the ovens were blazing; one could hear the grinding of the potters' wheels; the molders and the glassworkers were at work. There were indeed several absences among the workers, almost all Protestant, some of whom had already taken flight. However, the majority, confident in their safe haven that was said to be associated with Palissy's enterprise, continued their work peacefully. Palissy himself, in the heart of his workshop, was in the process of modeling a charming statuette, and, absorbed by his creation, seemed totally unaware of what was happening outside.

In the modest chamber that had been given to the visitor, the tranquility was the same. Esther and Miss de Senneville worked with ardor, needle in hand, to adjust at the newcomer's waist one of Esther's dresses; it was important to find bourgeois clothing for Josèphe that was in keeping with her new role, and Esther did not hesitate to offer her Sunday best. Moreover, in this distant province, where the luxury of coquetry had not yet made much progress, there was not much difference between the clothing of a middle-class lady and the daughter of a country gentleman. Therefore, the changes necessary were neither lengthy nor complicated.

While manipulating their needles, the two young women chatted. Miss de Senneville, though retaining her reserve, had slightly relaxed her initial coolness. The gentleness, the modest grace and the vibrant intelligence of Bernard's daughter seemed to have temporarily disarmed her.

They were speaking of the unfortunate events that were in preparation. Josèphe, lowering her eyes on her work, asked with a degree of embarrassment:

"At least, Esther, did Master Hamelin find refuge in the home of that artisan friend of your father's?"

"What? Miss, did I not inform you? Yesterday evening, Pastor Hamelin could not enter the home of Master Savinien, the plumber, for the excellent reason that Savinien had left the city…. Another bourgeois of our religion, to whose home my father had thought of taking him, had decided to also leave today…. Thus, he returned here and we settled him the best we could in a quiet corner of the house."

"What are you saying, Esther," asked Miss de Senneville with vivacity; "Master Hamelin is here? You have already seen him, no doubt?"

And her eyes sent fiery darts in Esther's direction.

"Indeed, Miss," replied Esther. "We crossed paths a short time ago; but we exchanged only a few words as he was afraid of being seen by one of our workers. He sent Daniel to obtain some information at the inn in the outskirts where you left your coach and its driver."

These explanations were given with a calm simplicity. Josèphe, who had resumed her task, spoke again, with some bitterness:

"If Master Hamelin is here, why has he not thought of finding some poor creature who, at his instigation, would leave her country, her birthplace and her family?"

"He is committed to you, Miss, and it is certainly for your security that he sent Daniel to the outskirts."

"Yes, but it is for you first…. You have known him for long?"

"Since my childhood; his mother, who had embraced the Reformist religion, lived in our neighborhood. When Master Hamelin, who had studied law and theology in Poitiers, came to Saintes, where he settled down and soon became pastor, my father established a close friendship with him…. We then passed several years without seeing each other."

"He loves you, however. And, on your side, you do not resist the marital union of which they speak?"

"I must obey the wishes of my father."

"His wishes?"

"His least desires are orders for me." There was a moment of silence.

"Esther," finally asked Miss de Senneville, in a neutral tone which belied the trembling in her voice, "I would have thought that you would have dreamed about a husband who was a young cavalier, gallant, fearless and chivalrous, who would have preferred you above all else!"

"One cannot have answers to all our dreams, Miss," Esther replied with a smile, "you have certainly have had some like me... but God condemns improper imagination, and we must restrict ourselves to the realities of life."

The conversation was interrupted by some light knocks on the chamber's door. Esther went to open and Hamelin rushed in.

The young minister, whose itinerant life and privations had long since given him a pale look, was even paler than usual, and his eyes had a look of sadness. Letting himself collapse in a chair that Esther had just brought forward, he said to Esther:

"Everything is turning against us. Daniel has just informed me that the driver of the coach, instead of leaving immediately, as he had promised, is still at the outskirt's inn. And worse, he chatted with the locals, among which was an agitated and dangerous man, the barber Toupinac; such that now our arrival in Saintes is a secret for no one."

"Really?" said Josèphe, without reaction.

"There is something else," continued Hamelin; "Daniel has learned that a gentleman on horseback, followed by two servants, entered the city this morning and immediately had himself taken to the home of the Governor.... According to information we were able to obtain, the gentleman is none other than Master de Senneville...."

"My brother!" cried Josèphe, who could not keep herself from trembling.

But she immediately added:

"Well, did we not expect to be pursued? Moreover, did you not tell me that Master Bernard is capable of protecting us?"

"I told you because he told me himself. Unfortunately, terrible changes have occurred.... Ah! Miss, it is not for me that I fear, but for you, for you only!"

"And why not for the honest artisan that you call your father, or for this young lady that you call your fiancée?"

"They are not, I hope, in any danger; my pain would be too great if I had to fear also for my beloved Esther.... But it is on you and I that will fall relentless hate and vengeance.... May it fall on me alone! May you escape without harm from this ordeal!"

"Without harm!" repeated Miss de Senneville somberly; "what could one think of a noble damsel who abandons her family to follow a young man... already engaged to another woman?"

These words were a subtle and terrible revelation for Hamelin and Esther. In the innocence of their spirits, such a thought had never crossed their minds. They exchanged troubled looks, full of consternation. Hamelin covered his eyes with his hands and murmured:

"Dear God! What have I done? You who reads into the depth of our hearts, you must know if I had planned such a shameful outcome."

They all fell silent. Esther, who had sensed the truth concerning Miss de Senneville, seemed to search for a word for this enigma. Suddenly, Josèphe let out an ironic laugh.

"By my faith!" she said, "I cannot accustom myself to the peculiarity of these new sects... this mixture of mysticism and worldly love, of tenderness for God and passion for a woman, confuses my thinking. Here, Esther," she added, interrupting her work, "let drop this stupid task.... What need have I for a disguise now? I no longer wish to hide.... If my brother comes to claim me, I am ready to follow him."

At the same time, she got up, approached the window, and began unthinkingly looking out at the street through the small panes of glass framed in lead.

Hamelin remained struck by grief. Esther rose in turn and took Josèphe's hand.

"Why this sudden change, my sister?" she said. "How is it that you, whose eyes have seen the light, have fallen back into your initial blindness? Were you scandalized by the innocent affection that Pastor Hamelin has shown towards me and which the blessing of nuptial vows will soon sanctify? Master Hamelin, better than anyone..."

"What is the point?" interrupted Josèphe drily; "Listen, I was brought up in the country, and perhaps I have a coarseness and ignorance of a peasant woman... When Master Hamelin explained, with his irresistible eloquence, with his inspiring look, with his unctuous and penetrating voice, the principles of the reform, I felt as though my heart had never beat for anything but God, that his mouth had never pronounced other than pious words; I listened with confidence and respect. His influence on me was immense; I abandoned everything to follow him.... But now I glimpse the truth. When he made me stirring speeches, when he gave himself to generous releases of his soul, when he moved me, exalted me, impassioned me at his will, it was you, Esther, that occupied his spirit, it was to you that he imagined he was speaking!"

There was something in Miss de Senneville's tone, something close to hateful or irritated, that gave witness to more violent sentiments than religious doubts. Esther felt it, but the subject did not permit her to discuss it. Hamelin, on his side, though expert on controversial matters, found himself in such a delicate situation, that he did not know what to say or do.

The silence persisted, when a great hubbub arose from outside. Josèphe leaned out the window, but immediately pulled back. Armed horsemen were posted in the street, in a manner to form a cordon around Palissy's home, and the musketeers, on foot, reinforced this line of sentinels. In front of the principal entrance, a group of magistrates, nobles and officers prepared to enter the home of Master Bernard.

"Well!" said Josèphe in her bitter tone, "we will not have long to wait to know our fate, and you will soon be freed of my cumbersome presence."

Esther, in turn, leaned out the window.

"We are lost!" she murmured; "the Taillebourg cavalry and Captain Raby's people surround the house. No doubt they know that you have taken refuge here.... I beg of you, Pastor Hamelin, and you, Miss, do not show yourselves. I will consult with my father to find you a shelter where you will be protected from the search."

"This is useless as far as I am concerned," said Josèphe resolutely: "I do not wish to be the source of danger or embarrassment for anyone. I repeat, if my brother comes to claim me, I will follow without resistance,"

"Miss, have you thought of the severe accounting that may be asked of you.... But you, at least, Master Hamelin," continued Esther, "agree to go into hiding.... *They* will be without pity for you!"

"Esther," answered the young Pastor dejectedly, "I have committed several grave errors, and God is punishing me. Let destiny have its way; Providence knows better than we do what we deserve."

Esther was about to insist, but a clamor coming from the house itself, as if Bernard's workers were preparing to resist, and other cries were responding from outside. In the middle of the tumult the male voice of Palissy soon emerged as he gave orders or protested against any act of violence.

'My father is in danger," said Esther; "I must go to him.... Please, Miss, rejoin my mother, who is in the next room, and consult with her to find safety.... You, Master Hamelin, hasten to the painter's workshop; therein is a hiding place which Miston, the supervisor, will show you.... Quickly, quickly.... My God, what is happening to my father?"

She rushed towards the stairway and disappeared.

The door remained wide open. The external tumult continued to increase. However, neither Miss de Senneville nor Hamelin had moved.

Suddenly, Josèphe came and placed herself in front of the young minister.

"Time presses," she said, "and the circumstances do not allow for delicacy of language.... You deceived me. When you spoke to me with such devoutness in your faith, when you exhorted me with such eloquence to leave my family that was tyrannizing me, I thought I read love in your tone, in your gestures, in your look. Love was there, but it was for another woman.... However, I am rich and noble, and I have also been told that I am beautiful…. Forget the artisan's daughter and we will resist misfortune together!"

She remained before him, straight, her face reddened, her eyes flaming. Hamelin, who had risen, backed away in surprise and horror.

"You are a demon," he stammered. "Who could believe…. Who could imagine…. Oh! I am cursed!"

"This girl does not love you," continued Josèphe, with biting irony; "she almost admitted it a short time ago. She is not worthy of you; give her up and…"

"I prefer death!" cried the Pastor impetuously.

And he fled in despair, while Miss de Senneville fell back in her chair murmuring:

"I also am cursed!"

IV.

THE CATASTROPHE

Palissy was working quietly in his studio, as we said, when the soldiers, on foot and mounted, arrived to surround the house. He would perhaps not have noticed this alarming situation, had not the agitation and the cries of his people attracted his attention. At the same time, someone came running to announce that several important persons from the city, among whom was the Governor, had entered the vestibule and were asking to see him immediately.

He hurriedly interrupted his work, and without even thinking about removing his leather apron, headed towards the main hall that normally was occupied by workers. There, an extreme confusion reigned. The workers, terrified, were arming themselves with anything handy. Mathurin and Nicolas, believing their father in danger, had seized staffs and were organizing the resistance.

When Bernard appeared, they all approached to receive his orders. To their great surprise, he exclaimed with authority:

"What is this my comrades? Why have you left your workshops? Each of you, return to your task.... I do not intend to pay a day's work to slackers!"

"But father, have you not heard?" said Mathurin, "Captain Raby's cutthroats are back, and with them those vicious Germans from Taillebourg.... We are going to be massacred, or at least thrown in prison."

"Well then, they will imprison us, or they will massacre us," said Bernard firmly; it is not with acts of violence that we achieve our ends. I maintain that one must never draw one's sword in the name of religion.... One can spill our blood, but it is forbidden to spill that of our enemies; the martyr is proof of faith.... My sons," he added, "it is for you to set the example.... I order you to throw aside those staffs."

Mathurin and Nicolas did not hesitate to obey; and the others, like the sons of the Master, rid themselves of their improvised weapons.

"Now," continued Palissy with a satisfied tone, "I repeat; return to your work. As for me, I will prove to you that there are means other than sticks, and even muskets, to make justice triumph."

And he left the hall. The workers did not dare follow him; however, they did not go back to their tasks since the persons who had been waiting in the vestibule had become impatient that no one had yet come to see them, and had entered at that moment. Bernard, having seen them, immediately spoke to one of his sons, who immediately left.

Among the new arrivals was, as we said, the Governor of Saintes, Master de Pons, whose demeanor did not bode well and a Presiding Judge in red robes, who, while waiting for the arrival of a Royal Commissioner, had been delegated by the Bordeaux parliament for the implementation of the edict, and filled for the city the function of Chief Justice. There was also a tall young man with the look of a country squire, a somber looking person, with coarse manners. He was dressed in gray, with a plume on his hat, and a long sword. No one in the house knew him; it was de Senneville, the brother and tutor of Josèphe.

A little further back were the two officers who commanded the musketeers and the thuggish cavaliers from Taillebourg. One was our old acquaintance Raby, as proud and robust as ever, although a slight stiffness under his collar was a reminder of the blow from a sword that had been previously bestowed upon him by Gaston de Massac. The other was an older German with a white beard who appeared no less brutal than the Captain. Both, wearing helmets and armor, with boots that rose over their knees, had their naked swords in hand. Outside, the stamping around of the horses, the clinking of weapons, the shouted orders in German or French, were evidence that the troops were actually on guard.

Nevertheless, this menacing apparition did not intimidate Bernard Palissy. He politely bowed and said with a mixture of malice and good humor:

"It is a great honor for me, Sire Governor, to see you here, you and so many respectable persons...."

"I would like to be coming to your home as a friend, as I have many times in the past, Master Bernard," replied de Pons with embarrassment, "but the truth is that I am here in the performance of my duties..."

"We are here in the name of the King and the Parliament of Bordeaux," said the Presiding Judge.

Bernard bowed.

"Very well, gentlemen," he replied. "I therefore await the orders of the King and the Parliament.... What does this concern?"

"You know very well, Master Bernard, "continued the Judge, "that you are subject to the conditions of the Royal edict that the tribunal has just ordered implemented. You belong to this unholy sect that repudiates God...."

The Governor hastened to speak:

"Sire Judge," he said, "allow me to remind you that this is not what concerns us for the moment. We are here due to a complaint against Master Bernard; he is accused of having provided asylum to a supposed minister of the Reformed religion, who by sorcery, or enchantment, had taken a noble damsel from her family...."

"Yes, yes, by sorcery or enchantment!" Interrupted de Senneville with violence; "I maintain that only magic could have affected the mind of a damsel of our house to that point.... But what is the reason for this delay? If my sister is here, deliver her to me immediately and I will remove her fantasies of world travel."

Le Pons made a sign to calm the ardor of the irritated brother.

"Do you hear, Master Bernard?" he continued addressing Palissy, "Irrefutable testimonies have established that the Huguenot priest or this lost damsel, or perhaps both are hiding in your home. You are therefore ordered to turn one or both over to us if you do not wish to see your home searched by the musketeers and the Germans.... Come now, Bernard, you know that I am your friend, and that I am here to assure that they do not treat you with too much vigor. Comply and reflect that all resistance could be disastrous."

At this moment, Esther and Palissy's two sons rejoined the head of the family. Mathurin and Nicolas exchanged looks with the workers as if to ask if all resistance was impossible, but Esther, although secretly upset, remained calm in appearance. She had confidence in the high intelligence, energy and merit of her father. She pressed herself against him, certain that he was their protection and salvation.

Master Bernard, in fact, did not stop smiling; taking from the hands of his son several parchments that the young man had just brought, he said quietly:

"I thank Sire Governor for his kindness.... But I will ask him, as well as the other honorable persons who are accompanying him, at whose house do they think they are?"

"Zounds!" responded de Pons in astonishment, "we are in the home of Master Bernard Palissy, the illustrious inventor of the *rustic figulines*."

"You are in the house of Monseigneur le Maréchal–Duc Anne de Montmorency, Constable of France," said Bernard unrolling a parchment. Everything here belongs to him, or at least, he takes under his protection everything that is here. My person, my family and my possessions are protected from legal proceedings or damages, either for religious reasons or any other reasons, as validated by this deed that bears the seal of the great Constable.... As for the soldiers present here," continued Palissy, turning towards Raby and the other Captain, presenting them with another parchment, "here is another safeguard document from Sire Count de la Rochefoucauld, Commander of the King's army for the provinces of Saintonge and Guyenne[22].

22 **Guyenne**, was an old French province which included Bordeaux. In the 17th century, it was united with Gasconny.

He expressly orders all the officers and soldiers in his service, to not only respect my person, my family and my possessions, but to protect them if necessary."

The documents were passed from hand to hand and created among the group of officials a great deal of agitation. It was to be expected that Bernard Palissy, the great artist, friend of so many illustrious persons, would invoke powerful protection, but no one could suppose that he would benefit from such a far reaching, complete and indisputable immunity.

Bernard felt his triumph and continued, still smiling:

"I can now ask these Lords who stand before me, in what capacity you come to the house of Sire Constable, if you are not here as guests and friends?"

A violent discussion erupted among the participants. De Pons, who, as we know, was now devoted to Bernard, attempted to cut the discussion short.

"Well!" he said briskly, "all that remains for us to do is take our leave. Our presence here would now be a transgression against the authority of Sire Constable."

"The Devil's horn!" said Raby, "the orders are clear and I would not like to have a falling out with Master Montmorency who is a rough fighter."

"And I, with the Camp master of de la Rochefoucauld," said the Captain of the German troops; "we would not touch our pay for six months."

This judgment by the leaders of the armed force seemed to carry the day. The parchments were returned to Palissy and the Governor was about to give the order to retire, when the Presiding Judge, who had been speaking with de Senneville, said with authority:

"One moment, Sires! I fully respect the orders of Sire Constable and Master de la Rochefoucauld, but these Lords have undoubtedly been misled, for they would certainly not condone heresy and sacrilege; I will denounce this situation to the Bordeaux Parliament so as to have these protective documents revoked as rapidly as possible, to allow the royal Commissioner, who should arrive soon, to apply the edict in Saintes as elsewhere."

"In the meantime, I see nothing in these parchments that prohibits us from accomplishing our current mission. The person, the family and the possessions of Master Bernard, according to these documents, must be held in respect.... We will not even concern ourselves with the workers, who, it is said, are almost all infected with heresy. But, once again, nothing prevents us from visiting this house, and if we find this so-called minister of a condemned sect, or the damsel whose mind he has troubled, they are to be immediately turned over to me."

The magistrate's presumptions were greeted with a general silence. Master de Pons said thoughtfully:

"The case is an embarrassment.... Sire Constable's document refers only to Master Palissy, his family and his possessions; there is no mention of outsiders who might be at his home, either as guests or for any other reason."

"About time!" exclaimed Raby; "Master Bernard has always been a bit much for us to digest, but if we can get our claws into that hypocrite of a minister who I have been after for a long time, and on that shameless Huguenot hussy…"

"You should speak better of a noble lady, Captain!" interrupted Senneville angrily.

"Sacrebleu! Noble or nasty, she is still a…"

As an argument was about to break out between the roughneck and the country squire, Palissy spoke out:

"I cannot accept this interpretation. My protectors had intended that this home should be a sanctuary; not only for me, but also for anyone it pleases me to receive. Therefore, if anyone acts with violence, I will file a complaint with the Constable."

In spite of his protestations, the officers and the soldiers prepared to begin the search in the work area. De Pons, recognizing the impossibility of stopping them, whispered to Palissy:

"Give in, my poor Bernard…. Passions are riding too high; the crime of which this man and woman are accused is too great to prevent justice being served…. Turn in the culprits because not even you can protect them."

"Never!" said Palissy heatedly. "I ask everyone who hears me to leave this house and cease troubling the peace of my home."

"Oh yes?" exclaimed Raby in a derisive tone, "And if we do not obey, what will you do, my man?"

"I will call upon your head the curse of God and…"

"The curses of your Huguenot God do not frighten us at all! Comrades," added Raby turning towards his soldiers, "Enough dawdling. Do not break anything, and do not take anything from the house, or you will know the *wooden horse*;[23] but we must find those Huguenots or else!"

The soldiers busied themselves preparing to implement the Captain's orders while outside, the exterior of the house continued to be guarded by the Germans on horseback as a swarm of musketeers and halberdiers[24] entered the workshop area.

His entire family, who were lamenting their plight, now surrounded Palissy; in the meantime, Mathurin and Nicolas had suddenly re-armed themselves with their staffs and were moving rapidly towards the workers who

---

23 **wooden horse**, was a sharply angled wooden device of triangular shape, pointing upward, mounted on a horse-leg like support poles, used for torture or punishment.

24 **halberdiers**, soldiers armed with halberds which were two-handed pole weapons.

had gathered into a compact group.

"Brothers!" cried Mathurin, with energy and eyes flaming, "will you help us defend your master?"

"Let us defend him…let us defend ourselves!" cried the workers; "down with the cutthroats!"

These men, so calm and docile previously, were taken with a sort of frenzy. Each had armed himself with some sort of tool, an axe, an iron spade; some had picked up bricks and tiles.

The soldiers responded with jeers at these menacing displays. "Bah!" one of them exclaimed, laughing, "those rascals have only stones and sticks."

"With a stone and a stick," replied Mathurin, "David killed the giant Goliath… to arms! Brothers; the sword of God and Gideon!"

Bernard had succeeded in freeing himself from the embrace of his wife and daughter.

"No resistance! No combat!" he cried; "God punishes men of violence…. My sons, I forbid you to strike anyone…. Comrades and apprentices, return to your workplaces."

But his voice was lost in the tumult, and de Pons, who also tried to make himself heard, did not have any more success. The soldiers were swearing while readying their muskets, which would have made many victims in this dense crowd. The workers were running about looking to position themselves; some had already begun chanting a psalm as a battle hymn. In a few moments, the two factions, in spite of the disparity in their forces, were about to hurl themselves at one another.

At that moment, from the far end of the hangar, came running a man dressed in black, bare headed and very pale, although he appeared calm.

"It is I that you are looking for," he said; "here I am, Sires, I am Pastor Hamelin."

Indeed, it was Hamelin. Hidden in a nearby room, he had seen what was happening, and was showing himself to prevent a horrific battle.

A cry of distress came from the side of the Palissy family; it originated from Esther.

"Wretch!" cried Bernard in turn, "what are you doing? Leave here immediately…. I must not be…"

Hamelin thanked his friends with a sad look and remained still.

However, there was no going back. De Pons, Senneville, and the Presiding Judge himself had recognized the Reformist minister.

"Yes, yes, it is he," exclaimed the Governor, prompt to take advantage of a situation that could end the conflict; "This is the dreadful man who is the cause of all this discord…. Soldiers, seize him!"

"It is he," exclaimed in his turn de Senneville, whose eyes were aflame with fury; "here is the infamous sorcerer…. But what has he done with my sister?"

"Seize this man," ordered the Judge, "and watch out for his tricks."

"I am not trying to escape, Sires," said Hamelin.

Raby and several of his soldiers jumped on him and restrained his movements. Raby said, while shaking him brutally:

"Do not worry, I will take care of him, Sire Judge; but by the Saints, what do we do with him now? Do we hang him from one of these beams, or what would you say to a good musketeer firing line...? It would be faster."

"No, no," replied the Judge with authority, "he must appear before a tribunal, after which, if he is found guilty, he shall be treated in accordance with what he deserves."

"Above all," resumed Senneville, "he must tell us what became of Josèphe.... Speak cursed magician," he continued placing the tip of his sword near the face of the Protestant. "Where is my sister?"

Hamelin, who the soldiers were in the process of tying up, did not reply and did not even seem to hear the threats. On the other hand, Bernard said in a pleading tone:

"For your self-respect as a gentleman, do not disgrace yourself with such a dark crime. Your sister will be returned to you."

"I insist that she be returned to me immediately!" replied the coarse country squire, clenching his teeth; "I will not allow that a lady that carries my name... speak, speak, speak, miserable Huguenot, or I will kill you like a dog!"

And he once again lifted his sword over the prisoner, who could not make any move to avoid the assault, but nevertheless maintained his silence.

A piercing voice cried out behind him:

"Coward! Coward! Shame on he who threatens an unarmed man!"

At the same time, Josèphe appeared, her features distorted, her clothing in disarray, her eyes flaming like those of her brother; her expression was animated; her pink nostrils were puffed; she was magnificent in her indignation, menace and revolt.

"My sister, my unworthy sister," roared Senneville, grasping her by her arm. "Abominable creature, I have you now, and you will no longer be allowed to dishonor our name.... Willingly or not, you will follow me to a convent with austere rules, where you shall be confined until the end of your days; it is decided."

"In taking this action, Miss, we are showing great indulgence," said the Judge, "as your conduct deserves much more severe punishment."

"And who asked for indulgence?" asked Josèphe in an arrogant tone. "Your convents only inspire horror in me; they are hideous prisons, where the soul is as captive as the body.... Why don't you reserve me for execution, like the poor minister of the Gospel? Like he, I am no longer Papist, I belong to the Reformist religion, and I wish to die with him."

This audacious profession of faith, in such a moment, was greeted by a general murmur.

"Did you hear her?" exclaimed the Judge, "she renounces God and she blasphemes."

"She is possessed by the Devil," said Senneville with a sort of dread. "Here is the effect of the sorcery and magic potions.... Shameless girl," he added, addressing himself to his sister. "Get a hold of yourself and consider that in the silence of the cloister you will be able to repent your errors...."

"While my family takes advantage of the money from my dowry!" replied Josèphe with irony. "Your customs are a superb invention to rid yourselves of girls from whom you inherit, is that not true, my dear and tender brother? But I repeat, the convent is abhorrent to me, and I prefer a hundred times death with this pastor who taught me the religion of my choosing; and now that he is abandoned, imprisoned, condemned in advance to execution, for me, he has become an angel of wisdom, devotion and charity!"

This time, the murmurs had changed to signs of indignation; some persons were covering their ears; others had turned away in horror.

"Be quiet! Be quiet!" said Senneville, "I could...you can see it, Sires," he continued, turning to the Judge and the Governor. "It is not she who is speaking, it is not a noble damsel, raised in the principles of piety and modesty. It is the malevolent spirit that has taken possession of her thanks to some infernal pact.... Could not someone exorcise this demon that possesses her?"

"It is not a demon that possesses her," said the Judge, shrugging his shoulders; "it is passion, mundane and vulgar, worthy of the one who inspired it."

Hamelin, silent until now, reacted in desperation;

"As God is my witness," he said, "I have never done anything to trouble this innocent soul! If I had guessed, if I had suspected..."

"Well, yes! I love him," cried Josèphe having reached the height of exaltation, "I love him and I do not care who knows it.... In the past few hours, I have understood myself clearly.... Brother," she continued with a strange tone of tenderness addressing the pastor, "if we had lived our separate lives, we would have always been apart. You would have always refused to let me share your life, but you cannot prevent me from associating myself to your martyrdom.... Now I will truly be your fiancée, as we will die together, for the same faith... perhaps on the same pyre."

"Will you be quiet, foolish girl!" growled Senneville.

"Who can impose silence on me? I am liberated from all earthly ties; I defy the hatreds and angers of this odious world.... Shame and malediction, therefore, on this greedy family that for lucrative motives, wished to condemn me to eternal confinement!... Shame and malediction on those powerful men who use their power to tyrannize others, and who, forgetting the charitable principles of the Divine Master, know no other method of persuasion than torture and execution."

"Will you not be quiet?" repeated Senneville, beside himself.

'You will not remove from my lips the expression of my contempt and my hate, odious brother... fierce soldiers... unrighteous judges...."

"So, you want it then?" screamed Senneville, "take that! and that!"

And the brute plunged his sword twice into the chest of his sister.

Josèphe stayed upright for another few seconds, an ironic smile on her face, trying to raise her arm in a final gesture of defiance and finally collapsing backwards in a pool of blood.

As Senneville, terrified by what he had just done, remained mute and motionless, the Governor exclaimed:

"This is an abominable act... it is a crime! Arrest the murderer!"

The Judge waved away the soldiers who were already moving forward.

"There is no hurry," he said; "Master de Senneville gave in to an overwhelming indignation upon hearing the curses and blasphemies of his sister... He will be judged later."

Esther, Mistress Bernard and several other women from the house, were leaning over Josèphe who lay quivering on the tiles in her final death throes. Esther was trying, with her handkerchief, to staunch the flow of blood that streamed from her two wounds. Josèphe recognized her.

"Thank you, little one," she stammered, "you see now, I loved Hamelin more than you loved him yourself!"

"Cease your earthly thoughts, Miss,' said Esther, distraught; "remember that you are about to appear before God!"

"He will judge me.... Brother Hamelin," she added in a barely distinct voice, throwing a last look towards the devastated young Pastor, "learn to die!"

Then her eyes closed and she expired in a final convulsion.

Esther, still kneeling next to the victim, persisted in trying to treat her; the Governor, who had been painfully affected by this tragic scene, soon resumed speaking, raising his voice:

"Now! Sires, our task is finished and, contrary to the orders of the Constable, we can no longer remain in the home of Master Bernard.... Everyone is to leave! The so-called Pastor Hamelin will be taken to the prison of the chateau.... Concerning the body of this poor creature, I suppose that the family will wish to claim it?"

"I do claim it," said Senneville, "I do not repent what I have done; but the remains of a girl of our lineage should not be left in the hands of these Huguenot peasants."

"Yes, let us go," resumed the Judge. "However, the heretics of this house are warned that they will not benefit for long of their immunity. We will return… we will return with new powers, and then it will be understood that the law is equal for everyone."

"Yes, yes, we will return!" said Raby snickering.

Some soldiers placed the body of Josèphe on a stretcher and took her away, followed by de Senneville, who was still mindlessly holding the bloody sword in his hand. Others dragged Hamelin, tied, showering him with curses and insults.

As the crowd was slowly departing, Master de Pons, lagging in the back, approached Bernard and said to him sadly:

"You see, Palissy, there exists an authority greater than mine against which I cannot fight. Have those workers that belong to the Reformist religion leave as rapidly as possible. If there are still days of security for you, there are perhaps none for those poor devils."

Immediately, the Governor hastened to leave, trembling that someone might have noticed this last conversation with the Huguenot artisan.

V.

SALVATION PLAN

A few weeks later, Palissy's situation, like that of that of his family, had become increasingly perilous. Following the advice of the Governor, and perhaps with his assistance, Master Bernard secretly arranged for the departure of those workers who belonged to the Reformist religion. Some, only the most devoted, like Daniel, had not wished to abandon him, and remained hidden in the production facility, considered temporarily a sanctuary. However, the ovens were still extinguished, all tasks interrupted, and the workshops remained deserted. Master Bernard and his sons went quietly about their business, and it was rare that women left the house to furtively shop for food and basic necessities in the neighborhood.

The persecution was taking increasingly fearsome proportions with each passing day. It spread throughout the Province with such violence that it soon evolved into the *Saintonge wars*. Palissy, although confined to his home, was a witness to terrible scenes that took place in the city. He said in his writings:

> 'If you had seen the horrible excesses by men that I saw during those troubled times, you would not have had a hair on your head which would not have bristled.... Certain devils would emerge from the Chateau de Taillebourg and would enter our city with sword in hand exclaiming: where are they? We must cut their throats! They would then go from house to house, stealing, pillaging, ransacking, reprimanding, ridiculing and enjoying the destruction with words of blasphemy against God and men.'

The *devils* were, as we know, Raby's militia and the German cavalry.

There was therefore a real danger for Palissy, or a member of his family, of being encountered by the rabble of soldiers, or by a fanaticized local population who were hardly less cruel. Only once did he dare leave his home. You will remember that Hamelin had been taken to the prison of the chateau for his trial. Master Bernard had the courage to go appeal to the judges, who knew and respected him, on his friend's behalf. He pleaded so successfully that he was able to arrange that the prisoner be treated as well as possible, but he was not able to obtain permission to see him, and his other requests were refused.

One evening, Palissy and his family, as well as two or three workers and servants, who lived with their masters on an equal footing, were gathered in a vast chamber, with the shutters carefully shut, illuminated by two resin candles. Master Bernard, seated in an oak armchair, was reading aloud from the Bible, interrupting himself from time to express thoughts inspired by the text.

Several blows, hammered on the exterior door in a particular and mysterious manner, made the listeners jump. Palissy closed his Bible and said calmly:

"I know who is there.... We will no doubt get some news, and may they be favorable to our cause! Mathurin," he added, speaking to his oldest son, "go to the door yourself."

He whispered a few more words to Mathurin, who nodded, took one of the candles from the table, and went out.

The young man soon returned, followed by a gentleman dressed in dark clothing, who, as was then the custom, had covered his face with the collar of his cloak, making it impossible to see his features. The stranger silently touched his hat, but remained in the shadows of the entryway.

Master Bernard had gotten up and moved hurriedly towards the visitor. He noted this reserve but could not keep from shrugging his shoulders.

"Hmm!" he said, "Always prudent!"

He continued with authority addressing his family:

"It is late. Everyone should retire in peace.... I must speak with... this gentleman. Esther and Mathurin may remain here."

Turning towards the stranger, he added:

"One is my adviser, the other is the executor of my wishes.... I will undoubtedly have need for both of them."

The servants and the family members, except for Esther and Mathurin, left and Palissy closed the door after them. The visitor then lowered the edge of his cloak and one could recognize the Count de Maulévrier.

The master of the house had him sit down and could not resist saying, with some irony:

"You are taking too many precautions, Sire, the persons around me are trustworthy."

"I do not fear treason, Master Bernard," replied the Count in embarrassment; "but only indiscretion and thoughtlessness. You disapprove of these precautions; however, what would be the point of confronting inevitable dangers? Wait until the excesses of the persecution lead to open revolt, which in my opinion, will be soon. Then, I will no longer hide; I will simply draw my sword, and Morbleu! I will prove…"

"You swear, my brother?" interrupted Bernard.

The other bit his lips. Palissy perhaps did not approve of the ideas that the gentleman had just expressed; however, he said softly:

"Let us leave that aside, Sire Count…. What is the news from the city?"

"Still bad. The Presiding Judge, still believing that his power is not sufficient, has referred the problem to the Bordeaux Parliament. Rumors are being confirmed that any time now, we shall see the arrival of a special commissioner, authorized to disregard the Constable's safeguard document…. So, if you believe me, Bernard, you and your family will leave Saintes while you still can do so."

"No," replied Palissy without hesitation and with firmness. "I do not want to abandon the many works that are here and that no one will safeguard in my absence…. Moreover, it would be an insult to my protectors to appear to doubt their credibility."

The Count made a gesture of distress. Esther, who for some time had been holding back a question of great interest to her, asked timidly:

"Do you know anything, Sire Count, concerning our pastor, Master Hamelin?"

Master de Maulévrier shook his head.

"Do not ask me, poor child," he replied, "if you do not wish to learn about things that will distress you."

"Good Lord!" said Palissy, "Hamelin, our friend, almost my son, Hamelin, has he been condemned?"

"Not yet, Master Bernard. Undoubtedly you were very eloquent when you went to visit the judges, at the risk of your own security, as they did not wish to take any decision concerning him; however, he will be transferred to Bordeaux in several days, and will appear before the Tribunal…. You know what that means!"

Esther hid her face in her hands.

"Master Bernard," resumed the Count de Maulévrier, "do you not have some news for me? You wrote to Paris to inform the Constable of the appalling situation you find yourself in and the contempt they are showing for his authority. The letter left a long time ago, and no reply has come back to you?"

"None," replied Palissy sadly, "although I sent it with a trusted messenger and my letter was urgent. Master de Montmorency detests our cause and I would not count very much on his indulgence for my family and for me…. However, I did warn him that my work had been interrupted and that, if no one comes to my assistance, there is a great risk that the stained-glass windows, the *rustic figulines* and the bas-reliefs that he had ordered for Ecouen will never be completed. This consideration should trouble him, and yet, as

I have told you, I have not received any response. I believed I could count on the support of a young gentleman who is with him in the role of clerk, or personal secretary. This gentleman, Master Gaston de Massac, had previously rendered to myself, and that poor Hamelin, significant services, but he was quite young at the time and no doubt now regrets his kindness."

"This is possible, Master Bernard, as the Massacs, father and son, are known to be fervent Catholics. However, I can explain why at this moment the son does not intervene in your favor with the Constable. The elder Massac is ill in his manor, several leagues from here, and the young man asked leave to join his father. He therefore left Paris and has arrived in Massac. He was recently seen there."

"Could this be true?" asked Esther; "so, this explains everything, and perhaps Master Gaston is unaware.... But is it certain that he has returned to Saintonge?"

"No doubt is possible on this point."

"And how does this concern you, my daughter, Esther?" asked Palissy.

"My God, father, this young gentleman has rendered us such services, as you acknowledge yourself.... So, he has returned... he has returned!"

And, retiring to the far end of the room, she began to reflect profoundly.

Bernard continued to discuss with Master de Maulévrier. However, the conversation did not last long, and the Count, after having repeated his warning, that the Palissy family should leave Saintes as soon as possible, and after stating that he would keep Bernard up to date of any news, left, taking the same precautions as when he arrived.

Master Bernard, having accompanied him to the exterior door, entered the room. He was anxious; in spite of the steadfastness of his spirit, what he had learned concerning Hamelin, dismayed him. He made a sign to his children that they should leave; Esther, instead of obeying, approached him.

"Father," she asked, "is it not true that without some powerful intervention, the poor pastor is lost?"

"I fear so, my daughter."

"And do you see anyon. among our secret or avowed friends who would act in his favor?"

"No one.... The danger of compromising oneself is too great."

"There is, however, dear father, a man sufficiently daring and devoted, to undertake the saving all of us, and powerful enough to possibly succeed."

"Who, my child?"

"Master Gaston de Massac," replied Esther, lowering her eyes, "the gentleman, the night of the Preaching, who provided safe passage to Master Hamelin."

Master Bernard furrowed his brow.

"You have an excellent memory, Esther," he replied; "but it does not appear that Master de Massac's is as good, or if he still remembers us, it is with hate or disdain."

"With your permission, father," continued Esther, blushing; "I hope that it is not true, and although he has never directly expressed any interest in us, nothing authorizes us to put it in doubt. If he had been in Paris at the moment that your letter to the Constable had arrived, perhaps we would not have waited in vain for assistance; but it is confirmed that he is with his father in Saintonge...."

"Eh, and what does that do for us? Come now, my daughter, what are you getting at? Do you really think that this young man would respond to our call for help?"

"I am certain," replied Esther, blushing even more.

She briefly explained the circumstances under which Master de Massac had given her a family ring, with the promise to come to her assistance as soon as she sent him this object of a pledge.

Palissy appeared to be increasingly annoyed.

"And this ring, do you still have it, Esther?"

She went to rummage in an old piece of furniture reserved for her use, and soon returned with the subject object. It was a heavy silver ring with an engraved bezel that could be used to seal a letter. Bernard examined it.

"Here is a remarkable story!" he resumed; "and why did you not speak earlier about this ring that a modest young girl like you should never have accepted?"

"I told my mother about it, but as she saw it as guarantee against all sorts of dangers to which we are exposed, she told me to keep it safely hidden."

"It is there that I recognize your mother, so timid, so inexperienced in worldly affairs!" said Palissy with an indulgent smile, "and as I would have rejected such a gift.... Well, Esther, what is your plan?"

"Nothing simpler, my father; a trusted person... Mathurin, and here he is, if he accepts, will take the ring to the Chateau de Massac, and explain to Master Gaston the plight in which we find ourselves."

"If my father permits," said Mathurin, who normally remained silent and respectful before Bernard, "I will willingly make this trip. Also, I owe an apology to that gentleman, which I had mission to guide, the night in question, and who I abandoned, in an excess of childish fright."

"It is that you were all children in that time," resumed Palissy, "and all that happened was childishness.... Now, Esther, you have often proven that you are sensible and prudent; do you really believe that upon simply seeing the seal, Master de Massac would leave his sick father and come protect Huguenot reprobates such as we?"

"Why not?" said Esther; "it is a chance to take considering our cruel situation. Have you not said yourself that we should not count on any immediate assistance? So, to save you, to save poor Hamelin," she added, breaking down in tears, "I don't know what I am capable of doing."

Hamelin's name seemed to change Palissy's thinking. He became pensive and walked around in silence. Finally, he stopped in front of his daughter.

"You are perhaps right, my child," he continued. "Your affection for Hamelin clarified mine, and we should not neglect any way by which we can tear our pastor way from the bloody hands which retain him.... Nothing opposes Mathurin from taking the seal to Massac as you suggest.... In fact, a number of our co-religionists are hiding in a neighboring village; your brother, while he is there, will get news from them and give them ours. This effort with the secretary of the Constable will, no doubt, give no result, but the fate of our friend worries me immensely.... May your will be done."

"Thank you, my beloved father," said Esther, throwing her arms around her father's neck.

"How she loves him!" thought Palissy.

It was immediately agreed what had to be done for the implementation of this plan. It was decided that the following morning the young man would leave the city and would travel to Massac on foot, which should be simple for him since he was nimble and vigorous. He would not carry any correspondence, for fear that he might be stopped and searched on the way, and they simply gave him the most detailed verbal instructions possible.

With everything arranged in advance, they separated, and Mathurin left to prepare himself for the trip, which seemed to be the last hope for the Palissy family.

VI.

THE PROTECTOR

Two days later, around midday, a young and elegant horseman, riding a handsome stallion that was covered with dust and appeared to have made a long trip, had halted in front of Master Bernard's home. The agitation in the city of Saintes appeared to be greater than usual that day, and the Palissy family, fearing insults, remained sheltered in their house. The gentleman, since one could guess that he was a member of the nobility from his healthy appearance and clothing, had hesitated a bit before finding the right house. However, he had undoubtedly received the correct information because he finally dismounted, and holding the horse by its bridle, lifted the heavy knocker several times to announce his arrival.

Not receiving a response, the stranger resumed knocking in a hurried manner, more with worry than impatience.

He was making so much noise that he did not hear a window on the first floor opening just over his head, which immediately closed again. At the same instant, Daniel appeared behind a small grilled window that existed in the majority of doors in those troubled times. After having taken an attentive look at the visitor, he asked in a defiant tone:

"Who are you? What do you want?"

"Open," replied the gentleman imperiously, "open immediately... by the Mass! I am a friend of Master Bernard."

This swearing; *"by the Mass!"* did not seem to the guardian to be a recommendation, and he grumbled with embarrassment:

"A friend! Again, one has to know..."

"Open, Daniel," said from behind him Esther who was running over, "It is, indeed, a friend... and one we have been impatiently waiting for."

"So be it," replied Daniel; "friends are so rare here that we do not make those who present themselves wait!"

And he released the bolts, while the traveler attached his horse to an iron ring that was fixed to the wall.

The door being open, the gentleman crossed the threshold saying:

"You will watch over my horse, valet.... But first of all, take me to Master Bernard... or a member of the family."

"I will take you myself, Master de Massac," said a soft voice coming from the shadows of the vestibule.

This voice made Gaston jump. He hesitated a moment, then advanced towards Esther, who was flushed and trembling. He took her by the hand and looked at her intently.

"Master Gaston," stammered the young girl, embarrassed, "is it possible that you have forgotten me?"

"Not for one moment, Esther; in spite of myself and all that separates us, I have never forgotten that night when you revealed yourself to me. It is rather you that has forgotten the stranger, the traveler...."

"Who has showered us with kindness, and each letter from the Constable was witness to his generous intervention.... But... excuse me! Master de Massac, where is my brother Mathurin?"

"When I learned from him the terrible dangers you were facing, I hastened to come on horseback.... Your brother wished to return on foot, so I am preceding him by only a few hours."

"Good... come and you will see my father, who, like all of us, is in great need of your support."

"Alas! Henceforth my support will not be very effective!" Gaston replied with a sigh.

He followed Esther, who had entered the complicated labyrinth of workshops, while Daniel, obliged to stay by the door to keep an eye on the traveler's horse, murmured while shaking his head:

"Hmm! a Papist. It is certainly not from there that we will find salvation!"

Esther continued with rapid steps towards her father's studio, and although she turned around fairly often, she did not appear to wish to resume the conversation. However, Massac, moving up beside her, said to her in a voice full of emotion:

"So, you kept my ring, dear child? On my side, I saw you, or thought I saw you in the marvelous painting and sculpture masterpieces that your father sent to Ecouen. I imagined finding your charming features in Rachel of the Bible, and Minerve of mythology, and although pride and my attachment to the religion of my fathers, prevented me from expressing the sentiments that filled my heart, I toiled only for you.... Over there, in the midst of the seductions of the Court, I compared you, so pure and so perfect, with those frivolous creatures...."

"Master de Massac," interrupted Esther, "allow me to remind you that time presses. Let us rejoin my father."

And she rapidly resumed walking; not only had all conversation become impossible, but Gaston had trouble keeping up.

Soon they stopped before the door of the workshop, and Esther, having given several light knocks, led her companion into the room containing Master Bernard.

The great artist, as we have said, went about his business as if he had no fear of seeing, at any moment, the arrival of a band of pillagers and assassins. His arms bare, wearing a leather apron, his hands full of clay, he was peacefully modeling a bas-relief; and thinking that only his daughter was there, did not even turn around.

Gaston, in spite of his admiration for Bernard and his tenderness for Esther, seemed suddenly put off when placed in the presence of this man in stained clothing, who had the appearance of an ordinary worker. At that time, one was not familiar with the methods used by artists, and the pride of social class was awakened in the young man at the sight of a sculptor occupied at modeling. He nodded silently and remained motionless by the door.

Esther informed her father of the arrival of Massac. Palissy immediately arose, and since the state of his hands prevented his reaching out towards the visitor, he bowed politely.

"It is a great joy to see you again, Master de Massac," he said in a friendly tone; "We have all reserved for you a deep gratitude…. And your noble father, how is he?"

"Much better, Master Bernard," resumed Gaston, heartened by the sincerity of this greeting, "and I was able, without inconveniencing him, to respond to this appeal transmitted to me by your son, Mathurin…. My father is still delighted to have the marvelous formula to cure *crowning* of horses, formula that he insists on considering the product of sorcery…"

"Sorcery!" repeated Bernard; "When will the Catholics, like the Reformists, stop seeing sorcery in things which are strictly the domain of experience and science!… But let us leave that," he added, indicating to Gaston a chair that his daughter had just brought over. "You are not unaware, no doubt, Master Massac, of the painful reasons that decided us to implore your aid? My letters to the Constable, your master and mine, remained unanswered…."

"It is undoubtedly that you sent them to Paris or Ecouen, while his Eminence is in Blois with the Court; and communications are so slow and difficult…. Moreover, it is not possible, Master Bernard, that you have not heard speak of what recently happened in Amboise."

He then explained the events that had occurred some days earlier and are known in history as the *Amboise Conspiracy*. It is known that it involved a plot between the Calvinists and some of the French nobility, to kidnap the young king, François II, from his mother, Catherine de Médicis who was dominated by the house of Guise.[25] The conspiracy having been discov-

25 **House of Guise,** Noble French Roman Catholic family that played a major role in French politics during the Reformation. They were particularly known for

ered, the majority of their leaders were arrested, although Condé, Châtillon, Coligny and other important figures suspected of complicity, managed to escape.

"The punishment from these dark machinations was not long in coming," continued Gaston, "and the heads of the guilty, I am told, are displayed on all the gallows of Amboise.... Since that time, a veritable reign of terror hangs over the Court and Paris and even threatens to spread through rest of France. The Queen-Mother and the Guises see conspirators everywhere. There is no one, noble or evil, Catholic or Protestant, who can believe that he is above suspicion. The most important personages are themselves suspect, and undoubtedly Monseigneur Constable would not have dared respond, even if he had received your message."

Bernard and his daughter were appalled seeing that their situation had been complicated in such a cruel manner. Esther exclaimed with despair:

"But then Master de Massac, you can do nothing for us?"

"I can die while protecting you, Esther, I came here for that... I have no order from Master de Montmorency; I am not even in his service at the moment since he gave me a month off.... Nevertheless, all that a determined man can do in your favor, I am ready to do and will do."

"Thank you, Master de Massac, this devotion would be dangerous for all and certainly useless."

"You are right, Esther," replied Palissy, "I could not accept it.... Did you really think, young gentleman," he continued with an indulgent smile, "that, alone, armed with your sword, you could hold your own against the *devils* of Taillebourg, if they were ordered to invade this house? Moreover, it is known that I hate rebellion and violence."

"Your Calvinist friends, Master Bernard, are beginning to demonstrate different sentiments.... I will serve you as circumstances permit, and I will install myself in the city, until we are certain that there is nothing to fear for you and yours."

This generosity, so simple and touching, generated a feeling of deep gratitude from both the father and the daughter. Master Bernard said with affection:

"A brave and loyal young man!... Well, Master Massac, under these conditions, I do not refuse your good services.... But it is not only my family and myself that are concerned. You could, no doubt, also come to the aid of a person that I love like one of my sons?"

"And who would that be, Master Bernard?"

"Our pastor, Master Hamelin, who is being detained at the Saintes chateau."

Gaston's facial expression suddenly changed.

---

their conflict with the Protestant movement.

"What!" he said in a dry and curt tone. "Do you speak of the supposed minister, who was recently the cause of a terrible scandal? Was it not Hamelin who, after having kidnapped from her family a young damsel destined for a cloister, had the impudence of bringing her to your home where a brother mortally struck the dishonored creature?He is not only pursued as a heretic, but as a corruptor of women.... Not one word about him, Master Bernard. I have often regretted the services I had performed for him at your request and that of Esther. He is a hypocrite who covers guilty passions with the veil of religion."

"You misjudge him, Master de Massac," replied Palissy, heatedly. "And you do not know the simple facts which have led to shameful slander."

He then explained how it had come about that Hamelin protected Josèphe de Senneville.

"So be it," replied Massac. "I am willing to accept that this man reacted to a misunderstood zeal; however, the scandal exists, and I will not interfere in this sort of affair.... Allow me to maintain my credibility, all my devotion for those that I love and respect.... I owe nothing to others!"

Bernard, seeing the uselessness of fighting against a negative decision, kept quiet. However, Esther, who had a secret awareness of her power over Gaston, said in a pleading tone:

"Master de Massac, could you remain indifferent to the fate of our friend, whom you have already saved once? If you abandon him now, nothing will save him from the final ordeal."

Gaston looked at her intently.

"Esther, Esther!" he said, "you admit that you love him?"

Esther did not respond.

"This is not of your concern, Master de Massac," resumed Palissy coldly; "all you need to know is that if Hamelin survives this danger, Esther will obey the wishes of her father."

"Then let him manage it!" replied Gaston, getting up. "By the Mass! I will not worry about him."

Esther appeared to be very agitated. Finally, she made an important effort within herself, and said to Bernard, with lowered eyes:

"My father, if, thanks to the intervention of Master Massac, or for any other reason, Hamelin recovers his liberty, I would hope that you would not follow through with the project conceived at another time."

"What are you saying, Esther? You had led me to believe that..."

"Previously, I would have obeyed you without a murmur, but you have heard what they said on the subject of this unhappy Josèphe de Senneville... In spite of myself, I could never see Master Hamelin, involuntary cause of this scandal, without imagining the poor creature that I held bleeding in my arms.... I will not hide, my father, that obedience would be for me totally impossible, and I beg of you not to impose it."

"I do not wish your unhappiness, beloved child, and if you really have such a repugnance for the man that I had chosen for you.... Besides," continued Palissy, "sadly, this discussion is useless, as Hamelin will never find freedom."

"He might recover it if Master Massac wished to take him under his protection."

Gaston tried in vain to meet Esther's eyes, but she pointedly looked aside with determination. Finally, he undoubtedly began to suspect in her a sentiment similar to his.

"Now, Master Bernard," he resumed, "I could not refuse your prayers.... Although I feel no sympathy for your heretic pastor, I will do everything in my power to rescue him from his fate, which he perhaps deserves."

"I knew it!" exclaimed Esther.

At the same time, she bestowed upon the young gentleman a look so frank, so full of gratitude, that Gaston was overwhelmed to the depth of his soul.

Palissy, who was of an extreme innocence regarding anything that did not touch science or art, did not understand what caused the sudden change in Massac's attitude. Joy kept him from thinking about this reversal:

"You will succeed, Master de Massac," he said. "You have as much courage as you do prudence and wisdom. Myself, if I were not such an object of revulsion and anger, I would have remained active. But since this persecution has begun, I have only ventured out once from my home, and I have found myself exposed to many insults.... Listen," he continued lowering his voice, "perhaps your arguments and entreaties may not be listened to any more than mine, and they will insist on sending Hamelin before the Bordeaux Parliament.... The best, in my opinion, is to help him escape."

"This method could be a good one. I am well equipped with money, and it would be easy to bribe a guard."

"If, in the execution of this project," resumed Bernard. "You need support, we are not lacking in secret friends who would give us assistance."

"I will go to the chateau to stay with the Governor. This is where my father and I usually reside when we come to Saintes.... There, I will be in a position to know what is happening, and I will come to you at the slightest alert."

While speaking, Gaston had made his preparations for leaving and was now heading for the street door. Bernard and Esther were accompanying him as a courtesy. While Palissy was giving him some final advice, Gaston said in a low voice to the young woman:

"Well! Esther, are you satisfied?"

She offered her hand, and Gaston took it bringing it to his lips. Esther hastened to withdraw it in confusion.

As they were approaching the door, a muffled hubbub came from the street. Daniel, as we have said, remained outside to guard Gaston's horse, and its presence outside Palissy's house had attracted a certain number of inquisitive persons. The public thoroughfare was a little crowded, when a traveler passed by, riding a mule, followed by a large escort. The traveler was tall and lean, with an unhealthy look and piercing eyes, wearing a long black robe and capped with a velvet mortarboard. He seemed to have made a long trip, and his robe lifted up revealed dust-covered boots, equipped with silver spurs. By his side, on foot, was the Presiding Judge, who was obsequiously showing the highlights of the city to the person in the black robes. Following them, and also mounted on mules, came several liveried lackeys and some scribes dressed in black.

This group was obliged to slow down due to the congestion in the street. When Palissy, Esther and Gaston appeared on the doorstep, they were obliged to wait as the procession went by and they became themselves the object of scrutiny. Following a word from the Judge, the traveler in the black robes stared fixedly at the father and daughter as well as Massac, who bowed respectfully as was the custom towards a person of great distinction. When he had passed, he turned his head several times to see them again, and from the liveliness of his conversation with the local magistrate, one guessed that they were the cause of an extreme preoccupation. Finally, the group disappeared around a bend in the road and the sound of the horses faded in the distance.

Bernard and his daughter noticed all these details with concern, but Massac had not paid any attention to it. As he was untying his horse and was about to mount, Palissy said to him in a low voice:

"What you must do, Master de Massac, do it rapidly. That traveler can only be the councilor sent by the Bordeaux Parliament with the title of Royal Commissioner, and his arrival means new harsh actions."

"Bah! Master Bernard," replied Massac, with the disdain of men of the sword for men of justice, "are you that afraid of those birds and their book of magic spells?"

He jumped on his mount, saluted father and daughter, and left at a gallop.

As soon as he had departed, Palissy, noticing that his neighbors were whispering in a hostile manner, hurried to enter and said to Daniel:

"Close well the doors, comrade, and do not open them again for anyone except for Mathurin, who should soon be here, or for the gentleman who you just saw…. As for us, we will go prepare for the hardships that God wishes to bestow upon us."

VII.

THE PRISONER

It is only in modern times that prisoners, merely accused, or already condemned, had the right to any compassion. At the time of this story, still reigned all the barbarism of the Middle Ages against those unfortunates who, rightly or wrongly, one thought necessary to deprive of their liberty. The heavy chains, the obscurity, the straw, the diet of bread and water, which, in our day, are no longer in usage in our prisons, were then a sad and ugly reality. In addition, if the crime of which the detainee was accused was particularly odious, or if a powerful enemy had pursued him, one added to his captivity all sorts of privations, humiliations and tortures to make life intolerable.

And so, Pastor Hamelin was very uncomfortable in the Saintes chateau. His cell was located in a lower part of a gothic tower, not far from the Governor's apartments, apartments that in spite of their sumptuousness, left much to desire from the point of view of comfort and hygiene. Moreover, the tower of the prison had an even more sinister look than the other buildings, and its massive ramparts seemed to defy the efforts of time and men.

The days following the arrival of Gaston in Saintes, Hamelin was alone in his cell. The dungeon was spacious but very dark. A little light came from small grilled opening recessed and placed high above. The prisoner sat on a stone bench placed below this, reading his Bible. He was not chained, undoubtedly as a special favor, but a piece of black bread and a jug of water placed on a small table and several handfuls of straw laying in a corner, serving as a bed, were witness to the fact that he had not been spared the other habitual rigors.

No external sound reached the dungeon. In all seasons a humid freshness prevailed, with an odor of mold as in cellars or underground passages. It was a veritable tomb, and the unfortunate detainee must have felt a loss of everything including hope.

Hamelin interrupted his reading occasionally to abandon himself to meditation. Occasionally, he would raise his eyes towards the ray of light that came from the small opening above and he moved his lips as though quietly praying, or he would even sing a psalm in a low voice. But whether praying or meditating, his features retained a serene expression.

Suddenly, from outside, came the grating of the lock, and the door, which was made of solid iron, rolled on its rusted hinges. Two persons appeared and exchanged words in a low voice; then, while one stopped and closed the door once more, the other advanced hesitatingly.

The prisoner had gotten up, seeing a well-dressed man, in a noble style, who could only be someone important, and bowed in silence.

Gaston de Massac, as one might have guessed, approached Hamelin, and in spite of his prejudice against the Calvinist pastor, he could help but feel moved by his air of suffering and sadness. In turn, he greeted the prisoner:

"God bless you, Sire," he said. "Although we have not met in a long time, perhaps you have not forgotten my name and my person?"

"I would certainly be an ingrate to have forgotten you, Master de Massac" he replied, "as you saved me from a great peril, my coreligionist and, in particular, me...."

"That suffices," interrupted Gaston, "I have not come here to discuss past services, but to render again, if possible.... I am here under the auspices of your friends, Master Bernard Palissy and... his family."

"Bernard!! My dear Bernard!" said Hamelin, with eyes tearing, "Ah! My fate must really affect him.... However, perhaps he is also in danger?"

"I fear so.... But I am in a hurry to accomplish my task... You are aware, Sire, that tomorrow, perhaps tonight, you will leave this prison under guard to be transferred to Bordeaux?"

"Indeed, I have been told this, and I can expect no pity from the Tribunal.... Due to human imperfection, I committed a grave error, without wanting to, and now I must answer to God!"

"It is not only in the eyes of God, Sire, that atonement is necessary.... Anyway, I am not your judge. On the contrary, I am here to save you.... Are you ready?"

"Save me!" repeated Hamelin; "what are you saying, Sire? It is an impossible task."

"Everything is prepared for your escape. I bribed your guard, and here is a disguise that you are going to wear." At the same time, he pointed to a package that had been placed in a dark corner of the cell. "You will slip out by this door, which I will leave ajar and you will leave the chateau and rejoin the countryside. Then, since you know very well this area, where you have many friends, and all the pathways are familiar to you, you will easily elude your pursuers."

Hamelin listened to him pensively.

"Indeed, once outside the city," he resumed, "I should be able to avoid the search… but to leave the chateau, I will have to get past two manned guardhouses, one by the city's archers, and the other by Raby's soldiers."

"When you leave the tower, you must not take the gallery on your right, which leads to the soldiers' quarters, but the one on the left; this one leads to the private apartment of Master de Pons, and there are only a few guards of honor on that side."

"The Governor's apartment! Is this possible? The door that communicates with that part of the chateau is always shut."

"You do not have to worry about this; it will be open."

"And then, going through the apartment, I cannot avoid being seen."

"No one will see you. Moreover, your disguise will justify your presence in this place."

Gaston went to get the package, opened it, and took out a *mandille*[26] or lackey's vest in the livery of de Pons.

The prisoner appeared stupefied.

"What is this?" he asked, The Governor agrees to…"

"If the Governor ran into you, he would sound the alarm and would double your punishments. Do not worry about knowing the authors of the plot of which you are the beneficiary. Think only about the fact that time presses."

Hamelin looked at him in silence; finally, as if speaking to himself, he said:

"A minister of the Reformist cult escapes from prison in the disguise of a lackey!… My miserable existence, is it worth such a humiliation?"

"Here are some strange scruples!" resumed Gaston impatiently, "Sacrebleu! Sire, I do not care if you remain in this cell or not; but I have promised some persons who have the weakness of caring about you.…"

"And among those persons," asked the pastor with vivacity, raising his head, "is that angelic girl, Esther Palissy?"

"Your fiancée, as they say?" murmured Gaston.

"She was by the wish of her father, if not her own."

"But you, do you love her?"

"Perhaps, too much; and I reproach myself for this tenderness like a crime."

"All the more because you have felt the same for a young woman which caused her tragic death."

Hamelin brought his hand to his heart in a painful gesture.

"Ah! Sire," he said, "You are cruel.… I have never been for this unfortunate Josèphe de Senneville anything but a minister of the Gospel, a disinterested protector. Perhaps I was missing in basic prudence; perhaps I should have thought of the inevitable consequences… but Esther, the wise

---

26 *mandille*, a type of coat formerly associated with poverty

and sweet Esther, does she believe the accusations which are my shame and desperation?"

"Loyalty obliges me to respond that even yesterday, Esther Palissy energetically protested against this accusation."

"Bless you for these good words.... So, if Divine Providence wrenched me away from the fate that awaits me, Esther would not refuse to become my companion?"

Massac did not answer.

"You appear to know something about this subject? Oh, please speak, Sire, I implore you to speak.... My decision will depend upon what you will tell me."

"Well, the same loyalty imposes that I be truthful: Esther Palissy, whatever the resolution, has clearly declared that she will never be your wife!"

Hamelin let himself drop down on a bench as if overwhelmed.

"So, why would I try to defend my life against those who menace me?... I must now only think about God, the refuge and consolation for those who no longer have a place in this world!"

And violent sobs racked his body.

Gaston could not help but feel a sentiment of commiseration witnessing such a real and great distress. He soon resumed energetically:

"Now, Sire, your ideas will undoubtedly change later. You must find strength.... Do you want me to help you put on your disguise which will easily fit over your normal clothing?"

"Thank you. It is useless.... I am staying."

"Have you not thought about avoiding the terrible torture.... ignominious?"

"The crueler the torture, the more commendable it will be before God and men to pay for the scandal I have caused."

"Once again, these hesitations make no sense.... Leave, I beg of you... in the name of Esther, herself!"

"Esther! Dear Esther! Master de Massac, you are full of generosity, and it is you, no doubt, that she loves. I have often suspected in her heart another affection than the one imposed by her father."

"What is the use of these considerations at such a moment?"

"If you love each other," continued Hamelin with a soft melancholy, "I will no longer be an obstacle for your union.... The souls of the elite, like yours and hers, do they not deserve in this world great bliss?"

"Your expectations, Sire, will perhaps not come about, and I fear... however," added Gaston in lower voice, "you have not wanted to follow my advice, and now it is perhaps too late.... Listen."

One could hear, behind the iron door, a whispering. After some discussion, the door was partially opened, and a man wearing a black and white outfit and the large brimmed hat of a Dominican, slipped through the opening, while the guard remained on sentry duty outside. In spite of the poor light in the prison, Massac recognized Father Desmazures.

He remembered the fanatical expressions of hate in the past by the Prior of the Dominicans of Saintes against the Reformists in general and against Hamelin in particular, and he had a sentiment of fear in seeing him appear. Thus, the peaceful, almost friendly greeting from the prisoner surprised him. Hamelin had arisen.

"Ah! My Reverend Father," he said with a sad smile, "the moment is not ideal for us to have one of our normal debates. Today my soul is in shreds and I would not be capable of properly replying to your argumentation."

"Well, Master Hamelin," replied Desmazures, "I have no intention of renewing our controversies, which, I have seen, have no results other than having you harden your position.... I prefer addressing myself to your heart and invoke your pity for yourself.... The Royal Commissioner, who has sovereign power, has decided that you will leave today, and he has just arrived at the chateau to personally oversee the implementation of his order.... We will be separated, and perhaps we will not see each other again in this world.... Hamelin, poor lost brother, can you let me hope that that you will finally renounce your errors?"

"Not more than you would renounce yours, my Reverend Father," replied the minister; "our faith, for one or the other, is unwavering; God will judge us both."

"It seems to me, Reverend Father," said Gaston with astonishment, "that you have not always spoken and acted in this manner with the Reformists?"

"This is very true, Master de Massac," replied Desmazures, looking embarrassed, "and you have been witness to fanatical actions which I deplore.... I was convinced that severity and torture could eliminate this dreadful heresy. I considered it my duty to show myself without mercy.... But this was a shameful illusion; the more the persecution became cruel, the more the number of heretics increased, and the more they became obstinate in their revolt. I understood then that persuasion and charity were only chances of succeeding."

"Well! if this the case, my Reverend Father, can you do something for this friend of Master Bernard?"

"Nothing," replied Desmazures, sighing. "I tried to speak in his favor at the chapter of the college of clerics to which I belong, but the tragic adventure of Josèphe de Senneville complicates in the most unfortunate manner the accusations against him, and the Royal Commissioner insists that the decision be taken by the Bordeaux Tribunal. Master Hamelin is lost unless he renounces his faith... or if he succeeds in escaping."

Gaston looked at Desmazure as though he doubted his sincerity. However, the simple and benevolent appearance of the monk reassured him.

"Helping him escape, Reverend Father," he said heatedly, "this is exactly what I was thinking about when you arrived. I can do it, and it would give Master Hamelin the time return to the good ways.... Unfortunately, a scruple prevents him; he would be ashamed to escape in the *mandille* of a lackey."

And he explained the means of escape that he had prepared.

"But perhaps," replied Father Desmazures with eagerness, "might he not have the same scruples about escaping in religious garments? I will give him my robe and my cap, which will make him sufficiently unrecognizable. Moreover, you told me that he should not meet anyone.... Accept, Master Hamelin," he continued in an almost supplicating tone; "time presses. I saw the wagon meant for your transportation arrive a short time ago. While you attempt to leave the chateau and the city, I will stay here with Master de Massac. I do not believe that my complicity could have serious consequences for me.... In any case, I am ready to accept them."

At the same time, the Dominican began taking off his outer clothing; Hamelin stopped him.

"Thank you! my Reverend Father," he replied. "Ah! It is by actions of this sort, rather than violence and anger, that one could attain my heart.... But Master de Massac did not understand the cause of my refusal; I cannot accept these acts of devotion from either one of you. My fate must be fulfilled!"

Desmazures and Massac tried vainly to have him to go back on his decision. He listened to them in silence but limited himself to shaking his head.

Soon a new noise was heard in a nearby gallery. This time it was the heavy steps of a troop of soldiers.

"Master Hamelin," said Father Desmazures with sadness, "you have waited too long.... Those who came to get you are here!"

The door opened, and the Royal Commissioner entered, followed by several musketeers, ushered in by the guard who was embarrassed and trembling.

This commissioner, who we had already seen at his arrival in Saintes, was a councilor to the Bordeaux parliament, renowned for his hate of the Huguenots. Religious fanaticism, combined with a somber jealousy of certain magistrates and the great authority he had been given, added to his despotic image.

He listened to the explanation of the guard, who sought to justify the presence of the visitors in the cell.

"We know," said the Royal Commissioner, "why the Dominican priest is here...but this other person, who is he, and what does he want?"

And he haughtily looked Gaston up and down.

"Who are you, yourself?" replied Gaston with no less pride; "I have the permission of the Governor to visit Master Hamelin."

"Ah! I recognize you," resumed angrily the councilor, whose eyes were getting used to the obscurity of the dungeon. "You are Master de Massac, gentleman to the Constable.... You can be a good Catholic like your master, but this is the second time that I find you in the company of persons who are not.... But it is not about you that we are here."

Then, turning towards the prisoner;

"You are," he asked, "Hamelin, the so-called minister of the so-called Reformed religion?"

Hamelin made a sign in the affirmative.

"You will leave immediately.... You," he continued, speaking to the soldiers who had accompanied him, "execute my orders."

They took hold of the prisoner and attached heavy chains to his feet and his hands. Hamelin made no resistance, but Father Desmazures asked the councilor with indignation:

"Are these not unnecessary cruelties, Sire? This poor man will suffer horrible tortures during the trip."

"He is no longer under ecclesiastic authority but civil authority, my Reverend Father," replied the magistrate; "and we cannot take too many precautions to assure that he cannot escape."

"Before treating the prisoner with such inhumanity," said Massac, "one should remember that we are here in the chateau de Saintes, where the Governor alone can give orders."

"The Governor knows perfectly well under whose orders I am acting.... Do not worry, young man; my powers are greater than you can imagine, and you may learn this at your expense, if you continue to favor the heretics."

Gaston was about to make an ill-considered response. Hamelin, who had great difficulty moving with the heavy chains, approached him.

"Adieu, Master de Massac," he said in a low voice, "and thank you for your courageous intervention on my behalf.... I pray my friends will keep an indulgent memory of me.... Tell them also not to bemoan my death, as I am counting on divine forgiveness, which is higher and grander than that of men."

Gaston attempted to stammer a few words of encouragement.

Hamelin turned towards Father Desmazures:

"And you too, my Reverend Father," he continued, "you have my gratitude and I bid you adieu...."

"Not yet, my poor Hamelin," replied the monk, whose eyes were wet, "I will accompany you to the wagon and I will help you carry these chains which are crushing you.... My God!" he added, as if talking to himself, "can error be outside the truth and still provide strength to the martyr?"

Soon, Hamelin, supported by the Father Desmazures, went out with his escort of soldiers, and the councilor followed to assure that his orders were rigorously followed. Massac, in turn, after exchanging a few words with the guard, hastened to leave the prison.

We have said that one of the nearby galleries communicated with the private apartment of Master de Pons, and Gaston, who had long been familiar with the corridors of the chateau, headed in this direction. By previous arrangement, that part of the old building was deserted and all the doors were open. The apartment itself seemed abandoned, and one saw neither a valet nor page. But Gaston knew where to find the Master of the dwelling, and after having crossed several silent rooms, he entered the Governor's study.

Master de Pons was indeed there and standing at the window that faced the main courtyard of the chateau, he was looking out through the glass panes. Recognizing Massac, he said sadly:

"Well, my dear Gaston, you did not succeed? This terrible Royal Commissioner arrived too early?"

"What! Sire," asked Massac with astonishment, "you already know..."

"It is not difficult to understand; see for yourself."

And Master de Pons led him to the window.

The unfortunate Hamelin, still supported by Father Desmazures, who was attempting to relieve him of the weight of his irons, had just reached the courtyard. This vast space, surrounded by lofty towers and old buildings, was already full of soldiers, some on foot, and others on horseback. At the center, was a sort of tipcart, similar to those used by farmers, and harnessed with two shafts; it was destined for the transport of the Calvinist pastor to Bordeaux. Two soldiers prepared to seat themselves with Hamelin in the wagon, and six of the German cavaliers, dressed in steel armor and equipped with lances would serve as mounted guards during the journey.

As soon as the prisoner appeared in the middle of this rabble of unruly soldiers, profanities and booing came from all sides. They shook their fists and showered him with insults. Perhaps things would have gone further than verbal insults had not Father Desmazures stopped the menacing demonstrations with an imposing gesture.

Gaston averted his eyes.

"Sire Governor," he said, "can you intervene on behalf of this wretched man, whom you know is condemned in advance to a horrible death."

"No, my dear Gaston," replied Master Pons, sighing, "I listened carefully to your escape plan when there was a chance of success; but now we have no choice but to live with necessity. The Commissioner showed me official documents which give him absolute power for the repression of heresy; if I dared undertake the slightest resistance, I would be shattered like glass."

During this conversation, the two soldiers had placed the prisoner in the wagon and seated themselves on a rough plank next to him. Then Father Desmazures, having embraced Hamelin, whispered some final words in his ear, and withdrew with tears in his eyes. The wagon, with its guard of cavaliers, moved off heavily and soon disappeared under the dark arch that led to the drawbridge.

Master de Pons and Massac remained pensive.

"This so-called minister," finally said the Governor, "perhaps merited his fate; but we must think, dear Gaston, about other Huguenots who matter to us much more than this one.... The Royal Commissioner, I fear, is planning something against Master Bernard Palissy."

"What!" you think that in spite of the safeguard documents that were provided by the Constable and Master de Larochefoucauld...."

"Since this damnable Amboise conspiracy, everyone is suspect.... Moreover, the Bordeaux crowd are very irritated with the Constable for his severity with the town following the recent events, and they would take advantage of the occasion.... It is important that Palissy leave Saintes with his family as soon as possible."

"I will try to convince him, but I fear that I will not succeed. Master Bernard has a will of iron upon which prayers and menaces have little effect."

"Give him this advice on my behalf: tell him that if he does not hasten to flee, his stubbornness may be very costly.... The Huguenots who lived in the city have almost all emigrated. Now that the terrible Councilor has gotten rid of Hamelin, he will undoubtedly wish to strike a major blow."

"I would still hope that he would not dare attack this famous artisan who is known throughout the kingdom.... But I will go immediately to the home of Master Bernard."

"Yes, yes, do not lose any time.... Who knows if the Royal Commissioner is already at work on this."

Gaston took leave of the Governor.

"Poor Esther," he was thinking while heading towards Palissy's home. "What good did it do her to call upon me for help? Everything is going badly, collapsing and perishing. I thought that I would be bringing her one set of bad news, but now I am bringing two.... I will, at least, have the resources to die defending her.

VIII.

THE EXPLOITS OF THE ROYAL COMMISSIONER

The sad predictions of the Governor did not take long to come true. The next day, in the early hours, several squads of Raby's militia arrived to surround Master Bernard's home and production facility, as they did once before. Soldiers equipped with halberds[27] or musketeers, were posted at each exit of the large buildings. Moreover, in spite of their agitation, these persons seemed peaceful, chatting and laughing with the neighbors.

In the house itself, no one seemed affected by this demonstration. Windows and doors remained shut; no smoke could be seen escaping from the roofs; no noise could be heard from the interior; one could believe that the home and the workshops were completely deserted.

The mercenaries seemed to have no other orders than to keep an eye on Palissy's home until further notice. Raby, dressed in his armor, with metal arm piece and breastplate, wandered nonchalantly from group to group, and undoubtedly considered this not to be a very serious assignment.

The bourgeois and the artisans, attracted by this military activity, did not dare ask the Captain, who was known for his brutality; but a passer-by who was carrying surgeon's kit, and seemed to be going about his business, was more audacious. He approached Raby and said in a friendly manner:

"By Saint-Côme, you got up early this morning, but I think that the birds have already flown the nest!"

Hearing himself addressed in such a familiar fashion, Raby made an angry gesture; but as soon as he recognized the speaker, his features relaxed.

"By the Devil's back! Is that you Master Toupinac?" he said with a loud laugh. "I don't imagine that you came here in the hope there would be a battle and that you would earn a few ecus patching up the wounded?... By God, if there are any Huguenots capable of fighting, they are not here."

"However, Captain," replied the surgeon-barber, "you have certainly not forgotten a certain sword thrust, following a certain preaching, a thrust which was certainly not administered by a good Catholic. You could not have forgotten the talented surgeon who, after having cleaned the wound

---

27 **halberd** is an axe mounted on the edge of a large spear, popular as a combat weapon in the 15th and 16th centuries.

with warm white wine, sewed up your throat so cleanly that you can today order '*trim your fuses!*' , or sing *Gaudeamus,*[28] without a problem."

"Yes, yes, you obtained a nice cure, Master Toupinac," replied the Captain, who mechanically brought his hand up to his neck-piece in memory of past injury; "and if I ever find the scoundrel who was responsible for that sword thrust, by all the horns of Beelzebub! I will certainly return the favor.... I do have certain suspicions, as there were not only Huguenots at that preaching, or at the very least among them, the most dangerous of all. Triple head of a wolf! If I could only be certain..."

The barber blinked.

"Search, search, brave Captain," he said, "and perhaps you will succeed in finding him.... As for us, members of the brotherhood of Saint-Côme, we must remain as discreet as confessors. As regards the wounded, our left hand must ignore who had been treated by our right hand.... And now, I must go bleed the good Canon Rénal, who has had a stroke.... It is not likely that you will need my services today; I repeat, Palissy has certainly made his escape, and it is a sad thing for me, Captain, because I would certainly have finally succeeded in converting him. God has blessed me with eloquence, and more than one sinner, who I could not cure with my lancet, died repenting of his sins after listening to me..."

"Good, good, Master Toupinac," interrupted Raby; "As for me, I will content myself with seeking your talents to plug the holes in my skin that had been acquired in a fight.... But really, do you think that Bernard and his crowd have cleared out?"

"Without a doubt; despite his pride, Master Palissy values his life like the rest of us."

"Sacrebleu! I would have thought... but," added the Captain upon seeing a group of persons moving towards the house, "we will know shortly if Master Bernard is, or is not, in his home."

The group he was speaking about consisted of the Royal Commissioner, the Presiding Judge, as well as several judicial officers, among which one remarked two bailiffs, their canes in hand. Behind them marched a contingent of curiosity seekers and disaffected persons who found irresistible any scandal or act of violence.

Raby turned his back to barber Toupinac and went to exchange a few words in low tones with the magistrates. The Councilor gave an order to one of the bailiffs who then lifted the heavy doorknocker several times and loudly exclaimed:

"Open, in the name of the King!"

The hammering had resounded throughout the building and extended, echo upon echo, to the furthest workshop. However, when the knocking

---

28 *Gaudeamus*, the name of a Latin medieval student song.

ceased, the deepest silence reigned in Palissy's home.

The magistrates and judicial officers looked at each other with concern, while Raby made a meaningful grimace. After another moment had passed, the bailiff knocked again, even more forcefully, repeating his exclamation; but with the same result, and a third try was no more successful.

"By the wolf's tail!" grumbled Raby, "the Huguenots have definitely taken flight."

"Alright, break down the door," ordered the Councilor; "we will inspect the house from the cellar to the roof."

Several workers, who had been brought along in case of this kind of problem, came forward, equipped with sledgehammers and iron crowbars. The door was solid; made of heavy timber held by enormous nails, but could not resist for long the efforts of these experienced men. They put themselves to work with zeal, and soon the hammering against the beams produced a din that was deafening.

Finally, the house lost its impassivity. A window opened and someone appeared on a small wooden balcony above the door.

This person was not a regular inhabitant of the facility but a gentleman of refined appearance, a cloak on his shoulder and a hand resting on the hilt of his sword. With the other hand, he removed his hat, and signaled that he wished to speak.

The Royal Commissioner immediately ordered the workers to interrupt their task.

The gentleman, whom we have undoubtedly identified as Massac, leaned out over the balcony:

"Who are you? What do you want?" he asked.

"By the King's orders!" replied one of the judicial officers, "Open, if you do not want to be punished for rebellion."

"The King's orders cannot be executed here," replied Gaston resolutely; "this house and its dependencies belong to his Lordship, the Duke Anne de Montmorency, and my master will punish whoever violates his dwelling."

Some of the participants appeared frightened by the responsibility that they faced. However, the Councilor lifted a parchment containing several seals, over his head and said in a loud voice:

"And I am the bearer of an order from the Queen-Mother, Regent, and his Eminence the Cardinal of Lorraine, by which I am instructed to have arrested, and delivered to the ecclesiastical or secular tribunals, all the heretics of the province of Saintonge, as well as any 'trouble-makers or followers.'"

"This order," said Gaston vehemently, "does not concern Master Bernard Palissy, retainer of the Constable…."

"It does not contain any exceptions" replied the Royal Commissioner; even further, it formally states: '*in spite of any safeguards, safe-conduct, or other immunities that they may have been given...* 'Therefore, I order that the bailiffs and soldiers here present seize Master Bernard Palissy, potter and inventor of the *rustic figulines,* so that whatever pleases the King or Justice may be done."

Gaston could not retain a movement of anger:

"And I affirm," he exclaimed, "that the Lord Constable, Master de Rochefoucauld and Master the Duke of Montpensier, who have all granted this great artisan, Master Bernard, their special protection, will make you regret your actions.... Shame on you!"

At the same time, he slammed the window shut.

The councilor and his accomplices were very embarrassed. Nothing proved that Bernard was in the dwelling, and perhaps these discussions had no other objective than to divert their attention, or to buy time. However, after a moment of hesitation, the workers returned to their task; and while the sledgehammers and crowbars slammed against the door, the house returned to its state of somber impassivity.

However, on the first floor above, in the room normally used by the family, numerous persons were meeting. Palissy was there with his wife, his daughter, his sons and their servants, as well as Gaston de Massac, whose peaceful intervention had just miserably failed. All were subject to feelings of terror that one can easily understand.

Palissy, in reality, had refused to accept the advice that Gaston had transmitted to him on behalf of the Governor as well as that of the Count of Maulévrier. He had not thought they would dare attack him; moreover, we know that he did not want to abandon his production facility where so many beautiful works of art were in process. However, he had wished that his family and their servants rapidly seek a sanctuary in the city, but neither his wife, nor his children, nor his servants had wished to abandon him. All had begged him to allow them to share his fate, whatever it might be.

However, at this time, there were only tears, despair and confusion in the room. Master Bernard, seated next to a table, holding his Bible, from which he had several times attempted to read aloud; but the state of agitation of the family, as well as the external noises, drowned out his voice.

Gaston, while on the balcony, had wanted to intimidate the aggressors, and especially learn what the charges were against them. The result of this effort worried him, and he searched in his mind some means of salvation. Palissy said to him in a calm voice:

"Many thanks, Master de Massac. You courageously exposed yourself to being fired upon.... But please, do not try further protests or resistance. You could be dragged into the abyss along with us."

In a plaintive voice, Esther said:

"We have already succeeded in getting you deeply compromised for

Hamelin, and today if you take our defense with such fervor…"

"I do not risk anything," replied Gaston, "My status as gentleman attached to the Constable will protect me from trouble…. Corbleu!" he added with concern, "the door will not resist that hammering for long!"

This observation was a result of the increasing din coming from the street.

"Master Bernard," resumed Gaston resolutely, "I do not think there is a real danger for your family and they will find powerful protectors in Saintes; it is only you that they are after, and it is you that one must save…. Now listen to me; while the crowd and the soldiers are busy with the main door, the other entrances to the production facility are only lightly guarded. Your sons, servants and I will surround you and we will suddenly exit by a small door leading into the alley. I have checked that there are only five or six soldiers on that side…. We will knock them over by surprise, and taking advantage of their confusion, we will leave the city. Once in the outskirts, it will be easy to hide you or get you a horse…. So, this can succeed…. My friends, are you ready?"

"Yes, yes!" they all exclaimed.

Bernard Palissy had not moved and a feeble smile played on his lips.

"You will be one day a brave general of a great army, Master Massac," he said, "but for now I would ask you to dismiss your troops as being too inexperienced…. My friends, my children," he resumed in a different tone, "remain peaceful."

As Mistress Bernard, Esther and his sons begged him to attempt this method of salvation, one heard a terrible crashing noise coming from the floor below them and the entire house shook; at the same instant cries of triumph came from the street.

"The door has given way," said Palissy; "We must be prepared."

Soon a clamor resounded inside the buildings; apparently the soldiers were invading the workshops. This event upset Palissy more than the rest.

"They will break everything and loot the rest," he cried, "unless I surrender myself immediately…. The hour has come…. Farewell, my wife, farewell, my children, my friends…. Have courage… and do not despair for divine goodness!"

At the same time, tearing himself away from the arms that retained him, he hurled himself towards the stairway.

The door had indeed been knocked down, and the soldiers, as well as groups of curiosity seekers, had penetrated Palissy's home, following the magistrates and the judicial officers. However, the invaders, not certain what they would encounter in the vast buildings which were unfamiliar to them, advanced slowly. The explosion of cries caused by Master Bernard's determination to surrender, further diminished their confidence, and they approached each other, preparing their arms, ready to repulse a possible attack.

In the vestibule, where there now penetrated a bright light, Master Bernard, followed closely by his family, suddenly appeared, and cried out in a firm voice:

"'It is I whom you are looking for, Sires, so here I am.... Spare my family, and I will humbly obey the King's orders."

Until this moment, the Royal Commissioner and those with him, had their doubts about Bernard Palissy being there. They were very happy to see him appear.

"Seize this person," the Councilor ordered.

"We have won," exclaimed Raby. "I claim the privilege of arresting this prince of the Huguenots myself; he who has defied us for so long.... Hah! I warned him that we would return."

With his hand in a steel gauntlet, he seized Palissy, who although tall and vigorous, did not consider resisting or escaping. Moreover, a dozen soldiers, without waiting for their chief's orders, had moved toward the famous artisan and now formed a solid circle around him.

In the midst of this tumult, Bernard was exclaiming:

"Spare my wife and my children. It was under this condition that I surrendered.... Above all; do not let anyone break anything in my workshops! The objects therein, which are for the most part destined for various churches, belong to the Constable and other important persons in the kingdom."

However, these exhortations went unheeded. Mistress Bernard, Esther, the two sons and the servants tried vainly to approach the head of the family, but they were roughly pushed away, and their calls, their supplications and their cries of desperation were mixed with the swearing and curses of the brutish soldiers.

Raby, losing patience, said to the Royal commissioner:

"Gads! Sire, what have you decided regarding this young Huguenot hussy whose screaming is piercing our ears? And these women who go off to the Sabbath at night, do we let them go free?... Sacrebleu! I agree with Toupinac, the little one is pretty enough for us to tear her away from the jaws of the Devil."

The object of this last observation was poor Esther, her face bathed in tears, who was still trying to reach her father. As the Captain approached her, curling his thick greying mustache, Massac suddenly threw himself between them.

"Brigand!" he exclaimed, "You should remember that your roguish gallantries do not suit you.... Once before, we stopped them in your throat; this time we might make them enter by your chest."

Hearing this allusion to the wound he had received several years earlier, Raby stared fixedly at Gaston.

"Cornebleu! it was you?" He exclaimed. "Well, I always suspected it, as you had a strange look the night of the preaching.... So! You are then a Huguenot?... One of those cowardly Huguenots who do not dare admit their faith and betray both sides! For a long time, I have had the burning desire to have a heretic of quality on the other end of my rapier, and by all the Devils, I will now satisfy my whim."

"And I," said Gaston, burning with fury, "I cannot wait to remove from this Province a chief of the bandits, an infamous cutthroat like you."

The two took defensive stances and their long swords crossed.

Duels were quite frequent at that time. One frequently encountered persons, who for the least pretext, or no pretext, would throw down a challenge. The spectators would make room so that the enemies could settle their quarrel. However, this combat presented monstrous inequalities. Captain Raby, as we have said, was armed to the teeth in armor, while Gaston de Massac was wearing a silk doublet with a velvet cape.

The rules of fairness would normally oppose a combat where the advantage was only one sided, but the soldiers in Raby's company did not have such scruples. However, the Royal Commissioner, obeying other considerations, exclaimed:

"Stop.... Captain Raby! Master de Massac belongs to the Constable.... I order you to..."

"Leave it be, Sire," replied Raby, continuing to spar. "He may well belong to the Constable, but he is still a Huguenot, as he has just almost admitted, I can bring him to reason, you will see."

In spite of this boast, Raby appeared neither the more skillful, nor the stronger of the two. Gaston's sword had already struck his helmet and breastplate several times and if he had not been protected by his armor, he would have suffered several wounds. On the other hand, Gaston, other than a minor wound to his shoulder, had not been touched, and thanks to his accuracy, his suppleness, his vigor, and his dexterity, he had evened his chances against the mercenary.

One could not judge what would be the outcome of this duel, when the Royal Commissioner said a few words in a low voice to those around him. Immediately a halberd fell across the two swords, and despite the protests of the two adversaries, the combat was interrupted. While the soldiers surrounded the Captain, and attempted to calm him, others came up behind Gaston and disarmed him.

Gaston managed to disengage himself.

"Rascals," he exclaimed; "you fear for your Captain, for he is accountable to God for a lifetime of debauchery and crimes! The coward will certainly reward you for saving him from this peril!"

"Back, my men!" exclaimed Raby, on his side; "I must terminate this disguised Huguenot. Five hundred thousand demons! I want revenge for the blow he gave me the night of the preaching.... He almost killed me by treachery!"

However, the two combatants being separated and contained, the Councilor interposed himself with authority.

"Captain Raby," he said, "when you are performing a public service, you must not think of your personal quarrels.... Moreover, Master Gaston de Massac is not only in rebellion against royal authority, but he is also suspected of heresy, and I order the judicial officers here present to arrest him."

The bailiffs hastened to obey and seized de Massac.

"I?" he exclaimed with indignation, "I, the secretary and friend of his Lordship, the Constable, I from a line of good Catholics, and a good Catholic myself...? it is a veritable folly, and by the Mass, it could cost dearly to those who do this."

"So be it," replied the Royal Commissioner, "I will be answerable."

Nevertheless, this severe action appeared to awake some apprehension among some of those present, and he added:

"By virtue of the authority vested in me, I have the mission of pursuing all heretics, as well as their trouble-makers and followers. Now, since my arrival in Saintes, I have always seen Master de Massac in the company of Huguenots, first with de Palissy and his family, and once again yesterday with that odious depraved supposed minister Hamelin, with whom he was perhaps plotting some intrigue. Now the brave Captain Raby accuses him of having participated in one of those abominable assemblies called a *preaching*, and having struck, him, Raby, with a sword.... Is this not true, Captain?"

"Yes, yes," replied Raby.

"And, I will not deny it," exclaimed de Massac with exaltation, "It is I, disgusted by the persecution, insults and cruelties imposed upon harmless cultists..."

"You hear him...he admits it!" interrupted the Councilor.

Massac wanted to continue, but an immense clamor drowned out his voice.

"He admits it! He admits it"" they repeated from all sides. "A gentleman of the Constable.... What infamy! Down with the Protestants! Down with the heretics!

In vain, poor Gaston struggled, ranted, and roared, but no one was listening, and the indignation against him increased.

Bernard, surrounded by his guards, became quite agitated.

"Sires," he exclaimed, "you are mistaken. I take God as my witness. Master de Massac is not one of us.... In spite of his humaneness, he has always pleaded the cause of our enemies."

And Esther, on the side, murmured:

"Please to God that they tell the truth!... But is it there that his zeal and devotion was supposed to lead this generous young man?"

A great noise had arisen from the interior of the production facility. Following the soldiers, many vagabonds had invaded the workshops, and devastation had begun.

These circumstances put Master Bernard Palissy in a state of desperation. Clasping his hands, he said to the Royal Commissioner:

"By all that is sacred, Sire, prevent these evil persons from destroying works which have caused me so much care and effort. The Constable will be very upset by this destruction;"

"These are ungodly works," said the Councilor disdainfully; "Most of them represent the false gods of paganism.... No matter! We will be watchful."

However, he gave no orders to stop the pillage, when suddenly, the crowd scattered, and a new group entered Bernard's home.

It consisted of Master de Pons, the Lord of Burie, the Count of Maulévrier and other important individuals, all secret or avowed friends of Palissy. The Governor, learning about the aggression directed against the famous potter, had hurriedly gathered them together to better enforce his authority, and was further accompanied by a dozen archers and some guards who were employed by the city and were completely devoted to him.

The sudden arrival of Master de Pons was very impressive as one could expect that a violent contestation was about to explode between the primary functionary of the province and the Royal Commissioner. The Palissy family seemed to gain courage.

"Ah, Sire Governor," cried Esther, "free my father.... free Master de Massac!"

"Give me back my poor husband!" exclaimed Mistress Bernard.

Master de Pons did not appear to have heard these touching entreaties. He had a furrowed brow, and his hand caressed the hilt of his sword; but he was pale and lacked the strength to support imminent battle. However, he said with much majesty:

"Who is in charge here, and how does one dare encroach on the authority of the Governor of Saintonge? How is it that the soldiers have left their quarters without my permission?"

The Councilor-Commissioner placed himself directly in front of him.

"It is I who gave the orders, Sire," he replied.

Directly after this first shock, Master de Pons, an excellent man, but of weak character, lowered the flag.

"That suffices Sire," he replied, "although it might have been a good idea to forewarn me.... But by the cross of Christ!" he added, looking at the prisoners, "how could you have arrested the great artisan, Bernard Palissy, servant to the Constable, and especially Master Gaston de Massac, son of my companion, the Baron de Massac.... This is a misunderstanding, Sire Councilor, without a doubt, a misunderstanding!"

"There is no misunderstanding," the Royal Commissioner replied; "both are guilty of heresy, and I have seized both, without worrying either about their social class or their relations. I will not oppose that an investigation be established before we turn Master de Massac over to a secular tribunal; as for Bernard Palissy, whose membership in the Reformist sect has been known for a long time and has become a veritable scandal for this country, I have decided that he is to be safely guarded and sent as soon as possible before the Bordeaux Parliament, like his friend, the infamous Hamelin."

Crying and lamentations broke out in that part of the vestibule where Palissy's family was located.

"Master Councilor," resumed the Governor, "if you permit, let us examine together before arriving at this conclusion...."

"Do not be concerned about me," said Master Bernard energeticazlly; "I am a Huguenot, and I do not hide it. Instead you should work on obtaining the release of that gentleman, Master Gaston de Massac.... Once again, he is not one of ours, I swear it before God!... Then, if I still have friends here," he continued, taking a softer tone, "I beg them to protect my wife and my children, who, in my absence, will be exposed to many vexations."

"You can have peace of mind on this, Bernard," said the Count de Maulévrier, putting himself forward with more courage than he had ever shown. "Your entire family will find sanctuary in my dwelling."

"She can also count on me, Maulévrier," resumed Master de Pons, delighted to give Palissy a proof of affection without openly challenging the terrible Royal Commissioner.

"Thank you, my good Lords!" exclaimed Bernard effusively; "and now if you are willing to grant me one more favor, prevent those vagabonds and villains from pillaging my house and destroying works which are the fruit of ten years' worth of efforts."

This time, the Governor dared show his indignation.

"What!" he exclaimed, "thieves and pillagers have entered here?... Archers of the City, chase and strike them with the shaft of your halberds, and if they resist, take them to the town prison, where they will receive a hundred lashes."

The archers, whom as we have said, report directly to the Governor, did not give him time to repeat the order. They entered directly into the workshop area and soon one could see the vandals fleeing, and one could assume that they had been relieved of their booty. The noise ceased in the building, and although some regrettable damage had been done, a great number of masterpieces, which today are still the admiration of the world, were saved from destruction.

Master de Pons, having made the necessary arrangements to assure that, during the owner's absence, the production area be protected from similar attempts, the Royal Commissioner indicated his intention of leaving with the prisoners. So, Palissy's family rushed forward to give them their final farewells. Raby's soldiers wanted to push them back again, but the Governor insisted that they wait a few minutes to allow such legitimate sentiments to be fully expressed.

The mother and the children took advantage of this permission and embraced Palissy. Their pain and their grief affected the most savage soul. However, Master Bernard maintained his serenity.

"Do not despair of the goodness and power of God," he repeated. "It takes him so little time to change the hearts of men, to bring calm after the storm!… May all his blessings descend upon you."

As he spoke successively to each of his dear ones, Esther found herself next to Gaston, still guarded by the halberdiers.

"Ah! Master de Massac," she said, her eyes filled with tears, "as I feared, you have fallen with us into this abyss of misery and despair. I knew well that your chivalrous zeal.…"

"It is not I that you must pity, Esther," replied Gaston; "I will not have any difficulty clearing myself of this ridiculous accusation, and as soon as I have returned to freedom, I will hasten to you to offer my services."

He was interrupted by Raby, who exclaimed in a jeering tone:

"Triple Devil! my man, if you get out of this, you will grant me first, I hope, a little round of conversation, and we will resume what we had started."

"I promise you to do so, Captain Raby," replied Gaston.

Seeing the Governor approach, Raby moved away. Master de Pons, after assuring himself that only the two young persons were close enough to hear, said to them with loquaciousness:

"All is not lost, my children: I will first take care of getting Gaston out of this bad situation. As for Master Bernard, as long as he stays in Saintes, he will have nothing to fear… and I will do the necessary to assure that he stays a long time!"

He could not say more; upon the order of the Royal Commissioner, they started walking and Massac was led by the halberdiers following Palissy. While the house echoed with the cries of the disconsolate family, a muffled murmur that arose from the street and soon spread throughout town along the path taken by the procession bore witness to the trouble caused by the arrest of a gentleman to the Constable and the famous potter.

IX.

THE BARBER'S SHOP

Bernard Palissy and Gaston de Massac had not been taken to the prison of the chateau where they would have been placed under the authority of the Governor. The Royal Commissioner had them locked up in the prison of the local authorities, where Raby's troops and the German cavalrymen guarded them. There, they were kept under absolute secrecy, and although they would have normally appeared before several judges, none were allowed to see them, and for several days, no one was capable of saying what had been decided regarding their fate.

However, in the meantime, a reaction in their favor had developed in the opinion of the inhabitants of Saintes. As long as Palissy, although menaced, remained hidden in his home and seemingly privileged by immunity, public opinion was against him. However, since Bernard was arrested, and his family has been obliged to search for sanctuary with charitable families, the sympathy of those who were quite hostile seems to have returned. They were thinking only about his righteousness, his wisdom and his artistic genius that was the pride of the entire city. As for Massac, whose name was so respected in the province, and whose position with the Constable of Montmorency appeared to place him above all suspicion, the accusations of heresy against him did not appear to be very serious. They blamed his incarceration on the personal animosity of the Royal Commissioner and the false allegations of Captain Raby, loathed for his moral corruption and brutality.

One morning, at an hour when the gates of the city were not yet open, Master Toupinac, the barber-surgeon, was in his shop, situated, as we know, at the far end of the outskirts of the city, not far from the ancient home of Bernard Palissy. The sun had barely risen and a fairly heavy fog hung over the neighboring river. However, it was market day, and the farmers were arriving with their carts and livestock, and while waiting for the gates to open, many of them stopped at Toupinac's shop. Therefore, the receipts looked promising for that day, if not for the surgeon, at least for the barber.

This shop did not have a luxurious appearance, and that of the poorest village shop today could be an example. It was at street level on a main thoroughfare and lacked a storefront, which facilitated both the entry of light and customers. Above the door hung an immense wooden shaving bowl, and a crude painting representing a military type being treated for a wound by a surgeon dressed in black. At the interior of the shop, were only a few sad pieces of furniture, two or three small mirrors that were attached to the wall along with some images of Saints, and finally a few wooden and straw chairs. On one table, quite dirty, one could see an earthenware jug and a large basin containing a quantity of stale water that served several purposes. However, in a showcase hanging near the entry were displayed, with ostentation, a dozen surgical instruments, with strange forms, highly polished, apparently very sharp, and which were designed to give an impressive image of the practitioner who would use them. Unfortunately, close inspection would reveal that they had never been used. They were there simply as a complement to the shop's other emblems.

In this shop, open to all kinds of weather and where the morning chill made itself felt, Toupinac and his boys, worked hard to satisfy their customers. The boys, or rather *apprentices,* were two poor lads, thin and frail, who probably rarely ate a proper meal, and were harshly treated, which was a tradition among barbers. They wore large aprons, once white, and for shoes, wooden clogs which constantly resonated on the tiled floor. Impossible to say if they had the opportunity to study surgery, or even if they knew how to read; but for the time being, they only thought about giving proper shaves and haircuts. Each was equipped with a pewter shaving bowl and a chipped razor and were doing their best to not do too much damage to their customers' chins to avoid insults or even physical punishment, which Toupinac was not stingy about distributing.

The owner took an active role in their work and really exhibited a superior dexterity. In a privileged corner of the shop, where the light was best, stood an old oak armchair, polished by usage, where the elite sat. It was this corner that Toupinac, in his omnipotence, had reserved for himself. He had, to perform his task, a superb copper shaving bowl, shiny as gold, and a royal razor adorned with silver and engravings. Moreover, the fortunate mortal who was served by Toupinac in person was the beneficiary of Toupinac's conversation, renowned for miles around, for its Gascony loquacity. Apprentices were not allowed to say a word in his presence; but when the master said something amusing, or that he thought was such, and began to laugh, the boys were also obliged to laugh, even if they were busy and did not understand the subject. This was the rule, and the poor devils were in trouble if they did not conform.

At this moment, three persons occupied the owner and his apprentices, while several others were lounging on benches waiting their turn. The person who was ensconced in the privileged chair in the care of the master was the large miller whom we had seen at the home of Palissy at the beginning of this story, and who was a friend of Toupinac. The first lad was occupied with a middle-aged man having the clothing and appearance of a journeyman. This man, endowed with a heavy beard, asked that it be made to disappear, which would certainly render him unrecognizable, and his mysterious air allowed one to think that he did not wish to attract attention. The third customer, assigned to the youngest of the lads, was apparently a simple farmer, coming to the market with the intention of purchasing or selling, and had judged it appropriate to bring metal to the virgin forest of his hair.

Moreover, this little crowd maintained a respectful silence, and conversation, following custom, belonged to Toupinac. The latter, while shaving the miller, was giving him the most interesting news in his repertoire, news that the others present were free to enjoy. "Cap de Diou![29] brother," he said, delicately holding the nose of his friend between his index finger and his thumb to scrape his upper lip, "in what a time do we live? A time of sin and Godlessness, neighbor, and we would be tempted to believe that the Antichrist would appear.... All the evil comes from not having listened to me.... Ah! if only they had listened!"

With an automatic movement, one of the lads gave a penetrating look towards the sky, while the other, interrupting the action of his scissors, made a gesture of admiration.

"As concerns this city's Huguenots," continued Toupinac, after having ascertained by a side-glance the sufficiently enthusiastic pantomime of his apprentices, "one does not know much yet. Our Lords of officialdom remain impenetrable. Besides, a good Christian such as I would not pry into such secrets.... I prefer telling you about intriguing things I have witnessed as recently as last night."

The audience became attentive. The miller took advantage of the moment the barber was strapping his razor to say, while spitting out shaving foam:

"Well, Toupinac, you want again to tell tales about cracked heads or pierced chests of those who came to you for repair?... We have heard all those, and you have the habit of getting several versions out of the same seed."

"Nothing like that, neighbor," resumed the barber, returning to his task; "You will see.... Last night, I was sleeping in my room upstairs when I was awakened by a loud noise. In our area, comrade, we are often subject to disturbances, and we always sleep with one eye open. Therefore, I sat up in bed and carefully listened. The noise was rapidly approaching; it came from the hoof beats of several horses mixed with the cadence of foot soldiers. As these troops could not come from the city since the gates would be closed

---

29 **Cap de Diou,** Gascon exclamation which translates to 'by the head of God.'

at this hour, this seemed to be a reasonably extraordinary event, you will agree. I therefore wanted to see what was happening.... I jumped out of my bed and went to open my window. However, since I had not put on either a doublet or breeches, the fog and the night breezes seemed to me devilishly cold.... You understand, comrade! Ha! Ha! Ha!"

"Ha! Ha! Ha!" repeated the lads, laughing on their side, one with a loud laugh in a low register, the other with a high-pitched laugh of a soprano.

Perhaps it was the amusing image of the owner naked that caused them to laugh harder than their training required, because a menacing *hmm!* abruptly stopped them.

"The night was very dark," continued Toupinac, while firmly scraping the miller's chin. "One could not see for more than two arms' length. The wind was blowing and my teeth were chattering; however, I held firm. When the troop arrived just across from the shop, I succeeded, by squinting my eyes, in seeing something, and this is what I saw...."

Here, a new pause, subtle and calculated, to allow their curiosity to reach its height.

"Oh!" said one apprentice.

"Ah!" said the other.

However, although both attempted to express by their exclamations the interest they were taking in the master's account, apparently, they failed because they only earned for themselves a tongue-lashing.

"You had better wake up, lazy oafs!" said the barber in a disdainful tone; "once you have well wined and dined, you only think about slipping between two sheets, and the sky could fall.... But it is to my comrade that I am speaking.... So finally, I could make out a group of horsemen whose spears and helmets shone in the night; then came a litter, with the curtains carefully closed, carried by two horses. Finally, behind the litter, came a troop of musketeers on foot, with their glowing fuses forming little red stars in the darkness. These people were moving forward cautiously without saying a word, and undoubtedly were doing their best to stifle the noise of their passage. Nevertheless, for a good quarter of an hour afterwards, after having returned to my bed, I could hear them moving away towards Jonzac."

This narrative by Toupinac was listened to with great attention. The man whom we had designated as a journeyman, seemed to have been quite impressed, and made several sudden movements that could have resulted in slashes to his face. As concerns the miller, whose grooming was finished, and who had regained the use of his voice; he said in a bantering tone as he got up:

"You are telling us quite a tale! Master Toupinac, with your curtained litter, your people on foot, and your people on horseback! You were dreaming, neighbor, and you were still asleep when you thought you saw what you described... so finally, where were these people who frightened you coming from?"

"On my place in paradise! Neighbor, as strange as it seems, they could only have been coming from the city."

"So, no doubt they just jumped over the moats and the walls?"

"The Governor could have given an order...."

"No, no, the Governor is too prudent to allow the gates to be opened in the middle of the night with the provinces far from peaceful. You have had a nightmare, Master, and you are subject to them, I think."

Toupinac became furious.

"This time, it is too much!" he resumed. "I repeat, I saw and clearly saw that the horsemen were the Germans, and the musketeers on foot came from here.... I could not swear that the large fellow who marched at the head of the musketeers was not Captain Raby, in person."

"You have seen too many things, comrade, with this heavy fog and obscurity.... Captain Raby, who has no more Huguenots in town to abuse, has certainly spent the night in some cabaret on Saint-Eutrope street, drinking and gambling, as is his custom."

"Sacrebleu! Neighbor, you will believe what you want, finally, but if those cowardly apprentices had not slept the sleep of brutes, they could tell you..."

Placed on notice, the poor devils pricked up their ears.

"Wait Master," said in a loud voice the one that had been shaving the journeyman; "now I remember that I heard the noise of the horses and the clanking of metal, and all that.... But we work so hard during the day.... Sleep was the strongest."

"And I," resumed the one with a high-pitched voice, "I was also awakened... and I smelled the odor of burned cord which escapes from the musket fuses.... I even thought I recognized a throaty cough that I would have recognized among a thousand, that of Captain Raby since he received the terrible wound which you cured with such dexterity."

Toupinac looked at the miller with a triumphant air. His apprentices, glorious in their success, were searching their imagination for some new lies to support the assertions of their master, when the flour merchant shrugged his shoulders and said:

"Keep quiet, you rascals.... Are you not ashamed? Toupinac should grind your bones after I am gone, I do not believe one word of your nonsense.... Nor his! Captain Raby has not left Saintes."

As he was confidently expressing this opinion, several of the customers who were sitting next to the door waiting their turn suddenly got up and began looking out onto the main road. One of them exclaimed:

"Attention! Here comes Captain Raby and his men, returning to the city…. If there are any Huguenots around here, they better start working their legs."

The persons inside the shop, including Toupinac, ran to the entrance. Only the journeyman, his face covered with shaving foam, remained patiently in his seat, waiting for the apprentice to decide that he had finished his task.

It was indeed Captain Raby and a dozen of his musketeers who were entering the outskirts of the city. Officer and soldiers, all were covered with dust, and appeared exhausted, as if having made a long trip.

"Hey, comrade," exclaimed a radiant Toupinac, "was I not right, and will you dare accuse me again of being a liar?"

Perhaps the canny miller never had a real doubt about his neighbor's story. However, accustomed from times past to the exaggerations of the little Gascon, he never lost an opportunity to contradict him and harass him with jests.

"Indeed," he replied coldly, "it is truly the Captain, one can recognize him from a hundred paces. I would also agree that it is musketeers from his company who follow him…. But where are the curtained litter and the German cavaliers that you were making so much noise about?"

"I agree, the Germans and the litter have disappeared…. Do you know what I suspect, comrade? Raby and his crowd accompanied them only a certain distance from the city; then they let them continue on their way, while they returned to Saintes."

"It pleases you to say this; but I persist in believing that the litter and the Germans never existed except in your Gascon head."

Toupinac was exasperated, as was often his custom, and he could not moderate his anger.

"Well! Morbleu!" he resumed, "Captain Raby is not unapproachable!… Moreover, he owes me since a long time for the healing of his wound, not to mention the patching up of a series of contusions, abrasions and bruises of all kinds that he accumulates in bars…. I will call out to him, and we will learn from him directly… you will see!"

At just that moment, Raby was passing in front of the shop, swaggering, with his fist on his hip. Toupinac call out to him from the doorway.

"Ah! Brave Captain, you look quite tired…. Would you do me the honor of resting a moment in my home?"

Raby hesitated, as if he feared that the barber might take advantage of the situation to claim some old debts. Reassured by the totally engaging smile of a brother, he relied with a hoarse voice:

"By Lucifer's horns! I will not refuse, because I feel absolutely broken…. Continue your way, you others," he added, speaking to his people: "I will rejoin you soon, but I will rest a bit at the home of my *friend* Toupinac."

The barber, very proud of such a title, brought Raby into the shop and settled him in the seat of honor. The soldier made himself comfortable, took off his metal helmet and placed his heavy sword across his knees; then, looking around him in an insolent manner, he resumed:

"Ah! So, Master, I hope that there are no Huguenots here? Corbleu! If any of these rascals were of *that religion*...."

"Huguenots, here, Captain Raby?" replied Toupinac; "who do you take me for? Never in my shop."

"Bah! If I remember correctly, formerly, one could run into that heathen, Bernard, in your place...."

"Do not speak to me about Master Bernard. He is a stubborn one who has never wanted to listen to me... a poor man, Captain! If the subject is not the *rustic figulines*, stained glass windows, literature, great speeches, philosophy or science, you can't get anything out of him. He is lacking in intelligence, and when a man lacks intelligence.... But let us cease speaking of this sad man.... For example, I was just chatting with my comrade, the miller, and my honorable customers, about the closed litter that you were escorting last night with assistance of the cavaliers of Taillebourg."

Raby gave such a start that Toupinac backed away in fright.

`"A closed litter!" exclaimed the Captain; "what closed litter? Ah! Do you have the Devil in your body? How could you have known...?"

"Parbleu! Captain, I heard and I saw, like others could see and hear, although it was a very dark night. As for the litter, it was too large an object to not see it four steps away as it passed in front of my door."

Toupinac's discovery greatly annoyed Raby and he sought some way to mislead the indiscreet barber. Unfortunately, he was lacking in imagination, and plausible lies did not present themselves to him. However, he answered firmly, without taking the time to reflect:

"By the Pope's mule! Master, one cannot hide anything from you. Moreover, we can agree now, and we will be able to agree more freely in several hours, that it was a well-curtained litter that we were escorting... thus my legs are folding under me as a result of following the horses on foot for more three leagues from here, where we let the litter continue on its journey."

Toupinac, hearing his all his assertions confirmed, looked at the annoying miller.,

"Ha! Comrade, now what do you say?" he continued; "Am I a Gascon, am I a liar? Did I have a nightmare or am I seeing things?"

"Well, what? I was mistaken," replied the miller blithely, "After all, I do not care.... We did not wager anything on this, so I have nothing to pay."

"Without a doubt; but in the future, you will remember that when the master surgeon-barber, Jean Toupinac, affirms something.... But for God's sake! Captain," he continued, turning once again towards Raby, "who was in the litter?"

Raby took a haughty air that hid his real embarrassment.

"Master Toupinac, I could reply that this is a State secret. However," he immediately added, "I want to tell you everything because you, as well as the other idiots who are listening, will imagine an unlimited number of tales…. In that curtained litter was… a woman."

"A woman" repeated the barber stunned; a woman from the town, then?"

"Yes… that is to say, no… It was a lady, a grand lady from the Court…. Sacrebleu! Peasants, do you think that one would have gone to such trouble and bothered an officer such as I for a bourgeoise?"

"But Captain, how is it that a lady of that class came to be in Saintes? This would have been discussed in town, and we hear everything in my shop."

"She arrived secretly…. And did not wish to be recognized."

"Well, finally, for what reason would this lady leave in the middle of the night with a cavalry and infantry as escort?"

"You may well be astute, Master Toupinac, but there are things that are beyond the comprehension of a barber. However, I can tell you that this lady, was having an affair in the city, which involved a young lover of high standing, and an older extremely jealous man, it was deemed necessary to have her depart as rapidly as possible with the appropriate precautions…. Ah! By the beard of Satan!" said Raby, interrupting himself when he saw smiles of disbelief appearing on their lips as he muddled though these explications; "Is someone here accusing me of being a teller of lies?"

He stared at each of them successively and demanded in a ferocious tone:

"Is it you, Master scraper of chins, would you be stupid enough?"

They were all struck by fear.

Some backed up to the wall stammering denials, others simply fled joining the crowd milling in the street. Only Toupinac, pale and concerned, attempted to calm the brutish soldier.

"Now! Now!" he said humbly, "what are you thinking, brave Captain. If we are smiling, it is because you have such a pleasing way of telling the story. And the story is quite amusing, you must admit."

"Fine!" replied Raby; "Triple head of a wolf! I will not allow anyone to mock me…. But that is enough of that. I must return to the city. However, if anyone in your shop dare say anything about this litter affair other than what it pleases me to say, I will personally close the mouths of chatterboxes and taletellers…. This is understood, is it not?"

"Yes, yes, Captain," replied the barber, redoubling his humility; "the story is strange enough that we need not change anything. I think there is no harm in laughing about a situation concerning a husband, a lover and a lady of the Court...."

"Decidedly, it would be better to not speak about it at all," Raby brusquely interrupted; "and if any of those idiots who were present decide to loosen their tongues regarding this affair, I will cut out their tongues, and their ears as well. As for you, Master Toupinac, if you say one word, I will return with a dozen of my fellows and break everything here. Now you have been warned.... So, go with God, or to the Devil, your choice!"

At the same time, the amiable and inventive Captain went out, his head held high, making his heels resound on the pavement.

After his departure, an embarrassed silence reigned in the shop. Toupinac was not sure what attitude to take; The miller said to him maliciously:

"Cape of Saint Laurent! Brother, he is quite brutal, your friend, the Captain; and for a moment, I feared he might slay you."

"Men of great courage like him, neighbor, have their excess of vivacity.... I wager that the next time we see him, he will want us to have a drink together."

"Good, if it is he who pays the wine.... But, after all, Master Toupinac, I do not believe in his Lady of the Court. And then we really do not know what was in that curtained litter that was so well protected."

The journeyman, whose grooming was completed and had just finished paying Toupinac, was heading towards the door. His freshly shaved face, which had become unrecognizable, reflected a mortal fear.

"Ah! I can, guess," he said; "and what will happen to so many innocent people if I am right?"

And, without giving the barber the time to ask any questions, he rushed outside and lost himself among the farmers headed towards the market.

X.

HOTEL MAULÉVRIER

During that same morning, several persons were meeting in a salon of the Maulévrier home in Saintes.

This salon, decorated with tapestries, was furnished with gothic furniture in old oak, and had a dreary look; two high windows that opened out onto a narrow and somber street, provided insufficient light. Moreover, the street was empty, and the tumultuous sounds pervading the city, which came from the market, did not reach them.

This silence, and the semi-darkness, fitted perfectly with the sad mood of the people occupying the salon.

Mistress de Maulévrier, the mother of the Count, a venerable old lady, was seated in a large armchair with the family crest and was working on a piece of tapestry. She was known as a good Catholic, but this did not prevent her from cherishing her son, whom she knew was attached to the Protestant religion, and who had great affection for the Huguenot family staying in her home. Esther and Mistress Palissy were knitting woolen stockings, seated a short distance away on low chairs, for at that time, one was always reminded of the difference of class. One of Bernard's small children was playing on the rug at the feet of his mother, while the others, under the supervision of Nicolas, romped about in a nearby courtyard. Mathurin, the eldest, who was standing near an open window, had been tasked with keeping an eye on what was going on outside.

Each time one heard steps on the street, Esther and her mother looked anxiously at the young lookout; but he responded each time with a negative sign, and the poor women returned to their knitting with a sigh.

After a number of these false alerts, Esther lost her patience.

"My God!" she exclaimed, "What is happening? Master de Maulévrier has been gone a long time and was to see the Governor, and if necessary, the terrible Royal Commissioner himself. He promised to bring us back news about out dear prisoners, whatever they were, and he has not returned.... Could something have happened to him as well?"

"Ah! My daughter," said Mistress Bernard, no less agitated, "we must be ready for anything. Daniel, on his side, has not returned. We sent him to warn the Baron de Massac about the danger that his son is risking, and he had promised to be back in Saintes last night. However, this morning, he is not yet back.... Who knows if he did not encounter the wrong people on the way?"

"This uncertainty is horrible," replied Esther; "Everyone who loves us, everyone who pities us, everyone who defends us, seem to be unpityingly stricken like us."

The Countess de Maulévrier said to them with kindness: "Courage! My dear ladies; impatience increases the gravity of things for you. Your messenger will surely arrive soon; he could have been delayed by unexpected circumstances so frequent during travel. As concerns my son, I know his prudence, and I do not expect him to be in danger. He is undoubtedly now occupied by some difficult negotiations of which you will soon know the result.... Do like me, remain confident; God protects those who serve him, no matter the sect."

"Countess de Maulévrier is right, my daughter," said Mistress Bernard. "Let us not yet despair. We have been assured that no harm will come to our poor prisoners as long as they remain in Saintes."

"Then let us have faith, my mother. Heaven is my witness that I only ask to believe!"

And Esther returned to her work.

Suddenly, Mathurin let out an exclamation of joy and hastily leaned over the balcony

"What is it, my brother?" asked Esther standing up. "Who is coming to us?"

"Master de Maulévrier," replied Mathurin, "and another person who I could not identify, but I suspect might be... We will see.... I do not want to give you false hope."

Indeed, one could hear the closing of the door to the street and two persons who were climbing the stairs. Esther cried out excitedly:

"Is it our beloved father?"

"My husband! My dear Bernard!" exclaimed Mistress Bernard.

And both rushed forward to greet the arrivals. Maulévrier was the first to appear, but the person that followed was not Bernard Palissy, it was Gaston de Massac.

The young gentleman, in spite of his three days of captivity, appeared well, and gave Esther a friendly smile.

Mother and daughter suffered a heartfelt shock at having their expectation dashed. Mistress Bernard did not have the strength to hide her disappointment, and fell backward, letting escape a feeble moan. However, Esther managed a modest curtsy to the newcomer and said with emotion:

"Thanks be to God! Master de Massac; It was for us that you braved those powerful enmities. Now you are free, totally free, true?"

"Yes, Esther. Thanks to the efforts and persistent zeal of Master de Maulévrier."

"I did not have great difficulty," said Maulévrier after having exchanged several words with the Countess. "The accusation against you was so absurd, Massac, that in spite of the ill-will of the Royal Commissioner, the Canons of the local Chapter, under the inspiration of Father Desmazures, unanimously decided in your favor.... Ah! We knew perfectly well that you were not one of us! Well, you were released and it was only justice."

"But my husband!" exclaimed Mistress Palissy, who could not restrain her anxiety. "Do you not have any news regarding Bernard?"

"None," replied Gaston sadly. "I was held under total security. I know nothing of my companion's captivity."

"And I was not more favored," said the Count. "As indulgent as they were with me concerning Master de Massac, they were impenetrable regarding Palissy. The Royal Commissioner, who I dared question regarding this subject, replied to me that *the public would soon be informed what had been decided regarding this accursed Huguenot.*' His manner in saying this forebodes no good."

"Therefore," resumed Mistress Palissy, "you cannot even tell me what they did with Bernard?"

"No."

"I am afraid that I know." said a new voice.

In the middle of the agitation, another person had entered without being noticed. It was Daniel, who as we mentioned, had been sent to the Chateau de Massac, who had just arrived. We do not need to add that Daniel was the journeyman who had stopped that morning at Toupinac's shop while awaiting the opening of the city's gates.

The absence of a beard had changed his appearance such that at first, they did not recognize him and looked up defiantly. However, Mistress Bernard was not perplexed for long.

"Daniel, here you are at last!" she exclaimed. "For God's sake, what have you learned regarding Bernard?"

"I cannot be absolutely certain, Mistress," replied the companion potter with embarrassment; "but I suppose... I suspect..."

"Then why are you saying something if you know nothing?" said Mistress Bernard with anger.

Gaston approached upon learning that Daniel had just returned from the Chateau de Massac.

"You have seen the Baron, my brave?" he asked. "How is he, and what did he tell you?"

"Although still suffering from the gout, he is not in a bad state, Sire," replied the companion: "and if he had not been restrained, he would have come here, although he is still incapable of riding a horse.... The Baron was upset but not frightened by your arrest, and he did not doubt, as events proved, that you would be rapidly released. Moreover, he provided me with letters for you, the Governor and other persons in the city."

"Give them to me!" said Gaston immediately.

And he began reading those addressed to him.

Meanwhile, Esther addressed the traveler with vivacity:

"What did you mean, Daniel, when you said that you knew something about my father. Do not worry about admitting the truth, as nothing can be worse than the mortal anxiety with which we are living."

Thus pressed, the messenger recounted how, the previous night, a mysteriously closed litter escorted by numerous guards had furtively left the city and had taken the road to Jonzac.

"Afterwards," he continued, "Raby claimed that a mysterious lady was in the litter; but one could not count on the word of such a miscreant."

"Ah, companion," asked Mistress Bernard, "what does this stupid story have to do with my poor husband?"

But Esther had grasped the connection that had escaped Mistress Bernard.

"What! Daniel," she exclaimed with horror, "Could my father have really been in that litter?"

The companion nodded affirmatively.

Master de Maulévrier, in turn questioned Daniel. Massac interrupted his reading to listen.

"No, no, this supposition is absurd," resumed the Count, more concerned than he let on; "never would Master de Pons have permitted that Bernard Palissy be taken out of Saintes."

"But perhaps," said Gaston sadly, "they acted without his orders or his knowledge.... Ah! If the suspicions of this brave man are well founded, I doubly thank God that I have recovered my freedom of action!"

"So, Master de Massac," asked Esther, "you believe.... Oh! My God! What have they done with my father?"

"He is lost! We will never see him again!" exclaimed Mistress Bernard with desperation.

"Do not despair," resumed Massac, seeking to reassure himself. "Nothing is certain in Daniel's suppositions.... No matter! Maulévrier, we shall immediately go to the Governor."

Mathurin, who had not moved from his position at the window, stopped them.

"There is no need, Sires," he said. "Here is the Governor himself!"

Indeed, a minute later, Master de Pons entered the salon.

He had come on foot, unaccompanied. Although he was of a certain age, he had walked rapidly, and appeared upset. After having bowed to the Countess, he spoke to Massac:

"Delighted to see you, Gaston! I was told a short time ago that you were out of their grasp, and I am very pleased; but why did you not come right away to tell me? Actually," he continued in a somber tone, "you were right to not be bothered about a person without authority such as I; a person that one defies, a person that one humiliates, a person that… I might as well return my responsibilities to the King, for I am no longer Governor of Saintes and Saintonge."

At the same time, he let himself fall into an armchair, looking overwhelmed.

"Perhaps we understand," said Massac, "the cause of your legitimate anger…. It undoubtedly concerns the curtained litter, which, this past night, left the city under military escort?"

"What!" exclaimed Master de Pons, "You already know? Yes, in spite of my express wish, these audacious persons dared kidnap Bernard Palissy[30] during the night and sent him to Bordeaux."?

"To Bordeaux!" repeated Esther in a heartrending tone.

"So, it was true!" said Mistress Bernard covering her face with her hands.

The two gentlemen looked at them with consternation.

"Sire Governor," asked Gaston, "did the Royal Commissioner really push to this point his disdain of your power?"

"This morning, he came himself, with hypocritical deference, to inform me of his decisions. He announced that you, Massac, had been set free, and had already left with Maulévrier. As regards the Master potter, knowing my excessive indulgence, he took it upon himself to send Bernard to the Regional Tribunal…. It was already too late to chase after the prisoner and return him to Saintes."

There was a silence; all the women, even the Countess de Maulévrier, were shedding warm tears.

"What to do?" continued finally the Count. "In two days, perhaps tomorrow, if they travel day and night, Palissy will arrive in Bordeaux… and we know that the Parliament is cruelly expeditious with the Reformists!"

Nicolas, Bernard's second son, had rejoined the family and had exchanged a few words with his older brother. Mathurin brusquely said:

"Excuse me my good Lords; but would it not be possible to rescue our father during the trip? They could not travel rapidly as the roads are bad. My brother and I could leave immediately, and at the risk of our lives, we might

30 **Author Berthet's original note**; It is important to repeat that all these details regarding Palissy, and those that follow are historically based.

find the opportunity…"

"I will accompany you," interrupted Daniel; "I too would not regret dying for my excellent master."

"Morbleu!" exclaimed the Count with intensity, "I would also be capable of…"

"All this is folly," interrupted the Governor; "Moreover, do you think that I could approve of an act of violence against royal authority?"

"Actually," said Massac, 'it is not in this manner that Palissy can be returned to his family.… I have another plan."

"What is that?" asked Master de Pons.

"Do you know where the Royal Court is at this moment?"

"In Blois. Just yesterday I received a dispatch dated from there."

"Excellent. I will leave immediately and I will be in Blois the day after tomorrow in the evening. My horse will carry me without stopping to the Chateau de Massac, which is on the way. After having embraced my dear old father, I will take a coach and present myself at the Court. There I will certainly find my master, his Lordship the Constable of Montmorency, who has great esteem for Master Bernard, and who would intervene very warmly in his favor."

"But do you think that he will succeed, Gaston?" said Master de Pons dispiritedly. "You see that his safety has not been respected."

"He will address himself to the Queen-Mother, Catherine de Médicis, and faced with this authority, the members of Parliament can only bow down."

"The Queen Catherine is under the influence of the House of Guise and especially the Cardinal of Lorraine.… Will his tortuous politics allow him to place under his protection a famous Huguenot such as Bernard Palissy?"

"I hope so… and I plan to use a sure way."

"May God hear you.… However, even the Queen herself would not dare interrupt the course of justice; she can only pardon someone once a condemnation has been pronounced. However, when Palissy, who is surrounded by such determined and audacious enemies, is condemned, do you think that they will let him have the time to await a royal pardon?"

Cries of pain emanating from both Esther and her mother, greeted this terrible supposition.

"Excuse me, good ladies," said the Governor; "Should not Massac be made aware of the difficulties of his task?"

"And I am not discouraged by these difficulties," replied Gaston resolutely. "Esther, Mistress Bernard, do not despair.… You will see Palissy again, I promise you.… I swear it!"

The mother hugged him, as she would have one of her children, while Esther, taking one of his hands, covered it with kisses and tears. Gaston disengaged himself, embarrassed.

He felt the need to hasten his departure; but he had to wait for his horse, which had remained in the stables of the chateau and which the Governor, when he returned, would send him. Moreover, the Countess de Maulévrier would not let him leave without taking some food.

As they prepared to leave, Master de Pons made various arrangements with Massac and the Count. It was agreed that they would correspond and mutually forewarn each other of new developments.

"Above all, Sire Governor," added Gaston, "seek means by which to hamper the proceedings against the unfortunate Palissy.... Our tactic is to gain time."

"I understand, Massac; by God's cross, you can count on me to make things as difficult as possible for these judges in Bordeaux. I know several of them and I will write them today. I will delay the sending of documents, I will disperse possible witnesses, and I will create as many problems as possible.... However, believe me, my dear Gaston," added Master de Pons, lowering his voice, "Get things going rapidly there at the Court.... We are dealing with men who are daring, fanaticized, with few scruples, and they could be capable of..."

The dignified gentleman did not dare finish his phrase. He embraced Massac, and after having rapidly taken leave of the other participants, he returned to the chateau.

Less than an hour later, Gaston's horse, held by a lackey, was waiting at the door. The Count and his mother and the entire Palissy family surrounded the traveler. The latter, taking advantage of a moment when he found himself standing with Esther at the embrasure[31] of a window, said to her with emotion:

"Once again I will be leaving you and God knows when we will see each other again. Have you ever asked yourself, dear Esther, from where I find the zeal to serve you and yours?"

The young woman blushed.

"But, Master de Massac, your natural goodness... and then the admiration inspired in you by the character and talents of Master Bernard..."

"It is true that I love and admire Master Bernard; but it is not only for him that I act and endanger myself. I still think, with indescribable pleasure, Esther, about the night we, still children, were seated before your humble fireplace, and the touching abandon with which you fell asleep on my shoulder.... When I found you again recently, even more perfect and desirable than ever, this child's love became a serious and profound love that will only end with my life. This is what I wanted to tell you, Esther.... And you, do you not have a word to sustain my courage for the mission I must ac-

31 **Embrasure**, an opening in a wall which is beveled on the inside, typically around a window or a door.

complish?"

"Sire…" stammered the young girl, troubled.

"Esther, did you deceive me when you stated that you did not love pastor Hamelin?"

"Oh! No, no; I was only obeying the wishes of my family. No matter, perhaps this poor martyr… Master Gaston, what do you expect from me?"

"I love you, Esther, and I will be much stronger facing the hostilities and perils if I could hope…"

"For heaven's sake, what are you asking me?" answered the poor girl, beside herself. "Are you forgetting the obstacles that separate us? Even if I were not the daughter of an artisan, and you were not a rich gentleman of noble birth, the difference in our religions…"

"Two hearts truly bonded, would they be hindered by such obstacles? Esther, Esther, why do you not say, as you once did: *Save my father and I will love you!*"

"Ah! Gaston, what can I say that you do not already know?"

Esther lowered her head and sobbed. Mistress Bernard, who understood nothing of this scene, approached hurriedly.

"Master de Massac," she said, "for pity's sake, do not delay for the useless complaints of this little one.… Every moment lost may be irretrievable!"

"I am ready," exclaimed Gaston, whose features were radiant; "Esther has just redoubled my ardor for this battle and my confidence in our success."

"In the meantime," resumed Mistress Bernard, "we have decided to all go to Bordeaux where we have relatives.… The voyage via La Rochelle and then by sea, is easy, even for the children. There, perhaps they will let us see Bernard, and our presence will ease his grief."

This decision, in Gaston's opinion, had a number of drawbacks; but he reflected that the stay in Saintes no longer provided the Palissy family with much security, and they would be less visible in a large city. He finally approved their plan and received the necessary information to be able to find them in Bordeaux if necessary.

They wished to accompany him to the street entrance. In the hallway, which was rather dark like most hallways in homes of that period, he felt a feverish breath against his cheek and someone whispered in his ear:

"You will save him, will you not? You will save him… because I love you!"

He turned; a slight figure was disappearing in the shadows.

Gaston, after having dismissed the valet who had brought his horse, hoisted himself up onto the saddle. As he had to restrain with some effort his impatient mount, he attempted a last look at his dear Esther's eyes, a loud voice made itself heard behind him.

"One moment, one moment, Cavalier! By a fox's tail, does one leave in this manner forgetting one's appointments of honor? You have a short memory for a gentleman."

The person who spoke was none other than Captain Raby.

At the sight of the mercenary, the members of the household hurried inside and closed the door. As for Gaston, his eyes gave a flash of hate, and he spoke in a firm tone:

"I have forgotten nothing, Captain Raby, but affairs of the utmost importance do not permit me to address our differences at this moment. But do not worry; you will lose nothing by waiting.... I remain willingly in your path!"

He continued to retain his horse, which was pawing at the ground and chafing at the bit.

"Bah!" said Raby churlishly. "We know these excuses, my little flower. You are undoubtedly starting to regret challenging me; you cannot fool me this way. I demand that you face me now! If not...."

He attempted to seize the horse's bridle; Gaston, who was an excellent horseman, caused his mount to bolt, while striking the captain's face with his whip.

Raby swore and drew his sword; but Massac, even if he wanted to, could not restrain his horse, which, excited by the sound of the whip, left in a gallop.

XI.

THE QUEEN

The story has now taken us to the Chateau de Blois, in a sumptuous gallery that leads to the apartment of the Queen-Mother, Catherine de Médicis. At the end of this gallery, a half-opened door permitted a glimpse into the royal chambers, reserved for the most important Lords and private audiences. Elegant pages, Swiss guards and Scots dressed in splendid armor were standing guard on each side of this privileged area, assuring that no one crossed the threshold unless they had the right to this honor.

It was morning, and the gallery was crowded with people. In addition to the colorful group of courtesans, the high magistrates in their black robes, bishops in violet capelets, and cardinals in red robes, there were a number of these ladies-in-waiting, 'all *beautiful, all capable,*' as described by Brantôme [32] and which was referred to as '*the Queen's flying squadron.*' In the Court of the last Valois kings these women played an important role and maintained constant high spirits. In addition, although the young King, François II, was currently quite ill with the illness from which he was to die a few months later, there was neither meditation nor sadness in this assembly. Courtesans, grandes dames and ladies-in-waiting cackled, laughed loudly and as the language at that time was no more refined than the morals, one heard, here and there, certain expressions that could surprise in such a place.

An eminent personage had just entered the Queen's chambers, having received numerous signs of respect as he passed. The man was elderly, but tall, robust and with hard eyes that did not lower easily. He was dressed with military simplicity, although several Order necklaces, most enriched with diamonds, jingled at his neck, below his heavy collar. Several gentlemen in his suite had accompanied him to the gallery but stopped there and were mixing with the courtesans, while one, the youngest, undoubtedly a favorite, followed his master into the Queen's chamber.

A large and flat wooden container that the young man carefully carried under his arm especially aroused curiosity. What could be in the container?

32 **Pierre de Bourdeille, dit Brantôme**, (1537-1614) Writer known for his caustic descriptions of soldiers, courtesans and important persons of his time.

It took no more than this to excite the chatterbox women and frivolous courtesans that filled the gallery. They interrogated the members of the retinue in vain; these could, or would not, provide any clarification, so suppositions of all sorts followed. Furthermore, the doors of the royal chamber had not been fully closed, indicating that the private audience was not a secret one.

The personage being received that morning by the Queen Catherine was his Lordship Anne de Montmorency, Duke and Peer, Grand Constable of France, who has played an important role in this story. As regards the young gentleman who accompanied him, and who carried the mysterious container, as you have certainly guessed, was our friend Gaston de Massac, and the formal Court costume embroidered with gold, and velvet jerkin that replaced his travelling clothes did nothing to spoil his usual attractive appearance.

Catherine was not yet in the large and magnificent room which served as her reception chamber and they were assured that she was with the King who had spent a bad night. The Constable seated himself while awaiting her arrival, and Gaston, having deposited the container in a corner, placed himself behind his master, to be near to receive his orders, or simply to answer his questions.

Master de Montmorency, despite his rugged appearance, was feeling certain apprehensions about the difficulties of the task he was to accomplish. In order to help the reader understand these difficulties, we must provide some details about this famous individual and his position at the Court.

Anne de Montmorency, although an unhappy general, was a fearless soldier. Voltaire affirmed that he was an honest man who thought with grandeur, However, Brantôme describes him as miserly, superstitious, and cruel. He proved himself to be one of the most ruthless persecutors of the Huguenots, and it was told that while reciting the Lord's Prayer, he gave extermination orders of Protestants, from which came a local proverb that said 'keep you from the Pater Nostre of Master Constable.' More recently, during an expedition where he had destroyed a Calvinist church, the Parisians had dubbed him 'Captain Pew-Burner.'

At the time of which we speak, he was already in disgrace with the Court which was dominated by the Guise family; and since they hated the Protestants, it would seem that to regain his influence, the Constable would have to redouble his persecution of the Reformists. However, we have undoubtedly guessed the motive that brings him to the Queen. Eager to save the life of an artist of the first order, motivated by the explanations of his young secretary whom he greatly appreciated, and who he was seeing for the first time after a long absence, he was here to request the protection of Catherine in favor of Master Bernard Palissy.

His situation was therefore extremely embarrassing, and even perilous.

Could his intervention in such an affair be badly interpreted, either by the Queen, or by the Guises who would jump at any occasion to demolish him? Could his remaining credibility disappear if this action failed?

These reflections occupied Anne de Montmorency as he awaited his audience and his anxiety was reflected on his swarthy features. In a futile gesture, he withdrew an ivory beaded rosary from his pocket to distract his thoughts with prayer. He did not succeed and soon grasped the rosary while making a gesture of anger with himself.

None of all this escaped the notice of Massac. He had known his master for a long time, and had a power over him, which explained why his services and his devotion were so needed. He took advantage of the moment that the Constable seemed disposed to listen to say in a low voice:

"Please, reflect, my Lord, about the insult to you in using Master Bernard…. You should not suffer because these people in Bordeaux now take revenge for the punishment you imposed on them following their revolt after the salt tax. Not recognizing your rights, pillaging your property, as they did in Saintes, and imprisoning your servants, as they did me. And then, good God! If they did away with the talented artisan, Bernard, how could the Chateau d'Ecouan, which it is said will be one of the marvels of the kingdom, be completed?"

This reasoning was of a nature to produce a major impression on Montmorency's spirits; but at this moment the Constable was not in his usual frame of mind, and since he was known as the most foul-mouthed person of the Court, especially with inferiors, he brutally replied:

"May the Devil take you, Massac! Because I allow you certain liberties, you have become arrogant and smug with me! Who asked for your advice? Are you going to give me lessons all the way into the Queen's chambers? Sacrebleu! If we were in the field, I would have you hung from a tree, or impaled by my lancers, to teach you respect!"

Gaston took no offense at this rebuff, the terms of which would certainly have shocked a person of the current generation. Used to the rough language of the military, he saw it more as a jest and recognized its inanity. However, he took care not to laugh and replied with apparent respect:

"I pray, my Lord, to remember that these observations all came from him and that I have the humble duty to reflect these to him as a mirror reflects an image…. As far as hanging me or lancing me, it would be better to leave that task to Master de Lorraine and his people who will miss nothing if the illustrious Constable does not protect his servants…."

"You are right; these Guises plot against my authority and attack my honor…. But Morbleu!" continued the Constable in a new surge of anger, "do you think that my request to Queen Catherine is of a nature to help me regain her good graces? May the fires of hell consume those who launched me into this affair!"

"The Queen is not always against the Huguenots, my Lord, and perhaps... if needed, do not forget to use the means that we have agreed upon."

"Well! Again, that ridiculous idea!" replied Master de Montmorency, casting a side-glance towards the container; "Just because you have learned Latin, Massac, you think that you know more than those who are above you.... Well, we could put it to the test."

"So, my Lord, do not forget.... Actually, here comes the Queen now."

And Massac, after giving a deep bow, stepped backwards to the entrance of the gallery.

Indeed, the doors at the other end of the chamber had just opened. A lady approached rapidly, with an almost impatient stride, towards the Constable, who in turn, stepped respectfully forward to meet her. It was the Queen-Mother, Catherine de Médicis.

At that time, she was around forty years of age and although her features were blemished by grief, and the cares of her shrewd politics, and while her eyes had a feline vivacity that did not work in her favor, she retained certain traces of beauty. Her dress distinguished itself by its simplicity in the midst of the courtesans covered with gold and precious stones. Since the death of her husband, Henri II, who had caused her much heartbreak with blatant infidelities, she had not abandoned her mourning. However, she did not wear her mourning of white, as did earlier widowed queens, who were for this reason called the 'white queens.' She was dressed in a black velvet robe, bereft of jewelry; and her wide head covering almost hid her hair that was beginning to grey. In spite of this austerity, there was in her posture, her movements, her gaze, a true dignity.

She held her hand towards Master de Montmorency who brought it to his lips, and said, with a slight Italian accent:

"God protect you, *my compère!*"[33] (This was the manner she habitually called the Constable.) "You have been neglecting for some time your good *commère*.... However, if it had not been for a man of your merit and standing, I would not have agreed to leave the bedside of the King, my son, this morning.... He spent a terrible night and the pains in his head gave him no rest.... Moreover, Ruggieri,[34] my astrologer, has advised me that the influence of the celestial bodies is not favorable to me today, and I had not planned to leave my apartments."

The superstitious Queen had seated herself in a chair decorated with fleurs-de-lis that appeared to be her usual place, while the Constable remained standing before her.

---

33 *compère*: Person forming a duo with another. (*f*) *Commère*.
34 **Cosimo Ruggieri** (15??-1615) was an Italian astrologer, influential advisor to Queen Catherine Médicis and reputed master of the occult, black magic and witchcraft.

This initial exchange greatly embarrassed Anne de Montmorency, who felt that the moment had been badly chosen to present his request. However, he replied:

"The unfavorable influences that your Majesty, my royal commère, has mentioned, are easily explained by the suffering of the King, suffering which greatly distresses me...."

"Queen Marie[35] is with him at this moment," resumed Catherine, not without a jealous anxiety, "and my son always seems to feel better when she is there.... I am anxious to rejoin them.... My compère, Master Constable, what is it that you have to say to me?"

Anne de Montmorency was about to explain the reason for his visit, when Catherine noticed Gaston, who was standing in a humble attitude, near the door of the gallery.

"Santa Maria!" she said, while her dark eyes shot sparks, "and who is this one?"

"Nothing, less than nothing, Madam," the Constable hastened to reply. "One of my gentlemen, in whom I have total confidence and who accompanied me because his testimony may be useful to me."

"All right," replied the Queen, "I had taken him for some flower from the Court here to spy on us, and I would have had him ousted by the pages."

At the same time, she leaned back in her chair with an air of boredom.

The Constable briefly explained that he was there to request the intervention of the Queen in favor of an artisan named Bernard Palissy, who, in spite of the safeguards that he, the Constable, as well as several other notables, had granted, had been arrested as a Huguenot and taken to Bordeaux, where he most certainly would be condemned to death.

"Your Majesty knows," he continued, "if I favored the Reformists... but this one is one of those rare men for whom one must make an exception; like the sculptor, Jean Goujon, and your surgeon, Ambroise Paré,[36] for the glory of the King and the kingdom.... Moreover, Master Bernard, inventor of the *rustic figulines*, belongs to me, and it is an attack on my honor to touch him without my agreement."

As he continued to speak, the Queen sat up in her chair, and her face flushed, and her eyes flashed like those of a viper about to strike.

"What! Master Constable," she asked, barely containing herself, "Is it for this that you had me leave the bedside of an ailing King, and that I allowed the Queen Marie? Really! I thought this concerned some serious matter of State and you speak to me about a miserable Huguenot who I do not care about. These Huguenots disturb the Church and the kingdom, Master

35 **Queen Marie**, Marie Stuart, wife of François II.
36 **Ambroise Paré** (1510-1590) French barber surgeon who served in that role for kings Henry II, Francis II, Charles IX and Henry III. He is considered one of the fathers of surgery, and invented a number of surgical instruments.

Constable, and it is not for nothing that edicts were issued against their detestable doctrines…. Let justice run its course and uproot this heresy…. The Royal Commissioner of the Bordeaux Parliament has only acted upon my orders."

She arose as if to dismiss the petitioner.

Anne de Montmorency, although rarely timorous in character, remained disconcerted. His pride might perhaps not allow him to persist; but an eloquent look from Gaston decided him to make one more attempt.

"I once again beg the Queen," he resumed, "to take into consideration that my dignity, the dignity of the Constable of France, would be compromised if one could, with impunity, abuse a person who belongs to him…. Furthermore, your Majesty undoubtedly knows of Master Palissy, the inventor of *rustic figulines*? He is a marvelous worker; sculptor, master glazier, painter and potter; he has all the talents."

"Yes… no," replied Catherine, annoyed and impatient; "I believe that I have heard speak of his *rustic figulines*, but your French artisans do nothing of interest."

"In that case," resumed Montmorency immediately, "my clerk can satisfy the curiosity of your Majesty…. Massac, show the Queen what you have brought."

Gaston hastened to open the wooden container from which he withdrew a large enameled dish; then he approached, and placing one knee on the ground, presented the dish to the Queen.

Catherine, astonished, first looked distractedly; but soon her gaze became focused and reflected an enthusiastic admiration.

"Santa Madona!" she exclaimed. "Now here is something of beauty!"

She took the dish from Gaston's hands, placed it near the window on a table decorated with Florentine mosaic, and studied it at length.

This enameled pottery, which we will try to describe, was a tableau in itself.

On a base of red sand, sprinkled with shellfish, snaked a bluish stream where played small perch with golden fins and brown crayfish with their powerful pincers. In the center, sprawled with gracious sinuosity, lay a grey serpent that seemed alive, so supple and sinuous was its body. On the large borders of the platter were lovely green frogs with fiery eyes, and slender lizards that seemed to be chasing after flies and butterflies. A large number of plants were reproduced with a striking accuracy that would delight a botanist. All these together formed a charming tangle. In the river; watercress and aquatic moss; on the bank, one recognizes fern, betony, germander and an oak tree branch with its acorns, a strawberry plant, maidenhair and celandine with its yellow flowers. And all this; sand, shellfish, crayfish, reptiles, flowered plants, are all fresh and glistening, as if wet; the animals living and swarming in the greenery; one has the impression of smelling the odor of the aromatic plants and sensing the freshness of the early morning flow of water.[37]

The Constable and Massac left the Queen to her contemplation. Now a smile was on her lips, her eyes sparkled with pleasure. With each detail that she discovered in this harmonious work, she gave a little cry, with the joy of a child. She had forgotten, in this moment, that she was Queen of France; She was no longer thinking of the suffering, the jealousies, and the anger that she had felt a few moments earlier. The emotion of art absorbed her completely. She only remembered that she was born in Florence and that she was a descendant of the Médicis, whose name was linked to all the artistic splendors of the Renaissance, and that the family instinct had just been awakened in her.

Master de Montmorency and his young secretary, respecting, as we have said, this admiration, which was taking proportions of ecstasy, remained silently aside. Catherine suddenly turned towards them and impetuously exclaimed:

"Who has done this? It is surely not a Frenchman! I recognize the refined and meticulous art of my dear Florence.... My ancestor, Lorenzo the Magnificent, would have swooned with pleasure at the sight of this marvel. Yes, yes, this is certainly a Florentine piece, and I would wager that it is the work of our Lucca della Robbia!"[38]

"With your permission, Madam," replied the Constable, smiling, "this dish is a *rustic figuline*, and was created by my retainer, Bernard Palissy. I already own much pottery of this type, and Master de Massac, who has visited Saintes a number of times, has seen him produce these."

Catherine looked at Gaston absent mindedly.

"And if her Majesty permits," resumed Massac, bowing, "I would dare tell her that Master Bernard Palissy is a humble worker, who, by his energy, his high intelligence, his immense knowledge, through labor, sacrifice and research, has created the new art form of which she is admiring the results."

"But then," exclaimed the Queen warmly, "Bernard Palissy is a genius who will be able to illustrate the reign of my sons.... My ancestors would have ennobled him and lavished him with wealth.... Did you not tell me that he was in prison and condemned to death by those fanatics of the Bordeaux parliament?"

"He is not yet condemned, Madam," replied the Constable, "but indeed

37 **Author Berthet's original note**: Palissy's dish, that we have just described, is the twin of one of the most beautiful Palissy pieces in the Louvre (n°136) and was owned by the author of this novel (*but now handed down to his great-great-grandson, translator of this work*).

38 **Luca della Robbia** (1399–1482) Italian sculptor from Florence. Della Robbia was noted for his colorful, tin-glazed terracotta statuary, a technique that he invented.

he is imprisoned in Bordeaux."

"What a shame," said the Queen with irritation, "that so many persons with talent and knowledge become Huguenots.... No matter," she continued resolutely; "we must get him out of there as rapidly as possible.... But how should I go about it, my dear compère? Saint Virgin! I will not permit an artist who can produce such beautiful works to be burned or hanged!"

And she returned to her loving contemplation of the dish.

Montmorency and his young secretary exchanged a look of triumph. The Constable then tried to make Catherine understand that the release of the prisoner presented inextricable difficulties. On one hand, one could not remove Bernard from the jurisdiction of the Parliament before he has been judged, and the Parliament felt very strongly about its prerogatives. On the other hand, even when Palissy has been judged, that is to say condemned, the King had renounced by edict in 1559, the privilege of pardoning those condemned for reason of religion; and should the Queen be disposed to transgress this edict, the tribunal would certainly hasten to execute the sentence without giving time for the grace to arrive.

Catherine, while listening to these explanations, became pensive and raised an eyebrow.

"Now this," she resumed with bitterness, "is what the policies of Master Guise and his brother, the Cardinal, have reduced us to! The King, himself, does not have the power to pardon a subject who, like Master Bernard, could become one of the glories of the kingdom! Well! My compère, there must be some way to rescue this poor man from the fate that awaits him."

"I only see one, Madam."

"What is it?"

"If Master Bernard Palissy, thanks to some function, belonged to the Royal household; he would escape the jurisdiction of the Bordeaux parliament, and would become inviolable to all."

"But I could not ask for better than having him attached to me!" exclaimed the Queen. "This method is easy and absolutely sure.... Well! Master Constable, Bernard Palissy was in your service; now he is in the service of the King. He had the title of 'inventor of the *rustic figulines* for the Constable.' He will now take that of 'inventor of the *rustic figulines* for the King *and* the Constable.' In addition, I hereby name him Governor of the gardens and Chateau of the Tuileries, that I am having built in Paris, behind the Louvre... We will send the decree this very day."

Upon learning of the eminent position to which Queen Catherine was elevating Master Bernard, the Constable initially had one thought; it was that now Palissy would now be filling the royal chateaux with his masterpieces in preference to the Chateau, d'Ecouen, and his ego as an art collector was seriously bruised. On the other hand, Gaston de Massac felt an overwhelming joy and had difficulty in restraining his excitement. He was about to fall at the feet of the Queen to thank her for this act of justice, and it took a personal effort to remain silent and in his place.

Anne de Montmorency, having surmounted his secret discontent, also wished to thank Catherine for the favors that she was granting his protégé, Bernard. The Queen interrupted:

"Now, now, my dear compère," she said, with a malicious smile, "it is I that gain the most in this affair, and my new Governor of the Tuileries will produce wonders.... But it is time for me to return to the King.... Master Constable, please see to it that the orders be sent with minimum delay. For this, see the Chancellor, Master de l'Hospital. Perhaps," she added, giving to her smile an expression even more subtle; "he may not be too difficult about a Huguenot.... There is not a minute to lose, as these gentlemen of the Bordeaux tribunal do not play around. I learned from a message received this morning that they have just condemned to the gallows with immediate execution a Reformist minister named Hamelin."

"Hamelin!" murmured Gaston, who could not help reacting with a heavy heart.

Catherine was anxious to leave; however, she could not take her eyes off the enameled dish that had remained on the table.

"Truly," she said with a timidity that was unusual for her, "I would like to show this faïence to the poor ailing King.... It will distract him for a moment... and the Princes, his brothers, will be amused as well."

"Madam," replied the Constable bowing, "such a trifle is hardly worthy to be offered to my royal commère. However, if Your Majesty..."

"I accept, Master Constable. I accept and I thank you.... Yes, I am certain that those lovely green lizards and cute frogs will amuse the King who is so bored in his bed,[39] and I will bring them to him without delay."

At the same time, Catherine carefully picked up the dish.

"Madam," said Montmorency, "if you permit, my gentleman will call a lackey...."

"Yes, so that one of those oafs, with his large ugly hands, breaks my superb piece.... Farewell, my compère and friend."

She then left with her light burden for the interior of her apartments, while the most important Lords waited vainly to be admitted, in their turn, for an audience.

The Constable and his secretary encountered certain difficulties in disengaging themselves from the crowd in the gallery. Members of the Court, both men and women, who wished to present requests, halted Anne de Montmorency after almost every step. Gaston, himself, had to deal with the coaxing of certain lovely and inquisitive ladies who absolutely wanted

39 **Author Berthet's original note:** It is known that François II was only 16 years old.

to know what he had carried in the container. Finally, the suite, having succeeded in regrouping, left the palace.

"Sacrebleu! Massac," said Montmorency, when they were able to chat freely, "You are sometimes right.... Without your excellent idea of showing the Queen a *rustic figuline*, I believe, may God damn me, that our poor Bernard, now Governor of the Tuileries, would have remained in great difficulty."

"As I was telling you, my Lord, the Queen may well have a dislike of the Huguenots, but she is a Médici, and the love of the arts is innate in the illustrious family.... Nevertheless, Palissy is not yet saved; we will have to suffer the slowness of the Chancellery in expedition of the orders, and it is far from here to Bordeaux. The impatient zeal of the judges of the Tribunal worries me; that unfortunate Hamelin, whose execution we just learned, left Saintes only a few days before Bernard Palissy, and you can see how much activity was put into his trial."

"Bah! Bah!" replied the Constable, with a loud laugh "Those damned Bordeaux people will think twice before acting against a person that I protect.... They will remember that when they revolted, I entered their city by a breach in their wall and had hanged more than a hundred of them.... God's blood! They know what to expect if one attacks the Constable!"

"Perhaps, my Lord," replied Massac, shaking his head, "will they not be even more relentless against your retainer.... Ah! How I wish that Bernard was out of their hands!"

XII.

THE CHAMBRE ARDENTE[40]

Bordeaux, which is today one of the largest, most beautiful and richest cities in France, was, in the sixteenth century, one of the most cramped, ugly and sad. Its magnificent wharves did not yet exist and ships were obliged to unload their cargo onto a muddy shore. It was surrounded by a wall and moats; furthermore, where exists today the magnificent Place des Quinconces, there was a vast and somber fortress named the Chateau *Tropeite,* and later, *Trompette,* that Charles VII had built to protect the city against the English. At the other extremity of Bordeaux, on the site now occupied by a large hospital, was a second fortress, constructed for the same reason, and named the Chateau de Ha. Between these two chateaux, each bristling with towers, ramparts, and turrets, were intertwined a thousand small streets that were tortuous, dark and cluttered with rubbish. These streets were inhabited by tumultuous populations where every day brawls exploded that were often quite bloody.

At the time of this story, these brawls were not due to hot southern blood, but more especially to the hatred generated by differences in religion. The Reformation movement had made great progress in Bordeaux. Accounts of that time state that there were seven or eight thousand Huguenots, secret or avowed, out of what was then a relatively small population. It was to fight against this new sect that the Parliament adopted methods of such incredible harshness. Each hour saw a new condemnation, that is to say an execution, as the execution immediately followed the verdict.

The Tribunal held its daily sessions in the Chateau Trompette and it was also in its courtyard that the sentences were executed. However, the modern principle that 'justice must be implemented in public' was not accepted at that time. It was very rare that the public was given access to the audiences in the chambers of justice, and only certain privileged individuals found room in the cramped galleries. In compensation, the spectacle of the execution was allowed to all comers as *'the good example'* and to make a lasting

---

40 **The Chambre Ardente** (burning chamber) also known as the 'Tribune of Final Judgement,' was an extraordinary court of justice in medieval France, mainly held for the trial of heretics.

impression. The crowds were free to witness the exploits of the executioner.

Yet, on a day that a Tribunal session was scheduled, no tools of execution had been prepared in the outer courtyard as a number of loafers and curious individuals stationed themselves in front of the fortifications guarding the main entrance of the Chateau Trompette. The drawbridge had been lowered, but archers were stationed under the first arch and only allowed those with good reason to enter the interior of the fortress. Occasionally, one saw some councilor in a red robe, arrive mounted on a mule, and followed by a lackey; immediately, the guards presented arms to greet the magistrate with military honors. The humblest employees were allowed to enter if they could properly identify themselves. As concerns those who were stopped at the entryway, among which were certainly persons simply interested in knowing what was going on inside, their solicitations were not listened to, and if they became too insistent, they would be pushed away by the guards with the handle of their spikes.

Such was undoubtedly the situation of a group of persons standing on the opposite side of the moat and who appeared to be lamenting their failure to gain admission to the chateau. This group included a small and wizened old man with a worried look who appeared to be a bourgeois from Bordeaux; then a charming young girl, in spite of her dark dress and linen cap; finally, two young fellows, the older of whom could not be more than eighteen years old. They were all speaking in low voices, and the young girl, her eyes brimming with tears, was saying in desperation:

"Uncle Balbein, they do not want to let us enter. However, I have the feeling that something horrible is about to happen behind those old walls.... Therefore, we must bring to their attention the letters of recommendation that we were given for certain important persons in Bordeaux. With these, we will undoubtedly obtain the right to enter the prison or at least attend the trial."

Uncle Balbein, who was one of those cringing persons that can be found at all times and in all countries, hastened to interrupt:

"Hush! Hush! My niece," he said. "Let us not speak about these letters because those who wrote them were seriously imprudent. They did not realize the state of crisis in which our poor city finds itself. If it became known who you are, it would be the end for all of you... and for me who gave you sanctuary in my home. We will see later; What the Devil! You only arrived yesterday evening! There has not been any time lost, I imagine."

"I want so badly to see my father again!"

"Patience! then, patience! I promised you, you and your brothers, to get you into the chateau; I will keep my promise, if you let me handle things. Indeed, it is time for the hearing, so some of my contacts will soon arrive...."

"But, uncle Balbein, several judges in red robes passed by and you did not speak to them!"

"Well! Would a simple tailor such as I dare address a councilor of Parliament and presidents with their mortar boards?"

"Uncle Balbein," said the younger of the two boys, "would you like me to try to slip between the legs of the archers when they are not looking?"

"And I," said the elder, "I am willing to shove around one or two of them to enter by force."

"No, no, do not move," said the poor uncle Balbein wiping his brow that was dripping with perspiration; "good heavens, these are real devils, and they will get me killed!"

One has undoubtedly guessed that the young girl and the two young boys who were creating so many concerns for the old tailor, were Esther and Palissy's two eldest sons.

The Palissy family had experienced delays during the trip from Saintes to Bordeaux, the capital of Guyenne, such that they had only arrived the previous evening. However, Bernard had been there for over ten days and there was much to fear that he would be tried in the very near future. To make matters worse, the long crossing had exhausted the travelers; the mother was suffering from a violent fever and the younger children were feeling more or less sick when they finally arrived at the home of Balbein, who, along with his family, received them with great cordiality.

The very next morning, although the mother was incapable of getting up, Esther and the older sons wanted to address the objective of their voyage.... But when the tailor and his family, who were timid Huguenots, learned of the intentions of the newcomers to make themselves known as the wife and children of Master Bernard, they became excessively alarmed. According to them, the wife and children could not avoid being arrested as accomplices to heresy, and in reality, due to the violent passions that perturbed the city of Bordeaux, these fears had certain foundations. For the same reason, Balbein, as we know, did not think it prudent to deliver to the addressees the letters of recommendation provided by Maulévrier and the Governor of Saintes to the Palissy family, and he first wanted to obtain certain information. However, giving in to the requests of his niece and nephews, he committed to getting them into the chamber where the Parliament held its sessions; we have seen the difficulties he felt in accomplishing this mission.

The tailor, therefore, began to regret having made such a promise, and was looking around anxiously, when he saw, headed towards the entrance, a big fellow, with dry yellow skin, dressed in black, with a worn jerkin and a short jacket on his shoulder. He carried a stack of papers and was walking, nose in the air, with the confidence often exhibited by the humblest of functionaries.

Upon seeing him, Balbein could not hold back a sigh of relief.

"Look!" What did I tell you?" he continued, "Master Leufroy will certainly grant us his protection."

"And who is Master Leufroy?" asked Esther.

"A man well placed, who has some friendship for me. He is the wax-warmer at the Parliament chancellery, responsible for affixing the seals on all the judicial documents.... an important role, as you see."

Esther did not understand the importance of the role of Master Leufroy; but since her uncle affirmed this fact, she had no reason to doubt it, and they approached the powerful wax-warmer. Balbein addressed him with humility.

"Master Leufroy," he said, bowing to the ground, "will you not allow me to inform myself about your precious health?"

The functionary stopped and answered in a haughty tone:

"Ah! It is you Master Balbein? I did not see you.... We have so much work today. The president and I are under great pressure; those damn Huguenots will make us lose our minds.... But we will pursue them to the end."

"And you would be right," replied the tailor with some embarrassment; "Here are my nephews and my niece who have arrived from the countryside and who are burning with envy to attend a session of Parliament; could you, you with all your influence, help us to obtain this favor?"

"Undoubtedly, I can, Master Balbein. Who could, if not me? Where would be the procedural acts, the sentences and the writs of execution if they did not go through my hands?... Yes, it is easy for me to have you enter the *lanterns*[41] but listen my friend," continued the wax-warmer lowering his voice, "I have to tell you one thing: certain persons claim that '*you have a bad religious odo*r,' and if your relatives were not better Catholics..."

"Saint Virgin!" said the tailor becoming pale, "is it allowed to speak of an honest man in this manner? How is it that you, who know me so well, did not close the mouths of these slanderers? Be so good as to accept a dinner in my home next Sunday, my worthy Sire; you will drink some of that Grave wine that you like so much, and I will explain..."

"Well, after all, this is empty talk," resumed Leufroy, "and does not merit any notice.... Never mind! We will chat about this next Sunday.... As for having you attend the audience at the Tribunal, nothing easier for you and your niece, but as for the two youngsters, it is another matter.... Introducing four persons at the same time into the *lanterns*, no one has that authority, not even the Chancellor, or the chief prosecutor!"

"Uncle," Esther said with some eagerness, "let us enter.... My brothers will wait here."

She spoke in a low voice to the two youngsters. Mathurin and Nicolas, though very annoyed, gave in to this necessity, and sat themselves down on

41 *The lanterns*, A special gallery allowing privileged individuals to witness trials in the Chateau Trompette. It is described in detail later in this chapter.

the edge of the moat, while Balbein and Esther left with Leufroy.

The latter was strutting with conceit.

"What I am doing is for you Master Balbein," he resumed; "I have always wanted the best for you, and except for a reason of heresy, you can always count on my protection.... And then," he added, giving Esther a smile, which was not much more than an ugly grimace, "you have there a niece who merits consideration... a very pretty girl.... Take my arm, little one.... I will introduce you to this house; as you will see, in the court of justice, I am home."

Esther, who was trembling slightly, placed her hand on the worn sleeve of the glorious functionary and they presented themselves before the guards at the door. Leufroy, indeed, only had to say one word, and the guards allowed him to pass with the two persons who accompanied him.

They crossed the drawbridge, passed through another archway and finally arrived at an interior courtyard which was quite vast but surrounded by buildings that were so high that the sun penetrated only an hour or two each day. Grass was growing between the flagstones and the base of the walls was eroded by saltpeter. Several persons from justice and some soldiers seemed to be wandering around aimlessly.

Esther, upon entering this courtyard, felt as though a mantle of ice had dropped on her shoulders. The windows in the buildings were narrow and had protective grills that made them look like prisons; the doors were equipped with enormous ironwork like the doors of a dungeon.

However, what really made the poor girl shudder was the sight, directly in front of her, of gallows, equipped with ladder, rope, and noose all ready for immediate use. Tears came to her eyes as she thought about this gibbet, which had perhaps been used on poor Hamelin, of whose death she had just learned, and she rapidly turned her head.

Then, her gaze fell on an apparatus with a strange shape that stood at a strange angle in the courtyard. This machine consisted of a long wooden beam, one end of which was equipped with an iron plate and heavy chains. This was balanced, at its mid-point, on a second beam which was planted in the ground in such a manner that the metal-tipped end could move up and down in a rocking movement. Underneath the end equipped with heavy chains were two sinister looking men who were at this moment preparing for an execution at the stake with wood, tar and sulfur.

Esther contemplated this machine whose use she did not understand with an astonished air. Leufroy saw her surprise and said, laughing:

"Aha! My lovely little one, you do not know what this toy is? It is an *estrapade*,[42] and it is used to burn those condemned to a slow death.... See, one attaches the condemned to the chain and lift him in the air; then one

42 *estrapade,* (Author Berthet's original note) an apparatus of this type once existed in Paris, and the spot where it was located is still called *Place de l'Estrapade.*

lights the stake and when the flames are intense, the patient is dropped into it. Then he is lifted up, and dropped again, and the process is repeated until death ensues.… It is ingenious, is it not? We call this *giving an estrapade.*"

Poor Esther almost fainted and hid her face in her hands. Balbein himself turned away in horror. These reactions only served to increase the wax-warmer's joviality.

"Ah," he said, "you are not accustomed, like us magistrates.… But I see from these preparations that there is a need for it today.… Let us hasten, duty calls. I wager that the president has already said a number of times: '*Where is Master Leufroy?*'"

The old tailor began to really regret having brought his niece to the Chateau Trompette. His distress, and Esther's as well, increased further, when a bearded man approached. He had a dreadful face and wore worn red clothing. It was the executioner.

He bowed to them, but feebly because it was rare that anyone bowed back, and besides, he did not really care.

"You are late, Leufroy," he said in a gravelly voice; "those gentlemen are already in their seats.… Nothing is advancing today.… However, I am ready, and they can let the populace enter when necessary."

"Good, good.… So, Master, we have an important case this morning?"

"I believe so, a noted Huguenot! But we have big affairs every day. I and my assistants, we barely have time to go and have a drink."

And grumbling, he went off to rejoin the persons who were preparing the stake under the estrapade.

"In truth," said Leufroy to his companions, "things advance slowly when I am not there.… Come quickly."

Esther and Balbein followed him automatically. He headed, at a rapid pace, into a new vaulted passageway and they plunged into a labyrinth of dark galleries and spiral stairways where reigned a deathly silence. At the far end of a Gothic corridor illuminated by slits in the wall in the form of crosses, they came to a small door that was ajar and that the wax-warmer pushed open without hesitation.

"Enter," he said in a low voice, "This will be perfect for you. Above all, be careful to not disturb the hearing! I will come to get you later."

Without waiting for a reply, he moved away and soon disappeared into the vast edifice which had no secrets for him.

Left alone, Esther and her uncle hesitated to enter this rather dark gallery, and one could barely see three or four other persons who had also obtained the favor of observing the session. The front of the loggia was open, permitting one to see the great light from the torches and to hear the murmur of voices which indicated a large number of persons below.

Esther, after a moment of hesitation, finally decided to move forward, and supported by the arm of her uncle, took a seat on a bench.

The gallery, on a wooden framework, was built near the top of two masonry pillars that supported the dome of an immense chamber. Its name of the *lanterns* came from a skylight that should have covered it on one side; but either it no longer existed, or it had never been built, and one could look down directly onto the chamber beneath the loggia. There exist *lanterns* of this type at the Paris parliament, and it was there that seats were reserved for privileged public to the Supreme Court.

Esther leaned over the railing, but immediately drew back, startled and horrified by what she had just seen. The setup for a court of justice for heretics was both imposing and frightening. At later times, they liberated themselves from the ceremonial aspects in use for these exceptional tribunals, designed to strike the imagination, but the Bordeaux Parliament's tribunal maintained the lugubrious pomp of the original institution.

The chamber did not have a single window or any other opening that permitted daylight to enter; one could have imagined being underground. The walls and the pillars that supported the dome were draped in black; also black were the benches, seats and table covers. A considerable number of candles and lanterns that gave off a smoky red flame burned as if around a catafalque, giving off a suffocating heat and foul odors.

The judges and the judicial staff that composed the tribunals were obliged to spend a number of consecutive hours in this sort of hell, and perhaps their own discomfort contributed to making them more aggressive and harsh with the accused. On the rostrum, one saw six councilors and a president in red robes bordered with ermine. The president wore on his head a velvet cap called a *mortar*, which was decorated with gold braid. The chief prosecutor, on his black chair, also wore a red robe. At the back of the chamber were the bailiffs armed with silver canes, archers and jailers charged with keeping watch over the accused. All this, men and objects, the black drapes, the red robes, the lighting, and the soldiers with their gleaming weapons, formed an image that was both singular and terrifying in character.

Understandably, poor Esther was initially stunned, but recovering her composure, gathered her courage and once again leaned over the railing. Moreover, someone was speaking directly below her and the president was questioning a person that she had not yet noticed since he was completely surrounded by guards. An outburst of voices made her shudder and, trembling, she became attentive.

The accused was a tall man, whose face was noble and intelligent, but had become cruelly pale from his stay in the dungeon. Nevertheless, his look was full of confidence, his voice strong, his bearing straight and he was easy to recognize. The hazards of chance had played their role; the person appearing before this terrible court of justice known as the '*Chambre Ar-*

dente' was Bernard Palissy.

The poor child let out a feeble cry, and standing, her arms outstretched, she appeared to want to speak. Balbein, who had kept an eye on her movements, and who had also just recognized Bernard, pulled her rapidly back and whispered in her ear:

"Keep quiet, for heaven's sake! Keep quiet!…or we are finished!"

Esther, for several minutes, was absolutely incapable of taking any action. She had fallen back on her bench and would have rolled on the ground if her uncle had not supported her. Further, her outcry did not seem to have reached the chamber. Only the persons who occupied the gallery with her were touched by it; but soon, absorbed by the events below, they forgot the incident

When the old tailor felt that Esther had recovered both her strength and her awareness, he hurried to speak to her again:

"If it is not for yourself, my niece, it must be for your mother, for your brothers, for the family…. We are lost if you do not learn to control yourself!"

"Esther straightened herself with an energetic movement.

"Uncle," she murmured, "I will be quiet, even if it kills me!"

And she placed her elbows on the railing, while biting on her handkerchief, to ensure that nature not betray her will.

What was happening in the chamber demanded her full attention. The president had just asked Bernard a question and he replied with dignity, but without boastfulness:

"It is useless, Sire, to utilize finesse of language or complicated questions to make me confess the truth. I am a simple artisan, but I cannot lie. I therefore admit, what I never sought to hide, that I am a member of the Reformist religion, and that I wish to live, and die, in this faith."

A stirring of the assembly greeted this avowal.

"Therefore," said the president with indignation, "you share the doctrines of this ungodly sect that in its clandestine meetings commit abominations and sacrilegious acts?"

"In our meetings, Sire, there are neither abominations, nor sacrilegious acts," replied Bernard. "We are indeed obliged to hide, since the practice of our religion is banned in public. But we restrict ourselves to the singing of psalms, and to encouraging each other in the love of God and Godliness…. As for myself, I do my best to serve the All-Powerful, and I respect the faith of others, as long as it is sincere and profound, even if it is contrary to my own."

In spite of the reluctance of the judges, this modest language seemed to produce a certain effect on them. The president hastened to resume:

"Finally, Bernard Palissy, you admit guilt to the monstrous crime of which you are accused?"

"I am a Huguenot, Sire."

From that moment onward, Master Bernard was condemned. However, the president wished to show moderation.

"I have been assured," he resumed, "that you have been living the life of an honest man, in spite of your heresy, and that you are a capable artisan whose works have often attracted the admiration of persons of quality.... Come now, can you provide us with any reason for indulgence.... You have nothing to say to lessen your crime?"

"Nothing, Sire, except that I belong to his Lordship the Constable of Montmorency. This Lord had placed me under his protection, which has not been taken into consideration; but I know that he is asking for me and that he will be extremely distressed to lose me."

Of all the excuses that Master Bernard could have put forward, none could have been worse. During a revolt that had taken place some years earlier in Bordeaux, a conflict had arisen between Master de Montmorency and the president of this very tribunal. The man in robes having had to incline himself before the man of the sword, he had retained a profound grudge. Therefore, he said impatiently:

"Master Constable has nothing to do with a court of justice of the Bordeaux Parliament, although as a Duke and Peer, he can sit with the Parliament in Paris. I do not have to worry about what pleases him."

He resumed after a short pause:

"Is that all that you have to say?"

"I would add only this, Sire," replied Palissy, whose voice had become less steady. "I am father to a large family, and if on my part I am ready to sacrifice my existence, this existence is precious to my dear wife and my poor children."

A reaction, sympathetic this time, was felt in the audience, and Esther could not suppress a sob, but the president made an imperious gesture.

"That suffices," he said. "Bernard Palissy admits that he is guilty of the odious crimes of sorcery and evil spells for which we have reason to reproach his infamous sect.... The matter is settled."

He arose, and leaning successively towards each of the councilors, he gathered their votes. Some pronounced a few words in a low voice; others simply touched their *mortar* to signify agreement. In any case, all seemed to be of the same opinion.

During this deliberation, which lasted only a few minutes, a profound silence had fallen on the chamber. One could distinctly hear the crackle of the flames of the candles and the lanterns. The observers held their breaths and wondered what horrible ordeal the judges would invent against such a hardened criminal. Finally, the president sat down, placed his mortar on his head, and opened his mouth to pronounce the sentence.

At that moment, a muffled sound came from outside. A door, hidden behind some draperies, opened suddenly and a flood of white light penetrated the chamber. A gentleman, covered with dust, wearing boots with spurs that were bloody, as though he had ridden a horse a long way, entered without hesitation, and exclaimed, while waving over his head a letter containing large wax seals:

"Orders from the King and the Queen-Mother…. Urgent orders for the president of the *Chambre Ardente* of Bordeaux!"

This unexpected event generated a general stupor over the audience and the judges. Esther, at the sight of the royal messenger, seemed to revive; she cried out without worrying about being heard:

"Thank God! It is Master de Massac! My father is saved."

It was indeed Gaston, who, realizing the jeopardy to which Bernard Palissy was exposed, only trusted to himself the task of bringing the dispatch, and arrived in Blois without setting foot on the ground.

The president had promptly recovered from his surprise. He demanded in a haughty tone:

"What is this, who dares disturb in this manner a court of justice? Archers, do your duty."

"Not one of you move!" said Massac forcefully, "or he will make himself guilty of the crime of lese majesty[43] and will be punished by death…. What I am doing, Sires, I am authorized to do. I have been instructed, at whatever hour or the day or night that I arrive in Bordeaux, to demand that immediately be remanded to me '*the honorable person, Master Bernard Palissy, inventor of the rustic figulines, Governor of the royal chateau and gardens of the Tuileries in Paris.*' Here is the edict. "

Mounting the platform of the tribunal, he presented the president with the letter that he had brought, and which was addressed by the Queen using the common formula: '*To the persons of our Bordeaux Parliament.*'

The president took it and made a sign to his councilors to have them read it with him. Nothing could describe the agitation caused by its contents. The order was clear and precise; it was signed by the Queen-Mother Regent, and countersigned by Michel de l'Hospital, Grand Chancellor of France. It had to be obeyed or be accused of treason.

However, one would have to know very little about the spirit of opposition and chicanery which parliaments prided themselves in at that time, to think that Bernard's judges would comply without a struggle. The president soon resumed, but in a honeyed tone which contrasted with his previous arrogance:

"Very well, Sire. The *Chambre Ardente* fully respects the royal will, but

---

43 **lese majesty**, a crime (such as treason) committed against a sovereign power.

there is one issue that must take precedent over that will; it is the law. However, it is certain that Bernard Palissy, the Huguenot, who appears before us at this time, belongs to Master de Montmorency. In spite of the qualifications that he is credited with in this edict, aforementioned Bernard is not attached to a royal person. Consequently, the intervention of the sovereign power is contrary to edicts and statutory regulations."

"He belongs to the King, Sires. I repeat, he is named to the responsibilities and activities mentioned in the dispatch, and therefore escapes from your jurisdiction.... Here are the letters patent."[44]

And he showed the president the parchment that named Bernard to the government of the Tuileries.

This new document was minutely examined, and the members of the Tribunal consulted again. Finally, the president resumed in a low voice, visibly annoyed:

"These acts are in good and due form; it only remains for us to obey.... What will the Councilor-Commissioner say?"

He added forcefully:

"The General Prosecutor for the Parliament has the floor, so that he may be heard regarding his indictments."

The General Prosecutor arose to ask that suspension of sentence be declared and that the accused be released after the King's orders had been recorded in the registers.

During the accomplishment of the judicial formalities, Gaston, who did not doubt the results, approached Bernard and hugged him, without the guards daring to oppose him.

"My dear Palissy, my wishes have been fulfilled.... I arrived in time!"

Master Bernard, despite his fortitude, remained dumbfounded and thought that he was in a dream.

"Master de Massac," he asked, "is this all possible? My concerns about my family, did they affect my mind? The edict from the King, a responsibility at the Court, unbelievable and overwhelming favors...."

"All this is real, Master Bernard; not only is your life spared and your liberty reinstated, but you are called to Paris.... You will be housed in the Chateau des Tuileries, owned by the Queen-Mother and she wishes to entrust you with important tasks. The most important Lords of the Court and the young King himself are all impatient to see the inventor of the *rustic figulines*."

Bernard said nothing, but his lips were moving and one could think that he was thanking God silently.

He seemed to be hardly listening when the president pronounced a de-

44 **letter patent,** Legal instrument in the form of a published written order issued by a monarch, president or other head of state which generally grants a status to a person.

cree that freed him from all charges and ordered that he be turned over immediately to the messenger of the King, Gaston de Massac. However, there was some agitation in the *lantern* that was over their heads, and a voice exclaimed:

"My father! My dear father, you have been returned to me!"

The face, pale but glowing, of Esther Palissy appeared above the railing, and two arms were reaching towards Bernard.

The president was too irritated to pardon this infraction of the rules of decorum.

"Who dares lack respect for justice!" he shouted, "Archers, bring this insolent person before the court to be judged immediately."

The archers were about to execute the order; Gaston de Massac, who had just recognized Esther, hastened to intervene.

"I request the indulgence of the president and gentlemen of the *Chambre Ardente*," he resumed; "it concerns a daughter who has found her father again, and this sentiment is honorable.... Moreover," he resumed confidently, "the safe passage that has been given to me for Master Bernard extends to all the members of his family, and therefore each member is under royal protection."

And he presented again the parchment.

"Oh, but I also am a member of the family," exclaimed someone at the end of the gallery.

And one could make out the stunned face of the tailor Balbein.

The president, impatient to terminate, did not persist in his severity, and said drily:

"Alright, the affair is closed.... The order of the King has been executed; the audience should not be further disturbed. Call another case."

And he added, in a caustic tone, leaning towards one of the councilors:

"Upon my life, I cannot wait until we are rid of this royal messenger. He will end up producing an edict of the King that we must carry the Huguenot on our shoulders in triumph through the streets of Bordeaux!"

All that was left for Gaston to do was to depart with Master Bernard and to retrieve the parchment belonging to Palissy, leaving the chamber preceded by the Captain of the archers, whose mission was to lead them to the external door of the fortress.

Palissy walked unsteadily, like a man who was drunk. On one hand, this change, so abrupt and unexpected, and on the other, the brisk outdoor air and bright daylight upon coming out from the gloomy *Chambre Ardente,* prevented him from perceiving things clearly. He could not understand Massac who was speaking to him loquaciously and answered him in monosyllables.

Only when he reached the courtyard did he begin to regain control of himself. Esther, who hastened to leave the tribune with the tailor Balbein, came to throw her arms around his neck. Father and daughter exchanged, for a few minutes, words interspersed with kisses.

As Gaston was watching them with a happy demeanor, Esther disengaged herself from Bernard's embrace, ran up and kissed him with innocent abandon.

"A thousand blessings upon you, Master de Massac!" she was saying. "The deliverance of my father, his new position, the honors, all this is your doing! In the midst of our anxieties, I never once had a doubt about you; I knew that you were at work for us and hope never abandoned my heart. However, you saw," she added, shuddering, "that an hour later…"

At that moment, they were standing in front of the *estrapade*, with its iron arm pointing towards the sky, stake ready, with sulfur wicks and bundles of firewood, while the executioner, seated a few steps away, was looking at Gaston somberly with an air of regret.

Gaston turned his eyes away from this sinister machine, and, leaning towards the young lady, said in a low tone:

"Perhaps, dear Esther, I may ask you soon for the reward for my services."

Esther fell silent, and blushing, returned to her father who was chatting with Balhein.

The news about the events at the *Chambre Ardente* spread rapidly in the fortress. Many persons, archers, employees, magistrates came running to see the royal messenger and especially the Huguenot Palissy, who, it was said, was going to become '*the favorite of the King and Queen-Mother.*' Among the curiosity seekers was Leufroy still wearing a black frock, streaked with red wax, frock that he wore in the exercise of his duties. He approached the old tailor, who had been running to and fro, making himself look important around Palissy.

"So, Master," he asked, "do you have the pleasure of knowing this Huguenot, who is Governor of a royal chateau?"

"Certainly, my friend; his wife is a Balbein and she is my niece… such that the great Bernard Palissy, Governor of… of that chateau of which you speak, is my nephew."

"Why did you not say that this morning? On the contrary, you were saying…"

"It was modesty, *compère*; one does not wish to appear as if one is showing off one's family."

"The fact remains," resumed Leufroy in a confidential tone, "that Master Palissy is a powerful man…. Listen, Master Balbein, if you would recommend me to him, and through his intervention, have me enter the house of the King, you would be rendering a service to a very good friend, as I am for you."

"We will see, my friend, we will see," replied Balbein in a disdainful tone; "you have shown yourself very hard on the Huguenots in recent times.... I will bring Master Bernard and his daughter to my home, where the rest of the family is staying. I will try to put in a good word for you at the first opportunity."

Leufroy thanked him warmly, while the tailor re-doubled in self-importance.

As they approached the drawbridge, there was a disturbance on their side. Mathurin and Nicolas, lost in the crowd milling around the approach to the chateau, breeched the guard post and rushed into the courtyard followed by the archers stationed at the gate. Having seen their father and sister in the distance, they had pushed past the guards and run to join them.

Breathless, they jumped into Bernard's arms, but the guards were close behind them and arrived as well.

"Get out!" shouted one of them. "Chase these idiots out and do not spare the blows."

Massac approached with an air of authority.

"No one shall lay a hand on these young persons!" he exclaimed; "they are the sons of Master Bernard Palissy, and they are under protection of the King."

The officer who was accompanying Massac gave a sign and the archers backed away respectfully. Mathurin and Nicolas had already put themselves on the defensive, but they realized with stupefaction that their escapade would remain unpunished.

"Divine Providence!" said Mathurin. "What has happened and how is it that…"

"My brothers, my brothers!" exclaimed Esther with exaltation, "you see the power of genius! The glory of our father protects us against the wickedness of men.… Praise be to God!"

And Palissy, preceded by the officer, and surrounded by his children and his friends, exited from this courtyard which should have been the theater of his torment.

XIII.

SHIPWRECK AT THE PORT

After having escaped the rigors of the Chambre Ardente, it was only up to Bernard Palissy whether he wanted to be celebrated by the Bordeaux population. The Protestants, as we have mentioned, were quite numerous in the town, and the failure of the dreaded Parliament secretly delighted many hearts. However, by prudence as well as modesty, the new Governor chose to remain in hiding. For several days, he shut himself up in the home of his relative Balbein, refusing all visits, and he rested with his family after the cruel emotions that he had suffered.

Gaston de Massac, staying at a neighboring inn, came to Balbein's home every day, and, in truth, he rarely left it. A chaste intimacy now reigned between him and the daughter of the famous potter, an intimacy that offended no one since all were aware of the expected results, although no discussion had yet taken place between Massac and Bernard on this subject.

However, this situation could not be prolonged. Gaston had to return to Blois to be with the Constable. Bernard, on his side, had to go to Saintes to settle certain matters concerning his production facility prior to settling himself in Paris with his family to begin the important tasks that Queen Catherine had planned for him. Massac therefore booked his passage on a ship leaving for Nantes; the Palissy family planned their departure for a few days later.

The evening before the departure of Gaston, the young gentleman had accepted the invitation to dine at the home of Balbein. Although the tailor was quite well off, it had not been a small affair to receive a future Baron, in spite of certain considerations that rendered things quite natural. The dinner was as sumptuous as it could be for a bourgeois of that time. However, the guests were sad and constrained; either by thoughts of the pending separations that occupied their minds, or for totally different reasons, and conversation remained subdued. Gaston in particular seemed dreamy, and his dreaminess was reflected in the soft and melancholic features of Esther.

The meal over, Massac said to Palissy:

"I leave tomorrow morning at the hour of the tide, Master Bernard, and this evening I will sleep aboard the ship. Although our separation will not be long, I hope, I would like to have a conversation with you now."

Bernard smiled.

"With me alone?" he asked while getting up.

"If Esther would like to join us…"

"Come, then, my daughter," said Master Bernard, "and let us go into this room, where we can speak freely."

Esther followed in silence.

The room they had just entered was large, and several four-poster beds constituted a sort of dormitory. Bernard offered Massac a seat and sat down himself, while Esther placed herself in the shadows.

Gaston seemed quite agitated. After a moment of hesitation, he said brusquely:

"Master Bernard, I ask you for the hand of your daughter.… Dear Esther, will you consent to becoming the Baroness de Massac?"

Perhaps the father and daughter expected a declaration of this sort. However, neither hastened to respond. Bernard finally replied with dignity:

"You do us a great honor, Master de Massac… but first, I think it necessary to consult Esther. Although a girl should accept the husband her parents think appropriate to choose for her, the question is of too great an importance.… Now, my daughter, you have heard the proposal of Master de Massac, what do you think?"

Gaston gave Esther a supplicating look.

"My father," she stammered, "I defer to your wisdom, your affection for me.…"

"That is not the question right now, it is your specific opinion that we wish to know."

"Well, Master de Massac has been our protector, so steadfast, so generous.…"

"So! You would not have, I see, any major objection to this plan.… Unfortunately," continued Palissy in an austere tone, "it is not the case for me."

Gaston was going to thank Esther for her consent, when Bernard's last phrase stopped him, and he waited anxiously for the decision of the head of the family. Bernard soon resumed with a sort of solemnity:

"Esther is right, Master de Massac. You have rendered us so many services, you prove yourself so above vulgar prejudices in wishing to take as your companion the daughter of a humble artisan, that a refusal on our part would seem to be monstrous and one of ingratitude. However, following divine law and our customs, it is not you that should have made this request.… I do not know what his Lordship the Baron, your father, and all your noble family…"

Gaston fidgeted in his chair.

"Master Bernard," he replied with embarrassment, "imagine that in recent days, I have not been able to go to the Chateau de Massac to discuss projects which are so dear to my heart. But the Baron has tender feelings for me, and I would not expect any obstacles from him. Although our backgrounds are very different, my parents could only cherish the charming Esther, who has all the noble qualities, and is the daughter of the famous Palissy.... Moreover, thanks to the esteem that the Queen Catherine has shown for you, Master Bernard, esteem that can only increase when she knows you better, you will surely be ennobled very shortly."

A light smile, which was immediately suppressed, crossed the potter's lips.

"I do not know if I would ever solicit such a favor," he replied. "I am extremely grateful to Queen Catherine for having snatched me away from the hands of the executioner and heaped me with riches. Therefore, I will dedicate a work that I will have printed shortly[45] and I will thank her as warmly as I can for her goodness towards me.... But right now, we are only concerning ourselves with the opinion of your honorable family on this project of marriage.... According to your own admission, you are not absolutely certain that this project would have his approval?"

Massac's discomfort seemed to redouble.

"Ah!" he exclaimed, "I would not doubt for a moment if..."

"Finish."

"If Esther and I were of the same religion; but I fear that my father... This is the cause of my mortal concerns!"

There was a new silence.

"You will find it not surprising, Master de Massac," resumed Bernard with an overtone that was increasingly stiff; "that what I think myself about this marriage is the same as what your noble parents could be thinking. I also, would not see any obstacles to this marriage if, you and my daughter, you had the same faith."

It was not possible that Massac and Esther did not often reflect about the chasm that the difference in religion had created between them. However, both appeared dismayed, as if the abyss had suddenly appeared before them for the first time. Gaston was very pale; Esther was bowing her head.

"My children," resumed Bernard with sadness, "you must choose between God and the world, between your earthly sentiments and your beliefs; it is not I who created this unalterable necessity.... Look into your heart, Master de Massac. To marry Esther, would you agree to embrace the Reformist religion?"

---

45 **Author Berthet's original note**: The work in question and Bernard Palissy's first, is entitled: *"Recepte véritable pour augmenter ses trésor, etc"*. The introduction contains a dedication which is a masterpiece of dignity and sentiment, in which Bernard gives his thanks to the Queen. It was published in 1563.

Esther waited anxiously for de Massac's response. The latter was passing his hand back and forth across his forehead; his features had a look of pain:

"Master Bernard," he replied in a faltering voice, "I know that among the Reformists there are men with pure morals and sincere convictions, and I like to think that in spite of certain differences in dogma, God will be merciful with them on judgment day.... However, my respect for the ideas on which I was nourished and the fear that I will bring mortal displeasure upon my dear elderly father..."

"I understand," said Bernard, sighing; "and you Esther, you cannot help but appreciate the advantages of the marriage which is offered to you; would you, to become the Baroness de Massac, embrace the Catholic faith?... Do not pressure yourself to reply, my daughter.... My personal opinions should not influence your decision.... Conscience is sacred; paternal power must incline itself before her. If you need several days, several hours to reflect...."

"I do not need to reflect," she replied, "If his Lordship the Baron de Massac would experience such pain in seeing his son in the Reformist religion, why would not my father and mother experience the same in seeing their daughter in the Catholic religion? I will not renounce the faith of my father and my mother. "

She threw herself into the arms of Bernard and hid her face.

Palissy pressed her against his chest, and turning towards Gaston, said:

"Poor children, I pity you with all my soul, and yet I agree with you both.... I could not have helped myself from reproaching the one of you who was weak enough to sacrifice his religion for his private affections.... Now all has been said between you, and you must not see each other again... at least until the God of the Catholics and the Protestants has given you the strength to overcome your dreadful feelings."

At the moment that Palissy had pronounced the words: '*you must not see each other again,*' the young persons could not retain the expressions of their pain. Esther had fallen into an armchair and given full liberty to her sobs. Gaston exclaimed distractedly:

"Is it possible, Esther, that you remained indifferent to my despair? Do I have such a small place in your soul? I had hoped that gratefulness would help you surmount certain scruples...."

"Gaston, why do you demand certain sacrifices from me that you are incapable of making yourself? Respect my scruples as I respect yours.... My father is right, we must not see each other again."

"Never, never," exclaimed Massac impetuously, "I will never give you up, even if I have the world, my family, and God himself against me!"

"Do not blaspheme, young man," interrupted Bernard, "and submit to necessity.... I knew that my daughter would not renounce her faith to listen to the sentiments of her heart; and I was also certain that you would not want to embrace the Reformist religion. You are destined by your birth and your superior qualities to great success and all the glories of this world. Embracing the Reformist religion brings its followers only persecution, prison, torture and often ignominious death."

"By the heavens! Do you think that persecution, torture and death frighten me? If it were only that…"

"There is also the fear of distressing your elderly father, and perhaps the lack of faith," replied Bernard. "It is already too much…. You see, Master de Massac, there is no way for us to get together. Let us separate, without bitterness and without anger…. You will be embarking tonight; accept our farewells…. Perhaps we will meet again later, and then the heat of the moment will have passed. Whatever happens, my family and I will never forget that our safety, our well-being and our prosperity come from you…. Once again; farewell."

He had risen and was holding his hand out to Massac: Massac did not take it and did not even notice that it was held out. He walked rapidly around the room. Suddenly he stopped in front of the young girl:

"Esther," he said, "was I mistaken? Those words which often escaped your lips, those looks, those smiles which caused me so much pride and joy, were they lies? You do not love me, you have never loved me!"

Esther could only respond with sobs.

"I see," pursued Gaston, "You are under the absolute influence of a fanatical father whose genius has dried up his heart…. Ah! if you had truly loved me, no obstacle could have stopped me, you would have been mine, in spite of heaven and earth!"

Esther appeared to make a violent effort within herself.

"My father has told you," she stammered, "you blaspheme, and your religion, like mine condemns blasphemy! Master de Massac, receive also my farewell."

Gaston hesitated a moment, then he cried out in a sort of frenzy:

"So be it! Let us separate for all time…. You practice a doctrine that is ungodly, and rigid, and extinguishes the noblest sentiments, shrivels the soul and replaces devoted love with logical egoism…. May it be damned and let the consequences fall on those that follow it!"

He ran out, crossed the main room where the family were awaiting the results of this discussion, and left the house.

This sudden departure could have given an idea of what had occurred. Nevertheless, Mistress Bernard and Balbein entered with eagerness into the room where remained Palissy and his daughter. The tailor, flattered by the greatness of his guests, did not doubt success, and exclaimed in a joyous tone:

"Well, Palissy, we already have the Governor of a royal chateau in the family. Will we not soon have a Baron and Baroness?"

Palissy pointed to Esther, totally inert in the armchair.

"Woman," he said to Mistress Bernard, "take care of your daughter.... And then, we will pray all together to God for two young persons who are truly to be pitied, for their misfortune is without remedy!"

PART THREE

THE GOVERNOR OF THE TUILERIES

I.

THE VISIT

The palace of the Tuileries, when built by Queen Catherine de Médicis, differed little from the one we have seen in our day, before a horde of cosmopolitan villains set fire to this monument to our national history. It was located outside the walls of the city, completely isolated from the Louvre, which, in spite of the superb constructions of Henri II, had more the aspect of a feudal castle. From a window of the façade, one could see the tower and gate of Nesle,[46] which stood on the left bank, where today, stands the Institute,[47] then the Tour du Bois[48] and Porte Neuve, both located at the vaulted entrance to the inner courtyard of the Louvre now known as the Carrousel du Louvre on the right bank. Between the fortified walls of the Louvre and the new palace, was an open field with a few structures of little importance. The principal structure was a tuilerie[49] that manufactured tiles and bricks, long after the construction of the royal residence, so long in fact, that up to the start of the reign of Louis XIV, one could still see in the courtyard of the chateau the worksites and ovens used in their fabrication.

The palace itself, as it was executed by the architects Philibert Delorme[50] and Jean Bullant, consisted of a central pavilion whose slate dome was round, and two adjoining pavilions, one on each side. The gardens, surrounded by high walls were separated from the main building by a wide avenue.

At the moment of our narrative, the gardens had barely been laid out and the young plantings could provide neither shade nor freshness. As for the buildings, they had the dazzling whiteness of new construction; several

46 **Porte de Nesle** was the gate of a defensive tower of the old city wall, built in the 13th century, which once stood across the Seine from the Palace of the Louvre and was destroyed in 1665.
47 **Institut de France,** built in 1795, the Institute is made up of five *academies*, the most famous of which is l'Académie Française.
48 **Tour du Bois,** (Porte du Bois) Tower built to protect the West side of Paris in 14th century and destroyed in 1670 along with the Porte Neuve.
49 **tuilerie,** tile factory. Its location led to the name of *Les Tuileries*, behind the Louvre.
50 **Philibert Delorme,** (1514-1570) French architect and writer and one of the great masters of the French Renaissance.

were unfinished, surrounded by huge scaffolding. Small houses and isolated trees that cluttered the surrounding area spoiled the noble appearance of the palace.

However, it was already inhabited. The Queen-Mother, anxious to have *"her own place"* frequently left the Louvre, which was occupied by her second son, the King Charles IX, and went to the Tuileries to sleep. She had installed there a number of persons in her service, and she appeared to like this residence, although she later rapidly tired of it.

In an apartment facing the river were housed, with his family, the Governor of the chateau and its gardens, Master Bernard Palissy. In addition to the apartment itself, the Queen had given him the usage of the *tuilerie*, where he set up his ovens and his workshops. Any doubt about this could be discounted since only a few years ago, it was discovered during excavations in that courtyard, the remains of those ovens with molds and utensils of a potter.

So, one autumn morning, a young girl, dreamy and melancholic, was at the window of Palissy's apartment. From there, she could overlook a part of the palace gardens. Before her flowed the Seine, whose banks had no wharfs and were covered with willow trees and poplars. Neither the Pont Royale, nor the Pont Neuf, nor any other intermediary bridge yet existed. A *bac,*[51] leaving from the place where starts the street of that name, deposited strollers on the bank, opposite the Tuileries. On the other side of the river, extended the Pré-aux-Clercs[52] and beyond this grassy plain could be seen the old ramparts and the bell towers of Saint-Germain-des-Près.

The young girl at the window, the reader has no doubt guessed, was Esther Palissy. She was then twenty-five years old. A secret sorrow, that neither prosperity nor the present splendors had succeeded in surmounting, gave her features a character of sympathetic sadness. Moreover, Esther, in the home of the Queen, surrounded by a brilliant and corrupt Court, retained the simple charm of her origins. She rarely went out. Occupied with the care of the household, she remained a stranger to the dissipation and intrigues of this new world. Leaning towards the strictness of Protestant women, she wore heavy and dark clothing and the ample head coverings of the ladies of Saintonge, and her beauty was like the rare flowers in the field that one must seek in the grass to discover.

Suddenly, Esther became attentive. Her look remained fixed on the garden under development, in which Master Bernard could apply his theories he wrote about in a *Delectable Garden.*[53]

---

51 ***Bac,*** a *ferry*, departing from the location of the current rue du Bac.
52 **Pré-aux-Clercs,** (the Clerk's Meadow) was a prairie on the left bank famous in the 16th century for the many duels that took place there.
53 ***Delectable Garden****: le Jardin Délectable,* published in 1563 as part of *'Recepte véritable pour augmenter ses trésor, etc,'* and dedicated to Queen Catherine de

Access was not yet permitted to the Paris public, but persons attached to the home of Queen Catherine had free entry. And although the plants, as we have said, were still young and spindly, the greenery and flowers were abundant.

At that moment, groups of gentlemen and ladies were strolling in the alleys. Most of the women wore crimson velvet dresses that identified them as *ladies-in-waiting* of the Queen, the '*beautiful and honest ladies*' of whom Brantôme told so many scandalous stories. The men, with their plumed caps, their ruffled collars, their short jackets embroidered with gold and their velvet and satin doublets, all appeared to belong to the Court. They seemed to be in joyous good humor, happy conversations were exchanged at a distance, gales of laughter broke out, and they did not worry about trampling the flowerbeds or taking flowers by the armful. A ray of sunlight illuminated this elegant crowd, adding sparkle to the gold and precious stones, and color to the feathers, velvets and satins.

However, Esther's attention was particularly on a young man, dressed in black, whose wide sword strap bore the coat of arms of the Constable. His manner was much calmer than the other courtesans, and Palissy's daughter thought that she saw him look in her direction several times. However, if this was the case, the stranger was not able continue his contemplation for long, as he became the object of the coquetry of the *ladies-in-waiting* who were frolicking around him.

One in particular, a tall blond, with a vivacious air and rose-colored lips, did not give him a moment of respite; she seemed to be mocking him and was throwing stemless flowers at his head. The young man dressed in black seemed to put up impatiently with her provocations, and his glances continued to be directed towards Esther's window. But soon, either the taunting of his companions excited him, or he gave in to some caprice and turned suddenly and chased, with a sort of affectation, the coquette who was running away after having thrown a fistful of rose petals in his face. He caught up with her, and after a brief exchange, he retrieved a knotted ribbon from her that he attached to the strap of his sword.

One heard a burst of laughter, and some applause; but Esther did not see more. She had backed away from the window and a chaste blush had covered her face.

"It is *he*, it is surely *he*," she was saying to herself. "He has returned to Paris since his Lordship the Constable has been named Governor, and I am sure that he recognized me as well.... Undoubtedly he wanted to defy me by reacting to the teasing of that shameless creature!"

She remained pensive for a moment:

"And why should I be surprised?" She soon continued; "these are the

Médicis.

customs of the nobility.... A poor Huguenot from the provinces, like myself, cannot pass judgment on these things. She would be offended by what the great Lords and nobles find simple.... Ah, why did my father bring me here?"

She went and sat at the other end of the room, and an abundance of tears flowed on her cheeks.

However, she did not abandon herself for long to her weakness. After having carefully wiped her eyes, she moved to a nearby room where she knew she would find her mother.

Mistress Bernard had also maintained, in the Chateau des Tuileries, her modest and laborious habits of a Saintonge housewife. At that moment, she was placing bread, fruits and cold meat in a basket.

"Daughter," she said to Esther, "Mathurin and Nicolas have already been here for lunch; but your father, completely absorbed by his work, does not think about eating. If we did not pay attention, he would let himself die of starvation. Would you take him his morning meal? You are the only one who can get him to eat when he is working."

"Gladly, mother," replied Esther; "but there are Lords and Ladies in the garden, and there are certainly some in the workshops."

"Bah! They are constantly harassing Bernard. However, he has to live. Shame on those idle people who prevent a poor man from feeding himself!"

Esther placed the basket under her arm and descended the grand staircase.

The courtyard, as we have said, was still cluttered with construction materials, scaffolding and heaps of stones. However, Esther moved forward without hesitation, carrying her basket with the grace of the *antique canéphores*[54], she reached the *tuilerie* where her father worked.

The workshops were not as vast, or as well installed as Saintes, although they had reproduced the same positioning for the ovens and the rooms for molding, glazing and the execution of new works. It was in this room that Palissy was generally to be found, and it was there that Esther headed.

She realized that she would soon find company at her father's workshop. Ladies in their crimson velvet dresses and gentlemen with their plumed hats were still in the area, chatting and laughing, much more occupied, in appearance, by their elegance than by the works of art that surrounded them.

At the entry of the workshop, whose door was open, stood a new group, and in the workshop, one could hear the murmur of several voices.

No one deigned to pay any attention to Esther. This young girl in a woolen dress, carrying a burden, could only be a servant, and barely a head turned distractedly as she passed. She was therefore able to enter the room that served as Palissy's workplace without difficulty.

---

54 *antique canéphores,* ancient Greek basket carriers.

However, Palissy and his sons were not alone. At one end of the room, in the place of honor, one could see sitting in a large seat of sculptured wood, a lady of a certain age, in a black dress and a widow's head covering. The father and his children were spreading before her plans that seemed to be those of the gardens, or they brought before her glazed vases, dishes or ewers which she examined with evident pleasure.... Queen Catherine, for it was she, came often to spend a few hours with Palissy to consult with him regarding the embellishments she wished to bring to the chateau, or to order stained glass windows or his superb potteries with which he now decorated the royal residences.

When receiving this noble visit, Bernard did not seem to be better dressed than when he was not Governor of the Tuileries, or before he was in the service of Catherine. In truth, he wore a simple jerkin and black satin breeches which outlined the male proportions of his relatively athletic body, and brought out the noble character of his head, almost bald, with a greying beard; but he still wore the leather apron of a simple artisan and his callous hands bore witness that he had recently been handling modeling clay. Although in his relations with the Queen he was always attentive and respectful in his manners and language, he was very much at ease. He expressed his thoughts as freely as if he was speaking to a bourgeoise. Mathurin and Nicolas, now young men, came and went in silence, executing the orders of their father.

When Esther entered, or rather furtively slipped into, the workshop, an animated discussion was taking place between the Queen and Palissy, such that only her brothers noticed her. She deposited the basket on a table near the door and waited timidly to be able to approach.

"I wish, Master Bernard," said the Queen with her slight Italian accent, "that you make for me as soon as possible, six vases which will contain perfume, for René, to reward him for his zeal in my service."

Bernard Palissy's face took on an expression of sadness. René, perfumer to the Queen, whom she had brought from Florence, was known as a dreaded poisoner, and had rendered, it was said, his services as such to the Queen more than once.

"I am always at the service of Your Majesty," replied Bernard. "However I dare to ask what emblems I should place on these vases as decorations.... They should not be flowers, butterflies or shellfish, as usual. I would rather suggest plants of hemlock or henbane, some snakes, some scorpions, with, here and there, some heads of Medusa and Gorgon."

Catherine felt the hurtful intentions of these words towards her favorite.

"You are only a nasty Huguenot, Master Bernard," she said angrily. "You, and several other miscreants, that I protect and that I encourage because of their superior talents, you take, in my presence, insolent liberties of language…. René is my loyal servant. He knows the properties of plants, metals and all sorts of prodigious secrets. You, who prides himself in knowing chemistry and who teaches public classes on this science, you could learn many things from him."

"With your permission, Madam," replied the incorrigible Bernard, "it is doubtful that I ever take any lessons from *Signor* René, for any reason!"

Catherine stamped her foot but ended up laughing and arose.

"You will execute my orders, Master Bernard," she said, "as well for the perfume vases as the other *rustic figulines* that I have ordered…. But it is time for me to go to the Louvre to see the King who must now be back from his *jeu de paume*.[55] Have them bring my litter."

A page, stationed by the door, ran to announce to the persons in the retinue, the imminent departure of the Queen.

As Catherine was casting a final glance at the statues, vases and items of all kinds that decorated the workshop, she noticed Esther, who was doing her best to hide in a dark corner.

"Who is that little one?" she demanded.

Bernard frowned. In the midst of the Court of depraved morals, he had always tried to avoid drawing attention to his family, and this was the first time that Esther had encountered the Queen. In spite of his displeasure, he could not avoid introducing her.

"This is my daughter who has come to bring me my lunch," he replied, "and I request on her behalf the benevolence of Your Majesty."

"Ah! It is your daughter?" replied Catherine; "Approach, little one…. By the Madonna! She would be very nice if she did not have those dreadful Huguenot clothes."

She held her hand out to Esther, who kissed it tremblingly. The Queen continued to look at her with indulgence.

"No matter!" she resumed, "this child pleases me…. And when you wish, Bernard, I will take care of her future."

This proposal, which would have overwhelmed with joy another father, caused Palissy a mortal embarrassment.

"Madam," he stammered, "I humbly thank Your Majesty; but Esther is a simple bourgeoise, with modest tastes. She is not used to… she would not know…"

He was getting confused in his excuses and the Queen could take offense at the disdain that someone was showing for her benevolent intentions. An unexpected circumstance distracted Catherine, who had taken a look at Master Bernard's lunch.

"What is this?" she exclaimed with indignation. "Ham, on a day of abstinence! Ah! Master Bernard, Master Bernard, you do too much, you and

55 *jeu de paume*, is a "hand ball game" originated in France, it was an indoor precursor of tennis played without racquets and using the palm of the hand.

the other Huguenots, that one day I will give in to certain requests, and we will finish once and for all with all of you.... You are trying my patience, I warn you!"

Palissy did not dare respond, and Esther hastened to make disappear, behind an earthenware bust, the offending victual, and cause of this reprimand. However, the Queen seemed to be no longer thinking about the girl and departed abruptly.

Etiquette required that Palissy and all the persons present follow Catherine to the last door of the building, and Bernard, like his children, could not miss this ceremony; therefore, they accompanied the Queen, remaining a few steps in the rear, as was the custom.

Under the neighboring hangar were the gentlemen and ladies-in-waiting that would make up the procession. However, the laughter and joyous conversation had ceased. Each was only thinking about fulfilling, in a respectful silence, the duties of his office, especially since one could see that the Queen was irritated and that the least infraction in obedience could unleash a storm.

Esther, as we have said, also followed the procession, and lost in the crowd, was trying to remain close as possible to her father. Suddenly, a plaintive voice spoke into her ear:

"Esther, dear Esther, do you now have for me only hate and disdain?"

She turned around. Massac had furtively approached her and their eyes met.

Esther lowered hers and did not say a word.

"Miss," resumed Gaston de Massac with an even more plaintive tone, "is it then true that I have become, for you, odious? I, however, cannot erase your memory from my heart."

A bitter smile touched the lips of Esther. Without responding otherwise, she gestured towards the knotted ribbon that Gaston still wore on his belt. Gaston undoubtedly knew that Esther was aware of the origins of that ribbon; but he did not hesitate for a second, he tore off the ribbon, threw it on the ground and trampled on it.

"It was a simple childishness," he murmured.

Esther continued her silence. However, Gaston's action had not escaped the notice of the lady-in-waiting from whom that light fabric had been taken. The tall blond partly emerged from the ranks of her companions, let out a peal of mocking laughter and said aloud:

"Look! Master de Massac is flirting with the servants!"

It was a bad idea having incited some nervous laughs from the other girls. The Queen had heard it.

"Who is it that is creating this disturbance?" she said impatiently. "Miss de la Billardière, is it you again? We are bothered incessantly by your gossiping."

Miss de la Billardière, embarrassed, hid herself.

They continued to move forward and the general hubbub covered the noise of chatting. Soon, Massac once again leaned towards Esther:

"Miss," he resumed, "I cannot hold back and I must speak with you…. I wish to inform you of things of the highest importance."

"What is the use?" replied Esther in a low voice, "we have nothing to say to each other…. Do you want to make me an object of ridicule before the ladies of honor of the Queen?"

And she ran to place herself on the other side of her father.

In the courtyard of the Tuileries was the litter, harnessed with two mules covered with superb decorative blankets, which awaited Catherine. As she was going to the Louvre, a few hundred of steps away, the persons in her suite went there on foot. The widow of Henri II climbed into the litter, without worrying whether she revealed her attractive leg, with its taut stocking, described by Brantôme, and of which she was so proud. But once she was installed in the vehicle, she delayed giving the order to depart, and again cast a look around her. It rested on the Palissy family, who humbly bowed, and in particular, on Esther, who was doing her best to remain unnoticed.

"Now, Master Bernard," resumed the Queen out loud, "We will speak again about your daughter. It would be a shame if your fierce 'Huguenotry' caused the damnation of her soul…. May God protect you all! And think, Master Bernard, about producing the masterpieces to justify, before my conscience, the protection which I grant to a heretic."

Palissy wished to reply, but was not given the time, and the litter was now moving with only several squires and pages following on horseback.

They were hardly out of sight, that the gallant conversations and the laughter, restrained by the presence of the Queen, resumed with renewed vigor. Miss de Billardière detached herself from the boisterous group of ladies-in-waiting and approached Gaston.

"And what! Master de Massac," she said in a simpering tone," will you not offer me your hand to go to the Louvre?"

"Excuse me Miss," replied Gaston brusquely, "but I am not going to the Louvre."

"As you please. However, you were saying… but, by my troth, one would think that you are neglecting the '*ladies in velvet*,' like us, in favor of the '*ladies in wool*,' like that daughter of the artisan Palissy."

Perhaps it is because the '*ladies in wool*' run away from the gentlemen, while the '*ladies in velvet*' pursue them too much," replied Massac dryly.

He saluted her and left with long strides.

Palissy and his children, following the departure of Catherine, hastened to return to the workshop. Master Bernard appeared disconsolate.

"My daughter Esther, what a shame that you came while the Queen was here! She took a liking to you and will want to convert you to her religion. You will want to resist, I have no doubt, because you are a good and wise girl; but Catherine does not accept that one resists her…. It will result in persecutions without end, and we will suffer grief, ruin and disgrace!"

Esther began to cry.

"Do not fear that I will betray my religion, father," she exclaimed, "for Queen Catherine, our benefactress, even if she were ten times more powerful!… But, why did we come to this royal house, where one hears only unseemly words or see things which are scandalous. Ah! in spite of past miseries, I was happier in our Saintonge!"

"Since these disastrous religious wars, my daughter," replied Palissy sighing, "Saintonge has suffered many ills; the whole country has been ravaged; our friends, Master de Pons and Master de Maulévrier, who belonged to different sides, perished, both of them, in these fratricidal wars…. And may Providence move us away from further misfortune!"

There was a silence. Suddenly, Palissy leaned towards Esther, who was continuing to sob, and said to her affectionately:

"You miss our beautiful Saintonge, little one. Master de Massac, with whom you were speaking a short time ago, did he give you some news about it?"

"What! my father, you saw?"

"Yes, I recognized the poor boy, who has helped us out of so many bad situations, and I would have spoken with him except for the respect due to the Queen…. Finally, what was he saying?"

Esther recounted, blushing, the short conversation she had with Massac.

"What could he have to tell you about?" resumed Bernard, "however you did well to not wish to listen to him…. Come now," he continued with a tone of encouragement, "let us not despair too much concerning the fantasies of our royal mistress. Perhaps she will forget you if she does not run into you…. And we will do everything possible to keep you in peace and prosperity, you who are our pride and joy!"

II.

THE PROPOSAL

In addition to the apartment and the workshop that Bernard Palissy occupied at the Tuileries, there was in rue Saint-Jacques, in one of those dark houses of ancient Paris, a lodging which consisted almost exclusively of a vast room at the end of a courtyard. The walls were lined with shelves on which one could see objects of natural history, minerals, crystals, petrified wood, dried plants and finally reptiles and insects in liquid preservatives. The totality constituted what was then called a *cabinet of rarities*, and these objects had been collected by their owner during his numerous trips. Labels with long and detailed descriptions, which Palissy described in one of his books, were attached to each of these curiosities, explaining their nature and origin.

It was there that on certain days, '*Master Bernard of the Tuileries,*' as he was called, gave public discourses on natural history, chemistry, agriculture and global physics, and a great number of distinguished persons came to listen to his lectures. One did not attend these free of charge. Bernard himself relates that he had placed posters at Paris intersections, which announced 'that he would collect at the door one ecu for each lesson, but that if he were found to be a liar, he would reimburse each auditor fourfold, that is to say four ecus.' The offer was naïve; however, in spite of the boldness of the new ideas presented by the genius potter, ideas that modern science now almost completely confirm, he observed that he was never contradicted, and therefore never had to pay the penalty.

It is in this house on rue Saint-Jacques that we find Master Bernard, two or three days after the events that we have just described.

One arrived at the 'cabinet of rarities' by one of those long and malodorous alleys that the architects of that time provided for Parisian ground-floor entrances. However, before entering, one crossed a small bare room, where an old fellow demanded from each newcomer the ecu imposed by the poster. This fellow was the companion, Daniel, the Huguenot worker that Bernard had brought from Saintes to Paris, so that he could share the good as well as the bad fortune of his master.

The meeting room, although quite large, as we have said, was of an extreme simplicity, with roughly squared beams as pillars, while other exposed beams supported the ceiling. At one end of the room, was a massive table on which Bernard placed the objects necessary for his demonstrations. The remainder of the room was occupied by several rows of benches destined for the auditors. These could not number more than a hundred, as there was concern that the University, very jealous of its privileges, might be annoyed by too great an affluence at these unauthorized conferences. However, one could see in the audience, several doctors' felt caps, magistrates' robes and even ecclesiastic robes, in spite of the well-known religion of the professor.

On the day we are describing, the audience was particularly large in number and select in quality. Master Bernard, dressed in black, with a white ruff collar with large gadroons,[56] had just finished his conference, to the applause of his audience. His clear speech and substantive instructions backed up by facts, had made a great impression on persons used to language which was pedantic, bloated and empty from the scholars of that time. Moreover, when an assertion by the speaker did not seem sufficiently clear, the disciples did not hesitate to demand further explanations, which Palissy willingly provided.

Among the persons who, that day, had listened with religious attention to the eloquent phrases of the master, there were two who merited special attention.

One was a man of about the same age and size as Palissy; he had the same fiery look, with a narrow, thin and pale face and a bare forehead. Their black clothing and white ruff collars were almost identical, and one might judge by something in his rigid and austere posture, that the stranger also belonged to the Reformist religion. He had taken a seat in the first row of the audience, and although he remained silent, he was evidently an object of respect for all in the assembly. Palissy himself seemed to be concerned about his opinion; he looked at him constantly, and at every sign of approval that he saw on the stranger's face, he took visible pleasure.

The other was a young gentleman, also dressed in black, who was leaning against a pillar near the entryway of the room, and who never took his eyes off the speaker. One could not observe his features as he had brought up to the lower part of his face, the folds of his silk jacket. We know that it was still the custom at that time to remain incognito, where men as well as women, willingly appeared on the streets, in broad daylight, wearing a mask. What should have been equally surprising was to see a young gentleman attending a course on science.

Bernard Palissy had just finished the lesson, and there was a commotion as everyone arose. While some headed for the door, others approached

56 **gadroons,** special form given to ruff collars n the 16th and 17th centuries. From *godron* in French.

the master, either to compliment him, or to question him. However, little by little, the room emptied, and soon there only remained two persons with Bernard Palissy, the stranger we described, and the young gentleman.

However, it was only the stranger that received Palissy's attention; he stepped towards him and grasped his hand affectionately.

"Ah! Master Ambroise Paré," he said to him, "have you done me such an honor to come and listen to me, me, a simple artisan, who does not even know a little Greek or Latin?"

"I did not listen to you with less pleasure, Master Bernard," replied Ambroise Paré, the illustrious scholar, who could be considered as the father of French surgery. "And you say beautiful and useful things from which I take profit.... Come now, compère, I do not know any more Greek and Latin than you do, although when they accepted me as doctor of surgery, they made me stumble through a Latin thesis, of which I understood not a word. I rose from the bottom, like you, Master Bernard; and while you were an apprentice with a glass-maker, I was an apprentice in the shop of a barber-surgeon where I shaved the villagers for one penny."

"Nevertheless, Master Ambroise, you are today counsellor and first surgeon to the King, our Majesty, who likes and respects you immensely!"

"Parbleu! Master Bernard, you are the inventor of the King's *rustic figulines*, and the Governor of the Tuileries.... And between you and me, there are not many doctors who know Greek and Latin, that are worthy of either one of us!"

The two friends, since they had been linked for a long time, burst out laughing, then spoke in low tones.

The young gentleman waited impatiently for the end of their conversation. Not being able to hold back any further, he approached Palissy and said in a hushed voice:

"Master Bernard, would you please grant me a moment of conversation?"

At the same time, he let drop the folds of his jacket and one could recognize Gaston de Massac. Bernard smiled:

"God protect you, my gentleman!" he replied, "I will be at your service in just a moment."

"I cannot stay any longer, Master Bernard," resumed Ambroise Paré, "but we will see each other again soon.... You know," he said, winking, "that the King and the Queen-Mother, will, next Sunday, dine in public at the Louvre?"

"I know."

"Then... it is agreed?"

"It is agreed."

They exchanged once again a mysterious sign and separated.

Palissy returned to Gaston.

"It has been a long time since we met, Master de Massac" he said with an affectionate tone, "and in spite of the manner in which we separated in Bordeaux, I am always happy to see you."

"You know that on my part, Master Bernard," replied Massac sadly, "I am not lacking in reasons to not forget you… you, and yours. I have never stopped thinking about your daughter Esther whom I love above all, whatever I do."

"Never mind," replied Bernard, "as there still exists an absolute impossibility…. However," he added in a serious tone, "it seems that at the Court, you are trying to sooth your sorrow."

"Ah! Esther has told you!" resumed Gaston flinching, "but she could not tell you, Master Bernard, that I arrived in Paris only a few days ago, and that since my arrival, I have been the object of provocations by one of the ladies-in-waiting, Miss de la Billardière. I have always rejected her advances and I suspect that this lady is a spy for the Queen-Mother who would like to know, through me, the secrets of my master, his Lordship the Constable. Moreover, the day that I was strolling in the garden of the Tuileries, I saw, from afar, Esther at her window, and excited by spite, exalted by a bad sentiment…"

"All right," interrupted Bernard, "you do not have to justify yourself…. But this is not a good place to chat, as we are likely to be disturbed by the curious who come to visit my cabinet of rarities. I am returning to the Tuileries and will go by way of the Porte Saint Germain and the Pré-au-Clercs where I will take the ferry…. We can chat while walking; would it please you to accompany me a part of the way?… Unless you are afraid to be seen in public with a common artisan, and a confirmed Huguenot, like me!"

"Master Palissy," said Massac effusively; "your company would honor any French gentleman, especially I, who reveres you…. Let us depart, and I will explain what I came to tell you."

They crossed the courtyard and the dark alley. In the first room, Palissy exchanged a few words with his retainer, who was charged with guarding the entry, and who showed, with great satisfaction, the ecus coming from the entry fee to that day's session. Bernard hardly seemed to notice, and, after having given some orders to Daniel, he stepped out with Massac, into the populous streets of the University district.

That district was one of the noisiest in the city. The students and the clerks who frequented it were boisterous, and the privileges they enjoyed, privileges that assured them, most of the time, complete impunity, prevented them from moderating their turbulence. Moreover, neither Palissy nor Massac, had much to fear from these undisciplined youths, and they plunged into the narrow, dark and muddy streets, full of movement and noise, which characterized sixteenth century Paris.

Master Bernard, knowing the area perfectly, chose the less crowded streets and soon resumed:

"Now, my young man, what has happened to you since we last parted?"

"I have led a sad life, Master Bernard, and you know why. His Lordship the

Constable had given me several important tasks. Then, I had to put my personal affairs in order, as I had the misfortune of losing, a few months ago, my honorable father.... Thus, as you can see, I am still in mourning."

And Gaston's eyes filled with tears.

"Therefore, you are now Baron de Massac, with freedom of will and actions?"

"This is true, and I have no other family except for some distant relatives that I do not care about. I have therefore resolved to retire to my hereditary manor and live there as peacefully as possible."

"You are very young, Sire Baron, to become used to such an existence.... You undoubtedly could not allow yourself to remain a stranger to this religious struggle."

"Yes, Master Bernard; I wish to remain neutral in these deplorable wars. My conscience forbids me to take up arms against my Catholic friends, but I could neither use them against the sect to which belong the charming Esther and Master Bernard Palissy.... As I have heard said many times, by you and other wise persons, it is not with swords and muskets, with prisons and torture, that one can convince the spirit, but with soft words, good arguments and reciprocal charity."

"Good, good, Sire Baron," replied Palissy in a satisfied tone; "here are noble sentiments that should be shared during these difficult times we are living.... During some recent wars, the Protestants surpassed the Catholics in pillaging, violence and cruelty, all absolutely contrary to the Gospel.... But," added Bernard in a change of tone, "these are serious matters that we cannot resolve while chatting in the street; and you still have not said, Sire Baron, what you expect of me."

"Oh! you cannot guess? Before leaving the Court and locking myself up in my chateau, I wanted to determine whether it was truly necessary for me to renounce happiness. I will not hide from you, Master Bernard, that after the humiliating refusal that I suffered from you and Esther in Bordeaux, I did everything I could to forget the person who rejected me; but distractions, travels, responsibilities, determination, all failed to help me overcome this love. All women, in comparison with Esther, appear frivolous, vain and unworthy of a serious attachment.... I love her more than ever, and perhaps, in spite of the hardness she showed over at the Tuileries, she may not still hate me.... If this were so, Master Bernard, why could we not renew an old project? The circumstances are no longer the same as they were in Bordeaux; today I am responsible to no one but myself, I can listen to the inspirations of my heart. Why would our religions separate me from Esther now? Why would we hesitate to unite, committing to respect each other's faith? Do we not have before us thousands of examples of similar unions?"

And Gaston began describing, with spirited eloquence, his plan.

Mixed marriages were not rare at that time. Love, which willingly rebels against obstacles, did not accept any more then than today the tyranny of religion, and, everywhere in the kingdom, one encountered families where husband and wife belonged to differing Christian communities. The marriage, which took place a little later, between the Protestant King of Navarre[57] (Henri IV) and Marguerite, daughter of Henri II and Catherine de Médicis, was one of the most striking examples.

Moreover, the moment was favorable for similar alliances. Following the first war of Saintonge, a sort of truce existed between the Catholics and Protestants. The King, the Queen-Mother and the Court felt they had to support a match involving a family which had as its head the Prince de Condé et Coligny,[58] and many marriages of this nature took place, either openly or in secret.

Palissy, on his side, despite the fervor of his convictions, did not lack in *tolerance*, (the word, however, did not yet exist), and we know that he did not want, for anything in the world, to assault the conscience of his daughter. On the other hand, he had total confidence in Massac, and finally he began to feel it necessary to shelter Esther from certain obsessions of the Queen, obsessions that the Queen had renewed that very morning. Consequently, without committing himself, he presented the gentleman with some questions as to how he would implement his plan.

"Nothing simpler," replied the Baron, "I found here an old chaplain from Massac. He loves me like his son, as he knew me as a child and he owes much to my family. I explained my problems, and he showed himself willing to marry me in secret with the woman I love but respecting the scruples and conscience of the future wife. Since the marriage will be performed in accordance with Catholic rites, it will depend on you that it be celebrated in accordance with 'the Geneva mode,'[59] on the condition that my own personal beliefs are also respected; I imagine that you have the possibility..."

"Yes, yes," replied Palissy; "When necessary, I will take you to a certain

---

57 **King of Navarre,** the Kingdom of Navarre was a Basque-based kingdom that occupied the land between present day France and Spain.

58 **Prince de Condé et Coligny,** (1530-1569) was a prominent Huguenot leader and general, the founder of the House of Condé, a branch of the House of Bourbon.

59 **the Geneva mode,** a reference to the influence on Huguenot ceremonies of John Calvin (1509-1564) French theologian, pastor and reformer in Geneva during the Protestant Reformation, and principal developer of Calvinism.

place and I will put you together with certain persons, such that 'the Geneva mode' will appear to you to be just as solemn as the Catholic rites…. Ah! Sire Baron, I will not hide that as far as I am concerned, I would place no obstacle to these arrangements."

"Could this be true, my dear Palissy?" murmured Massac, elated, and crying with joy.

"Do not thank me too rapidly; I must first consult with her mother, and above all, Esther…. That little one has her own ideas. She seemed to be irritated with you because of that lady-in-waiting, and these young minds heat up easily."

During this conversation, Palissy and Massac had reached the ancient Porte de Saint-Germain or Cordeliers, which was part of the oldest wall of Paris built under the reign of Philippe-Auguste.[60] They had passed the abbey of Saint-Germain, which with its impressive ramparts and soldiers wearing metal helmets guarding the gates, resembled more a fortress than a convent, and they now entered the Pré-aux-Clercs.

This popular spot for promenades, where university youths had so often exercised their undisciplined humour, was certainly in fashion, although it no longer retained its original appearance. The distinction between the 'Grand' and the 'Little' Pré-aux-Clercs was no longer possible. The canal that had separated them, called the Little-Seine, where school children came to fish[61] had now been filled. The 'Little' Pré was now covered with houses and inns, and a similar fate awaited the 'Grand' Pré in the near future, and one already saw much construction in the middle of the trees and greenery. This consisted almost exclusively of cabarets, dance halls and houses of pleasure of all sorts; the noise did not cease, neither night, nor day. However, the Pré-aux-Clercs had fresh air, space, and shade; considering the rarity of public space in the interior of the city, it was the only place where the Parisian public could frolic freely.

It was indeed the case that day as the Pré-aux-Clercs was a spectacle of activity. One could hear singing, dancing and laughter in all the houses; here and there, persons were drinking, playing dice and cards or arguing.

Basochiens[62] in red outfits, students, with their writing kits hung on their belt, monks of all types, soldiers with buffalo hide boots, crested helmets and long swords, bourgeois dressed in wool, gentlemen dressed in silk, and especially women of all types, most with insolent expressions, all forming a turbulent crowd, some elements of which could frighten peaceful persons.

---

60 **Philippe-Auguste,** Philippe II (1165-1223), King of France, had the wall built to protect Paris while he participated in the Third Crusade of 1189-1192.

61 **Author Berthet's original note,** the rue de Seine in Paris is exactly where the canal was located.

62 *Basochiens* were law clerks from societies originating in Paris formed during the Middle Ages for vocational improvement and common amusement.

In the open spaces, were played various bowling games and handball. Persons ran, wrestled and tumbled about on the lawns. One could even hear, behind certain bushes, the clashing of swords from duels between *gentlemen of honor* who often killed each other, sometimes only to keep their hand in.

However, Bernard Palissy and Massac were accustomed to such scenes, and besides, they were too occupied by their discussion to pay the slightest attention. They had taken a tortuous path,[63] bordered by trees, along which one encountered, from time to time, a cabaret, and they headed towards the place on the river where the ferry was located, just across from the Tuileries.

"Master Bernard," resumed Gaston, "I cannot believe that Esther, as severe as she might be, attaches an importance to a frivolous gallantry. You should have no trouble explaining that I am forgivable. However, I will be in boiling oil until I know her decision, and I will be most grateful if you can shorten my ordeal."

"That is just as well, Master de Massac," replied Bernard, "since, I must admit, the situation of my daughter at the Court requires a rapid solution."

He then explained to Massac the interest that the Queen was taking in Esther, and the fears of what this interest would entail.

In sharing his concern, perhaps Bernard wanted to evaluate the effect it would have on Massac. The Baron replied with vehemence:

"You are right, Master Palissy; the place for this chaste child is not in this promiscuous Court, where there are intrigues, foul language and evil actions. Having been brought up in the provinces by severe teachers and a stern mother, I could not put up with these abominable customs. It is for this reason that I have given notice to his Lordship the Constable and wish to return to Saintonge.... Moreover," he added, lowering his voice, "I am wary of this secretive Queen, who perhaps wishes to utilize Esther in some machinations of her politics.... It is therefore important, Master Bernard, that you remove your dear daughter from this malignant influence as soon as possible."

"Well spoken, Sire Baron," said Palissy joyfully; "you see things in their true light. And there are not many young men, who, for the woman they are seeking, disdain the protection of a powerful queen.... Come now, why would I wait any longer to know the opinion of Esther and her mother on your plans? They must both be at the Tuileries awaiting my return; I will speak to them and urge them to take a decision immediately."

"Do that, my good Bernard," said Massac, "as the Queen is stubborn, and time presses.... But while you go discuss my fate, I repeat, I will be suffering a cruel anguish.... Why do you not let me accompany you? I can defend my cause directly with Esther."

"This is not possible; certain things cannot be said in your presence. I

63 **Author Berthet's original note**: the rue du Bac, in our day (1875), retains the sinuosity of that old pathway.

even request that you do not cross the river with me; tomorrow, you will learn what we have resolved."

"Ah! tomorrow I will have died of fever and worry!"

They had just arrived on the banks of the Seine. At the spot where today stands the Pont Royal, there was, on the edge of the water, a little house half hidden under the willow trees and the poplars. It was the house of the ferryman, and the ferry, which came and went constantly, as we have said, was the only mode of communication between the Pré-aux-Clercs and the Tuileries.

As the boat was on the other side of the river, they had to wait for its return. Palissy and Massac strolled on the shore. Master Bernard, seeing the growing perturbation of his companion, said to him, smiling:

"See here, Master de Massac, I have pity for you and do not wish to see you languish.... Look over there," he continued, stretching his hand towards the palace; "do you see that window on the top floor, on which there is a flowering shrub?"

"I see it," replied Massac.

"That is the window of my daughter's room."

"I know."

"What! You know... Hum! The shrub is a rare plant that was given to my daughter by the master gardener. Well, you will remain here, and in one hour, you will look once more at the window. If the shrub has not moved, it is because my daughter's answer has not been favorable, and you will have to accept this as a Christian and a kind-hearted man. If, on the contrary, the shrub has disappeared, nothing opposes your coming immediately to join us. The guard at the door will have been informed, and you will find there all the family disposed to greet you.... Have you understood me well?"

"Yes, yes; thank you Master Bernard," replied Gaston, vigorously shaking the potter's hand. "If I must wait two hours, even three hours..."

"I think that one hour will suffice.... But here is the boat which approaches.... Goodby, then Master de Massac, and if necessary... farewell!"

"Not farewell! Master Bernard, let me rather hope..."

Palissy was not listening to him. He had just joined the persons that jostled to find place aboard the boat. His modest clothing was not of a nature to give him privileges, but the ferryman saw him and hastened to part the crowd, saying in a respectful tone:

"Make way; this is Master Bernard from the Tuileries!"

And thanks to his celebrity status, Palissy boarded the ferry without difficulty, and was given the place of honor.

Soon the boat departed, and during the entire crossing, Bernard could see the Baron, standing on the shore, following him with anxious eyes.

III.

AN ENCOUNTER AT THE PRÉ-AUX-CLERCS

The Baron de Massac could not decide to move away from the part of the shore from which one could observe the chateau. Palissy had not been gone ten minutes and had barely the time to arrive at the palace, and Gaston was already dismayed to see that the shrub at Esther's window had not moved. Watches, at that time, were rare, being heavy, massive and impractical. The young gentleman was therefore incapable of knowing with any accuracy when the specified hour had elapsed. He was promising himself, however, to not leave his observation post until he had received the blessed sign, even if he had to stay until nightfall.

He ended up strolling up and down the shore with a deeply preoccupied air. He remained indifferent to the graceful movements of the swallows flying over the river, the flitting of the breeze over the water's surface and silver-leafed willows on the shore, or the singing of the ferrymen who were travelling up and down the river. He did not even pay attention to the joyous groups that frequently passed him, and he did not consider responding to the meaningful winks launched in his direction by strolling ladies dressed in satin and silk, in spite of the edicts of Henri II against lavish spending.

We could not say how much time Massac had spent on watch, but it seemed to him that at least three hours had elapsed since Palissy's departure, when he saw coming towards him several persons who were headed for the ferry.

One of them was a big fellow, of a certain age, as he had a swarthy face, lined with wrinkles and a large white moustache. Nevertheless, he was wearing brand-new clothing, but of an already outdated style called *half and half,* that is made up of two differing colours, thus half of his doublet and leggings were of a daffodil-yellow colour, and the other scarlet-red. The entirety was enhanced by gold and silver stripes, shoulder braids, and a ribbon of roses draped over his shoulders, arms and down to his buffalo leather boots. A large ruff and a hat topped with an enormous feather completed this extravagant outfit. The man gave the appearance of being a soldier out celebrating, and his sword, as long as a roasting spit, contrasted with the splendour of his clothing. He appeared drunk and had on his arm a fierce-looking woman, pretentiously dressed, with a withered face, a hoarse voice and who was laughing loudly, showing that she also was on her way to inebriation. Behind this couple, walked a little bourgeois, dressed in brown, a purse on his belt, who was trying to look all the more serious than his companions, thus demonstrating cynicism.

This type of encounter was frequent in the Pré-aux-Clercs, and when the group passed next to Gaston, he was avidly looking at the window and thought he had seen a movement which was a good sign. He had not noticed them, but the bourgeois dressed in brown had stopped and was staring at him, made easier by the fact that Massac had not thought it suitable to bring his coat up to his face. Someone exclaimed with a Gascon accent:

"God's blood! I am not mistaken…. It is a gentleman from our home-land…. *Adiousias*[64], Master de Massac!"

Addressed in this manner, Massac, in spite of his preoccupations, turned brusquely; the bourgeois was Toupinac, the barber from the village near Saintes.Gaston rarely had the occasion of seeing him and was surprised to be so well known. However, the customs of the time and his natural polite-ness, obliged him to exchange a few words with this 'countryman' who presented himself in such an unexpected manner.

"So! It is you, Master Toupinac?" he said distractedly. "You have left Saintes?"

"Cape of Saint-Côme! Sire Baron," replied the barber-surgeon taking a whining tone. "I was obliged to leave my poor home in the village because those of the religion burned it down during the last war! I was ruined and my apprentices, after having become Huguenot to torment me, sent those rascal heretics on my trail…. Not knowing what to do next, I accepted the proposition of Captain Raby, who was going to Paris to recruit a new troop of 'regulars' for which I would become surgeon. Unfortunately," he contin-ued, winking while making a movement of his shoulder towards his com-panions, "the Captain, instead of finding some men, thinks only about losing himself."

And the little Gascon began to laugh at his play on words.

Massac, upon hearing the name of Captain Raby, remembered immedi-ately that an old dispute existed between him and the soldier, and this was not a good moment to settle it. So, he turned away rapidly and said with volubility:

"Fine, delighted to have met you…. Unfortunately, I am on business…. Farewell, then, Master Toupinac!"

He wanted to slip away, but the Gascon retained him.

"One moment, my gentleman." he resumed, "I request your assistance,

64 *Adiousias*, Gascon form of greeting roughly translates to 'May God be with you.'

you must have many contacts in Paris, and I would like… Captain Raby," he continued, addressing the gaudily dressed man who had stopped a few steps away, "a little patience please… this is a gentleman from Saintonge, Master the Baron de Massac!"

Upon hearing the name, the soldier straightened and said in a hoarse voice:

"Huh! What? Massac!… Triple head of the Devil! I think I know that gallant. I have to see, Sacré bleu, I have to see this!"

He cast off the woman, who did not appear offended by this discourteous action, and advanced towards the Baron.

The latter, unless he ran away, could no longer avoid a disagreeable encounter; he remained still. He raised anxious eyes towards the window at the Tuileries, and, either his problem made him see what was not there, or his wish had really been granted, as it seemed to him that the shrub was no longer in place. However, he did not have the time to make sure. Raby, whose yellow and scarlet outfit highlighted his hideous features, planted himself in front of his nose muttering:

"Massac! I knew it…. Oh! yes," he added immediately in a firmer tone, "this is my man, the one I have been searching for a long time, and who owes me sweet revenge! Horn of Beelzebub! My youngster, we will not separate without a fight to the finish this time!"

Gaston hesitated to react, as was merited by Raby's insolence. The barber, who was looking at each of them with surprise, exclaimed:

"Well! Captain, then you know Master de Massac? Indeed, I think that I remember…"

"Do I know him? And he knows me well too, that little flower. For, when he knows I am somewhere, he hastens to go elsewhere…. Finally, since my patron Saint arranged for us to meet at the Pré-aux-Clercs, it is so that we settle our quarrel without delay…. And it is not necessary to say '*my dear friend,*' the moon and the sun are the limit!"

Raby unsheathed, with some difficulty, his formidable rapier. The Baron did not move and answered coldly:

"Once again, you come at a very bad time, Captain Raby; it is true that there exists, between us, an ancient commitment, but for the moment you are here for pleasure, and I am taking care of a very serious matter. Nothing prevents us from putting this encounter off to another day… tomorrow if you wish."

"Nay!" resumed the Captain, whose insolence was doubled by the calm of his adversary. "We know, my nice lad, that you slip between the fingers, like an eel, when we think we have you…. No, for God's blood, not tomorrow, not later, but today!"

"I repeat, Captain Raby, that I cannot accept a duel with you at this moment.... I am expected.... Besides," added Massac with irony, "you could not do battle with a gentleman in that clown's costume. Finally, everyone here can see that you are drunk and that my advantage over you would be too great if I answered your challenge."

The noise of this altercation had drawn some spectators, and it was to these, like Toupinac, that the Baron was speaking. Upon hearing it said that he was drunk, Raby fell into a violent rage.

"Drunk, me?" he exclaimed. "Who says that I am drunk? Who thinks so? Is it you, miserable barber? Is it you, *the old one*? Is it you, *the red-head*?... If one of you dare claim that I have drunk too much, I will skewer him like a roast of pork!"

While speaking, as was his custom, he brought the point of his sword successively up to the faces of the spectators, such, that all, including the barber, moved back in fear. The drunkard, delighted with his demonstration, turned towards Massac, and said in a tone half taunting and half menacing:

"You can see, my little one, that you are alone in your opinion, and not one of these rascals would confirm that Captain Raby is drunk.... Therefore, no more hesitation, a thousand muskets! It is time for you to draw your sword, triple tail of Satan!... Or else, little boy, I will whip you with the flat of my sword!"

That was too much; Massac jumped at this insult. In turn, he drew his sword.

"I take you as witnesses, honorable people," he exclaimed, "that it was the repeated insults of this drunkard that obliges me to accept his challenge.... On guard, then Captain, if this is what you want... but let us do it quickly, because I am in a hurry!"

"Parbleu!" replied Raby sniggering, "am I not awaited by my charming beauty? Patience! my dear," he continued turning towards the dreadful hussy, "this will not take long!"

Toupinac, who had no idea of the cause of the quarrel, was despairing, and urged the two adversaries to at least move to a more isolated place than on this shore full of people. However, the Captain was too exasperated to delay the combat, and Massac, on his side, did not for all the world, want to lose sight of the Tuileries.

Therefore, the fight began immediately. For the third time, Massac crossed blades with the brutal soldier, and he was anxious to finish with it. Nevertheless, prompted by a sentiment of moderation which was in his loyal nature, he did not want to take the advantage he had from his cool head and superior fencing skills. Consequently, he remained on the defensive, waiting for the opportunity to disarm Raby and end the combat without the letting of blood.

He realized rapidly that his adversary was not to be underestimated.

Raby, although drunk, and perhaps because he was drunk, demonstrated a vigor and fury which required constant attention during the action. A circle of curious onlookers observed the combatants, but as persons used to seeing such a scene, they remained still and silent, apparently very satisfied with the free performance that they were offered.

Raby understood the restraint that his adversary was applying towards him and this increased his anger. Breathless, and already bathed in perspiration, he circled constantly around the Baron attempting to surprise him, while the Baron, with a calm and extreme precision, parried his feints, completely frustrating his attacks.

While pivoting on himself, Massac momentarily faced the Tuileries, and with an almost involuntary movement, cast a glance in that direction: and he had an almost dazzling vision.

The shrub had disappeared; the window was open, and in its frame, in the sunlight, a lovely young girl anxiously observed what was happening on the other side of the river. This gracious apparition was, could only be, Esther.... Esther who had accepted his proposal, Esther who awaited him, was surprised by his lateness, and undoubtedly called to him with her wishes.

A sudden pain punished Massac for his distraction. Raby had struck him with the point of his sword, which fortunately, only grazed his ribs, tearing a part of his doublet. Blood flowed and the spectators could have thought, for a moment, that the Baron was disabled.

This was not the case, however. The warning was not wasted, and Gaston protected himself more carefully. Raby, intoxicated by his fleeting triumph, wanting to finish him off with one assault, rushed towards the Baron, but did so awkwardly, as the thrust was parried easily and he impaled himself on Massac's sword, which pierced his chest and came out on the other side.

Fatally wounded, the unfortunate Captain dropped his sword, staggered and finally fell backwards, hurling a terrible profanity.

Massac remained still, shocked by his victory. As Raby was writhing on the sand and no one thought of helping him, Gaston said to the barber:

"Do your work, Master Toupinac, and see if you can ease your companion's pain.... Although he is a terrible person, I regret that he obliged me to fight him. Is there anyone here," he said looking at the spectators, "who does not recognize that I acted with the greatest moderation in this affair?"

"Yes, my gentleman," replied the individual who Raby had referred to as the 'old one.' "It was the Captain who picked the fight, and if you had wanted, the duel would have been much shorter."

"This is true, added 'the redhead.' The gentleman could have pierced his stomach ten times, but he did not wish to."

Massac, satisfied by this testimony on his honor, wiped his blade with a tuft of grass and replaced it in its sheath, then used a handkerchief to staunch the flow of blood from his side, and threw his short jacket over it.

Toupinac had kneeled down to examine the wounded man, but he soon arose and said in a muted voice, while shaking his head:

"Nothing to be done.... Master Ambroise Paré himself would not have the knowledge. The poor Captain will not survive."

Then, true to his old role, he once more leaned towards Raby and spoke several words, this time wise and appropriate, to urge him to think about the salvation of his soul. Raby responded only with a horrible profanity. The barber, having persisted:

"May the Devil... choke you!" stammered Raby.

At the same time, he clenched his fists and attempted to strike his consoler in the face; but he lacked the strength and his arm fell heavily as he exhaled his soul in a final spasm.

The body remained stretched out on the naked ground and appeared all the more hideous in its brilliantly coloured outfit, soiled with blood and dirt.

"The poor man," said Toupinac, "died the way he lived, a blasphemy on his lips.... But good Lord!" he added, a look of consternation on his face, "what will become of me now that I have lost my protector and my friend?"

"And I, then!" exclaimed the horrible woman, who stood quietly at a distance during the combat. "I will never find another man like him! It has been only two days that we have known each other, and we could not be separated. Ah! my brave Captain, I will never forget you, never!"

And she threw herself in tears on the Captain and appeared to cover him with kisses. When she arose, the purse that he carried on his belt, as was the custom, had disappeared, and his pockets were later found to be empty. Moreover, the grieving lady, as if incapable of supporting such a painful scene, hastened to lose herself in the crowd and was never heard from again.

At that time, there existed almost no police in Paris, so the impunity of duellists was total. Every day, one found, either in the city, or at the Pré-aux-Clercs, the bodies of persons killed in a duel, or otherwise; and, unless the victim belonged to a powerful family, who felt it appropriate to pursue the murderer, no judicial enquiry was made on an event of this nature. Massac, therefore, had nothing to fear about being held accountable for the death of the Captain; but the sight of the body caused him indescribable discomfort, and in addition, the gracious apparition could still be seen at the window of the Tuileries.

He approached the disconsolate barber and almost emptied his purse into Toupinac's hands.

"See to it that this unfortunate receives a Christian burial," he said. "As for you, come find me tomorrow at the inn of the *Cheval-Blanc*, where I am staying, and we will see what can be done to help you."

Toupinac put the money in his pocket.

"Thank you, by all our country's saints!" he exclaimed. "You are a generous Lord, and I hope…"

The Baron was no linger listening. He saluted the '*old one*' and the '*red-head*' who appeared to be very unhappy at not been having offered a jug of wine at a nearby cabaret in recognition of their favourable testimony. Then he ran to the spot where the ferry landed.

Fortunately, the boat had just disembarked people and was at its mooring. Massac jumped aboard and said to the ferryman:

"Right away! I am in a hurry."

A golden ecu accompanied this order, and the boat immediately left the shore.

During the brief crossing, Gaston did not take his eyes off the window where Esther Palissy was waiting. Nevertheless, prior to the landing, he decided to look back for a final view. Everything on the other bank had resumed its customary look. The strollers were coming and going, as though the slight emotions generated by the duel had already been calmed. However, in a cluster of reeds, one could glimpse a multi-coloured object that had been carelessly deposited there.

Several minutes later, Massac entered that room in the Tuileries, from where the desired signal had originated. He found there Bernard and his daughter who appeared to be waiting impatiently for his arrival. Esther took a few steps towards him.

"What is happening, Master de Massac?" she asked. "Divine Providence!" she immediately continued, "despite the distance, I very well saw what has just occurred…. You fought a duel, and you were wounded!… How could you give in to vain preoccupations regarding your honor at such a moment?"

"Esther, dear Esther," said the Baron, falling to one knee, "my wound is slight…. Forgive me!"

And he recounted how he had come to be in the obligation of defending himself.

The rigid young lady tried to stammer out some further reproaches, but Bernard interrupted her:

"Ah! my child," he said, "can you prevent that the customs of our times be combative and ferocious? Master de Massac is a gentleman and acted as a gentleman…. Embrace your fiancée, Sire Baron," he added with a smile, "and let us agree, without delay, on what we must do. This place does not suit you any more than it does my daughter; after only a few days of being here, you have been involved in a gallant affair and a duel which resulted in someone's death…. I prefer, for the two of you, a calmer and happier existence!"

Peace was thus re-established. Massac sat near Esther, and they dis-cussed at length the projects to come in the near future.

IV.

THE CHAMBER OF CATHERINE DE MÉDICIS

It was the custom, under the ancient monarchy, that the King and members of the royal family, dine in public on certain days; that is to say, the town's population was permitted, on those days, to wander around the tables while the princes and princesses were eating. This custom existed particularly at the Court of the last of the Valois,[65] and a dinner of this type, which a good number of Parisian strollers planned to attend, was scheduled to take place at the Louvre, the Sunday following the events at the Pré-aux-Clercs.

A few moments before leaving for the ceremonial feast, the Queen-Mother, Catherine de Médicis, was attending to her toilette in her chamber at the Tuileries. She preferred this chamber, still imperfectly decorated, to the one in the Louvre, where she was constantly bothered by unwelcome visitors and petitioners.

The bed, an enormous four-poster, where slept the widow of Henri II, was surrounded by a golden railing which divided the room into two parts of about equal size. In the exterior portion, there were several ladies and maids of honor, but at the interior, there was, with the Queen, only an elderly chambermaid who was called Dame Marguerite. Catherine liked her very much and wished to be dressed only by her, a preference which astonished many because Dame Marguerite, although very loyal to her mistress, was known to be Huguenot, and judging from the seriousness of her bearing, her austere clothing, her puritan manner, public opinion was not in error.

Furthermore, Catherine, as we have already seen, did not display great luxury in her clothing, and she exaggerated the rigors of her widowhood in dressing with simple dark-colored fabrics. She barely consented to wearing a dress of black velvet for major ceremonies, and it was in such a modest outfit that she attended the weddings of her sons Charles and Henri.

It was a similar black velvet dress that she had selected for the public dinner at the Louvre, and she was chatting familiarly with her chambermaid, but in a low voice so as not be overheard by the ladies on the other side of the railing. Old Marguerite, despite her appearance of inflexibility, had an

---

65 **Valois,** The House of Valois was the royal house of France from 1328 to 1589, and thus in power at the time of this story.

air of finesse, a finesse which comes from discomfort and persecution. She spoke little, but a singular smile occasionally crossed her lips that could lead one to guess that her thoughts, though supressed, were no less lively and bold.

This confidential chat had lasted some time when the Queen impatiently said to her maid:

"Saint Virgin! That is enough about your accursed Huguenots… and try to not put my wimple on askew…. You always have something to ask me for these heretics, who are, for my son and me, wicked retainers. The fact is that that I shower them with benefits and they thank me with the darkest of ingratitude…. Now, for example, your friend Bernard Palissy, who I saved from the hands of those people in Bordeaux and who I have named Governor of the Tuileries; how did he show me his gratitude? I took an interest in his daughter, a lovely child, that I met by chance in his workshop, and I wanted to take charge of her future, save her from heresy…. However, Master Bernard told me yesterday, with an embarrassed air, that he thanks me for my generous intentions regarding the little one, but that she was ill, was remaining in her room, and on the advice of Ambroise Paré, first surgeon to the King, he was sending her to the countryside…. Do you think that I am deceived by such a pretext? Good Lord, I am not used to having my goodwill disdained."

"Ah, Madam!" replied Marguerite, "One must only ask Master Bernard to produce beautiful things in pottery and glass and he will give you satisfaction for this, I think. However, why do you not let him manage his family as he wishes?"

While saying this, the old chambermaid had that special smile that we mentioned earlier. The Queen, very perceptive herself, noticed.

"Why are you laughing, crazy woman?" she said with bitterness. "Upon my life! You share common cause with all those Huguenots, and perhaps you are yourself Huguenot…. Yes, you are; as one never sees you at Mass!"

"I am constantly retained by service to Your Majesty."

"You seem to be devoted to me and you take advantage of the fact that I am attached to you by habit… but you won't escape me that way…. Do you never go out to a preaching?"

"Never," replied Marguerite.

"There is something about you which is not forthright… well, swear to me that you say the truth!"

"Religion forbids to swear, but I confirm, once again, that I never go out to a preaching."

Catherine looked at her with such fixedness that the old maid was obliged to lower her eyes. However, the Queen was still not convinced; she nodded her head and pursed her lips, saying drily:

"That is good... finish dressing me."

And for the remainder of the toilette, not a word was exchanged between the mistress and the chambermaid. Nevertheless, Dame Marguerite did not seem the least alarmed by the Queen's bad humor. This terrible Catherine, whose perfidious politics inspired so much fear, usually exhibited a great weakness towards those who lived in her intimacy, and her anger towards them never lasted for long.

Indeed, a stifled laugh, which came from a group of ladies-in-waiting, appeared to act as a diversion for her thoughts. She turned and said cheerfully:

"I hear giggling. I wager that Miss de la Billardière is there!... When one does not see her, one can guess her presence.... Approach, Miss!"

The culprit, not very repentant, detached herself from her companions and came to place herself in front of the railing.

"Will you always be the silly one?" said the Queen in a low voice while Dame Marguerite was placing a final pin. "However, my sweet, I would like to know where you are with that gallant Master de Massac, the secretary of my compère, Master Constable!... It is not possible," she added, smiling, "that he resisted those beautiful eyes, those mischievous manners, that make Miss de Billardière the idol of the Court.... Come now, what has he said to you, my dear, about the affairs of State?"

As can be seen, Catherine de Médicis, although for the moment on excellent terms with the Constable Montmorency, did not neglect any method of obtaining information, and her ladies-in-waiting were rumored, with good reason, as being agents of her secret police. The tall blond pouted and replied in a tone which was half mocking and half respectful:

"Your Majesty has apparently too high of an opinion of those 'beautiful eyes' and 'mischievous manners' of which she speaks, Master de Massac did not care at all about them."

"Are you going to act with prudery and discretion with me?" asked the Queen, fixing the young woman with her piercing gaze. "When you want, you are irresistible.... You must have taken the wrong approach, no doubt.... One should better prepare the lure and the bird will let itself be caught."

"Ah! Madam, Master de Massac seems to despise me, and has slighted me several times.... For that matter, everyone knows that he will be leaving the service of the Constable and has asked leave to return to his province."

"What! He no longer belongs to the Constable?... No matter! it would be good to know..."

"What could I know about him? He is not a gentleman like the others. He is always reserved, serious and uncommunicative... and really, I would not be surprised if he were Huguenot!"

The spirited young lady knew no epithet more outrageous than that of 'Huguenot,' and it was, at the Court, the one they threw at each other during disputes. This name, pronounced perhaps by chance, sufficed to put Catherine in a thoughtful mood.

"Huguenot!" she repeated, "everything which offends me, everything that hurts me, is Huguenot! I cannot speak, nor do something, without finding a Huguenot acting against my actions or my words…. When will this insufferable obstruction cease?"

She reflected for a moment, then made a gesture, as if to dismiss a troublesome idea, and resumed:

"Let us go, ladies, it is time for us to leave. Undoubtedly, the King is already awaiting me!"

Immediately, all her 'flying squadron' was in the air. The double doors opened and one could see, in the neighboring antechamber, a large number of persons who were to accompany the Queen-Mother to the Louvre.

Catherine began to walk, leaning on the arm of Miss de la Billardière. As she was passing by Marguerite, she said to her in a low voice, but this time in a jesting tone, shaking her finger at her:

"Ah! if I thought that you went to a preaching!…"

Everyone having left, Marguerite assured herself that the antechamber was deserted, and went to post herself at the window that gave out on the courtyard. The Queen and her ladies had mounted in their litters and were moving away with their brilliant escort of horse guards and pages.

Dame Marguerite followed them with her eyes until she could no longer see them. Certain that no one would return for a forgotten object and that she was alone in this part of the chateau, she closed the huge door and removed the key, as her position authorized her to do, and lowered the portières.[66]

At this point, her attitude changed. She seemed to straighten, and that smile, which we have mentioned several times, became a silent laugh. Approaching the wood panelling, she touched a hidden button and the panel opened. It was by this means that Marguerite could enter her mistresses chamber, at any hour of the day or night.

She, herself, occupied a rather cramped room positioned between the sumptuous ceremonial chambers, and illuminated by a small round window facing the garden. From this recess, she could hear the silver whistle that the Queen used to call her when she required her services. A small stairway, winding and obscure, connected with the palace's kitchens; one could enter and exit in this manner without having to give explanations to the guards and pages who congested the large apartments.

Dame Marguerite took from her room a branch of green leaves, taken from a shrub in the garden, and descended the secret stairway. At the bottom

66 **portières,** are hanging curtains placed over a door, or over the doorless entrance to a room.

of the steps, she opened, using a key from the bunch attached to her belt, a small door which gave out onto a courtyard full of debris and construction material. There, she negligently tossed the branch on the ground; then, leaving the door ajar, she climbed back up to the Queen's chamber.

All this was done rapidly, without hesitation, as if Dame Marguerite followed a procedure which had become familiar.

"Now *they* can come!" she murmured with satisfaction.

She sat down, placed a pair of enormous glasses on her nose; and taking a Bible out from her pocket, began to read.

However, she was not allowed much time at this occupation. Several light knocks were sounded in a certain manner on the panel of the woodwork. The old maid ran over, and pronounced, through the door, a strange word which was certainly a password; someone answered with a word just as strange; then the panel turned on its hinges and a man entered the chamber.

"God keep you! my sister Marguerite," he said in a friendly manner.

"Greetings, my brother Ambroise," replied Marguerite. The visitor was Master Ambroise Paré.

"I am the first to arrive, I believe," he said quietly. "I was in the chateau, and saw the Queen leave for the public dinner…. Moreover, the green branch is on the ground next to the door…. Ah! will the assembly be numerous?"

"Yes, by the grace of God!… You are aware, Master Ambroise, that today we have a special ceremony?"

"Palissy warned me…. Upon my word! Dame Marguerite," continued Paré, laughing, "when I see all of us in this chamber, it seems to me that we are like mice lodging in the ear of a cat!"

Dame Marguerite did not have time to answer, as there was again knocking. After repeating the same formalities as for the first visitor, she introduced the second one to whom Ambroise extended his hand.

From that moment on, the chambermaid was occupied only with identifying and receiving the persons arriving as for a meeting. Each seemed to have some degree of importance at the Court, and among them were several ladies. Soon, between twelve and fifteen persons were reunited; and between their clothing, mannerisms and language, it was not difficult to identify Protestants. It became even more certain when one of them, an elderly man, with a venerable aspect, went to the Queen's prie-Dieu,[67] opened a Bible, and began singing, in a muted voice, a French psalm that the others repeated with great precaution.

The event that we are describing is rigorously a historical fact, and illustrates resoundingly how the methods of suppression are useless as re-

67 **Prie-Dieu,** is a type of prayer desk primarily intended for private devotional use, but may also be found in churches.

gards faith. Days after the ruthless Queen Catherine de Médicis ordered the massacres of Saint Bartholomew, there was a Huguenot *preaching* in her chambers at the Tuileries under the auspices of her governess, Marguerite,[68] while she was dining with the King at the Louvre. It is for this reason that Marguerite was smiling earlier, when her mistress accused her of going to a preaching; she was not going there, it was the preaching that came to her.

We have even retained the names of the majority of those who participated in the Protestant services in the royal chambers on certain Sundays. In addition to the surgeon Ambroise Paré, one could find the sculptor Jean Goujon who was working on the large caryatids[69] of the Louvre and was occupied with such a task at the moment of the Saint-Bartholomew massacre, when he Sundayswas killed by a musket shot while on his scaffold. Then, there was the architect Durceceau, Lord and Lady Feuquères, the mathematician Jean Viret, Lady d'Uzès and a poet named Sauxay, a great friend and admirer of Bernard Palissy. It was Sauxay, in an ode dedicated to Bernard, after having spoken of Colossus of Rhodes and the Pillars of Hercules, who wrote:

> But all this does not approach
> The rustic figulines
> So many and so well painted
> And dexterously imagined

Finally, the elderly man who presided over the ceremony, as its pastor, was the Minister Merlin, chaplain to the Admiral Coligny.

As the participants were ending the singing of the psalm, in muted voices, which thanks to the drapes and portières, could not be heard outside, someone again knocked at the wood panelling using the accustomed code. Immediately there fell a great silence, not because they feared a treason which would have placed everyone in great danger, but because they were awaiting the arrival of persons who, that day, would play an important role in this secret assembly.

Indeed, Dame Marguerite having opened the door, several couples entered.

Entering first came Master Bernard Palissy, holding the hand of his daughter, Esther, pale with emotion. Neither one or the other, in spite of the seriousness of the circumstances, were dressed more formally than usual, as it would have been dangerous to draw attention by excess. Esther had relaxed her usual austerity and was charming in a silk dress which corre-

68 **Author Berthet's original note** : See 'Etudes sur a vie et travaux de Bernard Palissy' by J. Salles, Nîmes, 1855. Mention is made of the secret *preaching* in the Queen's chambers.

69 **Caryatids**, are in classical architecture, draped female figures used instead of columns as a support.

sponded to her new status. Behind them came the Baron Gaston de Massac, in a black costume, giving his hand to Mistress Bernard, who in a new dress with a hooped skirt, seemed embarrassed by her appearance, poor woman, and was not sure where to set her eyes. Bringing up the rear were Mathurin and Nicolas Palissy, dressed like the young gentlemen of the time, and very proud to attend the marriage of their sister in the royal chamber.

As you have surmised, no doubt, marriage was the subject of the moment. The preceding evening, the ceremony took place in accordance with Catholic rites, at the home of Massac's former chaplain, and now it was about to be renewed following the Calvinist rites, to satisfy the conscience of each spouse. Protestants had no prejudice against mixed marriages and accepted them readily. However, some Catholics considered them an impiety and there was a real danger for those who contracted one when the fact became known.

The assembly looked upon Bernard Palissy and his family very favorably; the opinion was more reserved as regards Gaston de Massac, who presented himself with a noble confidence without affectation. Master Bernard, taking his hand, while on the other side, he held that of his daughter, presented the young couple to the assembly:

"My brothers and sisters," he said, "here are my children, and I ask you to join me in asking, on their behalf, the benediction of God.... One of them," he continued, indicating Gaston, "does not belong to our Church, but he is upright and generous, by our standards, and I have no fear in conferring to him the happiness of my beloved daughter, Esther."

"My brother Palissy," said one of those present, "your wisdom inspires our entire confidence; however, we cannot forget that our entire existence will henceforth depend upon Master de Massac, who now knows the secret of our meetings, and is not one of us...."

The suspicion contained in these words brought a flush to Gaston's features.

"Sire," he said with dignity, "do you think that if your existence was menaced by the object of this meeting, that I would have nothing to fear for mine?... I am full of respect for the faith of my dear Esther and for that of her friends.... I affirm this, upon my faith as a Christian Catholic and on my honor as a gentleman!"

This response, in spite of its pride, did not seem to displease the Protestants. Pastor Merlin had the young couple placed before him and addressed them with a lecture on the obligations of marriage. Merlin was known as one of the most eloquent persons of his time, and at this moment he demonstrated an impeccable tact and appropriateness. Artfully bypassing issues of dogma that could offend one spouse or the other, he remained on the terrain of pure morals, and expressed himself with a loftiness of thought and spiritual fervor that moved the assembly. Esther shed warm tears, and Gaston, electrified by these noble words, did not notice that they came from the mouth of a heretic.

The allocution finished, they proceeded to the marriage ceremonies 'in the Geneva mode' as was then said. Dame Marguerite went to get, in the Queen's chapel, two gold candlesticks, each with a burning candle, and placed them in the spouses' hands. The latter then responded to the customary questions, and following several prayers, all was done. The assembly intoned a final psalm in the place of a benediction.

Massac, in spite of his joy at finally being united with his dear Esther by indissoluble bonds, felt a little uncomfortable among these Huguenots against whom he retained tenacious childhood prejudices. However, this discomfort did not last long; the psalm had not even finished, that someone was knocking at the door of the wood panelling and a breathless voice exclaimed from outside:

"Dame Marguerite, alert!... Here is the Queen."

The singing ceased immediately, and everyone arose with concern. Marguerite ran over to open the panel. The person giving the warning was old Daniel, who had been placed as a sentry on the approach to the palace during the preaching.

Without entering, he repeated from the doorstep:

"Alert! My brothers.... The Queen is returning from the Louvre."

"Already!" murmured Marguerite.

The time had passed quickly during the ceremony and the speeches, and that day the public dinner had been prolonged less than usual. The old chambermaid ran to the window and lifted imperceptibly the curtain; indeed, she saw the royal cortege arrive in the courtyard.

"May the almighty God protect us!" she said in terror; "leave my friends, leave quickly, if you do not want to sleep tonight in the dungeons of the Châtelet or the Bastille."

"And yourself, Dame Marguerite," asked Master Bernard, "do you not also have something to fear?"

"Oh! me..." replied the maid.

And a sardonic smile completed her phrase.

They hurriedly headed for Marguerite's small room in order to reach the service stairway and leave the Tuileries. However, as that many persons could not leave at the same time without attracting attention, it was decided that the persons foreign to the palace would leave first, while those like Ambroise Paré, Palissy and his family, who belong to the house of the Queen, would wait in Marguerite's room for a favourable moment to leave. The majority of the others hastened to descend.

While they were going down the stairway, a woman, arriving in the other direction, mixed in with them. It was Miss de la Billardière. She had been sent in advance to give the order to Dame Marguerite to open the large apartments so that the Queen would not have to wait. Miss de la Billardière was very surprised to meet so many persons on this little used passageway known only to the servants. She examined the individuals with curiosity, but in addition to the fact that the stairway was very dark, the men had covered their features with their coats, while the women hid their faces using velvet masks which upper class ladies often wore in the streets. The lady-in-waiting therefore recognized no one.

Increasingly intrigued, she reached the top of the stairs. Dame Marguerite was still in the royal apartments to make disappear the traces of the assembly, but in her room, were, as we have said, Ambroise Paré and the Palissy family, habitual guests of the chateau; there also, however, was Gaston de Massac, who no longer wished to separate himself from his spouse.

At the moment that the lady-in-waiting entered, Palissy and Paré were chatting in low voices; the Baron, sitting next to Esther, was holding her hands in his and was saying sweet words to her to which Esther was listening with a smile. Miss de la Billiardière stopped in front of the couple and exclaimed in a mocking tone:

"Oh! now the daughter of Master Bernard dresses like us!… She is not ill as the Queen has been told?"

Esther moved rapidly away from her husband, got up and fixed the new arrival with an irritated look. However, since neither one answered, Ambroise Paré hastened to intervene.

"She is indeed ill, the sweet child," he said with irony, "and the proof is that here is her doctor."

"Now, see here, Master Ambroise," replied Miss de la Billardière in her little impertinent tone; "as wise as you are, it would require a much younger doctor than you to achieve such a cure!"

And she left with a burst of laughter. Massac, outraged by this impudence, was about, in his anger, to let escape some impudent phrases. Fortunately, he did not have the time. One could already hear the voice of the Queen in the next room, and Miss de la Billardière had left by the door in the panel.

Indeed, the Queen, followed by only a few ladies, had arrived at her chamber by coming through the large apartments, and was reprimanding Marguerite. She appeared to be in a particularly bad mood. Her son, the King Charles IX, usually very submissive to her wishes, had that day shown certain aspirations of resistance, and it was for this reason that the public dinner had finished so early. Moreover, upon returning home, Catherine, who was distrustful as well as observant, took only one look to recognize that all was not as it should be, and the obvious embarrassment of her chambermaid increased her suspicions.

"What is going on?" she asked severely; "I almost had to wait at the door…. Marguerite, what are you doing? Nothing is in its place, and one smells the odor of wax as if someone had been burning candles. You were not alone a while ago…. Who could come to my chamber when I am not there? It would be an audacity!"

"Madam," stammered Marguerite, "I was tidying up the furniture, and you arrived so suddenly…"

"You had not been warned? Had you not seen that foolish de la Billiardière who I sent in advance? She may well have long legs, but she prefers at all times to use her tongue…. That silly girl probably stopped off somewhere to chat with one of her admirers!"

At that moment Miss de la Billiardière arrived.

"May Your Majesty pardon me," she said. "I ran into such a crowd on the service stairway, and I had difficulty battling my way up to Dame Marguerite's."

"What?" asked the Queen, "a crowd in Marguerite's room?"

"It was," explained the old lady, "several persons from the palace who came to visit me, at the only time that my service allows me a little liberty."

"There were," resumed Miss de la Billardière, who hated the Queen's favorite, "many unknown persons who seemed to be hiding…. I saw in Dame Marguerite's room, where they probably still are, Master Ambroise Paré, then Master Bernard with all his family, including his daughter, who seems in full health; but there was also Master de Massac, first gentleman to the Constable, and that one does not belong to the palace, I believe."

Catherine flinched.

"Massac!" she repeated; "then he has not gone as they said? What does he want?… So? Is my compère Constable concerned about my secret affairs?… Have Massac come here," she ordered. "Have Master Paré, Master Palissy and the others come here as well."

Miss de la Billlardière hastened to go out, while the Queen began to examine everything around her with an inquisitive air. After a moment, the lady-in-waiting returned; she had found no one in Marguerite's room, and the door communicating with the stairwell was closed.

"They are gone!" she exclaimed, "one would think that they took fright. If Your Majesty so orders, I will go down and get information…."

However, the Queen had just found on her prie-Dieu an object that she hastened to hide with her hand. When she turned, she was extremely pale, and said abruptly to the lady-in-waiting:

"That suffices, Miss; before executing an order, wait until you receive it…. Everyone is to leave!… Dame Marguerite will serve me."

Miss de la Billardière and the other ladies were struck by the change in her voice. There was nothing to reply, and after having bowed, they left by the large door.

They had barely left the two alone that the Queen let her anger explode:

"Miserable creature," she cried out, waving the object that she had just found, "do you recognise this?"

It was a Protestant Bible that one of the participants in the preaching had left in the haste of his flight.

Dame Marguerite was not disconcerted.

"Master Ambroise or Master Bernard could have left this book here," she replied; "Your Majesty knows perfectly well that both of them are of 'the religion!'"

"Such an abomination in my home, on my prie-Dieu! Exclaimed the Queen, throwing down the book with horror.

Marguerite hastened to pick up the book and make it disappear.

"Ah! Madam," she said, keeping her composure, "it is simply the Holy Scriptures, but in French."

The Queen was at the height of her exasperation.

"Old impious woman!" she scolded, "I wager that this heretic book of spells belongs to you!... You merit my having you burned alive at the Place de Grève[70] as a sorceress!... But I want to know what happened in my chamber a while ago. Aside from Palissy, who was there?"

"There was the family of Master Bernard as the young daughter will be leaving and the dear young child wanted to say goodbye to me.... And then there was Master de Massac, who the Palissys knew in Saintonge, and was going to accompany them.... That one, no one will accuse of being of 'the religion' as he is attached to the Constable, a leader of the Papists... the Catholics, I mean!"

"Once again, Miss de la Billardière saw a great number of persons."

"Well, does Your Majesty believe the chatter of that scatterbrain? That young lady only looks at her lovers, and she has some from both religions, without counting the miscreants who are from neither."

These explanations were given with such assurance and calm that the Queen seemed to be reduced to silence. However, she felt that something was being kept from her, and she fixed Marguerite with a look of frightening acuity. Soon, she threw herself into a chair and said aloud, as if talking to herself:

"She is lying to me.... I wager that she is lying to me. Every one betrays me.... I am surrounded by traps and dangers. My God! Would you leave me prey to the machinations of my secret enemies?... But I will know the truth," she added in a menacing tone. "I will consult Ruggieri, my astrologer, regarding certain persons.... Ah! Ruggieri was right this morning

70 **Place de Grève**, is now the Place de l'Hotel de Ville (Paris City Hall), but was remembered as being the site of most of the public executions in early Paris.

when he assured me that the conjunction of the star Antares and the moon presaged a treason for today."

And she remained a moment plunged in her musings, as sometimes happens. Finally, she raised her head and resumed in a gruff manner:

"Now, Marguerite, while waiting that I decide to throw you into a dungeon, undress me. This velvet dress is crushing me."

Marguerite smiled her special smile, but she kept quiet for fear of spoiling her cause and hastened to complete her task.

Meanwhile, Master Bernard and all his family, which now included Gaston de Massac, had sought refuge in the workshop at the tuilerie, whose access was forbidden to the uninitiated. One has guessed that the Palissys, as well as Ambroise Paré, upon hearing the Queen's angry voice, beat a hasty retreat, certain that Dame Marguerite would find a way of calming her redoubtable mistress. Ambroise had left the chateau, but the Palissys were not without concern regarding the consequences of this alarm, and were expecting at any moment, to see an officer of the guards arrive to give them the order to appear before Catherine.

"You see, my son Massac," Bernard was saying with sadness, "the life that we lead here. The favor which supports us has the fragility of glass, and the slightest of shocks can break it…. We here, we know how to put up with it all; but this sweet and timid Esther, now your wife before God and man, could not resist for long under these perpetual anxieties. Therefore, in spite of the painful void that will be created by her absence, it is important to take her away as soon as possible."

"You anticipate my wishes, my father Bernard," replied the Baron with vivacity; we will leave, my dear Esther and I, this very evening."

"Tonight?!" repeated Esther.

"All the arrangements have been made," continued the Baron. "My wife will travel in a good litter and I will be on horseback. We will be escorted by four lackeys, armed to the teeth, who will protect us from any bad encounters during the trip. We will travel in short stages, and I hope that we will arrive in Massac without incident. Moreover, I have a safe passage from the Constable, and no one would dare to stand in the way of our travel."

Esther gave free reign to her tears.

"Ah!" she murmured, "to be separated from my beloved father, of my tender mother, of all those that I hold dear!"

"And I, my love?" said Massac with a tone of reproach.

"Oh! Pardon me, Gaston. Would I be worthy of you if I could leave my parents without cruel heartache?… But you, my father," she added, "do you not fear anything from this Court divided by religious hate, intrigues and hostile feelings?"

"Do not worry about me, my child," replied Master Bernard, "as soon as you are in a safe place, I will not fear either for myself or for those of mine that remain in my care. The Queen is a fanatical Italian; she is a forceful woman, but she retains, from her heritage, a taste for the fine arts which dominates her fanaticism. As long as I can produce superb glazed pottery, coloured stained-glass windows, statues and can design magnificent gardens for her castles, she will not let anyone touch a hair on my head, even if I am the most committed Huguenot."

"Ah! my father, your genius has saved us many times, but will it always save you?"

V.

THE RETURN

Several years have passed.

Friday, twenty-two August 1572, all of Paris was still celebrating the marriage of the young King of Navarre (later Henri IV) to Marguerite, sister of the King Charles IX. One knew that the marriage was a guarantee of reconciliation between the major political and religious factions, whose mutual antagonism had cost France so many tears and so much blood. Henri de Navarre, Protestant, had married the daughter of Henri II and Catherine de Médicis. The religious quarrels were therefore going to cease. On the occasion of this peace, all the Huguenot leaders who had presented themselves on the fields of battle, had come to Paris where they had received a most attentive welcome from Charles IX and the royal family. In addition to General de Coligny, the true leader of the reform, and the young Prince de Condé, who was helping the King of Navarre, there were, either at the Louvre, or at the various inns of the city, a considerable number of Protestant gentlemen, and although the celebrations were coming to an end, there continued to be new arrivals.

On the day of which we speak, it was perhaps to this category of traveler that belonged the gentleman who arrived at the Croix-de-Lorraine Inn, located on rue de la Croix-du-Trahoir (today, rue de l'Arbre-Sec.) He had a modest style and was accompanied only by a servant who was to bring back the horses. His baggage consisted of one suitcase and two horse pistols that the innkeeper, who rushed out to receive him, wanted to carry himself to a room in the house.

As they mounted the stairs, the master of the lodging asked, in an obsequious tone:

"You will undoubtedly wish, my gentleman, to have something to eat?"

"Yes, I am exhausted. I have come from a great distance, and for the past thirty hours, I have not left the saddle."

"You are here in Paris, I suppose, for the marriage celebrations. It is a little late. However, they say that there is an important reception at the Louvre this evening."

"I do not care," replied the stranger, coldly.

"What would you like for dinner, my gentleman. Some ham? Some chicken?"

"Rascal!" said the traveler, frowning. "Are you forgetting that today is Friday? You will not serve me meat."

"You are therefore not…"

"What business is it of yours? But go prepare my dinner."

The innkeeper bowed out smiling. His ploy had worked and he knew that the newcomer was Catholic.

A quarter of an hour later, the traveler came down from his room and sat down in a dining room of dubious cleanliness, where his dinner awaited him. He had, with items withdrawn from the suitcase, suitably modified his outfit, and looked quite well dressed. After having rapidly finished his dinner, he appeared ready to go out.

"My gentleman," asked the innkeeper, "what are your orders for the day?"

"The most urgent is to indicate to me a barber who can accommodate me."

"You will find a few steps from here at a shop-sign for '*the Conversion of the Heretics*,' *a* barber said to be quite capable."

"That will do."

"Please, my gentleman, would you not tell me whom I have the honor of lodging in my house?'

"Baron de Massac, formerly first gentleman to his Lordship the Constable de Montmorency."

This time, the innkeeper bowed down to the ground.

It was, indeed, Gaston de Massac, who after several years in Saintonge, had returned to Paris, and judging from his mysterious and preoccupied demeanour, he was here for an important affair.

As soon as he left the inn, he headed for what was called the Place de la Croix-du-Trahoir, although it was hardly more than a crossroad, but Paris did not have many large squares, as we have previously said). The Baron passed near a fountain that King Francois I had erected in the middle of the public place, and which was later moved to the corner of rue Saint-Honoré. At the end of the crossroad, marked by a stone cross, he had no problem identifying the barbershop that had been described to him.

Without hesitation, he entered the shop, where there were already a number of persons. As newspapers, to inform people about the state of affairs, did not yet exist in Paris as well as in the provinces, it was at the barber's that one learned about events and discussed them. Also, there was a crowd at '*the Conversion of the Heretics*' and perhaps Massac was not displeased to hear the latest news, as he sat down on a bench and lent an ear to what was being said.

On that day, one placed more caution and reserve than usual on the conversations. Although one spoke only about the reconciliation taking place between the Catholics and the Protestants, resulting from the marriage of Henri de Navarre and Marguerite de Valois, a sort of uneasiness existed among those present where the two religions were about equally represented. It seemed that no one dared clearly express his opinion and everyone seemed to be on the defensive. They satisfied themselves with descriptions of the superb celebrations that were being held at the Louvre or at the Hotel de Ville, and to repeat the small talk attributed to the leaders of both parties.

This reserve was fair game for the Master Barber, who, while shaving and shearing his customers, gave free reign to his tongue, and by himself covered the noise of individual conversations. One will not be surprised to learn, as you may have guessed, that the barber was, once again, none other than Toupinac.

"You see, my masters," he said in a confident tone, while waxing the long moustache of a gentleman with hard and devious features, "there will never be a reconciliation between Papists and Huguenots, as long as we have not demonstrated to the heretics the error and madness of their doctrines. To accomplish this, one does not need great clergymen, or experienced theologians who can only speak Latin, but practical men, men with a natural eloquence, like…"

"Like you, right?" replied the gentleman in a mocking tone while getting up, his toilette completed. It is certain that this is the claim of your shop sign!"

"Ah! by the Mass! Why not me as well as another?" said Toupinac assuming an air of importance. "I was an army surgeon, and I can say with pride that I often had occasion to…"

"Bah!" as eloquent as you might be, your arguments for conversion are not as convincing as mine."

"And what are yours, Sire?"

"An arquebus[71] bullet… in the right place!" he replied, and the gentleman left hurriedly.

The little Gascon, for a moment, remained speechless by the sharpness of this reply.

"What a hothead!" he finally said. That was Master de Maurevert, who belongs to Master de Guise."

"Maurevert! A cursed Guise follower!" repeated another gentleman, dressed in brown, equipped with a long sword, and appearing to be a Huguenot. "Maugrebleu! Had you said so earlier, I could have discussed with him in the manner he likes best!"

71 **arquebus,** was the first firearm with a trigger. A heavier version known as a musket, appeared in Europe around 1521.

And he left to follow Maurevert to look for a fight.

As the master barber prepared to resume his verbal harangue, his eyes fell upon Massac. He looked at him fixedly to let him know he recognized him. However, he gave no sign as he presented the protective sheet and said:

"Your turn, Sire."

Gaston sat down, and after briefly giving his instructions to the barber, allowed his face to be lathered in silence. He had hoped to maintain his incognito when Toupinac said to him in a low voice:

"Does Master de Massac have a reason for not wanting his presence in Paris known?"

The Baron smiled.

"None, Master Toupinac," he replied in the same low voice. "However, I would appreciate your discretion as I do not particularly want my name to be shouted over the rooftops."

It took no more than this to loosen the barber's tongue, and he began, with volubility, to recount his own affairs. He explained how after having rendered final services for the 'unfortunate' Captain Raby, he had used the money resulting from the Baron's generosity to rent a stall to exercise his specialty; and how, thanks to its profits, he had established himself in this shop where business was prospering.

Fortunately for Massac, the barber had much to do at that moment and soon found himself obligated to pass on to another customer. Gaston took advantage of this to straighten his clothes, and having generously paid his expenditure, wanted to leave. Toupinac nonchalantly interrupted his work on another client and approached him with a mysterious air.

"Sire Baron," he said to him in a low voice, "I am in your debt, and I wish to give you some good advice.... Will you be in Paris for long?"

"No Master, in two or three days I plan to take the coach.... Why this question?"

"I cannot really say, except that for the time being there is a 'bad atmosphere here in Paris.' Finish the business which brings you here as rapidly as possible and depart without further delay."

"Once again, what do you mean?"

"Do not ignore my warning.... It is known that you are a friend of Master Bernard of the Tuileries, and that you have certain connections with the Huguenots.... I repeat. There is a *bad atmosphere*."

Gaston wanted to insist to obtain an explanation, but the barber placed a finger on his lips and returned to his work.

While entering the crowded crossroads next to the shop, the Baron was thinking to himself:

"I believe that Toupinac is well-intentioned. What I see and hear here redoubles my fears.... So! I must not lose a minute; I will go to the Tuileries to see Master Bernard."

He headed for the river going towards the Porte du Bois which was near the Louvre.

He was already near the spot where later would be built the Pont Neuf, when the detonation of an arquebus was heard, followed by a great rumbling which resounded behind him, coming from the rue des Fossées-Saint-Germain-l'Auxerrois.

Massac had automatically stopped, as did a number of other passers-by, but during those troubled times, such incidents were quite common in Paris, and he was going to continue on his way. The gallop of a horse made him turn his head. On the horse was a man with a pale face, and a frightened look, who was urging his horse through the crowd, without fear of crushing pedestrians, and who soon disappeared. It was Maurevert, who Gaston had just seen at the barber's and who had been said to belong to the Guises.

An extraordinary agitation developed in the area. People were running and pushing each other; swords were beginning to be drawn from their sheaths. At the same time, one heard appalled voices which were exclaiming:

"To arms! To arms, good people…. Admiral de Coligny has just been assassinated!"

Massac needed to inquire carefully about what had occurred. He joined the crowd that was rushing towards rue des Fossées-Saint-Germain-l'Auxerrois. He was one of the first to arrive and he saw an old man, clothed in black, whose appearance was both majestic and venerable, covered with blood, and leaning on two gentlemen. A dozen other men, who made up his suite, sword in hand, were noisily searching a house from which the arquebus shot had originated. The old man was the Admiral Coligny. Upon leaving the Louvre, where he had gone to amuse himself by watching the King playing handball with the Duke of Guise, he was returning to his hotel located on rue Béthisi, a few steps away, when the arquebus shot coming from a window, wounded him in the left arm and cut off his index finger of the right hand. His people, as we said, were in the house which belonged to Villemur, an old tutor to the Duke de Guise, to search for the assassin, but they found only the arquebus which was still smoking. As for Maurevert, he had jumped on a horse which was waiting behind the house, and Massac had seen him fleeing at full speed.

That part of the city was occupied, at that moment, by Protestant gentlemen who had come to Paris with Coligny and the King of Navarre. The majority of them came running, equipped with armor, a sword or escopette[72] in hand. The rue Béthisi, that the Admiral had found the strength to reach on foot, had filled with armed persons, both noble and bourgeois. People were

---

72 **Escopette,** a small hand-held version of the arquebus.

agitated; shouting and menacing each other. Completely contradictory versions were being heard. Some insisted that the Admiral was dead, and others that the wounds were not serious; some rejoiced, others becoming angry or lamenting. There was total confusion, and exasperation, which could result at any moment, in a terrible fray.

Soon the crowd was violently pushed aside by Swiss guards and royal musketeers who came from the Louvre. These soldiers were escorting the King Charles IX, his brother, de Duke of Anjou (later Henri III), his sister Marguerite, the new Queen of Navarre, and finally, the Queen-Mother Catherine de Médicis. Behind them, among the members of the retinue, one could see Ambroise Paré, medical kit under his arm. The King, who was still playing handball when he received the news of the assassination attempt, wanted to immediately visit the illustrious victim, bringing all his family. Perhaps due to his haste, he did not have a coat, and one could see his long and lean body, beardless face, sparse hair and a sickly and wan expression, as was reproduced in the bust by Germain Pilon.[73] He seemed very animated and was speaking excitedly with his mother; but one could only hear the horrible swearwords with which he usually punctuated his sentences. Catherine, on the contrary, comfortably aged in her widow's attire, was quite calm, although very pale; and she examined the crowd to evaluate the impression that these events had on them.

All these important persons were walking rapidly and entered the Admiral's house. History tells us what happened there. The King showered Coligny with caresses, called him 'his father,' swore to have the assassin pursued, such that the Admiral and the Protestants, reassured, banished their distrust. Ambroise Paré, who, after having dressed his wounds, declared that he took responsibility for the life of his patient, succeeded in calming everyone, and even before the King and the royal family had returned to the Louvre, the crowd had begun to disperse.

However, the Baron de Massac, engrossed by a specific thought, was saying to himself agitatedly:

"Perhaps this assassination attempt is only the work of a lone fanatic, but perhaps also it is a prelude to even more terrible crimes to come.... I had better not lose another minute to see Palissy."

He headed back towards the Porte du Bois, and as it was not far away, it only took him a few minutes to get there. However, a cruel disappointment was awaiting him. They had closed the gate and the drawbridge was up.

He approached one of the guards and asked if it was still possible to enter or leave Paris. The guard, softened up by the gift of an ecu, answered that by the express order of the King and the provost of the shopkeepers, all

---

73 **Germain Pilon,** (1535-1590) French sculptor whose work, principally monumental tombs, is a link between the Gothic tradition and sculpture of the Baroque period.

the gates of the city had been closed; that they wanted to prevent the escape of the Admiral's assassins, (and he appeared to snigger as he gave this explanation) and finally, they did not know when the gates would be reopened, but in any case, this would not be until the next day.

Massac, distraught, had to retrace his steps.

"My God! he thought, "what will Esther say?... I feel, I am sure that Palissy is in the greatest danger, and I cannot give him advice that might perhaps save him.... What purpose has this difficult journey served!"

VI.

SAINT BARTHOLOMEW'S DAY

The next morning, when the Baron de Massac arose, the agitation in Paris seemed to have totally calmed down. Several Protestant gentlemen from the retinue of Coligny and the Bourbon princes lodged at the Croix-de-Lorraine, the previous evening, had shown themselves to be very anxious and very exasperated. Now, they no longer had the same attitude. The news concerning the Admiral continued to be excellent. It was said that Charles IX had very rudely received the Duke de Guise, presumed author of the assassination attempt, and had given formal orders to capture de Maurevert and put him on trial. In short, all sources of trouble had disappeared, and the events of the previous day would likely be shortly forgotten.

Massac soon went out to verify the situation for himself. An apparent calm reigned in the area around the Louvre. At most, here and there, one could see groups of idlers peacefully exchanging news. In the rue Béthisi, fifty of the King's musketeers, under the orders of Cosseins[74], had the mission of protecting the Admiral; the majority of the leaders of the Huguenots were even kept in their lodging 'for their security.' The menacing demonstrations between Catholics and Protestants had ceased, and everyone was now only thinking about their own affairs.

The Baron soon had another proof of the appeasement now apparent in Paris. News had spread that the gates of the city had just reopened; and, indeed, when Massac hurried to the Porte du Bois, he had the satisfaction of seeing that the drawbridge was down and movement was now free with the exterior. He hastened to take advantage of this, and a few moments later, he had arrived at the Tuileries.

The palace was now completely finished, and numerous Swiss guards in colourful costumes, armed with halberds, were guarding the approaches. But it was not in the palace that Gaston wished to enter. He hastened to the workshops of the tuilerie itself, whose access was open to anyone, and where he counted on finding Bernard Palissy. He was not disappointed. In

---

74 **Cosseins**, though commander of the guard protecting Admiral Coligny, actually participated in his assassination when the signal was given to begin the massacre.

the modelling workshop, Bernard Palissy, assisted by his two sons, Mathurin and Nicolas, was quietly at work.

At the sight of Massac, he arose and came to greet him.

"You here, my son?" he exclaimed with emotion. "Good Lord, has something happened to Esther?"

"No! no! thank heavens," replied the Baron, embracing him. "Esther is safe at home in the country."

"And the children, how are they?"

"Wonderful. Bernard, the oldest, is becoming a charming elf, and little Berthe is growing beautifully."

The Baron then embraced his two brothers-in-law, and Palissy had him sit by his side.

"Ah! my dear Gaston," he was saying, "what a joy it would be for my poor wife, whom we had the misfortune of losing two years ago, to see her beloved daughter so rich and so happy!…but how did you find the courage, in these disastrous times, to leave Esther to come to Paris?"

"It was only for you, my father Bernard, that I undertook this voyage," replied the Baron. "Over there in Saintonge, the most sinister of rumors have spread regarding the plans of the King and the Queen-Mother. It is said that the marriage of Henri de Navarre is a lure to attract the Protestants to Paris where they will all be massacred. The fears on this subject are so great that the Rochellois[75] sent a delegation to the Admiral to beg him not to come here; he did not listen to them, and yesterday's terrible event proves how right they were."

"Bah!" replied Palissy, shrugging his shoulders, "the assassination attempt against the Admiral was the work of a lone fanatic, and Master Ambroise Paré, whom I saw this morning, assures me that the wounds will be healed in a few days."

"Beware, my father, of paying a high a price for your blind confidence. The fact remains that my dear Esther, learning of this news, felt greatly worried about you. She begged me to leave immediately to come and get you. Your youngest children, since the death of their mother, have been entrusted to the care of your family in Bordeaux. However, you, and your two sons, are particularly in danger in this royal palace where everyone knows your religion. I requested for the three of you, and for myself, safe-passage documents from Marshall de Montmorency, the son of the late Constable who had helped us in the past. These were immediately granted. Thanks to Sire Marshall's current situation, these documents will be equally respected by Catholics and Protestants. Agree therefore, to leave with me…. I beg my brothers Mathurin and Nicolas to add their entreaties to mine to persuade you."

75 **Rochellois,** inhabitants of the city of La Rochelle, located in the South-West of France.

The faces of the two young persons expressed how much such a proposal pleased them; however, they waited respectfully for their father to make known his opinion. Master Bernard was smiling.

"Come now! Massac," he resumed, "you have let yourself be frightened by false rumors; at a distance, you judge things badly. Do you really think that a King of France would listen to such villainous advice? As for the Queen Catherine, who has already saved my life in Bordeaux and made my fortune, she never has shown herself as benevolent towards me as at this moment. Just a short while ago, she came to the Tuileries with the Duke d'Anjou, Master de Biragues and other Lords. After having held a meeting, she came to the workshop, as usual, and ordered a large basin adorned with *rustic figulines* to be used as a holy-water stoup in the chapel of the Chateau de Blois. You do not know her well if you think that she would let anyone harm me before I completed her fantasy!... And as she knows that I need my sons to be able to successfully complete such a work, they have nothing more to fear than I do."

As one can see, Palissy shared the confidence of the Protestant leaders in the promises of the King and Catherine. But the sons and Massac were more aware of what was happening than the old artisan, so absorbed in his own daily tasks. They begged him to accept the offer. Master Bernard resisted, laughed and became angry. He could not abandon his work. This flight, without a real reason, would be his ruin, and would cover him with ridicule.

"Furthermore," he was saying, "the sons of the Constable are enemies of the Guise and suspects of the Court. How do you know if the safe-passage documents from the Marshall might not bring down upon us the hate of Catholics and Protestants?"

This objection did have some validity; Massac himself had already noted that the protection of the son of his former master, in the midst of the extreme violence of intense passions, might not necessarily provide protection from all dangers. However, he continued to beg Bernard to leave, when a new event came to change the situation.

One heard heavy steps under the hangar which precedes the workshop and a dozen Swiss guards attached to the Queen-Mother appeared at the door, halberds in hand.

Their officer, an old German mercenary with a white moustache, leaning on a cane with large silver head, moved towards Palissy and his sons.

Master Bernard knew this officer, whose name was Captain Zelter, very well. He was the usual executor of the Queen's wishes.

Zelter, after a sort of military salute, said with a barely intelligible German accent:

"Meinherr Goufernor, the Queen commants you to come mit me, you und your younk sons abrentis... Schnell... Order of Queen!"

"What is this, Captain Zelter?" asked Palissy stunned. "I saw my royal Mistress this morning; she was very gracious with me, as always, and gave me a new task. I do not understand…"

"Not need understant… Obey… Her Majesty commants."

"However,…"

The young people and Palissy, on their side, raised their voices and wanted to protest. But the Captain made a sign to his soldiers who, advancing nimbly, encircled Bernard, his sons and his son-in-law.

Attempts at resistance would have been folly. Palissy said in a firm tone:

"The Captain is right; it is not for us, servants of the Queen, who may disobey her orders, whatever they might be…. Mathurin, Nicolas, prepare yourselves…. Captain, I will follow you."

He removed his leather apron and covered himself with his coat, while his sons finished their preparations of departure. Gaston was despairing.

"Courage! my son Massac," said Master Bernard affectionately; "I cannot believe that the Queen-Mother has bad plans against us… at least as long as I have not completed the basin and other important works which she has given me to do. You, do not remain any longer… and if my life is not spared… tell Esther that I call down upon her, and you, all the heavenly blessings!"

The Baron wanted to reply, but Bernard embraced him and went to place himself in the middle of the Swiss guards who already encircled his two sons.

"You, leaf schnell, my chentleman," said the Captain to Massac; "no orders for you, but leaf schnell!… schnell!"

The halberdiers moved forward with their prisoners. They left the modelling workshop and the Captain closed the door and removed the key. At the same time, someone brought him all the other keys from the Tuileries and he gathered them carefully together and placed them in a pouch.

"But, in the name of God! Sire," said Massac to the Captain, when they were in the courtyard, "where are you taking Master Bernard and his sons?"

"Not ferry far," replied the old mercenary, chuckling, "but you, leaf schnell, schnell!"

Two of the Swiss guards crossed their halberds to prevent Massac from advancing. He stopped, almost crying from rage and grief.

"Farewell, my father… farewell my brothers!" he exclaimed a last time.

Bernard and his sons turned to send him a friendly wave; soon they entered, with their escort, into the palace by the door of the Pavillon Sully,[76] which closed behind them.

Massac was not thinking of leaving. He expected to see the Palissys taken from the palace to some prison in the city. But the guards, who formed

76 **Pavillon Sully,** also known as the *Pavillon de l'Horloge,* located in the center of the West wing of the Cour Carrée of the Palace of the Louvre in Paris.

a cordon around the palace, addressed such menacing signs towards him that he was obliged to decide to return to Paris. In addition, daylight was fading; the drums and the trumpets, which could be heard coming from the Tour du Bois, announced the closing of the gates, and obliged him to hasten there as rapidly as possible.

Just in time; the drawbridge was lifted behind his heels, and travel between the city and the Tuileries was interrupted once again.

It only took a few steps for the Baron to notice the sinister changes that had taken place over the past few hours in the physiognomy of Paris. The apparent calm had ceased. The Louvre was packed with soldiers who were moving around on the platforms of the towers, behind the battlements of the walls. In the surrounding area, numerous troops, French companies and Swiss guards, under the orders of the Duke de Guise, were stationed in the streets and were starting to prepare bivouac fires. A little further, a public gathering was forming, from which came a menacing clamor.

Upon arriving at the Inn of the Croix-de-Lorraine, Massac found new reasons for concern. Jean Choron, Provost of the shopkeepers, following the express orders of the King, had sent the 'district captains,' (the national guard of that time) to get the names of all the Protestants who were staying at the various inns. At that moment, a District officer, escorted by several bourgeois militiamen, was recording the names of the guests at the Croix-de-Lorraine. Massac was obliged, like the other travelers, to identify himself to the officer, and show the safe-passage document that he had received from the Marshall de Montmorency. However, judging from the slight grimace the municipal officer made when examining this passport, Massac understood that the recommendations of his protectors, once so powerful, had decidedly lost their prestige.

These formalities completed, the officer and his people were about to leave, when one of the bourgeois of the local guard, a little man whose face disappeared almost entirely under his immense metal helmet, and who was dragging a pike that was about three times taller than he, leaned towards Gaston and said in very low voice:

"If you wish to believe me, Sire Baron, you will go out from here as little as possible over the next few hours…. In case there is a fight, you can seek refuge at my place, at '*the Conversion of the Heretic*s.' There, you will be safe."

Massac recognized under the warlike attire, the weasel-like face of the barber-surgeon.

"Thank you Master Toupinac," he replied. "This is the second time that you have made the effort of giving me advice, excellent I am sure. However, would it not be wiser to tell me what is about to happen, what I have to fear and…"

"Hush! Hush!" said Toupinac mysteriously. "We are 'countrymen,' Master de Massac, and it was thanks to you that I was able to re-establish my affairs in Paris…. I am not an ingrate…. Do not forget any of my words…. And then," he added in even a lower voice, "in case of a public tumult, do not forget, when going out, to attach a white handkerchief to your left arm, and a white paper cross to your hat…. Did you understand me?"

"Perfectly; I would like to know…"

Toupinac, without answering, re-joined the other bourgeois of the militia who made up the escort for the District Officer. One minute later, they all left the inn while making their pikes resound on the cobblestones.

Massac, after having dined at the table hôte where his fellow guests, especially the Protestants, were quite taciturn, retired to his room and soon went to bed. The fears he felt about Palissy and the muted sounds which came sometimes from the street, kept him awake for a long time. Nevertheless, he finally fell into an agitated sleep full of dreams.

He was sleeping, when around two o'clock in the morning, the large bell in the church of Saint-Germain-l'Auxerrois began to ring. Immediately there was a loud noise of men and horses in the surrounding streets where there still reigned an intense darkness.

One heard, from all sides, screams, musket detonations and pitiful moans. The bell from the palace clock soon mixed its dismal chimes with those of Saint-Germain-l'Auxerrois. Armed men ran here and there screaming like fanatics:

"Long live the Mass! Death to the Huguenots! The King orders it; kill! kill!"

It was the 24th of August, Saint Bartholomew's Day, and the massacre of the Protestants had begun. Admiral Coligny already had his throat cut on the rue de Béthisi by the agents of the Duke de Guise and by the soldiers that had been assigned to his protection. The Louvre, where lived a number of Protestant princes with the King and his family, was the theatre of innumerable assassinations. The vicinity where the Huguenot gentlemen were lodging, as we have said, was invaded by the musketeers, the Swiss guard and the bourgeois of the militia. They assaulted almost all the houses and forced down the doors. From the Louvre area, the massacre was going to spread, like a burning fuse, to all the other districts, right up to the far reaches of Paris.

Massac, awakened with a start, listened for a moment to these various sounds, and rapidly guessed the truth. Jumping from his bed, he searched for his clothes by groping since he had no light and no way to get any. He succeeded, however, in getting dressed, he buckled on his sword and slipped his pistols in his belt. Thus equipped for any eventuality, he wanted to leave the room. He then realized that he was well and truly blocked in his room and that the key had received a double turn in the lock.

He began to bang violently against the door which proved to be extremely solid, and called out with all his might. Other inhabitants of the house seemed to be in the same situation and were calling out on their side. But no one was thinking of answering them, and the tumult that was occurring in the inn itself, perhaps kept anyone from hearing them.

A troop of armed persons, among whom one could recognize the District Officer and several of the bourgeois from the militia who, the previous evening, had visited the inn, had just entered the house. As Massac's window gave out onto the courtyard, he saw the glow of the torches that they were carrying. The innkeeper was acting as a guide, and they rushed up the stairs, dragging their arms and yelling: "the Mass or death!!"

The group stopped in front of Massac's door.

"Who is staying here," asked one of the invaders to his companions.

"The gentleman from Montmorency," answered another, "and it is said he is a good Catholic."

"Hum! Those Montmorency share common causes with the Protestants.... We will see later.... Let us begin with the Huguenots."

And they passed.

Soon, horrible cries, mixed with the clinking of swords, and explosions from muskets could be heard from the neighboring rooms. They were attacking all the Protestant gentlemen in the Croix-de-Lorraine. The house trembled with each detonation; the smoke and the powder were spreading everywhere, and in the midst of these acidic emanations, one could already smell the odor of blood.

During these terrible scenes, Gaston was like a madman. He paced in his room, letting out cries which were lost in the uproar. He wanted to throw himself out the window into the courtyard; but his window was at a considerable height and the obscurity did not permit finding a manner of escape. Moreover, all help would soon prove to be useless for his unfortunate neighbors; the noise of struggle had ceased; the task of death had been accomplished, and the group, who either had forgotten Massac, or had other more urgent work, plunged turbulently out of the inn.

The same scene was repeated in the entire neighbourhood. The clamor, the detonations and the moaning could be heard everywhere, in the middle of the silence of the night. Massac now remained struck with stupor, and such was the horror that he felt from these monstrous assassinations, that he had stopped thinking about his own danger.

Several hours elapsed in this manner; the first rays of light could be seen when the Baron heard a key grinding in the lock. He jumped up and took a defensive position. One lone man entered and Gaston recognized Toupinac under his warlike attire.

The barber appeared broken with fatigue. The hand that was holding the heavy pike was covered with blood.

"Sire Baron," he said in a breathless voice, "you are not safe here. *They* have left, but *they* have announced their return.... You must come with me, and I will save you."

"Wretch!" said Massac in indignation, "you took part in these heinous crimes...."

"No, no, Sire Baron. You have to appear to be howling with wolves, but I cleaned and staunched the wounds without making any.... Come, there is no time to lose."

"Where do you want to take me?"

"To my place, and you will stay there until this rebellion has calmed down."

At the same time, the barber made Massac understand the gravity of the situation. Although Catholic, Massac was a stranger in Paris, and had only suspect references; he had everything to fear in the middle of this terrible disorder. The Baron, after some resistance, finally agreed to follow Toupinac.

As they were about to go out, the barber exclaimed:

"One moment! Ventrebleu! I was forgetting... you cannot take ten steps outside of this house unless you take certain precautions."

He attached a white handkerchief to Massac's left arm; then taking out of his pocket a cross made from white paper, he fixed it on the hat of his protégé, after showing him that he wore these signs of recognition himself.

"Now," he said, "do not forget to yell: 'Long live the Mass' at every occasion. I will yell... whatever is necessary. Let us leave."

He took charge of the small suitcase that Massac had taken the trouble to prepare, and they left the room.

The inn was deserted and silent. The innkeeper and the valets seemed to have joined the cutthroats. On the other hand, the stairway, the vestibule and the courtyard carried the traces of the bloody struggle. A thousand objects blanketed the floor. At any moment, a foot would collide in the shadows with a body, already cold, which blocked the passage.

Upon leaving the inn, and, in the street, the same spectacle of pillaging, killing and extermination presented itself to the eye. Some unfortunates were fleeing in all directions, pursued by a howling crowd of armed persons. The slaughterers spared neither women, nor children, nor the elderly. Everywhere were wounded and dead. Certain hideous scenes occurring in 1793,[77] or those, not less hideous, of the recent 'Paris Commune'[78] could give cur-

---

77 **1793**, reference to the 'Reign of Terror' during the French Revolution which historians consider having started in March 1793 and ended in July 1794 with the fall of Robespierre.

78 **Paris Commune**, refers to a socialist and revolutionary government that ruled

rent generations an idea of similar atrocities

Massac and his companion passed almost unnoticed among these groups. They carried the crosses on their hats; the barber cried at the top of his voice: 'Death to the Huguenots!' They were each well-armed and seemed ready to defend themselves. They only had a hundred or so steps to take before reaching the home of Toupinac.

Finally, they arrived unhindered at his door. The barber had hardly knocked when it opened half way and he, as, well as Gaston, slipped inside the shop. There stood his apprentices trembling, but Toupinac did not stop. He seized the hand of his guest, who, struck with fright by all that he had seen, seemed incapable of reacting or speaking, and had him climb up a dark stairway, leading him into a small and poorly furnished room.

"Sire Baron" he said to him, "this is not a very nice room, I agree, but no one will come looking for you here. I will see to all your needs, and my boys, who are devoted to me, will help me to defend you, if such becomes necessary…. Now, if you will excuse me, it is important for me to be seen in my shop."

And he hastened to go downstairs.

We will not enter into the details of the events that took place during that terrible Saint-Bartholomew's day. History devotes numerous and painful pages to it. We will only say that Massac was obliged to spend a long time shuttered in his solitary and sad room. The massacres, although not occurring with the same intensity as the first day, continued for the following week, and even during the entire month. Whenever Toupinac had a free moment he would come up to spend it with the prisoner. The latter eagerly questioned him about what was being said in the boutique, about the well-known Huguenots who had been victims of this catastrophe. It was in this manner that he learned of the tragic deaths of the sculptor Jean Goujon and that of the learned philosopher Camus,[79] both friends of Palissy. But it was Bernard Palissy himself that preoccupied the Baron, and he had tired of asking for news about him from his host.

"I know nothing," Toupinac always replied; "It is said that the King wished to spare only his premier surgeon, Master Ambroise Paré, whose ministrations are absolutely essential to him. As for Palissy, our compatriot, who belongs to the Queen-Mother, no one has been able to give me any news…. The gates of Paris are closed; we do not know what happened at the Chateau des Tuileries…. Ah! why did the poor Bernard not listen to me in the past when I tried to convert him?"

All this did not reassure Gaston as to the fate of his illustrious father-in-

Paris from 28 March to 28 May in 1871. The regular French army suppressed the Commune in what is known as 'The Bloody Week' beginning 21 May 1871.

79 **Petrus Camus**, (1516-1572) a Protestant convert, he was an influential French humanist, logician and educational reformer.

law, and the time passed for him with a deathly anxiety.

VII.

LAST FAREWELLS

One morning, while the Baron was day-dreaming gloomily in his room, he heard footsteps on the stairway, and saw Toupinac enter with a Swiss guard from the royal palace. Gaston, although he did not doubt the loyalty of his host, thought of an attack and jumped for his sword. The barber simply smiled, and after exchanging a sign with the guard, left the room.

Massac did not know what to think about the visit, when the newcomer spoke to him with an accent which was anything but German:

"Sire Baron, my brother, so, you have escaped this terrible carnage?"

Gaston examined the supposed Swiss guard, but under the multicolored jerkin and felt cap, he recognized Mathurin, the elder son of Palissy.

Gaston embraced him cordially.

"My dear Mathurin," he exclaimed, "our father Master Bernard, does he still exist?"

"Yes, thanks be to heaven, and he misses you as much as you miss him. He sent me to bring back news about you, at all costs."

At the same time, Mathurin sat down and recounted to his brother-in-law all that had happened since their last meeting.

When, on the eve of the Saint Bartholomew events, the Captain of the Swiss guard had come to arrest Palissy and his sons, it was not, as could be feared, to take them to a prison. They had simply been brought to the Tuileries, and they had been forbidden to go out. As the Queen was then living at the Louvre with the King and her other children, the Chateau des Tuileries was pretty much deserted. Other than Palissy and his sons, there were Dame Marguerite and a few old servants. Undoubtedly, Catherine, before striking this blow that would horrify France, had wanted to shelter them from these events and had them carefully protected by the Swiss guards in her own palace.

However, those who had been protected in this manner, found that they were not sheltered from terrible anguish. The immense clamor, coming from the Louvre as well as the city reached them as well. From their windows, they even saw the King himself shoot with an arquebus at Protestants who were fleeing along the Pré-aux-Clercs. The river, red with blood, swept along thousands of the dead, of both sexes and of all ages.

One will understand the distress of Master Bernard, when he thought about all his friends who were perhaps among the victims. But no one generated more of his concern than that of his son-in-law Massac. The turmoil having calmed down a bit, the Queen had sent orders that morning that surveillance of the prisoners in the Tuileries could be relaxed. Bernard and his sons, whose grief was devouring them in their solitude, had gone back down to their workshop, and Palissy, impatient to have news of the Baron, made an arrangement with one of the Swiss guards assigned to his protection. This individual, secretly attached to the Protestant religion, had obtained for Mathurin a Swiss uniform, and Palissy's son had been able to leave the tuilerie to search for Gaston. He had first gone to the Croix de Lorraine inn, whose owner had connections with Toupinac, and it was in this manner that he had found the refuge of his brother-in-law.

Massac listened to all these details with an extreme satisfaction. As he did not tire of questioning Mathurin, the latter said to him:

"Before returning to the palace, my brother Massac, I must pass on a message that my father asked me to give you, if I had the good fortune of finding you…. These last events will undoubtedly lead to a terrible war. Within a few days, the entire kingdom will be in flames, and your return to Saintonge will become very difficult, perhaps perilous…. My father therefore requests that you leave without delay."

"Does Master Bernard believe that I can already start my voyage?"

"Who knows? However, the difficulties will be greater when armed gangs from one or the other parties are roaming the countryside."

"So be it, my dear Mathurin; I am ready to take that risk; but first I wish to see Master Bernard and bid him farewell."

"Do you mean it? How will you enter the Tuileries? The Swiss guards have the strictest of orders."

"Did you not tell me that you have agreements with several of them? If they let you go out, why would they not let me in?"

Mathurin, after several objections, finally gave in.

"In reality," he said, "it would be a great consolation for my father to see you one more time."

Massac was ready in a minute and they called Toupinac, who frowned when he learned what it was about. However, he did not oppose the departure of his guest, and the two brothers-in-law, without going through the shop which would have raised suspicions, exited into a neighbouring street.

Calm was almost re-established in Paris. any of the boutiques remained open and the bourgeois went about their business as usual. One came across houses, from time to time, whose windows were broken and doors torn away as witness to the recent devastation. Here and there, on still humid cobble stones, one noticed red stains, and even on certain corners, one could see half-naked and disfigured corpses that the gravediggers had not had time to remove. However, Massac and his companion reached the city gate without difficulty. The Swiss guard uniform worn by the young Palissy, appeared to be sufficient protection for the Baron, quite capable of defending himself in case of attack, and soon they reached the Tuileries.

Numerous sentries were watching over the palace; but at the entry to Master Bernard's workshop there were only a few Swiss guards under the orders of an anspessade.[80]

While Massac remained further back, Mathurin went to negotiate with the chief of this small post. We do not know what arguments he used to obtain relaxation of the orders; but the fact remains that after some negotiations, Gaston and his brother-in-law were allowed entry to the tuilerie.

Master Bernard, pale, worn, aged by ten years, was seated in his workshop. Surrounded by the objects that were normally the subjects of his studies and occupations, he was not considering resuming his work. His head lowered on his chest, he had abandoned himself to the saddest of reflections while Nicolas, his second son, leaning against a pillar, looked at him despondently.

At the sight of his son-in-law, he arose and ran to him with open arms.

"Massac, my dear son, you have been returned to me! My heart has been broken by the loss of so many friends, so many men, righteous and brave, whose blood has flowed like water. However, in the middle of my grief, I can still experience joy!"

He pressed the Baron against his chest, crying.

"Thank you, good father," replied Massac, deeply moved himself. "I had much more to fear for you, you whose religion was specifically singled out for the anger of the persecutors!"

"*She* has again spared us," replied Bernard with a bitter smile. "God, who holds in his hand the heart of kings, has permitted that for personal and miserable motives, *she* has spared us, mine and myself. Does *she* not need us to produce that basin for the Chateau de Blois and all the other works she has ordered from me?... Who knows, however," he added in a somber tone, "if grief, indignation and despair will prevent me henceforth from conceiving, acting and even understanding."

At the same time, he gave a kick to an unfinished vase that was in front of him, shattering it. Never had Bernard, always in control of himself, shown such violence.

"Dear father," said Massac, "if such is the case, why, as I have already

---

80 **anspessade**, was a kind of French police officer that had been used in the foot soldiers, below the corporals, and yet above the common sentinels, between the 16th and 17th centuries.

suggested, would you not abandon Paris and the Court. Why would you and my brothers, not come to Massac? You would live there, happily and in peace, near Esther and our children...."

Palissy shook his head; he appeared ashamed of his moment of anger.

"Forget these words which escaped me, Massac," he continued; "I am not able to renounce my trade. As for this woman who holds me in a sort of slavery, how can I do without her presence and her support? Yes, she is a secretive, treacherous and cruel Italian; yes, I should hate her, as she has deprived me of my best, my most illustrious friends. But as odious as she is, she is a Médici; she loves what is beautiful and she understands art. She has already saved me in Bordeaux; she has protected me a second time during these terrible days. When, from time to time, she comes to sit in this workshop, where you are sitting now, to watch me work, when she says to me in her majestic voice: 'This is very good Master Bernard, I am pleased!' Then I feel deeply moved and I redouble my efforts to be worthy of her praise.... Look, my son Massac, whatever horror I feel for this Queen with bloody hands, whatever contempt I have for my own cowardice, I am incapable of leaving here. I remain attached to my works, like a serf to his glebe,[81] and I will stay here until my redoubtable protectress has me thrown in a dungeon or massacred ruthlessly like so many other martyrs!"

He stopped, choked with emotion, and remained silent for a moment. Massac once again attempted to shake his resolve, to convince him to flee. Palissy soon interrupted him.

"Let us not think any more about me, Massac," he resumed, "it is for you that it is important to leave as rapidly as possible. Just as well, perhaps the Queen had her reasons for allowing me to come down to my workshop today.... I know her.... In the midst of sinister political intrigues, in the midst of these massacres, in the midst of all this blood and of these tears, she is still thinking about works of art, and it is not impossible that she will come here...."

"What! Do you think..."

"There you are! As I was saying!" murmured Bernard.

Indeed, the door had just opened and Queen Catherine entered with rapid steps.

She was absolutely alone. A strange smile touched her lips; however, her face bore signs of fatigue, and one could see that her hair had greatly whitened in a short time.

She gave no notice to the presence of the other persons who were in Palissy's workshop, and who were keeping themselves respectfully at a distance.

"Master Bernard," she said with agitation, "you must know of the great

---

81 **glebe**, land to which serfs were attached and which they had to cultivate.

victory which has been achieved over heresy, and you cannot ignore that this was accomplished by the will of the King...."

"And with the advice of Your Majesty, Madam," interrupted Palissy averting his eyes.

"This is possible... I won't deny it," replied the Queen proudly. "The fact remains that once again, I have covered you with my protection, but my patience, like divine mercy, can finally grow weary. I must now warn you that, if you do not return rapidly to the true faith, you will be treated like the other heathen...."

"In that case, Madam," replied Palissy firmly, "it is useless to let me languish.... I will never renounce my religion; I am prepared to immediately share the fate of so many noble martyrs."

Catherine threw him an irritated look.

"Head of iron!" she exclaimed. "Do you forget that your antichrist of Calvin... well, that was the reply that the Reformist Ambroise Paré dared to give to my son! That suffices; we will see if two obstinates, like you, will defy for long the royal Majesty.... We will prevail over this insolence, and if you persist in this impiety..."

The Queen suddenly stopped speaking, looking fixedly at an object that was on the table.

"Well! What is this?" she exclaimed.

She got up and went to examine the object that had attracted her curiosity. It was one of those large dishes like the ones that Palissy produced for his princely clientele; this one, in addition to the usual decoration of reptiles, green plants, fish and shellfish reproduced with an amazing accuracy, had as its base a floor of golden sand of such a richness, such a vividness and with such a harmonious balance, that never has such a splendid pottery struck the eyes.[82]

Catherine took it in her hands and contemplated it with enthusiasm.

"Master Bernard, here is your masterpiece, and none will surpass this degree of perfection.... For whom is this incomparable marvel?"

Palissy could not retain a smile.

"Your Majesty therefore finds it a success?" he continued. "Indeed, I am not displeased with it.... It was destined for the Chateau de Chaulnes."

"Master de Chaulnes will not have it." Said the Queen emphatically. "I want this masterpiece, and although I am ruining myself in construction, you will have my treasurer pay you what pleases you.... Do you hear, Master Bernard? This dish belongs to me."

Palissy contented himself with a sign of agreement.

"Come now! Why are you not working?" resumed Catherine with vivacity; "nothing should have been touched here; I had specified that your

82 **Author Berthet's original note**: the dish described is now in the Louvre, in the section Palissy under number 138. (collection Sauvageot).

belongings be respected.... Are you not going to work on my basin? Why not give it a floor of golden sand like the one that produces such a beautiful effect?"

"Ah! Madam," resumed Palissy despondently, "how will I have the courage to work when my heart is broken and when I tremble for my family, my children and myself?"

"Oh! you," said Catherine with a sly smile, "you know perfectly well that despite the reproaches and the threats, you are sheltered from all aggression... And as regards your sons, we have not put too much pressure on them because of their religion.... But now, who is that one?" she added, looking at Massac.

The Baron bowed.

"He is also part of my family, Madam," replied Palissy; "he is my son-in-law, Master de Massac."

"Yes," said Catherine, still smiling, "the gentleman of my compère the Constable, the pretty flower that was so cruel with my ladies-in-waiting.... Approach Sire.... Are you as good a Catholic as they say?"

"I oblige myself to be so, Madam; however, the horrible events of recent days..."

"Peace!" the Queen interrupted roughly. "I find you quite brazen! Do you permit yourself to question the intentions of your King... and mine?... Come now," she added in a softer tone, "in consideration of this old stubborn Bernard, I wish to do something for you.... You have nothing to ask of me?"

Massac bowed again deeply but continued to keep his silence.

"Ah!" said Catherine, pursing her lips, "the son-in-law scorns my generosity like the daughter and the father!"

"No, no, madam, he does not scorn them," said Palissy with alacrity. "Massac has no ambition other than living peacefully in Saintonge with his wife and children. The only thing I dare ask Your Majesty on his behalf, is a passport, so that he can travel in perfect safety a portion of your kingdom, as the safe-passage that he has from the Marshall de Montmorency cannot protect him sufficiently in the middle of the revolt which is in preparation...."

"What are you saying, Bernard?" resumed Catherine, flinching. "Are you crazy? Is a revolt possible? Thanks to the vigorous methods that the King has employed, there are no more Huguenots; they have all been exterminated!"

In those first moments, the Queen-Mother, Charles IX and the Court actually believed that the Protestant heresy was finished. However, several months later, the most terrible of religious wars exploded in France, and never had the throne of the sons of Catherine found itself in greater peril.

However, Palissy limited himself to responding, lowering his eyes:

"The decrees of Providence are impenetrable!"

The Queen remained pensive several moments.

"Bah!" she said in a light tone, "the dead do not return... unless they had been evoked by some magical power, and in that case, they would not be able to use either swords nor arquebuses!... You are daydreaming, Master Bernard.... As concerns your son-in-law, Master de Massac, I want to give you satisfaction. All he needs to do is to present himself, today, at my chancellery, and he will be given a passport."

The Baron thanked her with a respectful gesture. The Queen prepared to leave.

"Well, are you happy now, Bernard?" she said with an affectionate tone, "Am I not for you a good mistress? Now I hope that you will return to your work with ardor. You will produce masterpieces for my churches, and you will begin with the basin destined for the chapel of the Chateau de Blois.... Do not forget to put the floor of golden sand.... God protect you, Sires!"

And she went out so hurriedly, that those present, who according to etiquette, were supposed to accompany her to the final door, had trouble keeping up.

Catherine having climbed into her litter for her return to the Louvre, Bernard Palissy said to his son-in-law in an affectionate tone:

"My dear Massac, take advantage of the favor of the Queen, and, as soon as you have your passport, leave without delay, leave tonight.... I ask this of you, in the name of our good Esther, in the name of my dear grandchildren."

"I will obey, Master Bernard, especially as I have had my fill of these horrors, and need to reimmerse myself in sweet sensations, in the tenderness of the ones who await me there.... Farewell then, my brothers.... My father, what shall I say to Esther on your behalf?"

"Tell her," replied Palissy with sadness, that I am here like the prophet Daniel in the lion's den.... As soon as God ceases doing miracles, mine and myself will be devoured!"

Bernard and his sons embraced Massac a final time. Then Massac went to obtain the royal passport and also took leave of Toupinac, whom he generously rewarded for his services. That same night, he left Paris at full gallop, imagining that he saw a haze of blood over the city.

EPILOGUE

Following the Saint-Bartholomew events, Bernard did not live for long in the Tuileries, the Queen herself, having abandoned this residence in favour of the hotel de Soissons, that she had built near the church of Saint-Eustache. During this period of his life, Palissy published several works and continued his conferences at rue Saint-Jacques. He lived near the Croix-Rouge crossing, in the rue du *Sépulchre*, today, rue du Dragon, across from the one that is currently named 'rue Bernard Palissy,' in the company of his sons, Mathurin and Nicolas, who even after his death, continued to produce glazed pottery.

But the bad days were not yet finished for the illustrious potter. At the time of the *League*,[83] he was denounced by Mathieu Launay, a member of the Seize[84], and thrown into the Bastille, normally a preliminary to the *public spectacle,* as the gallows were called. Palissy was at that time, almost eighty years old. Queen Catherine, his protectress, was in the South of France, hindered by continued troubles.

Palissy had been languishing for a long time in the state prison, when one day the door of his cell opened, and he saw enter a person whose historical appearance is well known; tall, thin, effeminate features with earrings and hair curled in the style of a woman. Under his little velvet coat embroided with gold, he wore the blue ribbon;[85] and a rosary of miniature skulls hung on his belt. The prisoner, broken and trembling, thin and gaunt under his long white beard, hastened to arise. He had just recognized Henri III, the youngest son of Catherine de Médicis.

According to the historian Agrippa d'Aubigné, the King said to Palissy:

'*My good man, it has been forty-five years that you have been in the service of the Queen, my mother, and me; we have put up with your having lived your religion within the fires and massacres. Now I am so pressured by* the Guises and *my people, that I will be obliged to have you burned if you*

83 **The League,** refers to a Catholic league organized by the Duc de Guise in Paris in 1576 to combat Protestantism during the religious wars.
84 **The Seize,** a special council created in 1589 from five members of the League to control Paris and were all-powerful until 1591.
85 **The Blue ribbon,** worn by the members of the highest knighthood; *L'Ordre des chevaliers du Saint-Esprit,* was instituted by Henri III in 1578 which was the origin of the *Cordon Bleu* we know today.

do not convert.'

'Sire,' replied Palissy, *'I have pity for you for saying you are obliged. You, Sire, and those who oblige you can do nothing to me, BECAUSE I KNOW HOW TO DIE!'*

We do not know what impression this proud response made on Henri, who did not have a reputation of having understood noble and superior sentiments. However, he did not carry out his menace against Master Bernard, who languished another year in prison, and died the following year, almost at the same time as Queen Catherine.

Happier than the memory of his protectress, a memory that comes to us charged with malediction and hate, while the memory of Bernard, the great artist, the personification of natural genius, is one that continues to grow in the respect and admiration of men. In our day, a statue of Bernard Palissy stands in the gallery of the new Louvre, two steps away from where he produced his masterpieces in his workshop next to the Tuileries.

THE END